HUNTER

THE DRUM AND THE DANCE

JUDITH ASHLEY

Windtree
Press

CONTENTS

Windtree Press

http://windtreepress.com

Publisher's Note: This is a work of fiction. Names, characters, places, and incidents are a product of the author's imagination. Locales and public names are sometimes used for atmospheric purposes. Any resemblance to actual people, living or dead, or to businesses, companies, events, institutions, or locales is completely coincidental.

Book Cover by Christy Caughie, Gilded Hearts Design

Hunter/Judith Ashley -- 1st ed.

Print ISBN 9781940064598

Ebook ISBN 9781940064604

❀ Created with Vellum

This book is dedicated to single mothers.

Whether you decide to complete the pregnancy or terminate it, parent the child or plan for adoption your life is forever changed. There is no decision you can make that does not bring with it times of worry and even despair. Whichever decision you make, I applaud you because I know it was not made lightly and you paid a price.

ACKNOWLEDGMENTS

My village for *Hunter* includes Lois Regn, Michele Mairesse, Kris Bella, Heather Jefferis, Linda Needham and Maggie Lynch. Christy Caughie's Gilded Heart Design's cover took my breath away! As always, Kelly Schaub's editorial eye makes the story and characters stronger.

Any errors are mine.

1 - THE FUTURE?

Fremont, Oregon
March 21, 2005
Spring Equinox

Hunter Compton looped her arm around her daughter Logan's shoulder and leaned close whispering, "They're fantastically happy." She was referring to Ashley and Daniel, the newlyweds heading out the door.

"The kids are really glad their mom and Daniel are married. I've never seen Rose so happy." Logan sighed.

Hunter heard the note of sadness in her daughter's tone and wondered for the billionth time if she'd made the right decision to never tell her anything about her birth father. "You'll have a great time at the beach with them." She kissed Logan's cheek.

"I know." Logan sat a little straighter, a bright tone in her voice. "Daniel said I'm supposed to take the kids to the Newport aquarium, shopping in Lincoln City, and we're even going to a couple of the glass blowing places and making souvenirs." A mischievous smile on her face, she laughed. "My instructions are to head out before lunch and not return before three. I wonder what the newlyweds will be up to while we're gone?"

"Special alone time." Hunter ignored her daughter's wink. "Once they're back home and the kids are in school, they'll have a routine to set up and special alone time together will be scarce."

"What about after the kids are in bed?" Logan asked her seventeen-year-old curiosity obvious.

"At the end of the day, parents are usually tired and staying up another three to four hours just isn't going to happen."

"Makes sense." Logan hugged her mom and stood. "I've volunteered to help Eleanor and Gabby with them tonight. Looks like they're getting ready to leave." Logan joined the other women who were herding the kids towards the door. While James and Anthony at thirteen and ten respectively were clearly delighted, Rose, now eight, was ecstatic and bounced from one person to the next saying her 'good-byes'.

Logan held out her hand. "Come along, Rose."

Hunter watched her daughter charm Ashley's youngest into her coat and out the door.

"She's so good with those children," Lily said, sitting down in the place vacated by Logan.

"I'm blessed in so many ways," Hunter said, fighting back a surge of envy seeing the look that passed between Lily and her husband, Jackson, whose palpable connection was noticeable.

Lily tucked her blond hair behind her ears, cleared her throat and in a bit louder than normal voice said, "Everything happened so fast today, I'd love it if the rest of The Circle took some time to catch up with each other before it gets too late."

"Excellent idea," Diana chimed in. "Madison Michelle is sleeping right now so it's a good time for us or," she looked over at Matthew.

"I can take her." Matthew reached for his three month old daughter. Diana's fingertips stroked M2's dark hair as Matthew expertly transferred her into his arms.

She has dark hair like her mom and dad but inherited Diana's violet blue eyes. And Logan has a dark strawberry blond hair, a mix of my chestnut and

Grant's blond. But her eyes are turquoise-green like mine. Strange, even though she knows nothing about him, I still see flashes of Grant in some of her mannerisms—especially her smile.

"I've a fresh pot of tea brewing for you ladies," Jackson announced as the men headed downstairs.

"Thank you, Jackson," Sophia said on her way to the kitchen. "I see a few of my brownies are left. Why don't you and Matthew finish them off?"

"We're good," Jackson replied.

Sophia's waist length brown hair was escaping the twist she had it in. As she wrestled it back into place, she looked over at the other women, her brow raised in question. "I can cut them into smaller pieces so everyone gets a bite or two or I can leave them for Jackson and Lily or maybe for Matthew to take in his lunch tomorrow."

"I vote they go to Jackson and Lily or Matthew because I've an early morning yoga class and do *not* need anything more to eat," Hunter said.

"I vote they go to Matthew. Neither Jackson nor I need more sweets," Lily added.

"I vote they come home with us so Matthew can have them in his lunch tomorrow. I can't eat them because M2 does not like chocolate. Cranky colicky baby is motivation enough to leave them alone," Diana said.

"I'll wrap them in foil for you." Sophia pulled the aluminum foil box from the drawer and set action to her words adding, "I'll bring the tea pot and cups in just a moment."

Hunter rose and headed across the great room to the kitchen area. "I can do that. Need to get up and move." She put cups on a tray, got the sugar bowl out and poured a bit of cream into a pitcher. "Between Eleanor and Elizabeth, we've all gotten used to cream tea. I remember when…." Her voice trailed off as she saw amused smiles on her circle sisters' faces. "What?"

"I remember when we first met ten years or so ago. Lily, Sophia and Elizabeth drank tea. Gabriella, Ashley and you preferred soda pop and I drank tonics," Diana said.

"That began to change a couple of years later when Ashley had breast cancer the first time. We were a fairly new circle but I think we all took stock of our health and made some changes." Sophia carried the pot of tea to where everyone sat on the couch or chairs in a semi-circle in front of the fireplace. She added the teapot to the tray already on the coffee table before settling into one of the chairs.

"We started to drink more herbal tea and cut back on caffeine." Lily smiled, adding, "Except for chocolate. That is one form of caffeine The Circle has not eliminated from our diet." She looked over at Diana, "Except for when it upsets a baby's tummy."

"And Gabby, Ashley and I shifted from soda pop to seltzer water," Hunter said. "I love the feel of the fizz in my mouth. Sometimes I'll add a slice of lemon or lime but usually I just drink it plain."

"We're all tea drinkers now." Diana began to pour.

"Catching up? Anyone want to share?" Sophia's gaze connected with each of the women sitting around the fireplace.

"I'll start." Lily took a green citrine stone from her pocket. "I'm looking forward to Ashley being able to help out with some of my clients. I know that may not happen before fall. Daniel told Jackson he had convinced Ashley to make an appointment with her oncologist when they got back from their honeymoon. If he has his way, she'll have the mastectomy if that's what the doctor still recommends. I know we'll get an update from her when she is back. While all is going well for her right now, there may be another stint where she'll need extra help as she recovers from that surgery and the rehabilitation that comes with it."

A moment of silence, everyone nodded in understanding before the citrine stone passed to Sophia.

"Spring Break is one of my favorites because I start planting my main garden." She smiled at Diana. "I'm grateful Matthew has a rototiller and easily made the ground ready. Actually peas were planted about a month ago so be prepared. The bounty from my garden is about to begin."

Diana spoke next. "M2 is doing so well and Matthew is such a great father. I'm back to teaching my classes on my own when Spring

Term starts. I'm ever so grateful to you two," Diana nodded indicating Lily and Sophia, "for covering for me this last term and fall term also." A soft smile curved her lips. "He's really looking forward to it being just the two of them. I'm ever so blessed to share this time as a new mom with a new dad who wants to be an equal partner in her care."

Hunter listened to her circle sisters share what they were planning to accomplish during the next few weeks. All eyes trained on her when it was her turn. "I've my Spring Recital coming up April 1st. Of course you are all invited." She turned to Diana. "Even Madison Michelle so do not think you need a sitter.

"The Recital is easy in comparison to preparing for Logan's graduation the end of May. It's hard to believe in just over sixty days she'll have graduated!

"And, she's been accepted into every college she's applied to." Sitting straighter, pride in every word, Hunter added, "April 1st is the date she's set for herself to make her final decision. I know she really wants to go to Bryn Maar or Vassar. Even though she's been accepted to those two schools, her scholarships only cover half the tuition, books and fees.

"Last summer when I realized where she'd set her sights, I added more classes at the studio. I've been saving as best I can but senior year expenses... ." Hunter shrugged and looked around at the other women. "They add up."

"You know you can put your name on the house totem list," Lily said.

"I know. I just don't feel comfortable doing that. It isn't my thing." Unshed tears glistened. "It isn't that I don't have my own strengths—I do. Seeing the energy of the land just isn't one of them."

Hunter plastered a smile on her face. "Logan and I'll be okay. I'm just having a bit of a problem facing a future without my girl." She sighed and looked around at the others. "I know she'll still be in my life, but she's been a constant in my daily life since I realized I was pregnant. I don't exactly know how I'm going to deal with coming home to an empty place once she moves on."

2 - CHOICES

April 1, 2005
Providence, Rhode Island

Grant Haywood Parker IV froze outside the boardroom door. The two men inside were talking about a Compton, something about a Hunter Compton. He knew the Knight-Comptons. His parents and the senior Knight-Comptons were members of the same social circle. His body tightened as an image of the younger daughter, Honey, surfaced.

What was that? This Hunter Compton has a daughter about to turn eighteen?

Another vision emerged. Honey's long legs wrapped around him, her lithe dancer's body matching his thrusts.

She'd been a virgin.

She'd been special.

She'd disappeared.

Disappeared and erased from the Knight-Compton family tree. Or was she?

Grant knew he should clear his throat, do something to alert the other men to his presence but he pushed ethics aside and eaves-dropped.

There was no other explanation. Hunter Compton had to be Honey Knight-Compton. She had a seventeen-year-old daughter and was exploring the possibility of tapping in to her trust fund.

He was a skilled corporate attorney, in the top ten percent of his Yale Law School graduating class. It didn't take a mathematical genius to count the time from that long ago summer to today. Almost nineteen years. If Honey had become pregnant, and he did remember times the condom broke, whoever this girl was, he was certain she was his daughter. Why? Because not only was Honey a virgin, their relationship had been exclusive.

Fury fumed through him but the sound of voices announced the others were arriving for the meeting. He forced his feet back several steps from the open doorway. A tuneless whistle on his lips, he retraced those few feet and entered the board room.

As he had surmised it would, the conversation abruptly stopped.

The two men from the law firm that oversaw the Knight-Compton trusts greeted him and the others as they came through the door. Burying the sensations memories of that summer evoked, Grant used his intellect to push business to the fore.

He was the youngest of the foundation trustees, an enviable position for the most part. A position he had worked hard to secure. A position that gave him access to people in positions of financial, political and social power which meant it was important to stay engaged with the discussions.

As the meeting droned one, he did listen and contribute but also doodled. At last count, he'd written the number eighteen a dozen times in varying ways.

The meeting concluded. The inevitable invitations to stop by the country club for drinks on the way home deflected. Grateful he'd just broken up with another long term relationship—well, she'd done the breaking up as they all had—he could checkout this Hunter Compton without explanations.

Striding out to his car, he ruminated on his marital status. He didn't blame any of the women for leaving. If he'd been looking for marriage as each of them had, he'd have left long before any of them actually did. *Where did that come from? I'm making it sound like I change women every few weeks. Sunny was the third long term relationship I've been in since—.*

Restless, Grant drove past his downtown condominium. An hour later he pulled into the garage attached to his house at the shore. However, a stroll along the sand didn't ease the edginess. Neither did the three fingers of scotch. Removing the frozen ramekin from the freezer, he heated up the small casserole of mac & cheese Mrs. Ripley, his housekeeper/cook kept in stock for him. He went through the motions of eating while standing at the French doors looking out at the rolling waves ebbing and flowing on the sandy shore.

Why did I come here?

It was just down the beach, by the curve in the bank where we'd meet up, where we made love. The years slipped away and the feel of her lips kissing her way along his jaw, down his neck, her hand stroking—.

"Enough!" he slammed the dish down on a table. "Enough!" he mashed a fist into the palm of his other hand. "You don't even know if this Hunter Compton is—." But he did know. On some level, he knew with a certainty that Honey Knight-Compton now went by Hunter Compton and she had a daughter who was almost eighteen and graduating from high school in a few weeks.

The question he struggled with had more to do with what he was going to do with the information.

He hadn't moved.

He hadn't left.

She was the one who hadn't contacted him. Hadn't let him know there was a child.

Why?

Maybe that was where to start. Find out why she never said anything to him. Find out why she took off. Find out why she'd been erased from all Knight-Compton family conversation.

But had she?

There was still the trust.

Not from her parents, Grant remembered. That money was put in trust for her by her grandmother. *I wonder if she even knows that?*

Grant paced before the floor-to-ceiling glass windows. It was after ten o'clock but his mind raced with memories and questions. At midnight, the only answer he'd come up with was he had to find her.

Check out the child for himself.

He trudged down the hall to his private suite of rooms where a sleepless night waited.

3 - GHOSTS FROM THE PAST

April 4, 2005
Twinkle Toes Dance Studio
Fremont, Oregon

*H*unter stood before the wall of mirrors and twirled in an informal pirouette. Her mind whirled with possibilities trying to explain her unease. The Spring Recital had gone off without a hitch, every student performed well and the audience included a few more people than her circle sisters and her students' families.

But something felt off. *The Smith College bombshell Logan dropped last Friday? It wasn't as out-of-the-blue when I think about it. She had mentioned Smith when we talked about East Coast schools.*

Diana's son, Bill, was a junior at near-by Boston College. Jackson's sisters and their families live in the area and would certainly welcome her. *I think I just pushed it aside because if she was going to school in the east, I wanted it to be Bryn Mawr in Pennsylvania or maybe Vassar in New York. Massachusetts is too close to my past.*

Energy surged through her and she twirled and leaped down the studio floor and back. A final pirouette followed by a modified retiré, a one-leg stand, arms out to her side, her right leg bent, the arch of her foot resting on the side of her left knee. Something still wasn't right but what it was eluded her.

She heard the chatter of voices as students for her morning yoga class came in. *I need to get the bell of the front door fixed so I know when someone comes in.* Hunter greeted each woman by name. Within five minutes, everyone was in place and the lesson began.

TWO MORNING YOGA classes and one afternoon dance class for adults behind her, Hunter waited for her younger students to arrive at three. These classes were forty-five minutes each and she scheduled them on the hour from three to six.

By the time her last class was over, it would be seven and she would be exhausted. A quiet dinner with Logan, catching up on her day and she'd be ready for bed.

The unease from this morning intensified.

Logan popped in the door and danced across the room. Grabbing Hunter's hands, she pulled her into the middle of the floor and started a dance routine—the first one she'd learned as a toddler.

I'm so blessed to have her in my life. A shaft of light pierced through the darkness that had enveloped her heart as they danced the simple steps. A smile on her lips, she kept pace with Logan.

As the dance ended, Hunter smiled over at the students in the doorway waiting to enter the studio.

Sheer terror froze her feet to the floor as a face from her past glared at her from the shadows. Hunter fought for balance to keep from tumbling to the floor.

What?! Frantic, once firm on her feet, she stared over the heads of her students—at nothing.

No face in the shadows.

No ghost from her past.

Unnerved, she sprinted past the incoming students to the hall to check—to make sure nothing was there. Stopping in the middle, she looked in both directions. *No, I'm imagining things. It can't be. He doesn't know—.*

"Mom?" Logan's hand on her arm, the urgency in her voice, helped Hunter calm her racing heart.

"I'm okay," Hunter assured her daughter. "I thought I saw something but—well, obviously I didn't. I'll be right back."

Hunter marched to the front and locked the door. "That'll keep the ghosts out," she muttered on her way back to her class.

GRANT HAYWOOD PARKER IV stood in the shadowed doorway of the next building. Impotent with rage, he clenched and unclenched his fists wishing there was something or someone to hit, to beat into a pulp, to smash to kingdom come. He wanted to holler and release the pain searing his heart, strangling his breath.

Of course he'd do none of it. Making a spectacle of oneself was beneath a Haywood Parker, especially a Haywood Parker the Fourth. He wasn't sure right then whether or not thirty-eight years of social etiquette lessons were helpful because his gut clenched and his head pounded so hard—.

His rental car was parked two blocks away. Driving right now was not a good idea. To burn off the fury, he walked, jogged actually—in his eight hundred dollar suit, two hundred dollar shoes and one hundred and fifty dollar shirt—his tie wasn't factored in because it had been a gift. Two hours later the fury was transmuted to frustration. He was hot, sweaty and lost.

Asking for directions back to Honey's studio, he listened carefully and started the long walk back. Hailing a cab crossed his mind but walking was the better choice given his level of agitation.

I have a daughter. When he left off the "that bitch kept her from me" part and just focused on the daughter part, the tension from frustration eased.

I have a daughter. While she looked so much like her mother did at that age, he saw a glimpse of himself in her smile. He didn't need a paternity test to know who the young woman who dashed into the dance studio was. Honey had been with no one but him that summer.

I have a daughter. The affection between mother and daughter was unmistakable. The little dance they did together was sweet and their laughter and joy in the moment was—.

I have a daughter.

There was a moment when he knew Honey felt his presence. He was against the far wall, looking into the studio over the heads of her students. Wreathed in shadows, when she looked his way, memories of that summer almost nineteen years ago surged. Chestnut red hair, exquisite turquoise-green eyes—she may have had a child but her body was strong, fit and she moved with even more grace than he remembered—still magnificent.

And his split-second physical response? Gut-clenching attraction.

I have a daughter and I'll never forgive Honey for keeping her from me. Never! He noticed people stepping to the side. *I'm scowling.* He looked at his reflection in a store front window. A reflection that told the world he was furious about something. Furious coated with physical exhaustion.

Calling upon those years of social etiquette lessons, Grant schooled his face to a neutral mien. The idea to walk in and confront her fueled him the last mile.

But when he tried the front door, it was locked.

Through his research he knew Honey and her daughter lived above the studio. Waiting for them to come out when he was so tired and hungry served no purpose. He decided to return to his hotel room and regroup.

He'd found her.

He'd confirmed in his own mind the girl was his daughter.

He'd find to make Honey to pay for her deception.

Grant stood at the window looking out at the river. It wasn't the same as the ocean view from his house at the shore but it beat looking out at a brick wall, parking garage or downtown street. He was glad he'd Google-earthed Fremont and checked in with the Chamber of Commerce. In his corporate world, half the battle was won if he was prepared with intel on the other side.

Before traveling to Fremont, he'd done some sleuthing and learned a bit more about Honey. Why he hadn't tried to find this history out before now was a thought for another time.

She'd taken off, well, the date wasn't certain because she'd laid a false trail. Honey had been gone almost two weeks before her parents discreetly tried to find her. Talking to a couple of her high school friends, he'd learned she'd told her parents she was staying with friends and then left. *Very resourceful the way she put money aside and also sold things.* By his calculations she'd had about a thousand dollars. In 1986 that was an enormous amount but not enough to take care of a pregnant seventeen-year-old for very long.

Grant didn't approach any of the Knight-Compton family directly. He did ask an investigator at his law firm to check and see if any of the current Knight-Compton servants were employed twenty or so years ago.

He hit pay dirt with that angle. A few casual questions about the family were mixed in with the stated reason for the interview: background check. There had been a big fight. Honey had been grounded to her room. A doctor had come to see her. Another fight. And then she was gone. Yes, the family did look for her but after a few months, they stopped. No, no one knew why.

Grant did.

Once Honey was four or five months along, the scandal of her being an unwed teen mother would have been enough. Her parents had turned their back on her. So at seventeen, she'd turned her back on her Knight-Compton roots and figured out how to make her own way in the world.

And by the looks of it, she succeeded. She owned a business that was doing well and raised a daughter on her own. Combing the school's newspaper and previous yearbooks, Grant learned Logan Compton was a good student and liked by everyone.

Still, she was his daughter and he'd been denied a part in her life for too long. That would end tomorrow. He put down the scotch-on-the-rocks and paced. The outline of a plan in mind, he poured the rest of his drink down the drain. *I need all my faculties in top working order.*

5 - CONFRONTING THE PAST

*I*t was Friday. When Grant had gone to bed Monday night, his plan had been to confront Honey the next morning. He'd waited in his car across the street from the studio, ready to storm in when Logan left for school. That plan changed when the two of them left together. Arm in arm they walked down the street, laughing, doing synchronized twirls every few steps.

Grant watched them until they turned the corner and were out of sight. Honey, no Hunter he reminded himself, was still a free spirit, still gorgeous, still full of life. The thought stabbed his heart. The women her age in their social circle had fully conformed to what was expected. Polite, refined, formally charming, predictable—even in the privacy of their homes, even in the privacy of their beds.

It wasn't that the women were frigid or didn't participate as sexual partners. They did. But in a formulated way. The carefree abandon Hunter and Logan displayed just now and in public would never do. Would never be accepted.

He pushed away the moment of awareness that Hunter wanted more for this child than she had had as one of The Knight-Comptons. *It makes no difference. Logan is my daughter. She had no right to keep her from me.*

Starting his car, Grant pulled away from the curb. He wasn't sure where Hunter was, but he knew Logan was going to school. For the fourth day in a row, he drove to the high school and parked in visitor parking.

The second day he'd parked here, he even got out of the car and started towards the building. His plan? Introduce himself to the school principal and ask to have Logan brought to the office.

Why didn't he?

Even though energized by the vision of doing just that, he'd turned back, got in the car and driven away. Logan was his daughter but from all he knew she had no idea who he was. School wasn't the place to introduce himself.

So this Friday, he followed the routine of the previous four days. He watched her leave. Drove to the high school and watched her go in. He sat for a time and imagined her in her first class, greeting other students, happy among her friends, excited she was graduating.

He was back there after school, watching her leave. On Tuesday and Thursday, with a couple of boys accompanying her, she went home. He could see in the upstairs windows that they were sitting at a table. He surmised doing homework. On Wednesday, like Monday, she went to the studio and, again an educated guess, helped her mom with the younger students.

Today she took a city bus somewhere with a group of friends. Or at least she got on the bus with other girls she seemed to know. *Tomorrow.*

Saturday, according to the Twinkle Toes flyer, Hunter had a full class schedule starting at nine and ending at four. Parked two doors down, he timed everything to the second. Exiting his car, Grant waited next to the studio's entrance for the next to the last class to let out. As the two o'clock students left and the three o'clock students entered, he walked inside with a couple of other parents.

It was an old building by west coast standards but not really so very old. Built as many structures were in the early 1900's it housed the business on the ground floor and the family above. Stairs to the living quarters were at the back of the building as was a separate entrance. He waited until her back was turned to slip past the entrance to the studio.

Settled on the stairs, pleased he could hear what was happening in the class, Grant waited.

Waited for the class to end.

Waited for his revenge to begin.

HUNTER LOCKED the door after the last student. She glanced around the front office area. Nothing looked out of place but the nagging sense of doom prevailed. And, if anything it was stronger.

What's wrong?

Even Logan was asking her that question, sensing something was going on. *Tomorrow The Circle meets. Maybe someone can help me figure out what's bothering me.* The prospect of Logan in college in Massachusetts was part of the problem but Massachusetts was not Rhode Island. *What if someone at Smith knows the family name?*

The idea of sitting down with her daughter and telling her the truth about their past—well, her brain just shut down. Over the years even imagining the conversation created swirls of nausea through her body.

Back in the studio, she picked up her horsehide drum. She loved the deep reverberating sound it made. Using her hand, she began a slow steady rhythm. Raising and lowering the instrument, she circled the room in a slow, shuffle step. She increased the beat's tempo and quickened her pace on her second circuit. The third time, she held the drum out to one side and step-step-twirled her away down one side of the room and up the other.

"Hello Honey, or should I say 'Hunter'."

Her heart stopped.

Her breathing stuttered.

She stumbled but grabbed the barre just before she tumbled to the floor.

The smooth voice with the New England accent was so familiar, a reminder of another place and time, a reminder of the past and why she was here in Fremont. Her heart pounded in her ears, louder than her drum could ever be.

Her personal nightmare's name? Grant Haywood Parker IV and he was here.

In Fremont.

In Twinkle Toes.

In front of her.

Life as she'd known it ended.

"Grant." Astonished at the sight before her, Hunter stared. Cold crept from her feet up through her legs, into her torso, curled around her heart, chilled her lungs.

"So you do remember me," Grant said, a sardonic tilt to his mouth. "I wasn't sure you would."

The screaming thought in her head was to ask him why he was here. She clenched her jaw to keep the words inside. It really made no difference, his being here changed her world beyond all recognition.

"Aren't you going to ask me why I'm here?" He lounged against the doorframe, his icy hard blue-grey gaze locked with hers.

To keep from wavering, her grip on the barre tightened. She shook her head.

"I came for my daughter," he said in a voice as cold as his look. "You know, the one you've hidden from me for—," he straightened and took a step towards her. "Yes, I remember now, over eighteen years."

"Are you referring to *my* daughter?" Hunter asked, her chin raised, looking down her nose at him.

"No, I'm referring to *our* daughter." Grant emphasized his point by speaking louder and taking another step forward.

"*We* do not have a daughter. *I* have a daughter. And unless you and your wife have had children—." Hunter glared at the man now five feet away.

"No wife, no children. She's mine." He fisted his hands on his hips. "Let's stop playing games. I can count. I know you weren't with anyone else that summer. There's no way she isn't my daughter.

"And, don't tell me I've no right to a place in her life. You deliberately kept her from me!"

A keening cry from the entrance to the studio stopped Hunter's retort.

Logan stood there, tears streaming down her face, arms wrapped around her stomach. "I hate you! I hate you! I hate you!" she screamed at them.

Before either Grant or Hunter could react, Logan bolted. Her footsteps raced down the hall, the front door slammed.

Silence.

Hunter jerked into motion. The icy cold of a moment ago replaced by a volcano of energy. She dashed out of the studio, out the front door, Grant hard on her heels.

No sign of Logan.

"You check that way," Hunter ordered pointing to one end of the street as she took off for the other.

They met up on the opposite side of the block.

No sign of her.

"Where could she have gone?" Grant asked a quiet intensity in his voice.

Hunter's throat constricted. "I'll check in with her friends," she managed. "She's never run off like that. I really don't know— ."

"If you have a list of names, I'll help call," Grant offered.

"You've done enough! She's my responsibility. I'll do it." Hunter spat her spine stiff.

Grant followed her to the front door of the studio, followed her in and locked the door when Hunter just marched on. He followed her down the hall and up a flight of stairs to the living quarters.

Hunter paused at the door to one of the bedrooms before going inside.

Grant, still trailing behind her, knew it was Logan's. One wall was covered with Fremont High School banners and pictures from her years in high school. Hunter stood looking at a note tucked into the side of the mirror.

"What's it say?" he asked.

"It says that even in the darkest night, I'll always be there for her. I'll always love her." Hunter choked out the words as her fingers traced the paper's edges. In her entire life, Logan had never run off like this. She'd gone to her room and slammed the door, once she even locked herself into the bathroom, but to leave? Anger at Logan, at Grant and at herself battled with the cold dread of fear.

Trying to find balance on the emotional seesaw was impossible unless she focused on what she could do. She fought the threatening sobs, the screams of anger and anguish.

"I will find her," she said her voice tense with resolve. She swiveled to leave the room and bumped into Grant.

He stepped aside. "Let me make some calls."

"And who are you to Logan?" Hunter challenged. "Why would you be making the calls?"

"I'm an old family friend," Grant said, looking into turquoise-green eyes, bright with tears and filled with fear. "Please, let me help. If someone wonders why I'm calling, I'm an old family friend, in town for a few days, and don't want to miss seeing her."

It sounded plausible.

If anyone could pull it off, Grant could.

"I'll make a list after I make one other phone call," Hunter said as she strode into the living room.

She picked up her cell phone and punched in a speed dial number grateful she didn't have to remember the number much less look it up.

"Hunter, so good to hear from you. Are we still on to carpool tomorrow?" Ashley asked in her soft southern accent. "The kids are sure looking forward to seeing Logan."

"There's been a problem, Ash. I'm not sure Logan will be available. Oh Ash, she's run off. I can't go into details right now, I've got to call her friends and see if I can find her. Please send prayers for her to be okay."

"Consider it done," Ashley replied.

Hunter hung up, tears threatening. She wished she could dance through this, pound her frustration and fear out with her drum. She fingered the small figurine of a stork on the end table. "Just a minute," she said and left the room. Within a minute she was back, a bright blue shawl covered with flying storks wrapped around her shoulders.

"I'm ready," she said, sitting down and opening her planner to the contacts section in back. Picking up a pen and two sheets of paper she flipped through and made their lists.

Every effort she made to calm herself and search energetically for Logan failed. Shoving the 'if only' thoughts aside, Hunter focused on the present. *I did what I did because at the time I thought it was right.* Internally she shook her head. *At least be honest with yourself. I was just plain afraid at best and terrified at worst. To get through this I have to believe she's okay and we'll work things out when we find her.*

Grant's voice as he began to make phone calls brought her back to the present. Looking at her list, she dialed the first number. "Hi this is Hunter Compton, Logan's mother. By any chance is she there?"

6 - HELP?!

$\mathcal{A}$shley called Lily. They quickly agreed that while Lily emailed Elizabeth and called Diana, she would call Sophia and Gabriella. The message left for Sophia who was either working in her garden or helping her sick friend: Send prayers to Hunter and Logan and if possible be at the studio in an hour. When Gabriella answered her phone, their quickly made plan was for Gabriella to stop by and pick Ashley up.

She also called Daniel and let him know he and the kids were on their own for dinner. Makings for hamburgers were in the refrigerator. "I don't really know what's happened, something about Logan running away. No," she agreed "that doesn't sound like her at all. Be sure and let me know if you see or hear from her. Use your best judgment about telling the kids or not."

Gathering her purse, jacket and cell phone, she waited on the front porch for Gabby. Looking out across the river to the Cascade Mountains beyond Fremont, she said prayers for both Hunter and Logan.

The drive across town to Hunter's dance studio was an agonizing twenty minutes. Neither Ashley nor Gabby had any idea what might have happened. Last week Hunter's Spring Recital went off without a

"

hitch. Logan was obviously proud of her mom and had been a big help.

"We'll just have to wait and see what Hunt says," Ashley said after another foray into 'what if' land.

DIANA HAD to wait for Matthew to get home because she didn't have a sitter for Madison Michelle.

Lily, Gabby and Ashley met in front of Twinkle Toes. They tried the door, it was locked. They knocked, actually banged on the door. No response. Ashley tried calling Hunter's number, it was busy.

"I've tried calling her five times." Frustrated at not reaching her circle sister she asked the others, "Now what?"

"Let's see what we can see from across the street," Gabby suggested, already crossing in the middle of the block. "I can see her," she called out. "She isn't alone."

Ashley and Lily crossed over to have a look. Through the upstairs window, they could see Hunter's head. She was looking down at something on the table, one hand was by her ear and the other shaded her forehead. "It looks like she's resting her elbow on the table," Lily remarked.

"Who's that with her?" Ashley asked. "All I can see is some guy with blond hair, or maybe it's gray?"

"He looked up," Gabby said and started waving.

Lily tried calling Hunter's number—busy.

Gabby continued to wave and gesture.

Ashley crossed the street and banged again on the door.

"He's noticed us," Gabby said, waving and gesturing an awkward pantomime to let them in.

Lily tried calling again when she saw Hunter's hand drop away from her ear.

"We're here to help, Hunt. Let us in," Lily said as soon as there was a connection.

Hunter looked out the window, turned to the man who stood and disappeared from view.

"Grant will let you in," Hunter said.

"She said Grant will let us in and then hung up," Lily told the others.

The door to Twinkle Toes opened and a tall, blond man stood to the side.

"I'm Ashley," Ashley said rushing inside.

"I'm Gabriella," Gabby said following close behind.

"Hi, I'm Lily, another of Hunter's friends. I don't believe we've met." Lily scrutinized the man before her as she held out her hand and stepped inside the entry way.

"Grant Parker, an old friend." He took Lily's hand in a quick shake.

"Let's go see what we can do to help sort things out. We've all known Hunter and Logan for many years. I think just over ten now," Lily chatted as she hurried down the hall.

She started up the stairs but then noted Grant lagged behind. "Did you relock the front door? My husband, Jackson, will be along shortly."

"It's safer to keep it locked," Grant replied. "I'll wait for him."

"I expect there to be a lot of traffic, Mr. Parker. As an old family friend," she carefully emphasized the last three words, "I'm sure you'd much rather be up here supporting Hunter than sitting downstairs by the door."

Lily hurried up the rest of the steps and into the room when she heard Hunter yell, "I don't know where she is! Don't you think I've called everyone?" Hunter choked out, a touch of hysteria in her voice.

"Then let's just sit down and regroup, Hunt," Ashley said in her soft southern accent. "You said Logan's been gone just over an hour now and she isn't answering her cell phone and hasn't called you back. Right?"

Hunter nodded.

"You've got a few more people here to help come up with ideas," Ashley finished.

"First things first," Gabby said, moving next to Hunter and slipping an arm around her shoulder. "We need to pool our energy here."

Lily and Ashley joined arms and linked with Gabby and Hunter. Slowing their breathing, concentrating on Logan, they energetically searched for her.

"She's so angry," Ashley said.

"She's so hurt," Lily added.

"She's so alone," Gabby said. "But what's most important is we all know she's alive—hurting, but alive."

"What happened?" Lily asked the question on everyone's mind.

"She—He—," Hunter said. Shaking her head, tears streaming down her face, she started again. "I—."

A keening cry sounded as she sank to the floor, doubled over, holding herself as if she'd received a mortal wound.

Ashley knelt beside her, her arm around her shoulder and pulled Hunter into her arms. "Tell us as best you can, Hunt. We're here to help. We need to know a little bit more than Logan ran off."

Lily looked up and saw Grant standing quiet, rigid and so self-contained he could be a statue in the room. "What do you know about all this, Mr. Parker?" she asked.

"She overheard parts of a conversation between her mother and me," Grant said. He turned away and looked out the window, his back to the women.

"And?" Lily prompted.

Grant spun around, speared Lily with his best corporate attorney glare. "Look, you may be Honey's friends but I don't know you and I don't owe you."

He strode from the room; Ashley shrugged her shoulders.

His footsteps sounded on the stairs; Gabby arched a brow.

As his footfalls faded down the long hall, Lily rolled her eyes.

"So, Hunt, I see two lists of names and numbers here on the table and they've all got lines through them. I take that to mean you and Mr. Parker have called everyone and asked about Logan," Lily said her tone and manner brisk and business-like.

"Must have been some kind of conversation for Logan to take off," Ashley said. "I can't think of much that would drive that girl away from you."

Ashley still had her arm around Hunter. She leaned closer and asked "Want us to guess, or are you going to tell us?"

27

7 - WHERE IS SHE?

"Grant is Logan's biological father." There, she'd said the words out loud. No screams, not even a theatrical gasp from the others. Hunter raised her head, proud chin in the air and glared at other women, daring them to—daring them to do or say something that would destroy what little remained of her.

Logan, her world, had run away. The Circle, her other world, had been a constant in her life for over ten years. Perhaps what was more important was these women were constants in Logan's life. *Perhaps she'll contact—no, that's too much to hope for.*

Winter Solstice seemed like another lifetime ago, but in reality just over three months had passed. That night, they'd asked for what they wanted. Rose had asked for Daniel to be her papa. Logan had wished she knew something about her birth father.

Both girls had gotten what they wanted. Rose was sublimely happy. Daniel and Ashley were married and adoption paperwork was in process. Logan was so devastated, she'd run away—something she'd never done before.

*If only...*the litany ran over and over in her mind. But she hadn't. It was never the right time, never the right place, never—never just right.

Hunter had left her past behind for a reason. Even today she wasn't sure if she'd stayed at home she'd have been able to withstand the pressure from her parents; pressure to have an abortion; pressure to place her baby daughter up for adoption.

Leaving meant she'd been free to raise her daughter as she wanted, protected from the stifling lifestyle being part of her parent's social circle required.

If only Grant hadn't shown up.

She wanted it to be all his fault but she knew it wasn't one hundred percent his doing. If only she'd said something to Logan years ago about him, something so she knew he existed, something her daughter could use to fill the emptiness, the gaping hole that she now realized on a completely different level had always been a part of Logan's life.

Everyone had taken a seat. Ashley held her hand but it wasn't enough. She was desperate to have this nightmare disappear; desperate to know where Logan was; desperate to what? *To tell the truth about my past.*

A blanket of calm wrapped around her. She swiped her eyes, a heart-torn sigh slipped from her lips. "No, I don't want you to guess."

GRANT EASED DOWN and sat on the steps leading to the upstairs. He was out of sight but could hear most everything. Thankful he'd calmed down enough to return and find out what he could do to find his daughter, he listened intently. Of course when a voice dropped to a certain level he was out of the loop, but he was smart and could pretty well fill in the blanks.

Ashley had asked a bombshell question and then there was silence. Grant knew the power of silence and used it relentlessly when negotiating contracts. The woman named Lily, whose husband was on his way, was more focused on him. *Someone to steer clear of.*

Hunter's voice was shaky but he could hear her. As she talked about that long ago summer, he saw them as they'd been: young sixteen almost seventeen and nineteen at the time. Happy and free. A summer spent playing beach volleyball, diving in the ocean, campfires at night. If she was beautiful then, she was striking now.

What is she saying? He tuned back in.

"He was my first," Hunter said.

The memory of the gift of her virginity socked him in the solar plexus.

"He was so careful, so gentle."

Was she crying?

"I know I was young but I was sure we were truly in love. That he felt for me the way I felt for him. I'm not sharing the details other than to say there were a couple of times when the condoms failed. I didn't think too much about it because when I got home, I always douched.

"Summer was over and Grant returned to Yale and I started my senior year. I'd never been real regular so when my period was late, I didn't think that much about it. But then I realized I'd never been so late.

"I couldn't go to our family doctor so I went to a clinic in Hartford, used a fake name and paid cash."

The quiet was disconcerting. Grant started to rise, to move up a few steps so he could hear better. He startled when the tea kettle pierced the silence.

Seventeen and alone. We'd celebrated her seventeenth birthday with a bonfire on the beach. August. One of those nights the condom broke. He knew Logan's birthday was in May and counting the months wondered if that transcendent night was when she'd been conceived.

He was finding it difficult to remain quiet and still. Every instinct screamed he should rush up the stairs and demand to know why she hadn't said anything to him. But he didn't. He'd burst into her life, created a chaos he hadn't even considered, and lost a daughter he hadn't had a chance to meet much less get to know.

"But you never said anything to Grant?"

It wasn't Ashley's softer Southern voice that asked and it wasn't the more business-like tone he associated with Lily. That left Gabriella as the one asking the question uppermost in his mind.

"There was a teacher planning day in late October and I did go to Yale to tell him. I waited outside the building where I knew he had his last class. When he came out, a blond was hanging on his arm. She turned her face up and he leaned down and kissed her."

He heard her sobs and quiet voices he knew were comforting her. *Who was the blond?* He had no memory of that girl or that kiss. His chest tightened, tears threatened. *If only... .*

The front door opened and Grant jumped up. He didn't want to be seen lurking, even though that was exactly what he'd been doing.

A tall man, about his height at six feet strode down the hall. Sable hair with a touch of gray at the temples, cold gray eyes that brooked no argument, a grim expression announced he was not happy about whatever was going on.

He took the offensive. "You must be Jackson, Lily's husband. I'm Grant Parker," he said, extending his hand.

Glad for his corporate background, he withstood Jackson's head to toe scrutiny without blinking an eye.

"Everyone is upstairs," he added, turning to start up the steps.

Grant had known Hunter for years because their parents were in the same social circle and that summer they were inseparable. What struck him as he entered the room was in all that time he'd never seen her despondent. Frustrated, even angry but the desolation he saw in her face—Never.

Of course she would be upset over Logan's running away but kids ran off or ran away all the time. He figured one of the friends they'd called knew where she was because she was with them. She was probably complaining about her mother having lied to her. *Was she telling them about me?*

Nothing really to worry about. She'd come home when she was hungry or definitely before dark. Why didn't they see that?

Both Ashley and Gabby glared at him when he entered the living room. Lily was enveloped in a hug from her husband. Even though he was right there, when Jackson stepped back from his wife, he took Hunter in his arms, holding her, patting her back, saying something so quiet he couldn't hear—something obviously comforting because

Hunter nodded, took the offered handkerchief, wiped her eyes and nose.

I should be doing that. But he couldn't. As much as he wanted to, he knew Hunter would not welcome his efforts to console her. From her perspective he was the reason all this had happened.

While he didn't think that himself, he was able to step back and look at the issue from her perspective. She had a point. Not a good one but one that would need to be dealt with. Grant was still determined to be a part of his daughter's life.

But first they had to find her.

He cleared his throat, leaned against the table and instead of telling them what to expect, asked, "Don't you think she'll come home on her own?"

"No, no we don't," Lily said. "In all the years we've known Logan, she's never done anything remotely like this. Not even close. She's always been respectful of her mom."

"She's never been late or missed a curfew or anything like that?" Grant asked the assembled group. "She seventeen, I find that hard to believe."

"There's a difference between being a little late getting home and calling your mom to let her know that and being gone over two hours. Do you have any kids?" Ashley asked.

He shook his head. Opened his mouth to speak but was cut off.

"Then you don't have the same experience to understand what's happening that we do," Ashley gestured to Hunter and Lily. "Taking off like this is not something Logan would do unless something was very, very wrong."

"Like mother like daughter?" Grant said looking directly at Hunter. "You just took off, disappeared."

Hunter's knees buckled, a stricken moan escaped. Jackson helped her to the chair and eased her down. Straightening, he sent a black look at Grant. "I'm not going to respond to that," he said and turned back to Hunter.

"I was pregnant and refused to have an abortion. If I'd stayed, they'd have taken her from me as soon as she was born. I'd have never even seen her. I-I-I just couldn't do that. She's... ." Tears overwhelmed and any other words were lost.

Grant knew her parents and it did make sense why they let her disappear. They knew she'd fight to keep the baby if they found her. And, after enough time had passed and they were certain the baby had been born, well, how would that be explained? What would the scandal of all that do to their image?

He was well aware of what that scandal would have done. Not that there wasn't a scandal associated with Honey's disappearance but they covered it up by announcing she was attending a private school in Switzerland for her senior year. *I need to remember to call her Hunter. She's reinvented herself and that young girl I knew all those years ago no longer exists.*

As darkness fell and they heard no word from or about Logan, he realized that if she was like her mother, she could disappear and they wouldn't find her. *No, we won't give up. We will find her.* He thought to affirm to Hunter that he'd be there until Logan was found but there was no room for him.

He turned to leave, to go back to his hotel room and hire a private detective when Jackson appeared beside him.

"Do you have any idea where she went?" Jackson asked.

"I'm not the bastard you think I am," Grant growled. "I'm going back to my hotel and hire a private detective. The police have the initial report but won't really do much until she's been gone longer.

"We know she had her cell phone, wallet with her student identification and a little cash. I took notes about what she was wearing so I can give her description to the private investigator. I'll make it worthwhile to start looking for her right away."

"A private investigator is a good idea." Jackson's brow furrowed. "The more people out looking for her the better.

"By the way, I didn't say you were a bastard or that I think of you that way," Jackson continued. "Just making sure—well, maybe I do think you'd try to lure her away. She's wanted a dad for a very long time. I just hope when we find her, you're the kind of dad she needs."

8 - A SIGHTING

Sophia hurried along the sidewalk towards the entry to Twinkle Toes. Light from the upstairs windows patterned the street. A frisson of awareness along her spine—she stopped and looked around. The sight of Logan scrunched in the doorway across the street startled. *What—? I thought Lily said she'd run away? I'd better get inside and see what's going on.*

Hurrying down the hall, Sophia worried she'd made the wrong choice. *Maybe I should have gone over to her.*

The debate still going on in her mind, she started up the stairs. When she reached the top of the steps, she stilled at the scene before her. Hunter sat in the overstuffed chair, clutching her legs, her head buried between her knees. Ashley perched on one arm, Lily on the other. Jackson was fussing in the kitchen, fixing tea or something.

"I came as fast as I could when I heard your message," she said to the others. "What's going on? What happened?"

"Logan's run away," Jackson answered.

"I saw her just now," Sophia said, still confused as to what was going on.

Hunter's head snapped up so quickly she almost knocked into Ashley's chin. "What? Where?"

"Across the street. She was across the street in the doorway." Sophia strode across the room to the window. "She was right there," she said and pointed to the entrance to the cleaners.

Hunter and Gabby sprinted across the room. Ashley followed a little slower.

"Where did you see her?" Lily asked.

Sophia pointed again to the only doorway that could be considered across from the studio. "No one is there now, but I know it was Logan. I almost went over to talk to her but wasn't sure what was going on and thought I needed to get updated first."

Hunter was dashing across the street, her jerky movements nothing like the graceful woman they all knew. Gabby branched off headed for the corner.

Ashley appeared moments later.

"We need to get down there," Lily said.

The three moved quickly, grabbing their own coats as well as ones for Hunter, Gabby and Ashley.

"Why didn't you bring her home?" Hunter turned and screamed at Sophia when she, Lily and Jackson caught up with her at the corner.

"I'm so sorry, Hunter. The message Lily left was that Logan had run off and to come over here as soon as I could. When I saw her, I figured she'd come back. I know in hindsight it doesn't make as much sense as it did to me at the time. I just didn't realize, didn't know what had happened, what was going on," Sophia said in a broken voice quelling the urge to wrap Hunter in her arms. Ashley and Lily were already doing that.

A hand on her shoulder—Jackson pulled her into a side hug. "Let's go back and regroup," he suggested. "We can check in with Grant and see if he's found a private detective yet."

"Who's Grant?" Sophia asked looking at Jackson.

"He's part of the reason Logan ran away. But it isn't my story to tell." His gaze rested on Hunter who was sobbing in Ashley's arms.

"Go ahead, Jackson," Lily said. "You and Sophia go ahead and fix something we won't eat. Gabby, Ash and I'll be along with Hunt."

~

ON A BUS HEADED into the downtown area, Logan slouched on the seat. Doubts churned in her stomach. *I know Sophia saw me. Why didn't she come and get me?*

As soon as Sophia had passed through the doorway, Logan raced off, zigzagging through the neighborhood business district to a bus stop a dozen blocks away. Her plan had been to go home but once outside, she just couldn't go in. What would she say? What would her mom say? And then there was the fact she had a dad.

She'd always wanted a dad. But when she came in the front door of the studio, she'd heard them yelling at each other. They sounded angry. But there was another emotion she couldn't identify buried in the anger.

Replaying the scene over and over, questions circled in her mind. Was this man a mean dad? A few of the kids at school had that kind of dad and when she thought of them, she was always grateful she didn't have a dad. No dad was better than a mean one.

Should she have stayed? When she'd stood in the doorway, they were fighting but he didn't have his hand raised.

Maybe—but the pain inside….

If her mom hadn't lied to her all these years, she knew she could have stormed in and confronted him. Stood next to her mom and demanded answers. But her mom had never answered her questions about a dad.

When she was little, her mom told her a story about God knowing she needed a little girl and sending her. She was seven when her mom found The Circle. The story changed a bit and it was the God and Goddess who sent her to her mom. By the time she was ten, she stopped asking because the story never changed.

Morning eventually came. Tired, hungry and chilled, when Logan saw people going into a Catholic Church she got off at the next stop. Sitting in the back, she witnessed her first Catholic Mass. After the service she joined the others, made small talk with two people who must have been the greeters if new people showed up. Two cups of coffee and three cookies later, she waved good-bye and headed down the street.

No one will think to look for me in a church. At nine she attended a Methodist service. Two more cups of coffee and a banana helped stave off the growl in her stomach. As she took her leave, one of the women approached and gave her a card with the address of a youth shelter on it. "Just in case you know someone who could use this," she'd said. Clipped to the card was a five dollar bill. Another woman handed her another banana and two oranges.

So much for blending in. Logan truly was grateful these two women noticed her and yet she was terrified they had. She stood outside the Episcopal Church until their eleven o'clock service started. Sitting in the back, she fought the urge to jitter. The caffeine had caught up with her.

I wish I had my charger. I could check in with my friends and see what's going on. There were many more things she wished for like her own bed, her warmer coat, gloves, scarf or hat. *What I want most is to have my mom back. I don't want a dad any more.*

She changed to tea and politely declined the offer of cookies after the Episcopal service. The rest of the day was spent traveling. Thankfully she had her student identification that also served as a bus pass. Making sure she transferred from bus to bus and used the light rail so the same driver never saw her, Logan spent the day traveling around Fremont.

Night was falling. She'd eaten the banana and oranges from earlier in the day. She'd been able to drink from the public fountains in the downtown area or from the faucets when she used a coffee shop's restroom.

The five dollars she'd been given earlier was still in her pocket along with the three dollars she'd had with her when she took off. Where was she going to spend tonight?

The card with the information about the youth shelter was in her pocket. She got it out, studied it and made a decision. She could find a doorway, she could go home, or she could go to the shelter.

Almost immediately she crossed sleeping in a doorway off the list of options. That was too scary to seriously consider. She couldn't go home yet. What would she say to her mom? Whenever she thought of her mom's deceit, all those years she'd yearned for a dad, thought he must be dead. Why didn't her mom tell her about him if he was alive? All those lost years. Tears spilled down her cheeks and dripped off her chin. *No, I can't go home.*

That left the youth shelter. Buses were running every hour and she'd missed one while she'd stood there deciding what to do. *I know about where this place is. If I stay on this street, another bus will come by.*

Logan started walking.

It was dark, the Youth Shelter full when Logan arrived. Homeless youths took advantage of a warm place to stay even if it was only a cot on the floor when the nights were chilly. Running water, the opportunity to shower, even do a load of laundry if one had a change of clothes were available.

None of that really applied to her. She did have a home but after walking three miles, Logan was exhausted. When told the shelter was full, she burst into tears.

"The Shelter is full but we have a drop-in center next door," the staff person told her. "Let's go see what's available there."

Staff at the drop-in center pointed to the day room where a television was on with the sound muted. A couple of other kids about her age sprawled on the couch. When she spied an overstuffed chair, she cried again.

There were some papers to fill out but when she left her address and phone number blank, they didn't insist or tell her she had to leave. A glance at the clock on the wall showed her she'd been gone over twenty-four hours. It felt like a life-time.

Having a dad was a dream come true but the man who was arguing with her mom was not what she wanted in a dad. *How could*

Mom have lied to me all these years? The enormity of that lie caught up with her. *I can't go home yet. I don't know what to say.* The idea to call Ashley or Sophia popped into her mind. *They're Mom's friends first.*

Here at the shelter she was safe. She had to leave in the morning but could come back tomorrow night if needed. And there were counselors here she could talk to.

Logan gratefully accepted the bologna sandwich and bottle of water from one of the staff. After using the restroom and washing up, she collapsed in the chair—her chair. Too tired to eat, she tucked the food in a pocket and fell into an exhausted sleep.

She woke up to the sound of her name being called. It was seven and time to leave. If she wanted to talk to one of the staff about what she wanted to do or if she needed help making decisions, she could make an appointment with one for later in the day.

It crossed her mind to go on to school, but Sophia worked there and she was positive her mom had called The Circle. *No, school wasn't a safe place right now.* Her senior project? Her plans to graduate? Her goal of going to college? All on hold.

She turned her phone on. She still had a little battery left. Calls from her mom? Twenty-five. Calls from a number she didn't recognize? Thirty-one. Calls from Lily, Ashley and Sophia? One each. *The Circle was trying to reach her. Maybe?* She shook her head. *They're Mom's friends first.*

Gathering her sandwich and water bottle, she left with the others. One of the guys fell into step beside her. "I'm DT," he said. "Want to hang out with us today?" His gesture included the other four kids who'd spent the night at the drop-in center.

What else did she have to do?

She ignored the churning in her stomach, the taste of fear in her mouth. "Sure."

10 - THE CIRCLE

Sunday while Logan was circling Fremont on public transportation, The Circle gathered at Sophia's. The only one physically missing was Elizabeth, who was in Ireland with Michael. Emails had flown back and forth between Lily and Elizabeth, who assured Lily that she and The Lady would send streams of love to all of them but especially to Logan and Hunter.

Daniel had James, Anthony and Rose with him. He, the children and Jackson were at Matthew and Diana's house. It was easier to take three school age kids there than to take one three month old anywhere.

Sophia stood at the entrance to her sacred space, a smoking smudge stick made up of cedar, lavender and sage in one hand, the bell Elizabeth had brought her from Ireland in the other. As the other women passed, she waved the wand so the smoke wafted around them while ringing the bell. Extra time was spent cleansing Hunter.

In all the years the women had been together, no one had ever seen their circle sister so destroyed. Hunter sat huddled over, withdrawn. Ashley and Gabriella, keeping close physical contact, flanked her.

Ashley reached out for the talking stone. "I know how hard it is to talk about secrets, so I want y'all to know I spoke to Hunter when I picked her up. She gave me permission to tell everyone what I know.

"One obvious thing we've all known from the beginning was Logan had a father. We also knew that was a subject not open for conversation. What we now know is the man, whose name is Grant Parker, has appeared. He's in Fremont. Yesterday he showed up at Twinkle Toes and confronted Hunter. It seems he didn't know he was a father because," she turned to Hunter, "I hope I get this right so you listen careful so you can correct me if I mess up. Hunt?"

Ashley waited until she saw a nod before continuing. "As I understand it, when Hunter went to tell this Grant guy she was pregnant, she saw him rather cozy with another girl so she left. Because her parents were trying to force her to sign papers placing the child for adoption or if she resisted, have an abortion, she ran away.

"What she told Gabby and me on the way here were her parents never bothered to try to find her. Her grandmother did hire a private detective who located her when she was about to give birth. Hunt made an agreement with her grandmother to send her a letter once a year to let her know how she and Logan were doing.

"She had one telephone conversation with her grandmother after Logan was born. Her grandmother told her there was a trust fund for her but she's never taken anything from it. Last month she contacted the trust officer to see what needed to be done to get money for Logan's college fees.

"How'd I do, Hunt?" Ashley leaned over and gave her circle sister a hug. "Hope it helped ease your way." She handed Hunter the talking stone.

What do I say? What do I do? Hunter's brain whirled with unanswered questions. Having Ash and Gabby on each side brought her some semblance of comfort. Gabby had shown up around midnight and insisted on staying, it was better than being alone but not by much.

With the weight of the stone in her hand, she took a deep fortifying breath, raised her head and gazed at these women who were her family and maybe her salvation.

"I-I-I really don't know what else to say." She hiccupped. "Logan's never done anything like this before. I can only imagine how shattered she is. I-I-I've let her down. I-I-I'm supposed to take care of her. S-S-She must hate me. I've left messages and she's not even called me back to say she's okay. I-I-I keep waiting for the police to knock on the door to ask me to come to the morgue to identify her body." A keening cry erupted and Hunter surged to her feet and sprinted out of the room.

"Let her go," Gabriella said. "She hasn't left the house, just left here. We need to come up with a plan. For one, I don't think she should be by herself. I'm not sure she can pull herself together enough to even teach her classes. And, I think we need to find out more about this Grant guy."

"I don't know if it would be better for her to come stay with us and have kids around or maybe stay with one of you?" Ashley nodded to indicate Lily and Sophia.

"I think that has to be her choice," Lily said. "Of course she's welcome to stay with us and if Jackson and I are gone, there is always Eleanor to keep an eye on her. I will say Jackson's mother gets quite a kick out of being a resource to the rest of us. It wouldn't be a burden at all because she won't be going to visit her daughters until May."

"Just because she's staying with whoever it works out to be, because I do agree that her being alone right now isn't a good thing, doesn't mean we can't spend time with her during the day," Diana said. "I've got a really good sitter now and would be more than willing to take her to lunch or a walk in the park or whatever."

"Who wants to go check on her?" Sophia asked. "We can't really move forward without her input."

Before Sophia had finished speaking, Ashley was up and out of the room. Five very long minutes went by before the two women returned.

"I told her what we were thinking, so she's had a moment to consider her options," Ashley announced, sitting once again with Hunter next to her.

"Who do you want to be with for the next little while?" Gabriella asked. "You do know we are all available and none of us will feel slighted if you choose another, don't you?" She waited.

Hunter looked over at her. "Right now I don't know anything." Her voice quavered on each word.

"Do you want to be around children or would it be better to only be around adults?" Diana asked.

Tears streamed down Hunter's face. "Madison Michelle is such a precious baby... ."

"Yes, she is, Hunt, but that doesn't mean it is good for you to be around her. Your decision needs to be what is best for you. Ashley and I both totally understand if being around our kids would make this horror more difficult for you."

"Diana's right," Ashley added. "You need to decide based on what's best for you." She paused before going on. "If I was making the decision for you, I'd choose Sophia or Lily's place with Lily's place being first. Why? Because Eleanor is there and I can personally attest to what a comfort she is in time of travail."

Hunter looked over at Lily. "She's right. Eleanor helped me when I was staying there after the accident," Lily said.

"She was the only one I could listen to when Dennis was so abusive and Matthew so protective," Diana added.

"We all know what she did to help the kids and me," Ashley said. "Without her, I don't know what we'd have done."

"I don't want to intrude," Hunter started.

"I believe," Ashley interrupted, "this is your time to accept our help with grace and gratitude. Most of us have had the pleasure of this lesson and I will remind you what was said to me more than once 'this is being offered, your job is to smile and accept.'"

"I don't like this." A frown scrunched Hunter's brows together.

"Of course you don't," Lily said. "None of us did. However, that was beside the point. What is important to remember is when all was said and done, we truly were grateful for the support."

Hunter's gaze traveled around the circle hoping to see doubt this was the best plan. They were united. Of course they would support her if she refused, they'd regroup and come up with another idea but the voice in the back of her head said they were right, she shouldn't be alone.

"I've my classes to teach," Hunter said.

"That's another thing to discuss," Gabby said. "Can you provide the level of instruction your students have come to expect? You don't even need to make the calls, Hunt." Gabby patted Hunter's knee. "We can make the calls, say something as simple as there's a family emergency and you aren't available to teach classes for a few days."

"But," Sophia added, "I think you need to cancel your classes at least for this week. Once we find Logan, you and Logan and probably Grant will need some time to sort things out."

"But what about school?"

Everyone heard the note of panic in Hunter's question.

"She can miss a week of school and it won't really affect things that much," Sophia said. "Her teachers know and like her, she's a good student. Yes, she'll have work to make up but she's smart and can easily do that. What's most important now is to find her."

"Grant told Jackson he was going to hire a private detective and he's staying at the Fremont Inn. I think we need to have Jackson contact him to find out where things are. We can make another plan once we know if he's already engaged someone," Lily offered.

"I agree with Lily," Diana said. "We also need to check in with the police although I can't imagine they've found anything out and haven't told you." Her violet-blue gaze met Hunter's turquoise-green one before catching the others' eye. "I haven't even met him but I do think it better if someone who's met and maybe exchanged a few words spoke to him first."

"Looks like we have the beginnings of a plan," Sophia said as she stood. Closing prayers were said before the women adjoined to the family room. They left the altar in place so they could come back before they disbanded.

Lily called Jackson who said he'd call Grant as soon as they hung up. No one had heard anything and that had the worry meters skyrocketing.

"I'll call you as soon as I've finished talking to him," Jackson said. "Just don't know if this will be a short or longer conversation.

"Also, Daniel and Matthew think we should go to his motel and introduce ourselves. You know, see if there is something he'll tell us that he won't tell any of you. What do you think?"

"Call him first and then we can decide. There are children to make arrangements for if that ends up being the plan. And, I don't know how Hunter will take it if we are seen to welcome this man now," Lily warned her husband.

"Talk to you soon. Love you"

"Love you, too," Lily said and hung up.

11 - LOST BUT NOT ALONE

Wednesday

*L*ogan stood across the street from Twinkle Toes. It looked different somehow. DT and two of his friends had brought her. Her plan was to sneak in while her mom was teaching a class, get some of her things: her phone charger, some clean clothes, her winter jacket, the money in her piggy bank. And food. She was so hungry. The sandwich at the youth shelter at night was not enough. DT had bought her a hamburger at McDonalds but she was uncomfortable accepting too much from him. *He's been so kind and helpful but I feel—it just doesn't feel right.*

"Logan? Logan, is that you sweetie?" a familiar voice called out.

"Hi, Mrs. Webster." Logan waved and turned to cross the street to the studio.

"Oh sweetie, your mom's not there. She's staying with Lily and Eleanor."

Panic struck, her heart raced. Logan whirled around. "What do you mean?"

"Why your mom has cancelled her classes and is staying with her friend. She's very upset about—," Mrs. Webster reached out and held onto Logan's arm.

"I just came by to get some of my things," Logan said, when Mrs. Webster seemed hesitant to say more. She turned to cross the street.

Mrs. Webster's hand on her arm tightened. "You can't get in, Logan. Your mom had a new security system installed Monday morning, state of the art, cameras and everything. You'll need to talk to her to get the new password code or the alarm will go off."

"Hey, Babe," DT called out. "Let's get out of here."

"Come inside with me, sweetie," Mrs. Webster implored. "I know we can work things out. Please come inside."

Choices. Choices. Choices.

Life was all about choices. Some choices felt good and others felt bad. Logan stood on the sidewalk. Neither of the choices in front of her felt good. *What should I do?* In the past she always had her mom or maybe one of her honorary aunts to talk to. Ashley and Gabriella were the easiest to talk to but so was Sophia.

Choices. Choices. Choices. No one to talk to about this choice.

"Hey, Babe." DT, now out of the car, ambled towards her. "Hey," he said in that low seductive tone that created shivers. "I'll take care of things. You don't need this."

Logan looked back at Mrs. Webster. "I'm sorry." Her head down and shoulders hunched, Logan turned and followed DT to the car.

No hope of getting her things.

No hope of getting her money or food.

No hope—.

ELEANOR ANSWERED THE PHONE, listened intently and hung up. Crossing her apartment, she opened the French doors leading into the main house. Hunter was curled up in a corner of the couch, a cobalt blue throw around her shoulders. The vibrant woman she'd known had been replaced with a defeated shadow.

Also in the living room was her daughter-in-law, Lily. There'd been lots of discussion about who should be there, who shouldn't. In the end, Hunter agreed to stay at Montgomery House but insisted there be no hovering. One or two people at a time was her limit, more and she withdrew. Even with only one or two people, she'd reach a point where she just curled into a ball as she was now.

"Hunter," Eleanor said once she stood in front of the couch. "I have news."

As if poked with a hot iron, Hunter leapt to her feet almost knocking Eleanor over. "What news?" Hunter asked, her voice a mix of anger and fear. "Where is she?"

While she had thought it better if they sat and had this conversation, Eleanor saw that was beyond Hunter's ability. She'd already passed by her and was pacing, arms and hands gesturing as she talked.

"Where—?"

"I am having a bit of a difficulty passing the news on with you on the move," Eleanor said.

"I can't sit still," Hunter announced continuing around the room.

"No, of course you can't," Eleanor replied. "What I came to tell you is that your neighbor, Mrs. Webster, just called. She said Logan had been there, on the sidewalk in front of her place. She talked to her and while she was not the Logan she's known all these years, she does not seem harmed or injured."

"Thank the Goddess." Hunter paused a moment before heading for the front door. "I need to go home, have a talk with that girl. Get things sorted out." She stopped in mid-stride and turned back to the stairs. "Thank you for everything," she said, her voice giddy with relief.

"My dear," Eleanor said, crossing to the bottom of the stairs where Hunter stood ready to spring up the steps two at a time. "There is more."

Hunter turned back, a frown on her face. She stilled and looked steadily at Eleanor. "She isn't home, is she?"

"No, she isn't. She was with some other young people. They had a car and one of the boys seemed a bit too familiar from what Mrs. Webster said. Called Logan "babe.""

"She was very concerned and told Logan a bit of a fib. She is already doubting her decision."

"What did she say?" Hunter asked, collapsing on the bottom step. Lily sat beside her, an arm around Hunter's shoulder.

"She told Logan you had a new state-of-the-art alarm system installed, with cameras and there was a new password code. She thought Logan would call you for the new code and you could talk to her.

"The boy she'd mentioned got out of the car and urged her to come with them. Mrs. Webster said she didn't like the looks of them and was worried they would come back at night and steal something. She said she wouldn't be surprised if the car was stolen because the license plates had been dirtied up so she couldn't see all of it. She did say it started with UT and ended with 9 and it was a black Audi four-door sedan."

"I think we need to give this information to the police and to the private detective," Lily said when Hunter didn't respond. "It might help them track her down. At least she's been coming back to your place. This is the second sighting since she took off."

"I should be home. Maybe if I was home...?"

"If you were home, Hunt, you'd be alone. I'm fairly sure part of the reason you are still somewhat sane is you have people around you who see that you have frequent hugs, words of encouragement and food to eat." Lily sat with one arm around Hunter's shoulders, the other resting on Hunter's arm.

"I think she is coming home to get something, not to see you. She knows where to find you." Lily tapped Hunter's arm when she started to protest.

"Logan knows you are with one of us and she has all of our phone numbers. Most important, she has your phone number and could call and talk to you directly. She has not called any of us nor has she called you."

A pain lanced Hunter's chest as if a hand squeezed her heart. Her elbows on her knees, her chin rested in the palms of her hands. Fresh tears streamed down her face. "I know you're right, Lily. I know the police need to be notified about her being by the studio. But I-I-I just can't face Grant."

"With your permission, Eleanor and I'll take care of it." Lily hugged her circle sister and added. "I also think we need to let everyone else know what's going on. We can make sure someone drives by on their way to and from places. It's possible one of us will spot her."

Curled over her knees, Hunter openly sobbed.

"I'm going to call Ashley," Eleanor said. "She among everyone else can best relate to how you feel."

Tears streamed from Hunter's eyes, snot dripped from the end of her nose, her chest constricted and her heart and lungs were squeezed to the point of agony. She knew why Logan didn't call her, didn't come home to her, didn't contact anyone else.

Feelings of betrayal surged at the memory of seeing Grant with another girl, leaving her alone to deal with her parents and her pregnancy. He knew them. Knew how rigid they were. Knew that image was everything!

This scenario was different. But the feeling of betrayal she knew Logan experienced was the same. Someone you loved let you down. Not just *let you down*. Those three words didn't begin to describe the depth of anguish that came with betrayal.

Logan had been gone five days. She had to pull herself together and help find her. Even if that meant she must spend time with Grant. Hearing what Mrs. Webster said about the boy Logan was with was more than disconcerting. It terrified her. The hope she might be staying with a friend died.

"I'll call Grant." It was as if another person spoke, but it was her voice saying the words. "You and Eleanor can let the police and others know." Hunter stood, wiping her face with the tissues Eleanor handed her. She stood tall, spine straight, shoulders back, chin up. Her voice quavered as she asked, "Do either of you have his phone number?"

12 - THE PAST IS NOW

*H*unter did call Grant. More than that, she asked him to come over so they could plan together how best to track Logan down. She even asked him if he wanted to stay for dinner. The latter invitation extended when Lily popped a note with the same words under her nose. She stuttered on the "would you" and the "like to stay" came out rushed, but she was proud of the calm in her voice by the time she got to "for dinner." On her own she added that Jackson was an excellent cook and his special marinara sauce was simmering on the stove.

As a mom, she'd done her fair share of worrying but now she was free-falling into full blown panic and terror. She'd been about Logan's age when she'd taken off, lived on her own, sometimes on the street, trying to make her own way—a pregnant teen on the run.

Her mantra, her prayer? *Please, please keep my little girl safe.*

The doorbell rang. Grant was here. Her chin high, her shoulders back she headed for the door to let him in. Lily was in with Eleanor, close enough to call if she needed them but far enough away to give Grant and her some privacy. Her heart racing, Hunter took a deep breath and opened the door.

*G*rant stepped into the Montgomery house, gave his coat to Hunter and shoved his hands in his pockets. Touching her in any way was not an advisable action whether it was to hold her or throttle her.

"Come in and sit down," Hunter invited. "I've made coffee. Do you still prefer it black?"

The simple question stopped him cold. "Yes," he managed to say as he walked to where she'd gestured. *She remembers.*

"I thought we'd sit here at the table. I have a map of Fremont and have already marked some places that might be useful for us to look at." Hunter set Grant's mug of coffee on a coaster on one side of the table and sat down across from him.

"What have you marked out?" He peered at the various colored marks.

"I've marked our home," Hunter said, pointing to a dot on the map, "and the homes of The Circle. This one is where we are now.

"I've noted her school, the homes of her friends." Again she gestured to different places. "I've used the bright green to show where she's been seen. And thought if your private detective had any information, someone who'd seen her or something like that, we could add it."

Grant knew she was trying very hard to appear calm, controlled and reasonable. *I remember she folded her hands just so when she was anxious. Still does.* He held back a smile as a sense of relief edged into his awareness.

"I've brought the notes from the PI. He hasn't really come up with much anything. He did find a couple of bus drivers who remember her. Not so much the light rail operators because they are separated from the cars." He handed her a list of places Logan had been seen and watched as Hunter added the information.

Finished she stood back, studied the map and considered the places her daughter had been, the places familiar to her. It wasn't that Logan was kept on a short leash but she and her friends tended to hang out at each other's houses or at school events. From time to time they went to the mall but seldom downtown.

"Does this tell you anything?" Grant asked, rounding the table to stand beside her.

"Not really. Do you mind if I ask Lily and Eleanor to join us? They might see something I don't."

"I know who Lily is. Who's Eleanor?"

"Jackson's mother. Through those French doors is a separate apartment where she lives when she isn't taking care of one of us," Hunter said, a wry smile on her face. "It's why I'm here instead of at home. The general consensus was being close to Eleanor would help."

"And has it helped?" She looked up at him and shrugged, a smile as sad as the look in her eyes sucker punched him in the gut. "The more eyes and ears the better," he said, stifling the urge to take her in his arms and assure her everything would be all right.

Hunter crossed to the French doors and knocked. A moment later she opened the door, stuck her head in and said something. It was muffled enough he couldn't hear the exact words but assumed she was extending the invitation to join them.

Lily and an older woman he assumed was Eleanor followed Hunter back to the table.

"I'm Grant Parker," he said to the older woman when she was closer. He extended his hand and she took it.

"I see bits and pieces of Logan in you," Eleanor said, her gray eyes taking in every detail. She leaned over the table and studied the map. "What have we here?"

Hunter explained the various colors to Eleanor and Lily. Grant stood to the side and observed the three women as they discussed what all the dots meant.

"I'd assume from the bus sightings she spent the first night riding around on buses and light rail," Lily said. "It's fairly common for homeless people to do this. She'd have her school bus pass so wouldn't have needed any money. She's smart enough to use the light rail and bus so she wouldn't be conspicuous and draw attention to herself.

"We can check in with Sophia, but I'm fairly confident this would be common knowledge among her classmates," Lily said.

"The private investigator checked the homeless youth shelter," Grant said. "She was there Sunday and Monday nights but hasn't been seen since."

Eleanor uncovered the pot on the stove and peered inside. "I do believe Jackson has enough sauce simmering here we can safely invite others to join us for dinner. The more ideas we come up with the sooner we'll find her."

"I'll call Sophia and leave a message for her. I think Gabby is back in Seattle, but I'll let her know also. She might have some ideas to share even though she isn't here." Hunter reached for her phone.

"Do we want to make this an event and invite everyone? That means the men and children will be here also?" Lily asked.

A wave of unease sliced through Grant. "Everyone" here was a daunting prospect. *She's your daughter. How you handled showing up is part of the problem. Suck it up.*

"I think we should do whatever is needed to find Logan. If that means the men and children are included, I'm good with it," Grant said. He turned to face Lily. "Do what you think is best. The longer she's gone, the harder it will be to find her and the higher the likelihood something bad has happened." He caught the stricken look on Hunter's face as he said the last words.

His grey-blue gaze caught her turquoise-green one. "I'm not trying to make this worse than it already is. I'm just saying out loud what we're all worrying about."

Hunter turned to look out the window and started making calls. Lily did the same. Eleanor moved next to him and patted his arm. "Thank you. It needed to be said."

"Are you from England?" Grant asked his voice shaky with relief.

"I am. And you are from New England."

"Rhode Island is where my house is. My work takes me from D.C. to Portland—Maine that is."

"And what do you do?" Eleanor's hand still rested on his arm.

"I'm an attorney, corporate-type," Grant said. It was comforting to have her hand on his arm and engage in this simple conversation.

"Has she changed much?"

He didn't have to look at Eleanor to see she meant Hunter. "We've both changed. It's been over eighteen years since we've even seen each other."

In the ways that matter? No, she hasn't changed that much. Still full of vibrant energy even in this darkest time. Still exciting to watch when she moves. Still beautiful in face and form.

"I would hazard a guess it has not been that long since you've each thought of each other." Eleanor patted his arm and stepped back. "I'm calling my son to let him know everyone will be here and see what we can do to help put this meal together."

Grant was poleaxed. Why, Hunter had not been on his mind in years, in decades. He walked to the end of the dining room table and looked out the windows at the vistas beyond. Part of the Fremont skyline, the meandering river dividing it, the faraway snow-capped mountains stretched before him. *You've never been able to commit to anyone. Why is that? I could never imagine growing old with them.*

His gaze landed on Hunter animatedly talking. Grant listened and decided it was Gabby or Gabriella because she was saying something about waiting to come home, she'd call later and let her know what everyone came up with.

I can see myself grow old with her. She's fire and sky and I'm water and earth. Growing old with her would not be boring.

Hunter turned at the knock on the door. When it opened, her eyes widened in surprise.

"I thought you were in Seattle." Hunter crossed the room and hugged her circle sister.

"I was but now I'm here," Gabby said.

"There isn't a lot of food left, but you can have first dibs on dessert," Lily offered.

"My homemade ice cream and sauces and Sophia brownies," Jackson said.

Gabby ate the spaghetti with Jackson's special marinara sauce and tossed salad. She finished off the last slice of garlic bread. Putting her dishes in the dishwasher, she clarified, "I get first dibs on dessert, for sure?"

"You do," Jackson said getting various flavors of ice cream and sauces from the freezer and refrigerator.

When everyone was dished up, adults at the dining room table and children at the kitchen island, Gabby asked for an update. Hunter showed her the map and described what the different colors meant. Gabby nodded and followed along, asking a question every now and then.

The evening wound down; the worst part of the day from Hunter's perspective. It was dark out and Logan was out there. She could only hope and pray she was okay.

Grant walked out with Gabby. Hunter heard him offer to take Gabby to her car parked four blocks away. Sophia murmured to Lily that it was very nice of Grant to see Gabby safely to her car.

Yes, Grant's offer was nice but Hunter knew what was behind the offer. Manners. The manners were inbred. Grant would offer to see any woman to her car, to her door, wherever she was going—not because he really cared about her or her safety except in a superficial way but because it was what was expected of any male Haywood Parker, especially a Haywood Parker the Fourth.

∽

That night, across town.

"Come on, baby, you know you're special to me. I promise I'll stop if you tell me to." DT murmured in her ear, his roving hands tracked across her abdomen, down her thigh and up the inside of her leg.

Her insides heated as his hand rubbed against her genitals. *I should tell him to stop but...*his questing mouth and hands confused her mind.

His leg replaced his hand and he rocked his thigh against her private parts. She should tell him no, she should push him away but then the words and actions to tell him she was a virgin and to stop floated away.

"I know you want this as much as I do." DT breathed in her ear, his hands under her shirt rubbed her nipples as his thigh rode her— *vagina. That's the word I want. He's ... .*

"That's it babe. That's it."

D.T, pulled her shirt up, exposing her breasts, unzipped her pants tugging them down her legs. His hand rubbed her genitals, a finger in her vagina, his mouth sucked a nipple.

"No," she screamed and tried to pull away. "No, no, no!"

Nothing happened. The screams were in her head. She opened her mouth to call for help, to tell him to stop.

Nothing happened. *What's wrong? Why can't I?*

Her pants were off now. D.T. stretched out, his weight holding her down. His touch gentled. His tongue in her ear then his lips on her throat while one hand still touched her vagina, the other fondled her breasts. "Babe, this is going to be soo good for you," he crooned. "The best you've ever had."

Logan floated away, detached from what was happening.

A sharp pain sliced deep. No longer floating, she was no longer detached.

A part of her mind knew DT was having intercourse with her.

How did this happen? Her mind was so slow, words were so hard to remember. Did she say "yes?" She couldn't remember. Maybe she did. She'd never said "no" to his kisses.

DT groaned. A liquid heat permeated deep inside and then he collapsed on her. Minutes later he rolled away. On his side, his head propped on one hand while the other stroked her face. "God, you're beautiful." He leaned over and kissed her, his tongue penetrating her mouth.

He drew back, his gaze raking over her nakedness. The urge to cover herself was strong but she couldn't make her arms move.

"Bet you're thirsty," he said. He helped her sit up and sip from the cup. The water had a bitter taste to it and burned going down her throat. "That's it," he crooned. "Drink it all and you'll feel better."

Warning bells sounded but Logan was at a loss how to respond. DT held her, kissed her forehead, urged her to sleep. "I'll keep an eye out for trouble. I'll keep you safe."

Tears slipped from the corners of her eyes and dripped into her hair as a fog crept through her body, enveloping her mind, leaving her in the dark.

15 - THE CALL

April 19th, 2005
Montgomery House

Stir-crazy! If she didn't get out of here, didn't move, didn't Do Something, she'd be committable. Everyone was so nice. Everyone was trying so hard to be optimistic. Everyone was walking around her on egg shells because she was wound so tight. So tight even she thought she might break. Of course that wasn't an option. She had to keep it together. She had a daughter. She had a business. She had friends. She had—.

Gabby stopped by every afternoon. She talked her into walking around the neighborhood for five minutes and then ten. They were up to fifteen minutes now and it helped a bit because the Montgomery house was in the west hills and the walkways were fairly steep. Stretching her muscles, burning off some of the tension helped keep her worst fears at bay—at least during the day.

Grant came by later in the afternoon and stayed for dinner. He hung around the kitchen while Jackson prepared the food. Hunter was fairly certain Grant had never before seen a snack much less a full meal prepared from scratch to table.

Logan had been gone ten days. Hunter wasn't really sleeping or eating much. She didn't care that she looked haggard. The police had come up with nothing. The private detective had uncovered no new leads and suggested Logan had left the area. The report Grant had shared with her stated Fremont was a way-station for runaway teens along the Interstate Five corridor.

Upon learning that, she'd barely made it to the bathroom to lose what little she'd eaten. The idea that her daughter, her Logan was somewhere other than Fremont shocked.

Sophia and Lily were on the couch. Grant was talking to Jackson in the kitchen. The men seemed to like that space even when not fixing food. She was pacing. Eleanor was just coming into the main house when the phone rang.

Hunter froze in her tracks, tense and alert when Eleanor answered. There was something wrong. She knew it in her soul. Eleanor turned and called everyone to gather round the phone, asking Lily how to put it on speaker.

"I believe you are on speaker phone, Gabby," Eleanor announced.

"Hi everyone. The good news is Logan's been found." Gabby's voice was calm. "She's alive and—well, that's the most important part. She's alive. A doctor friend of mine is checking her out. With the right support, Logan'll be okday. She's a survivor."

"What's going on? Where are you?" Hunter challenged her breathing harsh. "Tell her I'm coming, okay? I'll be there as fast as I can…." Her words tumbled over each other before fading at the end.

"It's Grant, Gabby. If it would help her, I can come also."

"It's too soon, Hunt." Gabby cleared her throat. "She needs some time to get her bearings again. Right now, Logan doesn't want to see anyone she knows."

"You've seen her, Gabby?" Lily asked. "You know she is okay?"

"You will tell me where she is!" Hunter's pain screamed through the phone line. "You have no right to keep her from me!"

Hunter shook off Lily and Sophia who were trying to talk to her. The hell she'd been through these past ten days had taken a heavy toll. Staying at Lily's she wasn't alone but she couldn't dance. Short walks were not the same. For her to clear her mind and figure things out, she had to be twirling and leaping around her studio or going for a long run.

"Gabby, Grant again," the authoritative male voice said. "I don't understand what's going on. Please explain things better."

He turned towards Hunter. "Honey, knock it off. Get over here and talk to Gabby. There's more going on here we all need to know," Grant stated as they stood around the speaker phone.

"But I've said all I can," Gabby said, her voice shaky.

"I will Never Forgive you," Hunter vowed.

Silence.

They stood staring at the phone—all they heard was silence.

16 - AFTERMATH

Grant marched towards Hunter, who was bordering on hysteria. The others, Lily, Eleanor, Sophia and Jackson just stared. They'd obviously never seen Hunter this way. But he had—oh, not quite this bad but certainly in high dudgeon.

"Stop!" he commanded.

"You bastard!" Hunter screamed. "It's all your fault!"

"I'll share the blame with you," he said in a deadly quiet voice. "Time to go."

"What do you mean? Time to go where?"

"Time to go back to your place," he said, matter-of-factly, hands on hips, watching her in case she swung at him.

The fight seemed to whoosh from her body.

He saw Lily start forward. He motioned her to stay put.

"You were here for support because no one knew what had happened to Logan. You can go home now. Start up your classes and keep yourself busy," he said his tone softer.

"I only know she's alive," Hunter snarled. "I don't know why she won't talk to me." Her voice hiccupped on the last few words.

"But you do know." Grant stepped closer. His matter-of-fact tone had a gentle current to it. "You do know what happened to her. You do know why she doesn't want to talk to you—at least not yet."

"No. I. Don't." Hunter challenged. She swayed and gripped the back of the couch.

He stood in front of her, his gaze riveted on hers and said nothing.

Hunter broke away and turned to the others. "You—." She saw the looks on their faces. Tears streamed and her voice shook, "No, no, no —not to my Logan," she moaned. Hunter sank to her knees, arms wrapped around her waist, head bent, her body racked with sobs.

Hunter's despair rent the air so palpable, so heavy, everyone froze. The first to thaw, Jackson wrapped his arms around Lily. Sophia and Eleanor clung to one another.

Grant walked the two steps to where Hunter still knelt on the floor. He pulled her to her feet and tucked her against his side. *She's where she belongs.*

Hunter had always needed to do something physical to work through problems. "You need to go home, teach your classes and do whatever else you can do to support her from a distance. You must find a way to move through the hysteria, Honey. When Logan comes home, you will need to be her mother without hysterics.

"Go pack. I'll take you home and stay with you as long as you want. In the morning I'll come back. We'll get you some groceries. And I can help you call your students—let them know you're starting classes up again."

"An alternative," Eleanor offered, "is I'll come by in the morning with groceries. You can give me a ring and I'll take care of it."

"I can stop by tomorrow around eleven and help notify your students." Lily crossed the room and stood in front of Hunter. "And Soph, can you come by after school?"

"Yes I can, and I'll bring dinner. I've got a casserole in the freezer along with some brownies and cinnamon rolls. They'll be thawed and ready for you for breakfast."

Lily and Sophia reached out and took Hunter's hands. "We'll help you pack." Lily led her towards the stairs.

Jackson had not moved. The considering look on his face Grant did not want to explore. He turned and watched the three women go up the stairs, Lily and Sophia obviously saying something to Hunter.

Eleanor's soft touch on his arm, he glanced down into her compassionate gaze.

"You are correct," she said, in that slight English accent she still had. "Hunter does need to go home and begin to pick up the pieces. But, I do not think it wise for her to spend too much time alone. She —," Eleanor's lips pursed and she said nothing more.

"I'll stay for a while tonight. Make sure she's settled a bit. I'll be back in the morning. I'm going to ask her for a key so I can get in without waking her. I can catch up on work, if she is still asleep."

"Maybe take her out for a run?" Eleanor suggested.

Grant grinned. "I know how to do that."

"Are you sure she'll go with you?" Jackson asked, the considering look replaced with a skeptical one.

"I'm not sure of many things but I am fairly positive my challenge that she can't keep up with me will do the trick."

Eleanor smiled. "Please call me tonight with the grocery list and let me know if you have a key. I will be by around ten with the groceries if I'm sure someone is up."

Footsteps sounded on the stairs as Hunter, Lily and Sophia descended. At the front door, promises of "see you tomorrow" and "call me tonight if you need to talk" accompanied long hugs.

Grant opened the passenger door for her before he stowed her suitcase and a couple of filled canvas bags in the trunk. Sliding in behind the wheel, he turned the key in the ignition. The car purred to life and the CD he'd been playing on his way here came on. One of the "oldies" with the songs of his youth—his youth and Honey's. A glance in her direction. Her eyes were closed, a few tears tracked down her cheek, her breathing shallow.

At least I don't have to worry about her jumping out when I stop for a traffic light. That errant thought was comforting. He considered telling her to change the music if she wanted but then didn't. Thirty minutes later he pulled into the parking space behind her building, turned off the ignition and waited.

It wasn't a long wait before she stirred, opened her eyes and sighed.

"We're here," he said.

"I can see that," she said but there was no rancor in her tone.

"Let's get you inside and settled, okay?" he asked, not sure if she needed a few more minutes before going inside or not.

Her answer was to unbuckle her seat belt, grab her purse and open the car door. He mirrored her actions, heading to the trunk when she headed to the back door.

Upstairs with the lights on, she wavered. He saw her hesitate before going past Logan's bedroom to the front living area. As soon as Grant deposited her belongings in her room, he retreated down the hall and closed Logan's door. Returning to the living room, he picked up a blank sheet of paper from the table in front of the window.

"I'll write things down, if you want to check and see what you need," he offered, sitting at the table, pen poised.

Hunter started with the refrigerator, tossing a few items that, because her nose wrinkled, he knew were spoiled. He added milk, cottage cheese and sour cream to the list. A wilted head of lettuce was also tossed and he duly made note of that adding "at least two different kinds."

"I think everything else is good for now." Hunter bagged the spoiled goods. "I'll just take these down to the garbage." She picked up the paper sack and started down the hall.

"Or I can do that when I leave," Grant said.

Hunter stopped at the top of the stairs and set the bag down. "Okay, the bag is at the top of the stairs, don't forget," she said, a flush coloring her cheeks. "I didn't mean...," her voice trailed off.

"No offense taken. I can't remember if I've ever even taken the trash out so reminding me when I leave is a good thing."

"About tomorrow," Hunter started.

"It won't do any good to tell me to stay away because that isn't going to happen. I can always follow Eleanor or Lily in," he said in a mild voice. "My preference would be that you lend me a key so I can come in and check on things if needed."

Hunter opened her mouth to argue.

He added before she had a chance to respond, "You don't know when you may be called away. If I have a key, I can check on things, maybe take care of something here for you."

Grant looked at the altar Hunter and Logan had made on a small table in a corner. "I don't know that she'll ever want to see me, Hon-Hunter. Let me do this for you and for her."

One of the crystals seemed to glow from within even though no light shone on the space. Mesmerized by the display, a conversation he'd had with Jackson, Matthew and Daniel about The Circle surfaced. *They have their own way of looking at the world. You'd do well to remember that.*

Drawn to the altar, Grant checked out the cobalt blue bowl in the center, surrounded by a circle of varied colored stones an inch or two in size. No two were the same. There was also an outer circle comprised of four taller crystals five or six inches in height, each now illuminated from within. Automatically his hand rubbed the warming spot over his heart.

This altar represented Hunter's view and he suspected Logan's view as well, given what was in her room. He'd noticed a cluster of rocks and crystal on a window sill and walls covered with pictures of sacred places: The Great Pyramid, Machu Pichu, Stonehenge. Personal photographs of a grotto someplace: a snowcapped mountain he thought was Mt. Hood, a St Bridget's cross with Celtic signs, and a stone circle. In that picture she was standing in the middle, her arms raised to the sky.

A spicy scent with a hint of cinnamon announced Hunter was near.

"Here," she said handing him a key. "This is to the backdoor. The security code is 0587."

He knew without her saying anything that was Logan's birth month and year. Grant took the key. "Need anything else before I go?"

Hunter shook her head but followed him to the stairs, reminding him about the garbage. He picked up the sack, only slightly surprised when she followed him down. She stood in the doorway as he deposited the bag in the dumpster. When he got in the car, she closed the door.

He stared at the backdoor, knowing it would not open again. The night air was cool but he rolled his windows down to breathe in some fresh air. His daughter had been found. She was alive but the nightmare was not at an end. The muffled sound of the beat of a drum reached him.

Grant started the car, rolled up the windows and drove off to his hotel room a few blocks away. It wasn't what he was used to and he realized his family and friends would be shocked. In some ways even he was shocked. But being close to Hunter, having a chance to build a relationship with his daughter was becoming much more important to him than appearances.

He pulled into the parking lot of the clean and cheap motel that did not have free cable or wireless. A smile on his face, he got out of his car and set the alarm. The idea that he was 'roughing it' crossed his mind. His smile turned into a chuckle as he dug his room key from his pocket.

When on particularly restless nights, he'd driven around Fremont looking for Logan. Cruising through areas where homeless people, their carts pulled close, slept in doorways or benches or just trudged through the night challenged. The alarming idea his daughter was out here coiled like a viper in his gut.

Rhode Island had homeless people also. He served on the Board of one of the non-profits that provided services to them and donated a sizable amount each year.

But here he really noticed them. Here because of a daughter he knew nothing about until a few short weeks ago, he was painfully aware of how much he had. Here he had an opportunity to take stock of his world.

Inside his small room, he pulled his cell phone out and dialed the private investigator. "She's been found. Send me your bill."

A second call was to Eleanor with the short grocery list. He added picking up some yogurt and maybe some fresh fruit, whatever was in season. "I'll see you in the morning," he told her. "I'll be there around nine."

Hanging up, he tossed the key to the backdoor of Twinkle Toes in one hand before putting it on the bedside shelf along with his car keys. He plugged his cell phone in to one outlet, his laptop in the other. A short debate about a shower, the water didn't stay really hot for very long in the morning, he decided on as long a shower as the water would allow before calling it a night and going to bed.

The mental list he made once in bed was long; the light coming in from under the curtains distracting. He thought of Hunter and congratulated himself on making progress in remembering to call her that. Sleep evaded. Starting at one hundred and counting backwards, he was somewhere in the fifties before the monotony of the task took over and he slept.

Grant was not surprised to hear the pounding drum beat or the music—the same song that was on the CD when he brought her here last night blasting from the studio.

He closed the door behind him, stood in the hallway and contemplated his next move. How to announce his presence without frightening her was at the top of his list.

Decision made, he sat on the bottom step of the stairs and let his imagination run free. The drumbeat was closer at times so he knew she was dancing. Memories of her twirling down the sand or a graceful leap over a piece of driftwood swirled. Movement always soothed her and it was obvious it still did.

He himself was a list maker. Sitting, preferably at a desk, pen and paper in hand was how he sorted things out. Pluses in one column, minuses in the other had served him well over the years. Of course there were notes in the margins, footnotes at the bottom, arrows rearranging the order of items on the list before he carefully copied it over on a pristine piece of paper. But Hunter? He'd never seen her write anything down until her plan was clear in her mind.

The music stopped.

He moved opening and shutting the backdoor a little louder than necessary to announce his presence.

Hunter appeared in the doorway to the studio. Her hair pulled up in a high ponytail, her face sheened with perspiration, her breathing rapid. She was even more beautiful when in disarray. His heartbeat increased even though he had done nothing more than take a couple of steps. His breathing changed, shallow until a deep breath released the lock on his lungs.

"You're here," Hunter challenged.

"Yes, just as I said I would last night, I'm here." He glanced at his watch. "I expect Eleanor will be here shortly. She seems to be very reliable."

"Are you implying I'm not?" Hunter said, hands on hips, chin raised.

"Don't let me interrupt you," he said, deliberately ignoring her jab. Picking up his bag, he started up the stairs.

"You can't just waltz in here," Hunter shrilled as she strode to the bottom of the stairs. "You aren't welcome here."

Grant just kept going up the stairs, into the living area and began to set up a workstation. He might be on leave but he still had clients and responsibilities to tend to. While he waited for whatever happened next with his daughter, he would keep himself busy. Work always helped him deal with whatever was going on in his personal life.

A sardonic smile twisted his mouth. *Personal life? Yeah right.* He'd observed Diana, Matthew and Madison Michelle and Ashley, Daniel with James, Anthony and Rose, even Lily and Jackson—his definition of a "personal life" was now very different. Even though he'd had a few serial affairs, he never had the connection with any of them actually with any female that he saw between these men and the women in their lives. For the first time in his adult life, he wondered if....

Hunter stalked into the room. "What are you doing?"

"I'm plugging in my laptop," he said as he rose from the bent over position.

"Why?"

"Because I have some work to do," he said, sitting down and turning the machine on.

"I don't need you here." Hunter paced from one end of the living area to the other.

"I think your women friends would disagree based on last night's conversation," he said amiably. Although his eyes were fixed on the screen as it booted up, he was very aware of where Hunter was. Her spicy scent now filled the room, wrapped around him and tugged. He resisted, keeping his eyes if not his focus on the laptop.

Eleanor's cheery "Hello" brought a sense of relief. He hadn't realized how tense he was, how rigid he'd been holding himself until she arrived.

"Let me help you bring things in." Grant jumped up and strode towards the stairs.

"That would be welcomed," Eleanor said a bright smile on her face.

There were two canvas grocery sacks, easily carried up the stairs because of the handles. Grant took them into the kitchen area, deposited them on the counter.

"I'll leave the next part to you," he said, looking at Hunter.

"Now for a proper greeting," Eleanor said, coming over and giving him a hug.

Hunter glowered, things banged on the counter as she unpacked the groceries.

Grant kept his back to the women. Even though his computer had booted up, he stared out the window sorting through the mental list he'd made last night. He wasn't surprised at Hunter's welcome, but he was surprised at how deflated he felt.

"That's a beautiful picture," Eleanor said.

Grant glanced in her direction and noted she was looking at his computer screen. He hadn't entered his security code and finished logging in so the screensaver was what she was talking about.

The slide show of screensaver photographs was on the slowest setting.

"Why that's lovely also," Eleanor commented.

"These are pictures of the view from my house at the shore," Grant said. It struck him then that all the pictures on this slide show were of places he'd spent with Hunter. "I've a few things to do now." He moved the cursor so he could log in. "Another time, if you're interested, you can see them all."

"I'd like that," Eleanor replied. "My husband, Archie and I loved the shore. Some of our favorite memories were of times there with the children and also just the two of us. Those pictures remind me of some of the places we stayed.

"Hunter? Are you okay?"

Grant dared a quick look over his shoulder at Eleanor's question. Hunter's stark, forlorn look tore at his heart. Why did these pictures bring him comfort, help him cope with the stress and demands of his work? Another question he had no easy answer to.

Right now, he needed to get busy and stay busy. Today was going to be harder than he'd expected. It wasn't that he thought it would be easy, he just hadn't let himself consider how much Hunter's pain would affect him. After all, she'd kept his daughter from him.

Reminding himself of her deception helped. He clicked through to his emails. Scanning the long list, he purposefully deleted anything that was not totally work related.

His daughter was alive. Hope he could to get to know her dimmed because the reality was she may never want to know him. Pain stabbed his gut and he sucked in a sharp breath to counter it.

A familiar loneliness welled. His fingers stopped typing, his gaze rested on the building across the street. The memory of his first time here, seeing Hunter's fingers trace the note on Logan's mirror burrowed deep. Had anyone ever said or showed him they were committed to or responsible for him? That if he were lost, they'd find him? That they'd come for him?

Grant sent out a prayer his daughter would be okay.

18 - MAKING PEACE

*H*unter excused herself and went down to her studio. This room represented accomplishment and hope. Her reputation was exceptional. Her classes quickly filled whenever she had an opening or added new ones.

At first she wanted to teach children, encourage and inspire them to become dancers. Over the years, that vision shifted. Not that she didn't want to inspire her younger students to become dancers, she did. But there was so much more she wanted for them: to love to dance, to move, to connect with their bodies, to see themselves successful no matter their skill level. Loving to dance, to move was enough.

Music added to her experience but she chose not to turn it on. She just needed to move, to let her mind run free, to wait for the Goddess to bring clarity to her confusion, for her mind to clear, for her path to stretch before her. For that to happen, she must step back from her fear and judgment.

Growing up she'd had ballet lessons, but the dance routines she created were a mixture of classical and modern dance and even included some steps from watching Fancy Dancers at a couple of Pow

Wows. One, two, three twirl; one, two three, twirl; one, two three leap, the pattern soothed as she circled the room.

Up one side and down the other, diagonal now, a zig-zag pattern unfolded. That was part of the gift of dance. She'd choreographed routines over the years and the old well-loved ones came to her without thinking. But then so did free-dancing. Her paced slowed but she didn't stop.

Logan. God, Goddess, Please keep her safe and bring her home to me. It is beyond time to explain. I pray she forgives me.

Another half-loop around the floor, her steps slowing even more.

Gabriella. Please forgive me, Gabby. I was wrong to blame you, to think you were not helping me by helping my daughter. I owe you more than I can ever repay.

Hunter stopped, bent at the waist and touched her hands to the floor. Sweat dripped off her nose making splatter marks on the varnished surface. She straightened, did a final twirl before walking to the wall of mirrors behind the barre.

A deep breath, turquoise-green eyes staring back at her, she acknowledged the hardest piece.

Grant. May you find it in your heart to forgive me. May I find it in my heart to share Logan with you.

She picked up a towel, wiped her face, neck and arms as well as the wet spot on the floor. Returning to the living quarters, she announced she was taking a shower and would like to talk to them when she was done. Without waiting for an answer, she went into the bathroom, shut and locked the door.

GRANT LOOKED over at Eleanor who was sitting in the armchair, a book in hand. He'd caught up on all of his emails, the most important one to his partners was terse "I will be gone longer than originally anticipated. Will keep you updated. Grant"

That should cause a stir. But he didn't care. He'd been in Fremont less than three weeks but already felt different. This morning he wore a pair of casual slacks with no crease, a short sleeved shirt unbuttoned at the neck, no tie. He was wearing running shoes not loafers or dress shoes. *When was the last time I just relaxed and kicked back?*

Back home appearances were everything. Even at his beach house he dressed in 'beach casual' which meant a crease in his shorts, shirt tucked in, shoes that matched the outfit. Of course he was clean shaven. *What would it be like not to shave for a week?*

Those errant thoughts were interrupted by Hunter coming out of the bathroom. She wore a dark green blouse that matched a dark green in the vibrant multi-colored skirt. Her feet were bare, toes unpolished. No makeup, her hair pulled back into a chignon, she took his breath away. His unwelcomed attraction to her hit like a sucker punch. So he did what he always did to cover-up his emotions and adopted a neutral façade.

"I have an idea." Hunter gestured 'a moment' and picked up her phone. She punched in a number, listened and then spoke. "It's me, Gabby. Please forgive me. I know you are doing what's best for Logan and I'm ever so grateful.

"I also want you to know I can't just sit here at home waiting to hear from you so I'm going to ask Grant to drive around with me to see if we can find you.

"Please give Logan a hug from me and tell her I'm thankful she's alive and hope she can forgive me. I love you both." She ended the call, stood straight and tall with a questioning look in her eyes. "Will you?" she asked looking right at Grant.

Would this woman never stop amazing him? The answer was clearly "no."

"You want me to drive you around looking for our daughter?" He knew he'd just upped the ante.

She hesitated and a crease appeared between her brows. A curt nod followed by a sigh. "Yes, that's what I want."

"You do know it will be impossible for me to do that and not ask questions."

She smiled. It didn't reach her eyes. It wasn't bright and sunny. It contained no mirth. It was merely an upturning at the corners of her mouth. "As long as you know I may not answer them," she replied with a hint of sadness.

"Which doesn't mean I won't ask again," he added.

"I would expect nothing less of you. You're a successful attorney, Grant. I don't expect you to change that now."

He turned back, quickly shutting down the computer. When he stood, he reached for his jacket on the back of the chair.

A voice called out from the back door. Lily had arrived.

A quick change of plans and they divided Hunter's class lists up. During her time down in the studio this morning, she'd made another decision. Adding classes would be done one or two at a time.

First to be restored: the after school dance classes for the kids. She enjoyed seeing them grow and gain in skills. Second: one morning class. She had three but was only going to add the eleven a.m. one for single mothers on welfare. Watching them gain confidence in themselves as they mastered a dance routine, seeing them become comfortable with their bodies and knowing they were a worthwhile person who could learn—that class felt right.

With four people making calls, the task was completed in less than fifteen minutes. She looked forward to starting her classes again on Monday. That gave her two days to search for Logan. And, since these classes were on Monday, Wednesday and Friday, she still had Tuesday and Thursday to search.

Optimistic for the first time since Logan dashed out, Hunter gathered purse, cell phone and looked over at Grant. "Ready?"

Shoulder to shoulder they walked down the stairs and out the door.

19 - THE SEARCH

Hunter was surprised when Grant told her to drive. Of course it made sense because she knew Fremont and he didn't. She agreed if they could use his rental car in case they found Gabby or Logan. Both knew her car.

Knowing Gabby was involved, Hunter first drove by the Murphy house where Gabby lived. The house was dark, locked up and as they walked around and peeked in windows it was obvious no one was home.

"I didn't really expect them to be here," Hunter said to Grant as they returned to the car.

"She doesn't want to be found—."

"Yet...she doesn't want to be found yet," Hunter interrupted. "She's with Gabby so I know she's being taken care of." She swiped at an errant tear and sighed. "If I really believe that why am I even out here looking?"

"Because, well, because you're you. Sitting still is not your forte," Grant said.

Hunter, a sharp retort on her tongue, stopped and stared. Her mouth opened but words stuck in her throat. Grant had walked a couple of strides further but now turned back towards her. In an instant the soft almost secret smile on his face morphed into a frown with question marks sparking his eyes. "What?" he asked, now obviously confused.

Why am I upset? The answer to her question unsettled. He remembered her, remembered her quirks like needing to move when worried or upset or even in celebration. The way she curled up in a chair with her left side towards the back and that she liked black cherry flavored soda. He'd been a bit surprised to learn she'd sworn off soda altogether.

They'd reached the driveway when they squared off. Hunter scanned her body for discord and other than her concern for Logan found none. "After over eighteen years it's a little disconcerting to find you still remember so much about me," she said deciding to be forthright.

"You remember a lot about me, too," he said.

Hunter decided to move the conversation onto safer ground. "Let's check out where Gabby last lived. I think she's kept in touch with one of her neighbors there."

They weren't there. Nor were they any place Hunter could think of. They drove by her work just in case they were hanging out at the office. A long shot they both agreed but one they willingly took.

Both were quiet as they drove through the Fremont High School parking lot and turned towards home.

"Does Gabby have any connections with homeless youth?"

"I don't think so, why?"

"The private investigator showed Logan's picture around down by the homeless shelter and a couple of kids said they'd seen her."

"What?" Hunter screeched, slamming on the brakes.

"Pull over," Grant ordered.

When they were safely stopped in a mini-mall parking lot, he continued. "You do recall I gave you several addresses where she'd been sighted."

She nodded.

"Those addresses were from the investigator I hired."

She nodded, her jaw clenched to keep from screaming.

"She was only seen for a couple of days after she took off. After that there was nothing." Silence filled the too-small space. "I thought you understood that."

Thinking back to that time, Hunter knew she'd been overwhelmed with grief and fear. It was realistic there'd be things she didn't process very well. "I don't know that Gabby knows much of anything about homeless kids." She pulled her phone from her purse and dialed a number.

"Hi Lily, no we've not found any trace.

"Yeah, it is hard.

"But I'm calling to see if you know anything about Gabby having a connection to the homeless youth programs. Logan was initially seen around the shelter but then disappeared."

She put her hand over the receiver. "She's asking Eleanor."

"Thanks, Lily. In love and light."

Hanging up she turned to Grant. "No, neither of them are aware of Gabby having connections with those programs. Lily used to work in child welfare but that was over a decade ago."

"Let's go see the area. We may get lucky," Grant's look of hope on his face sounded in his voice.

Hunter started the car and drove towards the downtown area while Grant checked his cell phone for an address. They parked and walked the two blocks to the building that housed the youth shelter and walk-in clinic.

"Let's check here first." Grant reached for the door knob to the clinic.

The scene before them as they stepped inside was difficult for them both as the idea their daughter could have been here assaulted them. At least ten teenagers were sprawled in every available chair as well as the floor.

A woman in a white lab coat was talking.

"...one at a time," she was saying when they stepped in. She stopped midsentence. Her gaze searched their faces. No welcoming smile but she did step around two youth hunkered down on the floor and strode the few feet towards them.

"I'm Doc S," the woman said. "I'm the doctor here at this clinic. We need to step outside if you please." She opened the door and gestured for them to precede her.

"I'm Hunter Compton."

"And, I'm Grant Parker." He extended his hand and shook the doctor's. Noticing Hunter hesitate before following his lead, he glanced in her direction, saw the fear and longing on her face. "Our daughter, Logan Compton ran away two weeks ago." He stepped closer, put his arm around Hunter's shoulder and hugged her to his side. "We've looked everywhere. We even hired a private investigator that learned she'd been seen around here for a few days after she took off. Two days ago her Aunt Gabby Montcreif called and said she was alive but we know nothing more."

He paused, still watching the doctor for any sign of recognition. There was none. It made sense that even if the staff knew something, if Logan had told this doctor or any of them not to talk, there was nothing he or Hunter could say or do to change that.

"We just want her to know we love her very much. We want her to come home. We'll work out whatever needs to be worked out," Hunter pleaded. "Please, if there is any way you can let her know how much we love her… ," She turned, her arms around his waist, she clung to him and sobbed.

"I-I-I'm s-s-orry, pl-pl-please t-t-tell her I'm—."

Grant wrapped his arms around her, her lithe dancer's body fit just right. Her spicy scent reminded him of other times, happier times. *Can we ever recapture them?*

"We know we are at the root of our daughter's running away. We want to tell her, to show her we're sorry. To make amends for-for everything." One hand caressed Hunter's back, the other held her firmly against him.

"You can write her a letter," Doc S was talking now. "We have a place for mail, notes, etc. Write it and leave it with me. I'll see it gets to the right place."

Hunter's sobs had stopped. She pulled away and he felt the loss.

"Do we have paper in the car?" she asked. Her tear-filled eyes, tear-stained face matched her tear-stained voice.

"I'll get you a pad and pen. Just write your letter and put it in the envelope I'll include. You can seal it and put it on the desk if I'm busy."

"We're grateful for your help, Doctor," Grant said.

"Thank you," Hunter added. "I pray to the Goddess she'll see our letter and know how much I love her and how sorry I am."

"How sorry we both are," Grant amended.

When Doc S returned she had two pads of paper, two pens and one envelope. "I think it will be easier if you each write to her. I need to get back inside."

A young woman approached. "Hey Doc, need some help today?"

"Clary, I always need some help," Doc S said. "Go on in." She started to follow Clary, then turned back and said, "Leave everything with Clary. She'll see that I get it."

Hunter and Grant had a choice. Sit on the sidewalk, find a coffee shop or restaurant or go back to the car. They chose the latter. Another decision: would they read each other's letter? While she wanted to read what Grant wrote she was concerned he'd not say everything he might if she insisted.

When she voiced that concern, he paused. "You may be right. Let's write our letters and then decide."

With that plan in place they put pen to paper. It still took them over twenty minutes to write their letters. Another decision made when they'd started: not to rewrite.

"I think it better that she see this wasn't an easy thing for us to do," Hunter said.

While he agreed, it went against the grain. Attorneys did not send out correspondence that had cross outs and in one place an arrow looping back to an earlier paragraph.

"Your daughter is going to read this," Hunter said. "She has enough to judge us for, I doubt it will be for how our letters look."

She'd just said "your daughter" out loud and to him. Emotions clogged his throat and filled his eyes. He didn't dare look at her or speak. *Your daughter*. He liked the sound of that.

"Let's take this back to the clinic." Hunter stuffed her letter into the envelope.

Grant cleared his throat, making sure he could speak. "You can drive and I'll hop out and run it in."

"I need to move."

"Then I'll race you," he said and laughed.

"I am not running through the streets with you chasing me," she huffed.

"Who said I'd be chasing you." He grinned. "You could be chasing me."

"It doesn't matter, we are not running. We can walk briskly."

Grant exited the car, envelope in hand and waited for her. He thought of rounding the car and opening the door for her but she was already out and stepping up on the curb. *I like her independence.* He took her hand, pleased when she didn't pull away. They strode down the street, dropped the envelope off with Clary and started back to the car.

"Where to now?" Grant buckled his seatbelt.

"Let's go back home." Hunter slipped the key in the ignition.

"Sounds good to me," he choked out.

"Are you okay?" Hunter asked.

"Yes," he managed, emotions as yet unnamed clogging his throat and blurring his vision.

Hunter pulled away from the curb.

Grant looked out the window as the streets of Fremont slid by, looked out at the streets of Fremont with the eyes of a dad.

Sunday
April 24, 2005

In the morning Gabriella and Logan took a short hike. The Circle had accommodated Gabby's request to change the time of their Ceremony to three-thirty. Before leaving their cabin sanctuary, they fixed a plate of cheese and crackers and chopped up the last bar of chocolate into bite-sized pieces for Gabby's contribution to the potluck.

Around quarter after three, they met up with Doc S at a coffee shop between the clinic and Sophia's. The plan was for Logan to hang out with Doc while Gabby went on to Sophia's where she would pave the way for Logan's return. When it was time for Logan to join The Circle, Gabby would text her.

After one long reassuring hug, Gabby turned back to Logan and gave her another quick squeeze before getting in her car and driving off.

Parking in front of Sophia's, Gabby saw Hunter's car in the driveway, a sign she'd arrived first. Reminding herself this was about Logan, Gabby slung her purse over her shoulder, picked up the plate with cheese and crackers and the small bowl of chopped chocolate and made her way to the front door.

Before she had a chance to knock, she heard her name called. Turning, she saw Lily wave as she got out of her car. As Gabby waited for Lily to join her, she fought down the churning bile rising from her stomach.

Lily's bright smile, quick hug and "So glad you found her and are here." helped calm the internal chaos.

A quick knock, Lily opened the door and entered first. Gabby stepped through the doorway right behind her. It wasn't a surprise to see Hunter hovering at the entryway to the great room and kitchen. What was surprising? Her smile of welcome.

HUNTER HAD WORRIED about how to greet Gabby, what to say, what to do. She'd talked to Grant, Sophia, Lily—well, everyone including Elizabeth with whom she'd exchanged a series of emails. All the advice was pretty much the same. "See how it goes. Say and do what comes to you as "right" and for everyone's highest good."

She'd been so angry with herself, with Grant and with Logan it had spilled over onto Gabby. Standing in the entrance to Sophia's family room, the damning question came unbidden. *Why was I so furious with Gabby who'd found and protected my daughter?* Hunter pushed the question aside knowing there was a reason she did not yet understand why it was Gabby instead of her who found Logan.

Seeing Gabby, seeing her hesitate, seeing the uncertainty in her eyes, Hunter acted on impulse. "I'm so glad you're here." Her arms outstretched, her long legs closed the distance in a couple of strides. "I am blessed to have you in my life." Her hands rested on Gabby's shoulders, her turquoise-green gaze locked on Gabby's hazel one. "Thank you for all you've done for Logan and for me." Hunter kissed Gabby's cheek, took the plate of cheese and crackers from her and walked beside her into the family room.

Once Gabby's contributions to the potluck were set down, her jacket and purse stowed, everyone gathered around. It wasn't silent, but Hunter found it harder and harder not to ask about Logan. *I'm to say what's in my heart.*

"What news do you have of Logan?" Hunter asked, an unwanted tear streaking down her face.

Gabby reached out, took Hunter's hand and gently squeezed. "Are we all here?"

The doorbell chimed drowning out her last word. Ashley rushed in. "Sorry I'm late. Daniel and the kids will bring my food by later. Oh, Gabby!" Ashley dashed across the room and hugged her. "What have I missed?"

"Shall we smudge and call in the energies, send out prayers?" Sophia asked.

Murmurs of 'yes' and 'of course' were accompanied by actions. Lily lit the smudge and circled the room cleansing Sophia's sacred space. Diana followed Lily ringing a glass bell Elizabeth had sent home from her first trip to Ireland. Ashley got a white cloth from a drawer in a side table and flicked it open to create the foundation of their altar.

One by one they smudged and entered the circle. Hunter took a small rose quartz heart from her bra and placed it in the east, a red carnelian heart from her pants pocket went in the south. Her lapis lazuli heart in the west and her selenite heart in the north finished her rotation around the circle.

Sitting in the east, Hunter steadied her breathing and stared at the rose quartz heart in front of her. Focusing on her love for Logan, for Gabby, for The Circle had kept her somewhat sane the last couple of days. That and dance. That and drumming. Best of all? Dancing to the beat of her drum.

Moving her body moved energy, moved her thoughts, moved her along the path of life. *And Grant understands that. It's why he insisted I go home when Logan was found. Still insists that I teach at least one dance class in the morning and one in the afternoon.*

When everyone was smudged, their sacred objects (fetishes, rocks, crystals and pictures) on the altar, they stood. Arms high overhead they prayed.

"May our time in this circle be one of love," Sophia began.

"May our time in this circle be one of inclusion," Diana added.

"May our time in this circle be one of healing," Ashley said.

"May our time in this circle be one of acceptance," Lily contributed.

"May our time in this circle be one of understanding," Gabriella said and paused before adding, "and tolerance."

"May our time in this circle be one of truth and love," Hunter finished.

When everyone was seated, Sophia picked up the snowflake obsidian stone and held it out. "Who wants to share first?"

"I'd like Gabby to go first, but I think it best if she and I go last so everyone has a chance to speak and be heard," Hunter said.

"Who has something to share that cannot wait until social time or our next circle?" Sophia took some time, visually checking in with each person. No one put their hand out to take the stone.

Hunter reached for the black piece of stone sprinkle with white spots that resembled snowflakes. *I can do this. I can speak my truth in a loving way.* She'd spent some time this morning drumming and dancing, deciding what to say. All that flew out of her brain. A wry smile, a slight shake of her head, she tried to recapture those words.

Futile.

Trust, trust, trust. Trust my words speak my truth. Hunter looked across their altar to Gabby who sat in the west, the void—the opposite direction from where she was in the east, new beginnings.

"I," she stopped to clear her throat, "I want to tell you in front of everyone how sorry I am for doubting your love for Logan and your love for me." She held her head high, looked straight at her circle sister. "When I, well, when Grant sat me down," she paused, a slight smiled on her lips, "and drilled me with questions as only an attorney can do, I knew in my heart, past the fear, past the guilt, past the shame, Logan was where she needed to be. And most importantly she was with the person she needed to be with.

"I wanted it to be me. I was desperate for it to be me because I'd promised Logan when she was little that I'd always find her if she was lost. In my heart I know she needed to be with you. I don't know why that's so, I don't always like that it is so, but I do trust that all is as it should be. Well, most of the time I'm in trust, not quite 100% but getting close.

"I am asking that you forgive me for all the hate I dumped on you. That I shouted at you. I hope you can. I know now that it was really the hate I feel for myself projected onto you."

Her gaze never wavered, even as the tears fell, even as she sat and waited. Waited for Gabby to forgive her, waited for her to say something, waited when all she wanted to do was get up and move, move, move.

A hand on her arm, she looked to her right and Ashley. "If you are waiting for Gabby to speak, she needs the talking stone," Ashley reminded her. "Or?" she held her hand out.

Hunter checked. Gabby's hands were still in her lap but unshed tears filled her eyes. She handed the stone to Ashley.

"When I hear your words about hate, hatred of others or hatred of ourselves, I'm reminded of a lesson we've all experienced over and over and over. To move away from hate, we must move towards love. I'm not saying it's easy. After all the things Art has done…. But, if I am to be the best mom to my kids and the best wife to Daniel, I must stay focused on love and when he pops into my mind for whatever reason, it is important for me to hold myself and even him in the light of love."

Ashley held the stone out, Diana reached for it. "And, the more we love, the more love we have to give and then the more love we receive. We've all known that truth from our early days but we are offered "opportunities"," she crooked her fingers simulating quotation marks, "to learn new ways to manifest that truth."

Gabby took the stone from Diana and held it gingerly in her hands, tumbling it from one palm to the other. "It isn't always easy to trust, even when we know we are loved. I was able to find Logan because when I was much younger, I lived on the streets. As bad as it was, and there were times it was really bad, it was safer than my home.

"I came off the streets over ten years ago, less than a year before we started meeting. When I can, I've volunteered at the youth shelter. I'm not a stranger to many of the homeless youth because I do outreach: walk the streets and talk to everyone I see about coming in, getting off the streets, moving forward with their lives.

"Trust when broken can be repaired. It takes time but it can be done. Sometimes it takes over ten years to trust enough to tell even a piece of the story. Sometimes the story just needs to be locked away in order to keep moving forward. Sometimes the story comes tumbling out and healing can begin if it is heard with love. I believe everyone here will be able to listen to Logan with love. To understand what she can talk about now and let what she is not yet ready and may never be ready to talk about be."

Gabby stopped speaking, her voice weary and old, she looked directly at each woman, her gaze finally reaching Hunter who reached over and took the stone.

"While I'm heart-broke you had that life as a child," Hunter started, "I'm ever so grateful now that you did. Ever so grateful you were the one who found her. I know I would not have been the right person because I wasn't ready to hear her." She handed it back to her circle sister.

Gabby's grip on the stone whitened her knuckles. "She wants to come here, to spend time with everyone, men and children included, to say what she's willing to say right now. One time. To say it one time only. That means no questions.

"She doesn't feel she can return home yet, Hunt. She believes it will be too hard for you not to ask her any questions, not to say anything about her time away, and it would do her in to see you cry." Tears now streamed down Gabby's face, dropping in mini-splotches on her top. "She needs to be in control of her healing process at this point. I can assure you she is making progress. Baby steps, but progress none-theless."

Gabby swiped her face with the back of her hand. Lily handed her tissues and she wiped her face and blew her nose. "We did talk about what she wanted to do, where she felt comfortable in staying. She isn't sure about where to stay. On her list are here with Sophia or maybe with Lily and Jackson because of Eleanor. We also talked about her staying with me when the project in Seattle is over."

"Will she ever want to come home?" Hunter's words wobbled as she spoke.

"I believe so. She just needs time. It's been less than five full days since I found her. She has a lot on her plate, lots of questions. Time to recover her physical and emotional equilibrium is what she needs. To be honest, I can't see her comfortable in coming home until she is further along in her healing process."

Gabby watched Hunter draw into herself and was grateful Ashley took Hunter into her arms.

"She doesn't know if she can go back to school, if she has the ability to catch up. I expect she'll ask Sophia to help her with that problem, which makes sense," Gabby quickly added.

"She has established a connection with a doctor at the youth shelter walk-in clinic and I don't see her agreeing to go to her family doctor any time soon."

"Can I hug her?" Hunter asked, "I mean when I see her, what should I do?"

Gabby handed the stone to Lily, stood and rounded the circle. She gently tugged on Hunter's shoulder until her circle sister stood. Enveloping her in a hug, she said, "Of course you should hug her. Of course you should touch her, tell her you love her, whatever is in your heart." She took a step back, her hands loose on Hunter's arms. "Just know she may not say back to you what you most want to hear. Most likely she won't say much of anything—but you?" Gabby squeezed her arms in support, "you must say what's in your heart."

Closing prayers were said with Gabby standing, her arms around Hunter, The Circle shifting to accommodate the change. "This is what I mean, Hunt. I moved, we shifted but we are still The Circle. Logan's moved, you will shift but you are still her mom, still someone she loves and needs, and in some ways you are someone she needs to get to know again. Just so you know, she is curious about Grant. Hopes he isn't a 'yelling dad' as she calls it. Her fantasy dad was someone she could talk to, who laughed, who did things with her. And, he was totally in love with you."

Hunter's laugh was brittle. *How am I going to do this? You must find a way. She is your daughter and you love her. Love. Love, love. I must stay focused on love.*

Gabby stepped away, slipped her phone from her purse and texted "thirty minutes".

Hunter paced through the family room. Sliding open the door, she stepped out onto the patio and marched across the yard. Grateful Sophia's garden had paths, she chose one and strode forth. *Move I need to move.* The trail meandered but she did not slow: a leap, a twirl, a quick dance step or two or three or maybe four. *Move, move, move.* She stretched, reached into the sky, drew the fragrant air deep in her lungs. Dipping as she twirled, she pushed herself faster.

In the sitting area at the back of the garden, she closed her eyes, lifted her face and arms to the sun and silently prayed. *Goddess give me the strength to be the mother I know Logan needs at this time. Help me stay strong. Help me see and hear through the light of love.*

Her heartbeat quickened, a little shriek sounded when she realized she wasn't alone. Not Logan—Grant. Strange she felt almost glad to see him. "Is she here?" Hunter said, rushing past him to head down the path.

His hand cupped her arm and held her still. "Not yet. I understand she's on her way. There is time to walk."

Grant was nervous. He hid it well. No outward sign she could detect like darting eyes, nervous ticks, but she knew—could feel the shifting energy swirling around him.

"Feeling better?" he asked as they made their way down the path towards the house.

"That is a question that today guarantees an 'it depends' answer. Better than…?" She left the question hanging in the air.

"Better than if you'd stayed still in the house with everyone else?"

She glanced his way and saw the smile on his face; a humorous smile that softened his attorney façade. "Yes, much better than that."

They reached the patio. Grant stepped in front of her, blocking her entrance. "A minute?"

She nodded.

"Just want to make sure we're on the same page. I was told to be here or I would have stayed away."

Hunter heard the sincerity in his voice and saw the conviction on his face. *He would have stayed away if that was what's best for Logan and for me.* "We are on the same page. We are doing what our daughter has asked." There was a level of comfort saying the words *our daughter*, a level of comfort she'd worked hard to develop. Hours of drumming and repeating the phrase had paid off. She'd also practiced in front of the mirror to make sure she didn't wince or have some facial expression that telegraphed how hard it was to say those two words.

"Let's go in and see where things are at." She waited for his reply instead of walking around him.

Grant stepped to the side, a slight bow, a hand gesture and "after you."

Head high, Hunter preceded him into the family room. Food was set out, a spirit plate with bits of what everyone had contributed on the counter.

"I'm not sure if we should wait until Logan gets here or go ahead, say prayers and eat," Sophia said. "Any ideas?" she asked looking at Gabby.

"I think it would be a good thing to wait, perhaps ask Logan to say the prayer and take the spirit plate out. Give her a chance to be among us but with something to do."

"That makes sense." Sophia fussed with the arrangement of food on the counter. "We can certainly do that."

"I think we should sing a song," Diana offered. She turned to Rose, Ashley's youngest. "What do you want to sing while we wait for Logan?"

"The waiting song. We should sing the waiting song while we're waiting." Bright smiles bloomed on everyone's face hearing Rose's words and infectious laugh.

LOGAN HEARD the singing before she reached Sophia's front door. Doc S, who'd gotten out of the car and walked with her, gave her a hug. "Singing?"

"They're singing one of my favorite songs. It's about The Lady Goddess waiting for everyone to come back to Her," Logan said, her voice shaky, her eyes bright with a teary mist.

"Then She is waiting for you," Doc said, her arm around Logan's shoulder. "You are a strong young woman. You know you are loved by many. I would hazard a guess to say you are loved by everyone on the other side of this door."

Logan nodded. "I am loved by everyone on the other side of this door." The love infusing each word of the song strengthened her. She straightened her spine, shoulders back and chin up, she turned and looked directly at Doc. "I'm ready. I can do this."

"I know you can." Doc's hand on Logan's shoulder squeezed in support.

"Thank you for everything."

"You have my phone number. If you need me, call me." Doc turned away, strode to her car and got in.

Logan waited on the porch, hand on the knob until Doc backed out and drove away. "I am loved by everyone on the other side of the door. I can do this."

GRANT'S FINGERS were crushed in a grip he wouldn't have attributed to Hunter; a grip that was a testament to her physical strength. Out of the corner of his eye, he watched her prepare herself for a reunion with her daughter. He knew she was reminding herself to stay calm because he was doing the same thing.

They were on the same page; both wanted what was best for Logan. He wasn't sure they were on the same page in terms of what that might look like. He still wanted to get to know her, be a dad to her and he didn't want it to be long distance. She'd been accepted to Smith College, a few short hours away from him. If she decided to go there, he'd be able to see her weekends, pop up and take her to dinner or a play in Boston, invite her to—. Those thoughts were quickly shoved aside when the doorbell rang once and the front door opened.

"We're in the family room," Sophia called out.

HUNTER STRUGGLED to walk slowly from the middle of the family room towards the entrance from the hall. A blur shot past her. "Logan, You're here, you're here!" Rose McDonnell's shrill of greeting reverberated through the room as the eight-year-old streaked across the room and launched herself at Logan.

Logan staggered under the onslaught but recovered quickly, wrapping her arms around Rose, a smile of relief on her face. A hug and kiss on the cheek and Logan set Rose back on the floor.

Hunter saw her daughter's lips move and wondered what she was saying to herself. *A question for another time? A question I'll never ask? Does it really matter? No. My daughter is here.* Her silent prayer: their relationship could be rebuilt. She had no hope it would be as it once was, she only hoped something positive came out of this nightmare.

"You cut your hair off." Disbelief etched on Rose's face as she circled Logan. "How come?"

"I just did. It's easier to take care of this way." Logan shook her head. "See, it stays pretty much the same. No tangles."

Across the space still separating them, Hunter saw a familiar stranger. No long strawberry blond hair pulled up in a high pony tail, no smile on her face or laughter in her eyes. She searched her daughter's body from head to toe, looking for something to tell her what had happened.

Tangible fear registered in Logan's posture. And, although the turtle-necked top, long sleeves, baggy sweat pants and shoes hid everything except her hands and face, those hands were telling. Twisted together in a pattern Hunter recognized of unambiguous anxiety.

A squeeze on the hand fisted around Grant's helped her gather her thoughts and act. She managed to cross the space only because her hand was locked around Grant's. The urge to grab her daughter, hold her close and never let go surged but she resisted, instead gripping Grant's hand even tighter as she wrapped the other arm around her own waist.

"I love you so much," Hunter said, standing in front of Logan, her gaze searching eyes that reminded her of her own. "I thank The Goddess you are safe." Tears flowed down her cheeks. With her free hand she swiped them away. "Can you ever forgive me?" She clamped a hand over her mouth, "I didn't mean to say that. I'm sorry."

Gabby stepped next to Logan, her steady gaze on Hunter. "Remember, your mom and dad are doing their best right now."

Logan nodded.

Grant pried Hunter's hand from his and tucked her against his side. "Your mother and I," his voice choked. He cleared his throat and started again. "Your mother and I want what is best for you and right now we're uncertain what that is. We want you to know we love you and are grateful you are here."

Gabby leaned towards Logan. "What do you want to do? We can eat first or you can say whatever it is you've decided to say and then we can eat."

Logan took a deep breath. Rose, still by her side, glommed onto her hand and tugged. "What?" Logan asked looking down at the youngster.

"You talk and then we eat," Rose said. "I'm only a little bit hungry. I can wait."

Logan smiled, ruffled Rose's hair and leaned down. "An excellent idea. I don't think I could eat anything right now."

"Do you want to stay in here or…?" Sophia asked. "We can make room in the living room or maybe out on the patio?"

"I'd like a circle and prayers," Logan answered. "Wherever that is easiest is okay."

"Let's go back to the living room," Lily said. "We can shift everything around so we all fit in."

"A double circle will work," Diana suggested and added, "If that's okay with you, Logan."

In short order the double circle was formed with the women and Logan in the inner circle, the men and children in the outer circle.

Hunter was very aware that Grant was there, sitting behind her. Logan chose to sit opposite her, in the West with Gabby on one side and Sophia on the other. Eleanor and Jackson were behind Lily, Matthew and Madison Michelle were behind Diana, Daniel and Anthony were behind Ashley with Rose and James overlapping and behind Sophia. The crystal bell and emerald green bowl on their altar brought Elizabeth and Michael into the circle even though they were in Ireland. Hunter saw the shimmer of energy she always associated with her circle sister and The Lady fill the room.

The women stood, arms raised to the skies, their feet shoulder width apart.

"May the light of love be with us this day," Gabby started.

"May we listen with open hearts," Lily spoke next.

"May we hear as clearly what isn't said as what is," Diana added.

"May we know in our hearts that with love all is possible," Hunter said, her gaze on Logan, hope looming as her daughter met her gaze.

"May we know with certainty that together we can accomplish miracles." Ashley looked at Hunter, a smile of encouragement on her lips.

"May we understand that with The Goddess, with her love and

support, we can forgive and grow and move beyond any and all adversity," Sophia finished.

The conviction of her words embraced Hunter's heart.

"Blessed Be," they chorused. A moment later they sat.

Gabby handed Logan the piece of multi-hued fluorite they often used as a talking stone.

Hunter steeled herself for whatever was to come. Grant's hand on her shoulder comforted. They were in this together. Come what may, whether for good or bad, she was no longer a single parent with it all on her shoulders. Looking across the circle at her daughter, no their daughter, a small part of her raged but a larger part was glad. She finally admitted there was a downside to being a single parent.

She was under no illusions that the road ahead would be easy, that she and Grant would agree on everything. What kept her strong on this new path? Knowing they both loved their daughter and whatever challenges they faced, underneath the strife and stress, they wanted what was best for her.

Hunter watched Logan shifted the stone from hand to hand. Time stretched, magnified in the silence.

Her gaze captured Logan's. Hunter smiled and nodded her encouragement. Logan's deep breath and soft sigh echoed around the room. She opened her mouth to speak. Hunter held her breath.

*L*ogan clutched the fluorite in her hand. Her stomach in revolt, her chest tight, panic loomed. Gabby leaned towards her, their shoulders touched. A brush really but enough to break the icy dread, banish the darkness and allow her to take a deep breath. Her gaze shifted between her mom and Grant who sat directly across from her. *They are in the east, new beginnings, new starts while I'm in the west, the darkness, the void.*

She cleared her throat to chase the last of the panic away. Although she was definitely nervous, with Gabby's shoulder lightly resting against her and Sophia's soft presence on her other side—"I love you, Logan," a little voice whispered from behind her.

"I love you too, Sweet Pea," Logan whispered back.

The soft giggle loosened the remaining nerves. She cleared her throat again.

"I know I'm loved by many," she began. "I did forget that for a while and needed to remember before I could come back. Most of you know how much I've wanted a dad, a father and when I first learned of Grant, I was very angry at my mom for not telling me about him. And I did not stop long enough to talk to her. I know she'd never do anything on purpose to hurt or harm me.

"In time I hope she and I can talk and I can hear what she says, hear with my heart as well as my ears, remember with The Goddess and God's help she loves me and means me no harm.

"While I was gone, I got into some serious trouble. I can't talk about what happened yet. I am grateful The Goddess was watching out for me and sent Gabby to find and save me when I thought all was lost."

Her quiet voice quavered at the end. She looked at each of the women and saw nothing but love and compassion. It was humbling to realize it didn't matter to them what had happened to her, she was loved, accepted. Her mom was still in the same spot, statue-like, so unlike her. It was then she noticed Grant's hand on her mom's shoulder. It didn't seem as if he was holding her in place, more like he was showing her he was there and she had his support.

"I'm better but still have a ways to go before I'll feel totally safe. The person who," she stiffened, took a deep breath and bit her lower lip before continuing, "the person who hurt me knows where I live. Right now he's in jail but at some point he'll get out."

There was a rustle of noise at that news. Logan took a chance and looked beyond the women to the other people, the men and Eleanor. Mindful of Ashley's children, especially Rose, she paused a long moment.

"My Papa can protect you," Rose said. "He's very brave."

Logan twisted around until she could see Rose. "Yes, he is very brave and is doing a very good job taking care of you, your brothers and your mom. I think he's really busy with all that."

"He could—," Rose started.

"Logan has many people here to protect her," Daniel said softly, his hand on Rose's shoulder. "If she needs us, we'll be there but right now we need to be quiet so she can finish."

Logan mouthed 'thanks' to Daniel. Looking back around the circle of men, she saw quiet determination on each man's face. On Grant's a pained anger underneath the outward neutral look.

"I know I can count on your help." Logan looked again at each person in the room. "Right now I need time and some space. I need to figure out how to go forward, what of my life I can pick up and move ahead with and what I need to let go."

She turned to Sophia. "I'd be ever so grateful if you could help me sort out school. I don't know what all I've missed and what I'd have to do, if it's even doable to catch up." The idea of not graduating clouded her mind, her throat clogged with the 'what if's' facing her.

"Of course I'll help you with that." Sophia slipped an arm around Logan's shoulders and gave her a side-hug.

Logan noted Sophia didn't assure her everything would be okay nor did she say not to worry. The panic roared back. *What am I doing? I can't—*

Gabby took her hand and held it. Sophia seemed to know she needed someone to hang on to also because she gave her shoulder a gentle squeeze.

"I-I-I'm sorry. I-I-I can't say any more." With Gabby and Sophia on each side, Logan stood.

"We'll close the circle for now," Lily said.

Gabby and Sophia raised one arm high, keeping the other around Logan as closing prayers were said.

The pain on her mother's face, the stoic look on Grant's somehow gave her strength. She stepped away from Gabby and Sophia and crossed over to her mom.

"I need a hug from you." Logan stepped into Hunter's arms. Being held by her mom brought her comfort but with an element of unease.

"Grant," Hunter said, "We need you here too."

Logan looked at the man who was her father. It would never be as it was but with the grace of The Goddess and God, it could be okay. "We do." Logan extended her hand.

In all honestly, it didn't feel exactly right but it did feel somewhat right to have her mom and Grant's arms around her.

"I read your letters," she finally said. "It made all the difference in the world to see the words on a page, to know you still wanted me no matter what."

"We love you," Grant said. "Your mother was totally lost when you were gone. And I, I grieved for a daughter I didn't even know." He stepped back a half-step, just far enough to look directly at her. "You are a brave young woman, much like your mother. I do hope you'll give me the opportunity to get to know you when you're ready." He took her hand, his touch so gentle it was as if he feared it would break if he held it more tightly. A little squeeze and he stepped away. "You and your mother need a bit of time. I'll be in the other room."

Logan saw Jackson lingering by the entrance to the living room. He didn't say anything to her dad but he did walk away with him.

"I'm so, so, so sorry, Logan," her mom was saying. "If I could go back, I'd—."

"Don't Mom, don't say you'd do it differently. I just need to know why you did it, why you decided not to tell me anything. Why you never told Grant about me?"

Her mom wrapped her in a hard hug, her spicy scent wreathed around her. These arms had always meant safety, this scent had always meant home but right now? Right now she needed some space.

Doc S had reminded her that it would be hard for her mom and dad and maybe the others to give her the space she needed. They'd talked about what to say, how to claim that space she needed.

"Mom, what about food? I'm really hungry." Logan leaned back. "Did you bring that great bean and avocado salad you make? I hope so because that's a favorite of mine." She looped her arm through her mom's. "What did Sophia make for dessert?"

Her mom stopped before they left the living room. Turning towards her, Hunter's hands on her shoulders, she leaned forward, locked gazes and said, "Always know I love you. No matter what happened, nothing will ever change that. You are part of my soul."

Her mom turned towards the family room, the chatter of voices welcoming. Logan stayed next to her mom and filled her plate. She decided not to say the prayer for the spirit plate and suggested Rose do it. A smile blossomed from deep within as the little girl held the plate and thanked the spirits of all the foods on the plate. *Rose has been through a horrible ordeal and look at her now. Maybe... .*

It was easy to drift off into a fantasy of what her life would be, a life not really affected by all that had happened. Gabby and Doc S cautioned her it was normal and would happen. It was normal but it was important to remember it was also a fantasy.

Sitting between her mom and dad—Grant really was her dad. More formal, more like Jackson than the other men the circle's women married. Logan stopped the image of her mom and Grant married, another baby in Hunter's arms. *I'd be a real big sister instead of an honorary one to Rose and Madison Michelle. Nope, that's another fantasy.*

Both her mom and dad turned to her, talking at the same time, asking her if she was okay. Startled, she jumped up and dashed across the room to where Gabby sat with Ashley.

Her breath came in harsh gasps as if she'd run for blocks as the panic slammed in to her. Gabby gathered her close. "You are safe. You are loved by many. You are safe. You are loved by many." The litany soothed. As the panic receded, the hot flush of humiliating embarrassment flashed across her face. "I-I-I... ," she stammered.

"Ssh," Gabby said. "You are safe and that is all that matters." Her arm around Logan's shoulder, she led her down the hall to the first bedroom. Inside she closed the door, leaning back against it. "Remember, this is normal. It means you are healing, making progress."

"I don't care," Logan screamed. "I don't want to feel this way!" She crumbled to the floor, wrapped her arms around her knees and rocked.

Gabby sat on the floor, her back to the door, her legs resting against Logan's. At a time like this, she could only manage being touch if it was light and from a distance.

Time passed. Footsteps sounded up and down the hall. Once they stopped but no one knocked on the door. Gabby hoped Lily or someone was doing damage control. Hunter must be beside herself with worry and grief. It certainly would be a test for her, for their relationship. Hunter had said she knew Gabby was doing what was best for Logan and that she knew it would take time, but knowing and experiencing were two very different things.

The sobbing had ebbed, the rocking stopped. It didn't matter that Gabby and Doc had told Logan she might feel this way, that panic might claim her and she wouldn't know why. And even though that had happened over the past few days, she'd thought it was because she hadn't seen or talked to her mom.

It never occurred to Logan she could be sitting in a room with the safest people in the world and get slammed by the overwhelming urge to bolt, to scream, to curl into a ball, to disappear, to float away on a tether of light and look down on herself.

But that's what was happening. She was tucked in the far corner of the ceiling looking down at her sobbing and rocking body. Gabby close but not too close.

A memory of being in the tent flipped through her mind. She'd been up at the peak, watching DT have sex with her, not there and yet not far enough away. She thought she should leave the tent but in the end couldn't leave her other self.

Gabby and Doc S called it dissociating. They'd said it was how we dealt with really bad things we could not protect ourselves from.

The tent, why didn't she leave? Bile surged up her throat at the memory. A wild look on her face, hands clamped over her mouth she leapt up. Gabby scrambled to the side and Logan dashed out. She made it to the bathroom across the hall just in time.

GABBY LINGERED in the hall until the retching stopped. "I'm still here," she said. "I can come in and help if you need it."

"No," was the muffled reply. "I can take care of myself."

"Of course you can," Gabby said. "I'm going to let Sophia and your mom and Grant know you're okay then."

She'd done just that, walked away without waiting for Logan's reply. In the family room, Sophia and Lily were there with Hunter. Out on the patio, Jackson stood with Grant.

"She's taking care of herself. Got a bit sick to her stomach. It happens and will happen for a while. And no I don't know for how long or why now," she said seeing the questions in Hunter's eyes.

"I can tell you this. She's come a long way since last Wednesday."

She hunkered down in front of Hunter, "I didn't say that to make things worse, Hunt. I said it because I want you to know she is better, is getting better, and will be better. It just takes time."

"What about counseling?" Lily asked.

"Right now she won't consider it. She knows there are counselors who have a lot of experience helping young women who've been through what she's been through. And no, I'm not saying anything else," Gabby said. "Hunt, it is Logan's story to tell."

Grant and Jackson had come back into the family room and were standing close listening.

Gabby continued. "We each have our own stories. It's up to each of us when and to whom we share those stories. Even if I know someone else's story, it's still not mine to tell. Remember all things are possible when we listen to and understand the words through the light of love."

"I'm going to go check on her. See how she's doing." Gabby rose. When she turned, Logan stood in the doorway to the hall, her pale face bespoke her pain and exhaustion.

Hunter crossed over to her and held her. With one hand she stroked wet strands of strawberry blond hair back behind Logan's ear. "Your dad's hair may look blond now but it has hints of red in it just like yours. You have his mouth. I can see his smile in your smile. I've seen bits and pieces of him in you since you were a baby.

"When you are ready to hear why I did what I did, I'm ready to tell you. You need to let me know because I love you so much I don't want to do anything to make your path more difficult." Hunter spoke in a soothing, gentle voice that Gabby could imagine was just the tone she used when Logan was little and needed reassurance from her mom that everything would be okay.

Grant had joined them, his bent head and their nods showing her he had said something.

The three of them turned towards Sophia, Lily and her.

"Tomorrow is a school day," Hunter started. "We are hoping it would be okay for Logan to stay with you tonight," she said looking at Sophia.

"Clean sheets on the bed and cinnamon rolls in the freezer. How does that sound, my girl," Sophia said in a too bright voice.

"Do you have enough of those cinnamon rolls to share?" Jackson licked his lips. He turned towards Grant, "If you've not had Sophia's cinnamon rolls you are in for a treat, that is if she has enough to share."

"It depends," Sophia said, "on whether Logan will help me make another batch tonight. How about it?"

"With nuts?" Logan asked a light in her eyes.

"With nuts," Sophia replied. "The cooks get to make those decisions."

"I'll help," Jackson said, a good-natured grin on his face.

"Too many cooks spoil something," Lily said. "Besides, we still have a couple of Sophia's cinnamon rolls left in our freezer."

"Logan, why don't you get that package out of the freezer. It is clearly marked. Your mom and dad can have them. I've got one already thawed we'll give to Gabby."

"They get a whole package and I only get one?" Gabby said a mock hurt on her face.

"You can come by bright and early in the morning and get a fresh one right from the oven," Sophia said.

"I'll check in with all of you in the morning," Gabby said. "If everyone is doing okay, I'm heading back to Seattle to finish that project." She turned to Logan. "I'll come home Friday night. You have my phone number and Doc's so we expect to hear from you if you need to talk."

Logan had retrieved the package of cinnamon rolls from the freezer and given them to her mom. Lily and Jackson had coats and jackets in their arms and handed them to Hunter and Grant.

"Mom?" Logan called out as Hunter walked to the front door.

Hunter turned back, grief and hope on her face.

"I'll call you tomorrow, okay?" Logan's voice cracked, her eyes filled with tears. "I love you, Mom. I'll come home as soon as I can."

Hunter nodded and turned back towards the door. With Grant's arm around her, they left, Jackson and Lily right behind.

Logan buried her face in her hands. "I-I-I j-j-just—," she stammered out between sobs.

"In time you will." Sophia wrapped her arms around Logan. "In time you will be able to do more than you can today."

"Remember you are doing more now than you did two days ago," Gabby said. "It just takes time and you have time."

"Can I take a shower before we bake?" Logan asked, scrubbing her face with her hands, quelling the tears.

"Of course, there are clean towels already out. Do you need a change of clothes?"

"I've got her things in the car. I'll go bring them in," Gabby said. "Logan," she called out to Logan's retreating back, "I'll put your backpack with your clothes outside the bathroom door and the other bag in the bedroom, okay?"

A muffled "okay," the door closed, the water turned on.

Gabby turned to Sophia. "She may take another shower before going to bed and another one in—."

"If taking one every hour helps, so be it." Sophia waved a hand in a vague gesture of assent. "How about a cup of tea and another piece of my chocolate cake?"

"Do you have any ice cream?" Gabby asked, smacking her lips.

"As a matter-of-fact I have a pint of Jackson's homemade vanilla bean," Sophia said. "I think that's enough for me, but I also have some of his homemade chocolate sauce and some whipped cream."

"That is way over the top," Gabby said, beginning to relax for the first time in several days. "I'm good with cake and ice cream."

Dropping the backpack outside the bathroom door, Gabby called out, "Soph has some chocolate cake and Jackson's homemade vanilla bean ice cream if you're interested."

"Don't eat it all, Gabby, I'm coming."

Setting the duffle bag in the bedroom she strolled back to the family room. It had been a challenging day but ending it with a friend, chocolate cake, homemade ice cream and a healing soul was a very good thing.

23 - AND THEN?

*H*unter said goodbye to the last of her morning students, locked the front door and returned to her studio. She crossed the dance floor to pick up her drum when a familiar voice stopped her.

"Do you still run or just dance?"

Grant had a key to the backdoor but still she was surprised to see him. *Perhaps he called? I always turn the phone's ringer off during a class.* Hunter strode back across the room, down the hall to the front and turned the phone's ringer on.

The five messages, all from her afternoon class, all saying they were sick, was not what she needed to hear. Her forehead furrowed, her jaw clenched, she stabbed the rewind button.

"What?" Grant asked a note of apprehension in his voice. "Is Logan all right?"

"About a third of my afternoon class is sick."

Just then the phone rang. Hunter answered it, responded to the caller with, "Not a problem, see you next week."

Turning to Grant she said, "Another cancellation." She exhaled, blowing an errant strand of her chestnut hair off her forehead.

"You could cancel the class." Grant leaned against the desk. "I can help make the calls if you decide that's what you want to do."

"I need the income. If Logan still wants to go to Smith, I'll need every penny I can—." Hunter stopped mid-sentence at the scowl on Grant's face. "What? Why are you looking at me like that?"

Grant stood, pulled a chair around so he sat next to Hunter at the desk. He grabbed a pad of paper and pen. "Look at it this way. Or at least consider what I'm going to say." His blue eyes met hers and locked.

"Here's the deal. Even excluding the fact that I can pay her tuition, books and fees in full," he stayed her exclamation with a raised hand, "You do realize your grandmother set up the trust for you, don't you?"

"She told me I had a trust and that if I let the trust officer know where I was once a year, no one would come after me, or try to take Logan away," Hunter said, a challenging note to her words.

Grant muttered something under his breath.

"What?"

"Let's start at the beginning. While I don't know everything, I do know this much. Your grandmother set up the trust. Your parents have nothing to do with it. In fact I'm not even sure they know anything about it because she named it the LHF trust and while it was listed in her will, it was administered separately from her other holdings.

"Second, the LHF trust owns this building. The monthly payments you make are to yourself.

"Three, the trust owns this block so the other tenants who pay rent, are paying it to you.

"Four, you could stop paying rent to yourself each month which would add—," he paused, a questioning looked directed her way.

Hunter sat stunned. If she didn't pay rent, she'd have another thousand dollars a month to pay towards Logan's college. "I didn't know." Her mouth formed an 'o', her hands dropped to her lap. "I never asked her about the trust or checked anything out. I was so determined to keep Logan away from everyone, to protect her from—."

The pain she saw in Grant's eyes stopped her from saying anything more. "I'm sorry," she started.

"You wanted to protect her from the stifling life, the impossible expectations, what you saw as the exact opposite of what you wanted for your child. You never considered I'd understand." Grant pushed away from the desk and paced the perimeter of the room.

"I thought you were involved with someone else. I thought I didn't matter to you, that what we'd shared and done—the entire summer was a lie." She watched him pace, saw him stop and stalk back to her. He leaned across the desk, his blue eyes burned with rage.

"You didn't trust me," he spat out. "You never gave me a chance to explain."

"You kissed her," Hunter yelled, now on her feet. "You had your arms around each other, you leaned down and the two of you kissed. Why would I have trusted you? Why would I have taken the chance? How would I know you wouldn't side with my parents, demand I have an abortion, demand I put my baby up for adoption or take her from me so your parents could raise her? How was I to know?"

She'd rounded the desk and stood toe-to-toe with him. "I saw you kissing her. I thought you loved me. And if you really did love me, like you said, you would not be kissing someone else."

The phone rang. Hunter maintained eye contact with Grant while answering it. "Yes, I understand," she said and hung up.

Grant was the first to look away, to step back. "I don't even know who it was. I've no memory of being interested much less involved with some blond."

"I know what I saw," Hunter emphasized. "I am not making this up."

"I'm not saying you are, just that I don't remember it. I know if you'd talked to me I'd have helped in any way I could. We could have gotten married."

Hunter laughed.

"I'm sure your parents would have been excited, thrilled even to have their darling son married at nineteen and a father no less," she said derision coloring her words.

Grant scrubbed a hand down his face. "It's the past and as much as I'd like it to be different, it is what it is. All we can do now is move forward, to make decisions that benefit Logan.

"You really are a wealthy woman, Hunter. Hold the class or not, but make your decision on what is right for you not on finances. You have enough annual income from dividends to continue your life here, to add studio space, to even teach for free." He turned and walked towards the hall.

"Grant?" Hunter called out the question to his retreating back.

He stopped but didn't turn back.

"It's a lot to take in. I need some time—the idea I don't have to worry about how to afford college for Logan is—well, I just need some time."

"Take whatever you need," he said and continued towards the back door.

Hunter strode to the doorway to the hall. "Grant?"

He stopped again.

Her heart beat a rapid tattoo and she gripped the doorframe to steady herself.

"You offered to help with the calls to cancel my afternoon class."

He started down the hall towards her. "I did do that. And I asked if you still ran."

She smiled. "Most days I get in a few miles." When he reached the office area, she handed him a list of names and numbers. "You take the even numbers and I'll take the odd after I change the outgoing message on my phone."

"And the check mark?" he asked.

She took the page from him and added two more check marks. "These are the students who've already cancelled."

"You change the message and your clothes, I'll start the calls. When you get back, we'll divide the rest of the list up if I haven't already finished." Grant turned away and dialed the first unchecked number.

Hunter bristled at the dictatorial tone, the dismissiveness of the order. It rankled he was right, that this was the most efficient way to cancel the class. She picked up the phone, dialed the number that allowed her to put in the code to change the message. A brief, "The afternoon class on Monday, April 25 is being cancelled due to the illness of several students. At this time the Wednesday afternoon class is also cancelled. For anyone calling to cancel a class, please leave a message and I'll get back to you with rescheduling information as soon as I can. For anyone else, please leave a message and I'll get back to you as soon as I can. Thank you for calling Twinkle Toes Dance Studio."

Upstairs she quickly changed into a pair of sweats and running shoes. Before going downstairs, she sat at the desk in front of the window and looked out. It still boggled her mind that she owned this whole block, that she had money to offer scholarships to children and adults who wanted to dance but couldn't afford it.

"Hunter," Grant's voice from the bottom of the stairs pulled her out of her reverie. "I've finished the calls, are you coming? Afraid I'll beat you?"

"On my way." She trotted down the hall to the stairs. A ray of hope lightened her steps. There were problems ahead, but in her heart she was confident they would be surmounted.

Out the back door, she turned, locked it and set the alarm.

"At the end of the alley, turn left, go straight three blocks, turn right. You'll see the park four blocks ahead. Got it?" Hunter tucked the key in her bra.

"Got it," Grant said.

"Meet you at the end of the loop around the park." Hunter sprinted off.

"I'll be waiting for you." Grant dashed after her.

*H*alfway through the run, Hunter's cell phone rang. *Logan.* She halted, bent and with one hand on her thigh, reached for her phone with the other.

Grant, who'd been trailing a few feet behind her saving his energy to sprint past her when the end was in sight, pulled up beside her. "What?"

She glared. He was barely winded and she was, while not winded, breathing as if she'd run a couple of miles which she had.

"Logan," she replied and answered her phone. "Logan, are you okay?" She knew worry resounded through the line but somehow couldn't keep her tone light. "Are you okay?" She glanced at her watch, noted the time was just past noon. *What could it be?*

"Hi Mom, I'm okay," Logan said in a rush. "I'm calling because Sophia and I want you and Grant to come for dinner. Will you see him?" she asked. "I don't have his phone number."

Hunter blew out a breath, straightened and gave Grant a thumbs up. "He called you when you were gone so it's in your phone but," she hurried to add, "he's right here. You can ask him yourself if he can make it."

She handed the phone to Grant and said in a loud enough voice for Logan to hear, "It's Logan with a question for you, I'll just run along while you two talk."

"Are you out running with Mom?" Logan asked.

"I am." Grant watched Hunter lope off. "What did you want to ask me?"

"Can you come to dinner tonight at Sophia's?" Logan asked, adding, "Mom'll do anything to distract you so she can win."

"Not a problem, I can beat her if I want to," Grant said. "And, yes, I can come to dinner tonight. I'll bring a bottle of wine."

"No need. Soph and I are good. Mom doesn't drink much wine either. Says it gives her a headache in the morning—sulfites you know. Can you even see Mom?" she asked and giggled.

"No, she's around a bend in the path, but I'll catch up to her," he said with confidence.

"Not if it's the bend just before the end of the loop. Can you see a lake with willow trees along the side bordering the path?"

"No, not from here and I don't remember seeing it so far. There's a row of benches along the path, a restroom and—,"

"I know where you are," Logan interrupted. "About a half mile to the end. See you tonight."

The line went dead. He tucked the phone in his pocket and sprinted off. No way was Hunter going to beat him this morning. Five minutes later he spotted her just rounding the curve in the path Logan had described. He ratcheted up the pace a bit. While he'd done some running most days since his arrival, he'd not gotten in his usual amount of miles nor his days at the gym.

She heard the steady beat of footsteps and knew it was Grant. He drew alongside her, slowed and matched his pace to hers. "Maybe we can start a new tradition," he said, taking a breath between every few words.

"What?" she asked.

He reached for her hand as they neared the end of the path, "We can cross the finish line together. It's called a tie."

They slowed and walked the last few yards, leaving the path together. Hunter floated, feeling as light as an effortless leap in the air.

In the past they'd run together, matched each other step-by-step, crossed the imaginary finish line in the sand at the same time. She glanced up at Grant, saw sweat lining his brow, his upper lip. His hand was dry as she remembered. No sweaty palms for Grant Hayward Parker IV. A giggle erupted before she quashed it.

"What?" Grant's blue-gray eyes squinted as he looked over at her.

"I'm famished and in need of a shower," Hunter said striding ahead. "Come on before I leave you in the dust."

"Like that will ever happen," he said jogging after her.

He gained her side and kept pace with her. At the back door, while she turned off the alarm and unlocked the door, he said, "I'm heading to the motel to get my own shower and change."

Hunter turned back, the invitation to come in and shower when she was done on her lips. The moment was lost when her neighbor called out "Hello."

"When you're done, come on back and I'll have lunch ready," she said, after a neighborly wave back.

"Sounds good." Grant clicked the alarm off the rental car, got in and drove off as Hunter went inside.

GRANT SPENT the afternoon with her, going over her financial future in more detail. With his coaching, she called the trust officer and got the login and password so she could see the trust account on line. Initially the trust officer was resistant.

After her second offer to answer any security questions, Grant had taken the phone.

"Grant Parker, here," he'd said. "I'm advising Ms. Compton in this matter. I do hope you can assist her."

He'd handed the phone back to her and everything had proceeded at a rapid pace. "I didn't realize you were so, so, so—." She had her hand over the receiver as she struggled for a word to finish the sentence.

"So competent?" Grant flashed that devastating grin that drew her back to eighteen years ago.

"That's as good a word as any," she'd muttered, grateful the trust officer was once again talking to her. She wrote down the information he gave her, thanked him for all his help, listened politely as he made a herculean effort to undo the botched job he'd done at the beginning. After a couple of minutes of his talking and no response from her, he asked if she was still there. She said 'yes' but had other tasks to attend to. She was polite and cordial as she ended the call.

By four Hunter was saturated in the details of the trust. "How will I ever?" she'd asked Grant her face etched with a mix of wonder and worry.

"You can talk to the trust officer and ask him questions"

"But I don't know him. How will I know he is telling me the truth and not dumbing it down?"

"If you think he may be doing that, ask me. I'll let you know if that's the case." Grant stood and stretched. "Time to go?"

"We can leave any time," Hunter said.

Grant drove to Sophia's while Hunter gave him directions. Logan greeted them at the door, a brief hug for each. She'd taken Grant's jacket and hung it on the peg by the front door. Hunter shrugged out of her jacket and hung it up at the same time. Logan lingered a moment longer and Hunter wondered what her daughter saw, what she felt seeing her mom and dad's jackets next to each other.

For her it was a surreal moment.

In the kitchen, Sophia was stirring a pot of homemade soup, the aroma of freshly baked bread hung in the air. Hunter breathed in the homey smells, knowing everything would taste even better. Fresh chocolate peanut butter cookies were cooling on a rack—Logan's favorites.

"Thank you again for the cinnamon rolls, Ms. Stewart. The best I've ever had," Grant said.

"Sophia is my name, Grant. Ms. Stewart only exists in the minds of my students." Sophia rounded the kitchen counter to shake Grant's extended hand.

"Logan? Why don't you see what your mom and dad want to drink?" Sophia said giving everyone something to do, to talk about.

Since dinner still needed another fifteen minutes to be ready and the table was already set, Logan offered to show Grant Sophia's garden. Hunter knew he and Jackson had been out on the patio yesterday but also knew they were not talking about the garden if they had talked at all. The men connected to The Circle were still sizing Grant up, assessing his acceptability to be in either her life or Logan's. She thought they were leaning in his direction because they were including him.

Hunter watched Logan and Grant through the sliding glass doors. Logan animated as she pointed out various parts of the garden. Grant leaned slightly to the side and she was positive he listened to every word and if she quizzed him on the way home, he'd be able to recount everything his daughter had told him.

Her stomach churned as guilt struck. She knew why she'd made the choices she had but she also knew she was derelict in some ways. She'd never really checked out the trust. She'd never talked to her grandmother after Logan was born—the annual letter with a picture the only communication. Her grandmother had stood by her but she had not stood by her grandmother. As a result, Logan would never know her great-grandmother.

Sophia rested her hand on Hunter's arm. "Penny for your thoughts?"

"I'm sick with worry right now. I don't know why we're here. I doubt just about every decision I've made since learning I was pregnant." Hunter's eyes brimmed with unshed tears.

"Would it be better to talk first and eat second?" Sophia asked.

"If you want Grant and me to do more than stir the soup around in the bowl and nibble on the bread?" Her words were bitter, her laugh lacked humor.

Sophia crossed the family room and called Grant and Logan inside. She gestured for everyone to sit. Hunter was surprised when Logan sat on the couch between them. Sophia sat across from them.

"Hunter said for her it would be better to talk and eat afterwards. What about you?" Sophia asked Grant.

He nodded, wariness in his posture.

Logan sat at attention.

Hunter's stomach rolled in protest.

"I did go to school today and checked in with Logan between every class. And, at one point, Logan talked to her counselor, Ms. L.

"This is the beginning of the third week of class Logan has missed. I'd already spoken to Ms. L who'd talked to each of Logan's teachers last Friday." Sophia exhaled a huff of air. "I know I overstepped, but I also knew when Logan came back to us, there would be questions about school so I asked Ms. L what she thought Logan would need to do when she was able to return to school."

"What does she need to do?" Grant asked grim-faced.

"The daily work she can most easily catch up with. The challenge is her senior project and she has two classes where her grade depends on class participation. She has failing grades in those classes because of the days she's been absent. I think those teachers can be convinced to modify those grades under special circumstances because they know she's been a willing participant until these absences.

"Logan, this is not news to you because this is what you, Ms. L and I talked about on the phone. You've had some time to think things over. Are you in the same place you were when talking to Ms. L or do you have other questions or thoughts?"

"I-I-I don't know that I can go back to school yet." Logan's initial stammer turned to a rush of words tripping over each other by the end. "I know Ms. L said the teachers would not ask me why I was absent but the other kids will. I," she exhaled and drew in a deep breath.

Hunter heard the panic and saw Logan lock her hands in a fist on her lap.

"You don't know what to tell them," Hunter said, covering Logan's hands with one of hers. "Some will ask out of curiosity, some will ask out of worry, some will ask hoping to hurt you with your words."

"How-how do you know?" Logan asked, her gaze locked on her mom's.

"Been there, done that," Hunter responded. "You know your dad's a big shot corporate attorney." Hunter caught Grant's gaze and grinned. "Let's give him a chance to come up with a good answer or two, maybe even three."

"If you had answers to the question "where were you?" you'd go back to school?

Logan swiveled towards her dad. "I'm not sure."

"The best answer is always as close to the truth as possible. You can say you found your father and it took some getting used to."

Logan smiled. "That would be the truth but there is more."

"Does anyone else need to know the rest?" Grant asked.

Logan unfisted her hands. She reached out to her mom and dad. "I know you will love me no matter what. I just can't talk about it. Ms. L said something about counseling but I got sick."

Hunter squeezed Logan's hand. She might pray whatever had happened could be undone but that was wishful thinking. *Maybe if I told her what I did when I ran away?* She looked at Sophia whose attention was riveted on Logan.

"Does anyone else at school need to know more?" Grant asked rephrasing the question.

"Not really," Logan said in a quiet voice. "But if I go to school, I don't want to bolt out of the room because I'm going to puke. I don't want to scream because I think someone is going to hurt me."

"Then you aren't ready to go back." Grant's voice was calm, the tone decisive. "If you are worried you may get sick or scream or have flashbacks or whatever, I don't think you're ready. But I'm one opinion and a fairly new addition at that. What do you think, Hunter?"

"I agree." She shifted so Logan now held her other hand and the one closest to her daughter rested on her back. "What do you think, Soph?"

"There are only five weeks remaining in school for seniors. Logan has missed all but the first week of the last grading period. I'm not saying she has to or even should go to school but there is or could be consequences. Ms. L plans on talking to all of Logan's teachers to see what they are willing to do so she can still graduate if she is not able to return to their classrooms. We'll have that information tomorrow or Wednesday at the latest."

"So the plan for tomorrow is?" Grant asked.

"Sophia brought home all the books from my locker. I plan on reading tomorrow to begin to catch up. Ms. L told me where they are in Government and English. I know what chapters they've covered in physics. Sophia is going to see if I can prepare a speech and give it privately to my teacher or on speakerphone to my class."

"What if your dad and I come by around lunch time? We can bring pizza or sandwiches. Especially if you are stuck on something having to do with government, I know your dad can help you with that."

"You could come running with us in the morning, see me beat your mom?" Grant said and winked at Logan.

"Yeah right," Hunter shot back. "You'd need a head start to do that."

"Mom," Logan said. "He's teasing."

"Grant does not 'tease' about winning. It is one of his favorite things."

"Maybe I've changed," Grant said a twinkle in his eyes.

"What's that saying about a leopard changing its spots?" Hunter asked, her finger on her chin, her head tilted in a thoughtful pose.

"Is there more to discuss right now or is everyone ready to eat?" Sophia asked. "We can make final plans for tomorrow after dinner, okay?"

Hunter was still on the couch, when the realization hit she might not see Logan walk across the stage and get her diploma. Her chest constricted. *It is what it is. I'm grateful she's with us. I'm grateful she's healing.* Hunter looked over at Grant who was in the kitchen sniffing the pot of soup. *In so many little ways, he hasn't changed.* Hunter crossed the family room to the kitchen, picked up the tossed salad and took it to the table.

Having difficulty staying focused on the dinner conversation, Hunter's mind sifted through the various ways The Circle had supported her today. Ashley's sent her love and courage in two different messages. Lily had called, offering to help out as long as it wasn't cleaning house. They'd laughed and made a date to have coffee. Jackson was in town, Lily'd added so if Grant wanted to come along, the men could hang out while she and Lily did whatever.

Would Grant want to spend time with Jackson? Hunter made a mental note to say something about the invitation on the way home.

There were moments when they were together time slipped away and they were the carefree teens from long ago. There were moments when she could feel him watching her, the attraction between them growing. Those were the moments when she needed distance.

He was a reminder of her past. How could they ever truly maintain a connection? The idea of even visiting Rhode Island, of seeing old acquaintances much less her family chilled her to the bone. Because of her connections within The Circle, she knew those people from her past were not truly friends.

And Grant here in Fremont? She couldn't fathom that. He still had that prep school, Yale look about him. His two sentences to the trust officer showed her how important and how respected he was. And women? She couldn't imagine him single. There must be someone back east waiting for him.

Hunter checked back into the conversation, spent the rest of the meal engaged in small talk, told Logan to call her in the morning and let her know what the plan was.

On the drive home, she broached the topic of coffee with Lily and Jackson. Grant was receptive. Perhaps not excited about the idea but definitely not rejecting it either. In the parking area behind the studio, she was out of the car almost before Grant came to a complete stop. "See you tomorrow?" she called out. "I'll be out running at seven."

She had the alarm off and door opened in record time. Turning she waved, a forced smile on her face, she waved a second time and closed the door. Locked, the alarm reset, she sank onto the bottom step. *My heart is pounding, my palms are sweaty. I feel like I've run ten miles. What is wrong with me?*

A question with either no answer or an answer she was unwilling to face. She put it aside and trudged up the stairs. She checked Logan's room, decided to pack up some of her clothes and take them by tomorrow.

Logan's main altar sat on a corner of her dresser, a smaller one on her window sill. Tears coursed down Hunter's cheeks as she carefully dismantled the latter. Using a cigar box for a container, she wrapped the small crystals in tissue. In the center of the box, she placed the now wrapped antique glass bowl. Placing the package of crystals in the center of the bowl, she added a small smudge wand and four apache tears.

Another tissue was used from the box on Logan's dresser to dry her tears. Hunter breathed deep and exhaled a gentle love-filled breath into the box before closing the top. *Something to bring her peace and healing.*

In front of the living room altar, Hunter raised her arms in prayer.

"May I know peace tonight.

"May my dreams be filled with joy and happiness.

"May I wake in the morning ready for whatever life brings my way.

"Blessed Be."

25 - PLEASE, NOT THAT

*H*unter woke in the morning without the alarm. Instead of leaping out of bed she waited the three minutes until the ocean wave sounds indicated it was time. A fullness in her abdomen signaled the onset of her menses, a reminder to take some tampons, pads and pain reliever to Logan whose cycle was generally about the same time as hers. She put the supplies in a pouch and set it next to her purse.

After a quick shower, she dressed and padded into the kitchen. Breakfast consisted of fresh blueberries stirred into homemade yoghurt and a blueberry muffin.

"It's me," Grant called out coming in the back door. "Are you here? Are you decent? May I come up?"

"Yes, yes and yes," Hunter replied.

He strode into the living room, his hair still damp from his shower. He'd shaved too. But there was something different about him. Her head cocked to the side, she studied him.

"Like what you see?" he asked that brilliant grin on his face.

"You look different," Hunter replied. "What have you done to yourself?"

"Showered, shaved, dressed, pretty much what I do every day"

Grant crossed the room to look at his face in the mirror over the couch.

"What do you see that's different?" he asked studying his reflection.

"It's probably the light or something." Hunter rinsed out her bowl and put it in the dishwasher. "Have you had something to eat? I've muffins and yoghurt or you can have toast. I do have some bread."

"Muffin sounds good and coffee?" Grant asked his hands clasped as if in prayer.

"You're in luck because I don't always make coffee in the morning. You can have what's left in the pot." She gestured towards the carafe.

Grant poured a cup of coffee, grabbed a muffin and, after turning it around, straddled a chair at the table. He took a bite out of the muffin, washed it down with a gulp of coffee and sighed. "Perfect."

What struck her then was how casual he was, how relaxed, how unlike the buttoned-down-East-coast-society man he'd been when he first arrived. No suit, no tie, no highly polished shoes. His hair wasn't styled and was getting a little shaggy around the ears or at least shaggy for him. He was wearing sweats and running shoes. His briefcase was probably in the car but it wasn't an appendage.

"Your phone?" she asked not seeing it on the table in front of him. In fact she hadn't seen it at all yesterday. Yesterday he'd used her phone to talk to Logan.

"Phone?" Grant glanced her way. "It's in my briefcase."

"What about work? People were always calling you when you first arrived."

"And that's why it's in my briefcase." He patted the chair next to him and she sat at an angle so she could see him.

"Do you know how many real vacations I've taken in the last eighteen years?" He had an unfocused look in his eyes as he looked through her.

She shook her head, but then said, "No, I don't."

"The summer we spent together is the last time I just did what I wanted. It isn't that I've not spent a week in St. Moritz, Monaco, London or on the cape. There are times I've not been at the office but the expectation that I would be catering to clients, looking for ways to increase my billable hours and be available when called was a constant.

"This is the first time I've separated my personal life from business, from work." His gaze met hers, a slight wrinkle between his eyebrows; he leaned towards her and spoke in a confidential manner. "I told them I'd check emails and messages in the morning and at night. The rest of the time, my phone would be off and I would not be at a computer."

"Is the firm okay with that?" Hunter asked seeing Grant as if for the first time. "Are they going to fire you?" She whispered in a conspiratorial tone.

"I doubt it. After all, my grandfather and uncle started the firm. But are they happy? Not at all. Have they threatened? Oh yes, if only veiled ones. Will I face some kind of backlash when I go back? Definitely.

"My secretary has been a trooper because they've preyed upon her and threatened her with dismissal. She knows absolutely nothing, not even where I am. I've no doubt they'll try something. I don't know exactly what and right now I don't care. I'll deal with it when I have to."

"Can she take vacation or something until—,"

"Told her to do that this morning. Emailed the president of the firm and told him I'd given my secretary time off with pay until my return. I'm sure he'll fume if not rant but I said if he didn't agree, I'd cover her salary from my own earnings."

"You can do that?" Hunter gasped as the reality of Grant's position in the firm and his financial resources struck.

"Yes, I can do that and I can pay for Logan to attend Smith or whatever college she wants to. However, remember you are a wealthy woman in your own right. You have the resources to pay for Smith yourself." He rested a hand on her arm. "I'd like it if we shared those expenses."

Hunter blinked back tears and fought to control her voice. "I'm still coming to grips with all you told me about the trust and everything." The disappointment on Grant's face lanced her heart. "I'm okay with us sharing Logan's college expenses but what's more important is whether or not she would like it."

Grant finished his coffee and muffin, rinsed out the cup and put it in the dishwasher.

"You've been well-trained," Hunter quipped.

"My housekeeper has done a good job has she?" he said closing the door on the appliance.

"No dirty socks in the living room?"

Grant stared at her, as if looking into her heart. "What do you want to know?"

"I was just teasing," Hunter said her face aflame.

Grant continued to watch her saying nothing.

"You seem to know more about me and my private life than I know about you," she said, chin high.

Grant crossed to the table and sat down. "I've been involved with four women in the past however many years. I've co-habited with them, enjoyed their company but never once considered making it permanent as in getting engaged much less married.

"Each of them broke it off when it finally became apparent I was not going to make more of a commitment than I already had. The truth is, while each was beautiful and accomplished in many ways, they could have been exchanged one for the other. Even spontaneous plans seemed structured."

As those final words were spoken, Hunter could only describe the look on Grant's face as sardonic.

"Spontaneous plans—is that an oxymoron or what?" He looked directly at her. "Does that answer your unasked question?"

She nodded. "It was the 'spontaneous plans' that did it. I'm not sure I wouldn't have become just like them if I'd stayed."

"Then I'm very glad you didn't." He leaned towards her, his intense gaze searching her face.

He was going to kiss her. Hunter was positive he was going to kiss her. His hand traced the contours of her face, his fingers brushed across her lips. She saw passion in his blue-grey eyes. Was he remembering how it had been between them? Her body was remembering: nipples taut, belly tight, heat in her core.

He leaned back.

He looked away.

He took a deep breath and exhaled on a rush. No, he was not going to kiss her. She had no doubt he'd wanted to but for whatever reason he pulled back. Her mind swirled with relief but her body sighed with regret.

"How about a run?" he asked a moment later. "Not a race just a leisure run?"

Hunter got up and started towards her room. "Give me a minute to get ready." Once inside her domain, she leaned back against the closed door. "He was going to kiss me. I wonder what stopped him?"

DREAD MIXED with horror coated Hunter's stomach, its tentacles crept into her bowels. Her throat closed with terror at the stricken look on Logan's face. She should have just started her menses yesterday or maybe today and by the look on her face, none of the telltale signs were evident.

With Grant right there, she hesitated to say anything specific. Instead she hugged Logan close, whispered "don't worry" in her ear and pasted a smile of encouragement on her face. At least that is what she hoped it looked like.

From the look on Logan's face, she'd failed.

"What's going on?" Grant asked, worry edging his voice.

Hunter noted he kept his neutral look on his face, so unlike when they were alone. "Just girl stuff," she answered, going for a light breezy tone.

"Ookkaayy," he said. "Should I leave or at least go into the other room?" His brow arched with the question.

Before Hunter could answer, Logan broke away and dashed to the bathroom, the sounds of her vomiting easily heard where they stood.

Grant's confused and concerned look prompted Hunter to say, "feminine hygiene" before she started down the hall.

Logan was hunkered over the toilet, dry heaves bellowing her sides. Hunter perched on the edge of the tub, taking a washcloth and wetting it in the nearby sink. "You do know stress can make women late," she said, amazed at how calm her voice was because inside she was screaming "Nnnoooo!!!!"

Her daughter slumped to the floor, spent from the efforts of ridding her body of the toxins. Hunter started to hand her the cloth but instead sat beside her, put her arm around Logan and rested her daughter's head on her own shoulder. With studied care, she wiped Logan's face, stroking the damp tendrils away from her forehead and cheeks.

"I can make an appointment with Dr. Jane?" Hunter said.

Logan shoved away, her head over the toilet, another dry heave racking her body.

"No, Mom. No, I can't see her. Please," she pleaded. "I'll be okay. I promise." She stood, flushed the toilet, bent over the sink and rinsed her face off before swishing water in her mouth and spitting it out. "I promise, I'll be okay. I-I-I—sometimes it feels like there's something evil inside me and I have to get it out."

"I promise, no appointment with Dr. Jane, then." She waited a couple of heartbeats before adding, "What about the other doctor you know from the clinic?"

Logan shook her head. "I'm okay, Mom. I'll be fine." She wiped her face and hands on a towel. "Where's Grant?"

"He's in the family room I think, or maybe out on the back patio. He's really intrigued with Sophia's garden." Gratitude mixed with lingering horror warred in her stomach. Gratitude that Logan had allowed her to be there, to hold her, had talked to her. Horror that her daughter might be pregnant at seventeen. Pregnant but not from a loving consensual joining. What Hunter surmised, what fit into the holes, into the silence was that while Logan was gone, she had been raped.

At that moment she was very glad that less than two hours ago

Grant had pulled away, had not kissed her, had not stirred the attraction that still simmered between them.

Logan wanted to change her shirt so Hunter went looking for Grant. He was out in the garden, meandering up and down the paths. Hunter called his name and waved. He was too far away for her to see the look on his face when she first called to him but she wasn't surprised to see his professional neutral face when he drew near. His eyes? His eyes looked haunted one minute and burned with rage the next.

"I propose we take a walk instead of running today. There's a great sandwich shop a mile or so away. We can see if something looks good and either eat there or bring it back and eat out on the patio," Hunter suggested.

"Or, we could drive there, order, come back and eat here and then go for a walk," Grant added. He turned to Logan who had joined them. "Two great options for you to choose from. Know if you don't like mine, I'll be devastated." He winked at Logan.

Logan gave each a considering look. She sighed and turned to Grant. "You don't have to worry about being devastated. I don't think I'm up for a long walk right now."

They ordered sandwiches to go. Back at the house, they sat out on the patio, ate, chatted about the garden and Sophia's peanut butter cookies. Why the cookies? Because Logan brought out a plate with two cookies for each of them. Hunter laughed at Grant's exaggerated moans of ecstasy as he demolished his first cookie and looked longingly at Logan's untouched ones.

"Don't even consider it, Dad," Logan said. "I've got homework to do and these cookies are my reward. Sophia did not say we could eat them all!"

"If I help you with your homework, may I please have another?" Grant bargained, looking every inch the corporate attorney.

Logan laughed. "It depends on whether or not you really help me or not. I've got work to do in Government and when Sophia comes home, two quizzes and a test to take."

Grant stood, reached out towards Logan. "Let's get to it. Those cookies are a great incentive."

"Ms. Lawford says Sophia could buy her own island if she sold them," Logan said taking her dad's hand.

"Who's Ms. Lawford?" Grant asked.

"An attorney we know. She's helped Diana and Ashley with stuff."

"She's right about the cookies and if Sophia added the chocolate cake on the menu, she could probably afford two islands."

Hunter stayed on the patio and waited until Grant and Logan were settled at the table, text books and paper spread before them. She'd heard the sharp intake of breath when Logan called him Dad, saw emotions fly across his face before the corporate attorney look slid into place. His professional training and years of "image is everything" practice had held him in good stead.

She focused on her breathing, calmed the churning in her stomach that while not comfortable was nowhere close to nausea. A few minutes passed as she dealt with the reality that Logan's moving forward really did include Grant. Stepping onto a garden path, she walked to the very back of the garden. Taking her phone from her bra, she turned it on and dialed Gabby's number.

"What's going on?" Gabby's worried voice had a bit of static in it.

"Can you ask the doctor friend to call or come by and see Logan?" Hunter watched the back door through the branches of a dogwood tree.

"I can do that. What's up?" Gabby asked again. "I know something going on, Hunt. You wouldn't be calling me in the middle of the day just to chat."

Gabby's voice was muffled but she thought she'd said something about an important call. A moment later, the reception was clearer when Gabby asked again. "What?"

Hunter's knees buckled and she looked for a place to sit down. No bench in sight, she leaned against the tree, willing her knees to hold. Tears streamed down her face and her throat constricted with pain.

"Logan's late," she managed

"How late?" Gabby asked.

"A day or two. But she's never been late before. I'm terrified, Grant's stricken. Although we haven't really said anything directly to him—he's not stupid."

"Logan?"

"Logan lost whatever she'd eaten. She's refused to see Dr. Jane. I don't want to get a pregnancy kit without her permission. I thought maybe if Doc S called her or stopped by to see how she's doing...," her voice trailed off as the sobs took over.

"I'll call her. And she did tell Logan she'd be checking on her so that isn't going to look suspicious. Don't know what her schedule is so it could be a day or two before she calls or stops by." Gabby sounded confident and in charge. "Your job, Hunt, is to stay calm and not let your imagination get away from you when you're around Logan."

"I know. Right at this moment, I'm glad she isn't at home because I don't know if I could manage that 24/7."

"You could if you had to because you'd do anything for Logan."

The bands of steel around Hunter's chest eased with Gabby's encouragement. She could do this if she had to. "Is it wrong to pray for a miscarriage if she is pregnant?" she asked.

"Absolutely not," Gabby said.

"I want to let everyone know but I don't really have Logan's permission," Hunter said and sighed.

"I don't think you need to let anyone else know about this possible wrinkle. Let's see what Doc S does. I know she'll see and talk to Logan as soon as she can work it in without it looking suspicious."

"Thanks, Gabby. I do feel better knowing that." Hunter shifted the phone to her other ear. "I'll let you get back to work. I'd say I'm sorry for bothering you, but I'd be lying." A soft laugh, another sigh. "You'll be coming home this weekend?"

"I'll be there Friday night. And I've talked to my boss. The project is wrapping up and I may not have to come back up next week at all. But if I do," her delight was easily recognizable in her voice, "it will be a short week. Maybe only a day or two at the most which is why they are thinking of pushing to wrap up this week.

"I'll leave here Friday night but it may be Saturday morning before I get there if we have to put in a really late night."

"Be safe," Hunter said, knowing Gabby would come home as soon as she could. "I'll start sending you safe driving energy at noon on Friday until I hear that you're back."

"You remain in my prayers, Hunt, as does Logan and Grant. Talk to you soon. I'll let you know if Doc S has something going on and can't stop by in the next day or so. If you don't hear from me, she'll be knocking on Sophia's door."

Hunter took some time wandering the garden paths, composing herself. Both Logan and Grant were astute enough to see she'd been crying if she went right back in. A half hour later, Grant stood in the doorway and waved. She knew he'd watched her from time to time as she'd walked, stretched, twirled and even done a couple of leaps. *I can do this. Whatever happens, I can be there for my daughter. I know in my heart we will survive whatever is before us.*

26 - PRAYERS ARE ANSWERED?

Wednesday

"Hey, Logan, Doc S here. Got your message. What's going on?"

Logan looked furtively over her shoulder to check where her parents were. Her dad was outside in the garden, her mom fixing a salad and sandwiches for lunch. "Be right back," she called out to no one in particular, starting for the hall.

In her room she closed the door and crossed to the window. "I'm late, Doc." She looked out the window at Grant wandering down a path. A bend in the walk. He disappeared. Tears coursed down her cheeks. "I've never been late. Help me, please. I can't have a baby," she sobbed. "I don't know what to do."

"You do know you can be late for reasons other than a pregnancy," Doc S said.

Logan heard the calm certainty in Doc's voice. *Maybe I'm not?* But that thought wasn't enough. She had to know for sure. "Please help me," Logan pleaded, her voice shaky, her white-knuckled grip on the cell phone cramping her fingers.

"Come to the clinic at closing time and I'll check you out," Doc said. "Do not come alone. And before you ask 'why?' let me say this. Even coming with someone will be difficult. To come by yourself will be worse because of the memories that will come flooding back. You're making good progress, but most of it will be undone if you come by yourself. Does that make sense to you?" Doc S asked.

"I don't know who to—."

"Your parents have been here before. You're staying with another woman who I'm sure would bring you if you asked. You have choices here, Logan."

"Mom knows I'm late." Logan sat on the edge of the bed.

"The choice is yours," Doc repeated. "Just do not come alone."

A soft knock on the bedroom door, her mom's voice announced "Lunch is ready."

Logan called out, "Please come in, Mom." She stood as Hunter came through the door. "Bye Doc, see you tonight."

Hunter's long strides crossed the room in a long second. She wrapped her arms around Logan, held her close. "What can we help you with?" Hunter asked.

Logan saw the blotches on her mom's top and swiped at her face, willing the tears to stop.

They didn't.

"I need to go see Doc S tonight," she said her voice shaky, a fresh spate of tears streamed down her face.

"What time?" Hunter asked.

Logan felt her mom's arms tense, felt her chest rise in a deep breath. "Nine."

"Not a problem," Hunter said.

Grant appeared in the doorway. He crossed the room and wrapped both her mom and her in his arms. He didn't say anything and Logan was grateful for that. Her mom leaned a bit and her dad's arms tightened.

Logan relished the comfort of being held by both her mom and dad for a few moments more. The panic receded. She didn't feel calm and content but she felt cared for and safe. *Feeling safe is more impor-*

tant than anything. Her stomach rumbled and Logan felt her mom's mouth turn up in a smile against her temple.

"Hungry?" Hunter asked.

Logan nodded. She waited for the arms to loosen so it would seem natural when she stepped away. First Grant had to let go and step back. When he didn't for what felt like the longest time, her mom smiled again. "Grant."

Her dad dropped his arms and stepped back. A million unanswered questions about why her mom hadn't told her about him or told him about her clogged her mind. *Mom has at least that many questions about what happened to me.*

Panic welled. She held on to her mom for long moments until she calmed.

Logan looked at Grant when her mom moved to the side. She saw his neutral look on his face but when her gaze caught his, a profound sadness lurked in his eyes. Or at least she thought it did. He blinked, turned away and started towards the door. "Who wants milk with their lunch," he said as he walked into the hall.

"I love you. Always know how much I love you." Hunter's hand rested on her shoulder. "Nothing will ever change that."

Her mom linked arms with her. At the doorway, Hunter held her hand, raised their arms and Logan twirled through into the hall. Blinking away unshed tears, Logan did the two-step with her mom down the hall. They shared so many little traditions, routines that brought smiles to their faces, laughter ringing in the air. *If I-if I'm, please Goddess and God please don't take my mom and dad away from me.*

"I DON'T HAVE to go in," Grant had argued, "but the two of you are *not* going down to the clinic by yourselves. At the very least I can drop you off outside and you can call me when you are ready to be picked up."

"It has to be Logan's decision," Hunter had said.

In the end, Grant drove. Hunter sat in the backseat, holding

Logan's hand. When they left Sophia was busy in the kitchen promising a fresh batch of cinnamon rolls and pecan sticky buns for tomorrow morning.

At five minutes to nine, they were parked directly in front of the clinic. Grant turned off the engine and got out of the car. He rounded the front, opened the back door, held out his hand to help Hunter exit. He almost lifted Logan out when she scooted close enough to the door. Wrapping his arms around her, he was devastated when she pulled away suddenly. Her dash for the curb and the hurling of her dinner eased his devastation but hurt in a whole different way.

When she straightened, Hunter wiped Logan's chin with a tissue and took her hand. Together the three of them walked into the clinic. They were barely through the door when Logan, hand over her mouth, sprinted for the waste basket.

Doc S exited the exam room just as Logan sank to the floor.

"I'll be with you shortly. One more." Doc S turned and smiled at a young woman sitting on a chair, her eyes wide at the spectacle before her. "Come along." Doc gestured towards the examination room. She handed a key to Hunter. "Bathroom with water, towels through there."

Logan huddled on the floor clutching the wastebasket weak from yet another bout of heaving. She leaned into her mom when Hunter began to wipe her face with damp paper towels.

At straight-up nine, Doc poked her head out. "If one of you would please see that the door is locked?"

Grant quickly crossed the small space and locked the door. The urge to leave was strong but he quashed it and resumed his seat.

Another round of vomiting, this time dry heaves.

Hunter lifted the wastebasket's plastic liner and tied the top closed. She positioned a new liner in the receptacle. "Here you go." Hunter handed the basket to Logan. "Just in case."

"Thanks, Mom." Logan rested her cheek against the side of the container.

"I'll get clean towels," Hunter said as she stood.

At that moment, the exam room door opened. Doc S preceded the young woman, who'd obviously been crying, through the small waiting room. Doc unlocked the front door and gestured outside. Grant turned and saw someone just outside the door. He figured she was from the Youth Shelter next door. The exchange was short.

Doc closed and locked the door.

"Mom," Logan stood next to Doc S, "you need to stay with Dad. Doc will take care of me, won't you?"

"I'll do my best," Doc said, gesturing to Logan to go ahead.

Grant checked his watch, impatient with hands that moved so slow. He wanted this to be over. He wanted to go back and redo how he had introduced himself into his daughter's life, back into Hunter's life. He wanted the feelings of helplessness to go away. He wanted—so many things crowded his mind.

Hunter, who had been pacing, perched on the chair next to him. Her hands folded in her stressful pattern.

He reached over and rested one of his hands over hers. She glanced his way, a sad smile on her face. The clock on the wall said the same time as his watch, mere minutes had passed since he last checked.

"What is going on? Do you have any idea?" he asked in a low voice.

"Doc is examining her and that always takes some time," Hunter said. "I'm sure she's also talking to Logan because it's obvious our daughter isn't doing well."

Finally the door to the exam room opened and Doc S stepped out. "She needs you now." Doc stepped aside, gesturing them into the examination room.

An element of surprise surged through Grant as he strode the few steps to where Logan sat at the end of the exam table. *I know what to do.* He stepped close, held her with one arm and wrapped the other around Hunter.

He knew enough not to tell her everything would be okay because he didn't know that to be true. What could he say? "I'm so proud of you." And "I love you." They seemed to be enough. Grant relished the fact that his daughter was leaning into him and accepting his hugs. He was surprised when Logan said in a false-sounding chipper voice, "Let's see what Sophia has for dessert."

In the waiting room, Doc was sitting at the desk typing at the computer. "Sophia was baking when we left. Can you come with us?" Logan asked.

Doc stopped typing and stood. "I'll take a rain check on Sophia's delicious desserts." She crossed to stand in front of Logan and her parents. Taking hold of Logan's hands, she said, "Remember you have a friend but you need to double check if that friend is steering you forward or not."

"And I am loved by many. I will work on double checking what my friend is telling me."

Doc shifted to physically include Hunter and Grant in the conversation. "With Logan's approval I can let you know the tests I ran here to determine whether she is pregnant or not are inconclusive. I've sent blood work in for further testing and, because I have this weekend off, it may be Monday before I get the results back. However, I will let you know as soon as I know."

Grant reached out and pulled Hunter and Logan close. He wasn't sure if he did that to support them or to support himself. Hunter leaned against him, her hand reaching across him to hold Logan's.

Logan's quick intake of air was her only reaction. He gently squeezed Logan's shoulder, enough to let her know he was there and supporting her, that he wasn't leaving.

"I know you love chocolate," Logan said in that too bright voice. "Sophia makes a decadent chocolate cake. If you come over Monday, to tell us in person, I'll ask her to bake one this weekend. I could buy my own Pacific Ocean Island if I practiced and could do it as good as she does."

"Something to aspire to," Doc said. "Let's see when the results come back first, okay?"

Logan nodded. Hunter and Grant said their thanks and shook hands assuring Doc S she was welcomed Monday night whether the test results were back or not.

In the car and headed back to Sophia's, Grant reached over and held Hunter's hand. Logan had lobbied for her mom to sit in the front seat. His heart thudded and he studiously avoided looking over at

Hunter. When she wrapped her fingers around his palm and squeezed he knew he'd done the right thing.

Several right things actually: the right thing to come to Fremont, the right thing to stay and look for his daughter, the right thing to come tonight. Putting those things on one side of the scales of justice with how he'd introduced himself back into Hunter's life on the other, the sides were not in balance but they were more in balance than ever before.

A confidence as a new dad swelled and feelings of inadequacy faded only to be quickly replaced with doubt. *So much ahead of us.*

Thursday

Never had Hunter been so conflicted. Even eighteen years ago when she'd learned she was pregnant her path had been clear to her. It didn't mean it was an easy path, only that she had few doubts. Especially once she'd seen Grant with another woman, she'd been determined to move on with her life, raise her daughter on her own.

She'd invited members of The Circle to stop by her place if they could make it. Although she would not talk about the possibility of Logan being pregnant, she did have other things on her mind. Sorting through the information Grant had given her on her financial situation and what options she had was her agenda.

Lily, Gabby, Diana and Ashley were settled comfortably on couches and chairs in her living area. Tea and cookies were within easy reach. Grant was with Logan. They were going for a walk or run and get a bite of lunch. She'd meet up with them at Sophia's later.

Hunter cleared her throat, took a deep breath and when there was a lull in the conversation, changed the subject.

"I'm grateful you could come by today because this is easier than calling and talking to you individually," she started. "Your love and support have sustained me these past couple of weeks since my world turned on end." Her chest tightened, her throat began to close and tears pooled in her eyes. She stood and began to pace, the turmoil of conflicting emotions driving her on.

"I just can't sit still right now," she apologized to the other women.

"As long as you don't expect me to always keep my eyes on you, do what you need to," Diana said.

Hunter stopped for a moment. "You can all close your eyes if that is helpful," she said a bit of a playful tone in the serious words.

"We'll manage, Hunt," Lily said. "Do what you need to do in order to say what you need to say."

"I've just learned I'm a relatively wealthy woman. I'm struggling to understand just what that means." She strode around the space before plopping down and looking at each of her friends.

"I own this whole block. I've been paying rent to myself all these years." She blew a breath out, slumped back against the cushions. "It's just so surreal. I've been worrying about how to pay for Logan's college. I've added classes. I've worked so hard—not that I regret any of that," she said, her words rushing out. "I just don't know that I would have done all that if I'd known. I don't know—."

Hunter's gaze took in the stunned look of the other women. "Well, you all look poleaxed which is exactly how I felt and sometimes still feel when I think of it."

"Why didn't you know this before now?" Diana asked.

"My parents never searched for me after I ran away but my grandmother did. The private detective she hired found me. I talked to her and agreed to send a letter once a year to let her know I was okay. She also asked me to let her know when Logan was born and if I needed anything.

"When Logan was born, I talked to her on the phone. I'd swear she said "a trust" had been set up, not that she'd set it up. I've always thought my parents set up the trust. After the year Logan and I lived in Los Angeles, I'd send the letters to my friend, Jorge, and he'd have various friends of his around the country mail it.

"I didn't know my grandmother knew I was in Fremont, knew when I was looking for a place for my studio and arranged for me to 'find' the perfect place. Before she died, she bought the building and put it into the trust she'd set up for me.

"The firm who manages the trust always took care of everything. I know it sounds as if I should have known and from what Grant has said, if I'd wanted to know I could have easily found out but I've never wanted to know, I've never wanted to face my family, I've never wanted to return to that constrictive life."

"And what do you want from us today?" Lily asked.

"Someone to talk to. Someone to help me sort out what is real and what is not. Someone to help me see the best path."

"Do you want to be a part of managing the trust?" Diana asked.

"I don't think so," Hunter replied. "From what Grant says, they've done a good job. I'm sure having the Knight- Compton name involved has helped." The pain in her chest intensified and she rubbed the space just under her breasts to relieve it.

"Do you want to access some of the funds?" Ashley asked, confusion infusing her question.

"That's just it. I don't really know what I want when it comes to the trust."

"What do you know you want?" Lily asked. "You look as if there is a war going on inside you. My guess is that one side of the war doesn't know what to do about the trust, but I think there is more to it than that."

On her feet again, Hunter marched around the room, stepping high. Movement always soothed, always helped her sort things out but it didn't seem to help today which was why she'd sought the counsel of others.

"What are you afraid of, Hunt?"

Gabby's quiet question stopped Hunter in her tracks. She turned to face her circle sister. "I'm afraid of losing everything, of losing Logan, of Grant taking her away from me," she whispered.

"How does the money figure into that?" Diana's gentle voice asked.

"It's tied to that life, my old life, the life that rejected her, the life that never accepted me because I didn't fit into the mold of what a Knight-Compton should be.

"I don't want her to be seduced into that mold because that's what she'd have to do to have a dad, to be a part of Grant's world."

"You think he'll risk the scandal and possible censure and risk to his position in his firm and in society to have her with him?" Diana asked.

Hunter nodded, standing at the window. Tilting her head a certain way, she could see a slice of Mt. Hood between two buildings across the street. It was a view that usually soothed but not today. Her demons had been uncovered, laid out in the open. She could lose her daughter, the most important person in her life to the people who'd turned their backs on her, shunned her, left her to find her way.

Memories of the dark times loomed.

She turned back to the others, tears streaming down her face. "The money I had ran out after a couple of months and I-I-I didn't always find work."

She turned away as shame washed through her. "I-I-I let myself be picked up by guys, went home with them so I'd have something to eat, take a shower, tell myself I was safe."

She turned, her gaze unseeing, her laugh ironic, a sound that left no doubt she was anything but safe.

"I was seven months along and no one seemed to want me. The last guy I'd been with had tried to beat me. I'd managed to get away but other than a frantic grab at my purse, the rest of my belongings were left there. I was desperate and began going from business to business at a small mall in a suburb of Seattle. I know I was bedraggled. It was raining. I was soaked to the skin. I had my jacket wrapped around me trying to hide my pregnancy, hoping someone would hire me.

"The last shop sold second-hand items. I remember thinking it would be a good fit because I was certainly used. The owner, Celeste, a grandmotherly type took one look at me and ordered me to sit." A shaky laugh, Hunter swiped at her tear stained face and sank to the floor. "She fed me, gave me a bed and dresser in a small room. She found clothes for me at Goodwill and other thrift shops. She took me to the welfare office so I had insurance so I could see a doctor and get some pre-natal care before Logan was born."

"She was your guardian angel," Gabby said her voice soft.

Hunter nodded. "She was. I thought that then and I think that now. I got a job teaching dance at a pre-school and I worked in the shop."

"What happened then?" Lily leaned forward, her voice gentle.

"Shortly after Logan turned two, Celeste became sick. It was cancer. I worked the shop for her, took her to appointments and took care of her over the next year. When it was obvious she wasn't going to survive, she told me it was time to sell the shop because she was going to move to Phoenix. There was a Hospice House she'd been accepted into and since her sister lived nearby, she'd have family with her at the end.

"She wanted me to get a new start and suggested Logan and I come to Fremont. I started applying for jobs around here. With the money I had in savings and the five thousand Celeste gave me when the shop sold, Logan and I moved down here. Celeste also gave me her old car saying she had no use for it where she was going. It was an old car but still ran okay. In the end it was a life-saver.

"I found an apartment and daycare for Logan. The job I got was across town. I could have taken the bus but that would have added another three hours to my day care bill.

"We struggled over the next two years until Logan started school and I no longer had to pay for day care. I remember how worried I got towards the end of the month when I skipped meals so Logan always had a full tummy.

"Knowing about the trust, knowing I could have tapped into it without my parents swooping in and taking her away, I swing between being angry and despondent." Hunter was once again on her feet.

"When you look at your life now," Diana said, "the studio, Logan graduating from high school—I'm purposefully leaving Grant out of the picture—do you have regrets about where your life is now? Who you've become? Who Logan was before Grant came into her life?"

Hunter stopped in mid-stride. "No, no I don't. Up until now, while there were hard times, I was proud I'd managed on my own."

"Then, since we cannot undo the past." Lily paused.

"Since I can't undo the past, why am I torturing myself with what's behind me now?" Hunter sighed, returned to her chair, plopped down, and stretched her long legs out in front of her. "Is it really that simple?"

"The concept is simple," Lily said nodding.

"The implementation not so much," Diana said and laughed. "Each of us has stories to tell about how we've let the past color our present and paint our future with fear. So, know you're human."

Hunter looked around at the other women, soft smiles of knowing lit their faces with compassion. "I don't know how things will—."

"None of us do," Gabby interrupted. "The other part of the process is to have faith that our highest good will be served as we move forward even if we can't see it to be so right now.

"From what you've said about your past, when you thought all was lost, a door opened. On the other side was a path forward. Why do you think that won't happen now?"

"I like to know where I'm going," Hunter said.

"Don't we all." Diana laughed. "On the one hand we think we'd be more comfortable if we knew for sure what the future held in store but looking at it another way—from a different perspective, by staying in trust that we are beloved children of The Universe, we are watched over and protected, and when we allow it, guided. Then our lives are full of more joy and happiness because we are not worrying about the future.

"From this different perspective, even when our thoughts turn dark, we know we will come out on the other side with new hope or joy or whatever it is we need. We also know because of The Circle, if we need someone along with us as we travel through the darkness, we will never have to do it alone."

"Does any of this help?" Lily asked, her head tilted to the side.

The darkness of Hunter's fear faded. Through the window a shaft of bright sunlight shot across the room illuminating a path that ended at her feet. When she looked around at Lily, Ashley, Diana and Gabby, appreciative smiles lit their faces.

"The Goddess has spoken." Ashley stood and walked to stand in front of Hunter her arms out in front of her. "The Goddess has spoken and reminded you to seek The Light. Thank you for sharing your darkness with us today."

Hunter stood and accepted the hug Ashley offered. Diana, Lily and Gabby joined in. These women would see her through the dark times ahead. She only had to ask, and if past experiences in watching other members of The Circle struggle were any indication, there would be times she wouldn't even have to ask, they'd show up.

Logan easily kept pace with her dad as they jogged the five mile track around the park's perimeter. She kept pace but was not relaxed. This was her neighborhood park. People she knew ran here. She remembered what Doc had said about the panic being her friend, alerting her to the possibility something was amiss.

A glance at her dad helped. She wasn't out running on her own. That thought terrified her. She stumbled and put her hands out to break her fall.

Her dad quickly reached for her, steadying her as she regained her balance.

"You okay," he said, his gaze checking her out, a worried look in his eyes.

"I'm good," she said and loped ahead.

He matched her pace but said nothing more. She did notice that he glanced down at her every minute or so. "I'm okay, Dad. Just lost my focus and tripped over my own feet."

If she thought that would appease him, she was wrong. He motioned to a series of benches about halfway between beginning and end. It was inevitable he'd want to talk. She was prepared to be peppered with questions over lunch. At least then she could take a bit of sandwich or a sip of her drink before she answered. Here? She'd have to figure something else out.

It occurred to her she could just tell him she didn't want to talk about whatever he asked about. She could say right now that she didn't need a break and would meet him at the end of the path if he did. But she didn't. *Why? This is what having a dad is about. My friends have said that sometimes their dads want to talk to them.*

They sat on the bench furthest from other people who were resting before finishing the course. The silence had an element of distress but she took a deep breath and asked herself what that distress was trying to tell her. The answer was vague, something about 'what if'.

Logan quelled the thought by concentrating on her breathing and the lake across the path. A mother duck and her ducklings swam to the edge under the willow's branches, her quack sounding harried as she hurried her brood along. *I wonder what?* When she looked skyward, she saw a red tailed hawk's lazy circles against the bright blue.

She nudged her dad and pointed upward and then, when she saw his nod, pointed to the mother duck and ducklings.

"She's keeping them safe from the hawk."

"And the hawk is looking for a meal for baby hawks that will go hungry if she fails to find something." Logan watched the hawk glide on the air currents.

"Want to sit and watch to see what happens or do you want to continue?" Grant asked.

Her heart pounding, Logan swiveled to face her dad. Her gaze searched his neutral mien.

"What?" he asked. "Did I say something wrong?" She saw the note of worry in his eyes.

"No, nothing's wrong, just thought you wanted to stop so you could talk," she said standing. She looked back at the hawk that had moved a bit lower. "I think she's spied something else," Logan said just as the hawk swooped to the ground on the other side of the lake.

She looked back at her dad. Grant stood next to her an amused look on his face. "Don't worry," he said. "I can ask you questions over lunch."

Logan sprinted past him, "Not unless you beat me to the end," she called out over her shoulder.

GRANT TOOK A MINUTE TO REGROUP. *How many times had Hunter said the same thing to him as she sprinted off? Too many to count.* He noticed the mother duck and her ducklings head across a corner of the lake staying close to the shore. The hawk was flying low, her talons gripping a hapless duck whose markings showed her to be another mother. *What would happen to the ducklings? Do father ducks take care of their young?*

He loped along the path clearly not in competition with his daughter. *That's different. I always gave chase and usually won.* He increased his pace to an easy trot. The warmth of the sun, the smell of freshly mown grass, the other people on the path, most with earbuds. A couple of them had their music so loud he could hear it as he passed them. *Not good.*

A mile from the end he saw Logan headed his way. He smiled and waved. She stopped and waited. *Maybe that's a better plan, let her come to me.*

"I was getting worried. Mom said you liked to win." Logan said, hands on her hips, a fierce look on her face. "Did you just let me win?"

"Got caught up watching the hawk. She found another duck. Must be a very strong bird to be able to fly up carrying that kind of weight." Saying words without answering the question was something he was very good at.

"I know you didn't answer my question," Logan said as she fell into step beside him.

"So, that means you'll have to ask the question over lunch since I can't," Grant said, easily keeping pace. "That was the bet wasn't it?"

Logan's shoulders relaxed. Her step lengthened. "It was."

They stopped at the sandwich shop closer to Sophia's. Grant noticed her tense when they passed the shop in her neighborhood. He guessed the kids sitting outside were ones she knew.

They both ordered the veggie sub with avocado. A large cup of ice water, napkins and chips in hand, they sat outside in the sun.

He waited, expected Logan to ask why he didn't search for her mom but she ate half her sandwich before uttering a word.

"What would you be doing now if you were home?" Logan asked.

Grant looked at his watch and computed the time difference. "Some days I'd be finishing up and other days I'd have hours of work left to do or some social event to attend."

"So on the days when you'd have work to do?"

"I'd be reading over briefs, documents of some sort, maybe doing a bit of research on the law. I've got an assistant assigned to me who does most of it, but sometimes I want to check something out myself or maybe she's gone for the day." *And sometimes I stay and make work for myself so I don't have to go home, so I have an excuse to be late to wherever I'm expected to be.*

"You're a corporate attorney so what does a corporate attorney do exactly?"

She'd be a good attorney: smart, good verbal skills and dogged persistence. "I look out for the interests of the corporations who are clients of the firm I work for."

"Like?" Logan leaned forward as if interested in what he had to say.

"Let's say the corporation wants to build a new plant. We'd check out the building codes, environmental studies, look for any restrictions that would be counterproductive to our client's plans. If there were restrictions, we'd negotiate with the governing body to change or waive those restrictions for our clients.

"We also do other things," he hurried on seeing the disapproval on her face. "We review product descriptions to make sure they are well-written and protect the company from frivolous law suits."

A thoughtful look on her face, Logan said, "So you protect corporations from the people who purchase a defective product and you help them by getting restrictions waived."

"There's more to it than that. Our review of product descriptions also includes making sure they are accurate so customers know what they are purchasing.

"Ready to go see what Sophia has to satisfy our sweet tooth?" Grant said, changing the subject. He gathered his basket up and bussed their table. Picking up his water, he started for the car. "I'm hoping for a couple chocolate peanut butter cookies." He switched off the alarm and opened Logan's door.

"What about you?" he asked a minute later after sliding into the driver's seat.

"Since I know what's in the cookie jar," Logan said, a secret smile on her face, "I'm not saying because it might, I'm not saying it will, only that it might, give you a hint." She laughed and buckled her seat belt.

After buckling himself in, Grant started the car and drove off. *She'd make a great attorney. I wonder if she's ever considered that.* "I know I said I wouldn't ask questions but take pity on me and let me ask one?" He said in a mock plea.

"One only and I don't have to answer it if I don't want," she bargained.

"Deal."

"What is your question?"

"I know the plan is for you to go to college. What did you want to study?"

"That was pretty good, Dad, only one sentence before the question."

"And the answer is?"

"I'm not sure. I've thought about being a teacher like Sophia or helping people like Lily does. Mom says I'm talented and could work at Twinkle Toes with her and take it over when she retires. I know I'm good with kids.

"The first couple of years have pretty much the same courses. No matter where you go to school you have to take the basics. I figured that would give me time to explore through electives and decide." Logan looked out the passenger window.

Hunter's car was parked at the curb when they pulled in front of Sophia's house. Logan stayed seated and added, "Diana's son, Bill, is studying International Business. He spends summers in Italy with Giovanni, an architect friend of Jackson's as well as in Ireland with Michael and Elizabeth. I love staying with Michael and Elizabeth in Ireland and I think I'd love staying with Giovanni in Italy." She unbuckled her seat belt but didn't move to get out.

"Right now, I can't even think about going to college. I'm not even sure I can finish high school and graduate."

"If you want to graduate with your class, we'll find a way," Grant assured her. "And if you need some time before going on with your education, we'll make that happen also."

Logan leaned over and kissed his cheek, "Thanks for saying that Dad." She scooted out of the car and ran to the house.

Grant sat immobilized, his hands gripping the steering wheel. The touch of her kiss faded, he shook his head to clear his brain. "If she wants to graduate, spend a year in Italy and Ireland, she will." He solemnly promised her.

Out of the car, he started towards the house. Hunter stood on the porch, the welcoming smile on her face faded. "Logan looked happy when she came in, you look grim. What happened?"

"Sorry about that." He stood on the step below her, their eyes at the same level. "Did you know Logan is considering taking a year off and staying in Italy and Ireland before going on to school?"

Hunter shook her head, a thoughtful look on her face. "No, I didn't. She'd be welcomed in either country. And, if she is—," she waved her hands unable to say the words aloud, "it might be for the best." Her hand extended, she waited until he joined her on the top step. "Thank you for telling me. I feel I'm walking on egg shells most of the time, not sure what to say, what topic is safe."

"I told her if she wanted to graduate with her class we'd make sure that happened. And if you agree spending time in Italy and Ireland would be good for her, we'll make that happen also."

He glanced down, saw Hunter swipe a hand across her face. It was a conscious decision not to ask her what was wrong. Because at that moment, he truly didn't want to know.

28 - FRIDAY

Hunter locked the front door behind her last morning student. It was not the best class she'd ever taught and she knew her students had noticed. One even asked if she was okay. The worry on their faces, the concern showing in their eyes, she stopped the class half-way through.

"I'm sorry I'm not at my best today." She let her gaze travel around to each student. "Here's what I'm proposing. We call it a day. You have the option of adding a class somewhere along the way or receiving a refund for this class's fee. The choice is yours."

"What about next week?" one of her regulars asked.

"Right now I'd say things are looking iffy," Hunter responded, a huff of breath accentuated her words.

"We could just agree to cancel it now," another regular student suggested. "That way we can make plans to do something else."

Hunter was grateful not only for the suggestion but also for how it was worded. The underlying message: give you time to get it together. "Thank you, that's an excellent idea." A genuine smile of relief flashed.

"We can call the others," the first woman said "You gave us a list of other class members, remember?"

"Yes, I do remember. While I appreciate the offer, I think I'll make the calls myself."

Everyone changed into street shoes, picked up bags and shuffled towards the front door. She knew they were curious but also knew no one would ask a direct question. Grateful that was the case, she chatted about the parts of the routine they could still do on their own as they filed out.

Alone, Hunter returned to the studio. Grant and Logan wouldn't be by for another hour. She turned the music on 'blast' and started to move. The throbbing beat pulsed through her and she let her body move to the sound. She was free style dancing, letting the beat resounding through her body move her up and down the floor. The repetition of movement soothed, her mind soared into the ether, into the calm, rising above the urgent woman dancing around and around the floor.

Peace enveloped her as she moved surely and swiftly up the floor and back. Sweat beaded on her forehead and then ran in rivulets as she continued circling the dance floor. Abruptly her pattern changed and she zig-zaged across the room. Her leg muscles burned, her lungs gasped for air but still she moved unwilling to give up the blessing of a quiet mind.

The music stopped with a deafening silence. She finished the twirl and halted. Logan and Grant stood next to the stereo system. Logan, an inscrutable look on her face, turned and left the room.

Hunter heard the back door open and close. Panic welled.

"She's waiting in the car," Grant assured her. "She hasn't left. I promise Hunter. Logan is waiting in the car."

Legs shaky from their workout, Hunter strode across the room, her body in its dancer's pose.

Grant handed her a towel when she neared. "We'll wait while you shower or we can get something for lunch and come back."

"I don't think Logan is ready to be here." In the hall, her gaze lingered on the back door. "I don't know if she'll ever come home."

"We'll wait while you shower." Grant's hand rested briefly on

Hunter's shoulder. "Take your time. I don't mind being grilled by her. Well, not too much."

Hunter swiveled, her gaze locked on his. "What do you mean?"

"Logan would make a good attorney. She worries around a topic, nibbling here and there before going for the jugular. Lots of questions about what I did when I wasn't working, what my hobbies were, etc. and then Zing 'have I ever married?'

"Most of the time I see where she's going and have an answer prepared for when she dives in. No mention of people, just activities —," he laughed. "She got me good with that one."

"What did you tell her?" Hunter asked unable to turn away, to head up the stairs until she heard his answer.

"The truth. I told her I'd never married, braced myself for her to ask 'why'. She didn't. Just gave me her 'Logan look', you know the one where she is obviously considering follow-up questions or mulling over your answer looking for holes."

Hunter smiled. "I do recall seeing that look more than once. She was seven or so when I first noticed it."

"Makes me think she knows something I'm fairly certain she doesn't," Grant added.

Hunter laughed and started up the stairs. "I'll be quick to save you from the inquisition," she shot back over her shoulder.

"Think I can't handle a seventeen year old?" Grant hollered up the stairs.

The bathroom door had closed, the water was running when he stepped out the backdoor. Logan was not in the car and his breath whooshed out as fear curled through him.

"I'm here, Dad," Logan said coming around the dumpster next to the building's parking spaces. "I couldn't sit still so I've been jogging up and down the alley waiting for you."

"Your mom's taking a quick shower." He calmed his breathing releasing the fear.

"She'll still take thirty minutes because she has the lotion and other things she does. What do you want to do while we're waiting?"

"Our options are to stand around out here, pace the alleyway, sit in the car, or go in and either hang out in the studio, the front office or go upstairs." He held his breath, watched her consider the options and knew for certain Hunter was right. She would not pick the last one.

"I'm good here or in the car. You choose."

"How about we walk up and down the alleyway a few times and then wait in the car? Sitting for thirty minutes isn't very appealing right now and while the company would be exceptional, the scenery leaves something to be desired." He gestured to the dumpster and the brick and cement walls of the buildings along the alleyway.

Logan was right. Almost exactly thirty minutes later Hunter appeared. No make-up, her damp hair pulled back from her face and secured by a white headband. She wore an ankle length skirt in a swirling pattern of reds, yellows, oranges and pink. Her tank top white, a wrap matching the skirt over her shoulders, sandals on her otherwise bare feet. She took Grant's breath away.

When her mother appeared, Logan scrambled out of the front and climbed into the back. As Hunter got in the car, a soft spicy scent filled the air. "Where to?" Grant asked, turning the engine on.

"Logan? What do you want to do?" Hunter asked, every nerve ending alert to the subtle energy in her daughter's eventual reply.

"I'm not that hungry. Why don't we take a drive?" Logan suggested.

Hunter heard the tentative almost child-like tone underneath the adult sounding words. "Why don't we show Grant the waterfalls? If we get hungry, we can certainly find something to eat at Multnomah Falls."

"I've seen pictures," Grant said. "I think seeing The Falls in person would be cool."

Hunter looked over at him as he backed the car out and drove down the alleyway. "Cool? I don't believe a Parker much less a Parker the Fourth is allowed to say that word."

Grant adopted his most austere East Coast tone. "The weather appears to be cool this evening. Perhaps a wrap is in order?"

"Daaadd," Logan said and laughed. "You sound funny when you talk like that."

"That's actually the way Parkers' and Comptons' talk." Shivers shuddered through Hunter as if she was in a freezer. He was teasing. Or was he? She couldn't get the cold tone, the formal wording out of her mind. Glad Logan took over as tour guide, Hunter looked out at the hills and mountains until the cliffs of the Columbia River Gorge rose around them.

At Multnomah Falls they had a light lunch because no one was very hungry. Hunter remained sitting on a bench looking up at the majestic work of Mother Nature while Grant and Logan hiked to the bridge. Feeling the mist as the wind ducked into the water worn niche before continuing on its way, she knew The Goddess was with her.

Logan and Grant waved from the bridge. She lifted her arm but they continued until she stood and, arm overhead waved back. Sitting again, she waited until they made the trek back to the viewing platform where she waited.

It was four thirty when they reached Sophia's. She was home from school. Her decadent chocolate cake cooled on racks, the mixer beat the frosting to a light confection and custard cream for the filling waited in a bowl on the counter.

"I've fixed something light," Sophia said when everyone was in the house, coats hung on pegs in the entry hall. "I've got a fresh pot of tea, some coffee and apple cranberry juice as well as apricot."

Hunter's phone rang as did Logan's. Both stepped away to answer, leaving Grant to make the food decisions.

Gabby was calling Hunter. "I can come by or not, it's your call."

"Come," Hunter said answering with the first word that came to her.

"See you shortly," Gabby said and disconnected.

Logan had gone down the hall to her room to answer her phone. She came back out, nervous and upset based on the wringing of hands, the nervous chewing of her lower lip, the tears glistening in her eyes. "Doc is on her way. She'll be here in about five minutes. She wouldn't tell me anything. Wouldn't—." Tears won and streamed down her face. "It isn't fair!" she shouted. "I don't want to wait!"

Grant paled and looked from Logan to Hunter.

Hunter strode to where Logan sobbed, her arms hugging herself, anguish etched on her features.

"Not much longer." Hunter tipped Logan's face so she could see in her eyes. She took the handkerchief Grant handed her and wiped the falling tears away. "It's been a really long two days. I'm very proud of how you've handled this time. Remember, no matter the outcome, I love you and am here for you."

A knock on the front door announced Gabby arrival. "Doc's parking her car. She'll be right in," Gabby said upon entering the family room. She continued over to Logan and Hunter, added her arms around them both. "Whatever happens," she started.

Logan pulled away. "I don't care if I'm not alone. I don't care if I'm loved by many. I don't want to be pregnant. I don't want that bastard's child. He hurt me, he—," Logan was shouting when Doc walked in the room.

"Right now, he is winning," Doc said, standing back. "He is pulling you into the dark."

Logan stopped in mid-rant, her stricken gaze locked on Doc.

"Wh-wh-what is it? Wh-wh-what does the test say?"   .

Doc took Logan's hand and guided her to the couch. She tugged and Logan sat beside her. Silence filled the room as Doc patted Logan's hand. "You are pregnant."

Hunter staggered. Grant reached for her and held her tight. Logan sobbed. Gabby, who had sat on Logan's other side, rested her hand on her niece's shoulder.

"You have options," Doc started.

"I want an abortion. I will not have this, this—." Logan voice shook with tears.

"I want you to come to the Clinic tomorrow and we'll discuss your options," Doc said. "This news is hard to even hear. Give yourself twenty-four hours to decide what to do."

"I will *not* have this-this. I will not have that bastard's—. He drugged me, he raped me, he hurt me." Logan's voice pitched higher, hysteria claiming her.

"We'll see you tomorrow, Doc," Gabby said. "We all appreciate your willingness to come and let us know this way. I know this wasn't easy for you." She reached out to her friend and held her hand. "Thank you."

Sophia stood next to Doc S, tears in her eyes, a foil wrapped package in hand. "Did you wear a coat?" she asked, her voice barely heard above Logan distress.

"No," Doc replied. "I didn't."

"I'll walk you to the door unless you want to stay longer," Sophia offered gesturing towards the hall.

"Thank you, Sophia," Doc said. At the front door she turned back, "Don't let her be alone. Even if she wants to shower, make sure the door remains unlocked and someone needs to knock and check on her every few minutes."

"That won't be a problem," Sophia said. On impulse she gave Doc a hug. "Thank you again. We are a strong circle of women. Whatever comes, we will do more than survive. We will hold Logan, Hunter and Grant in the light of love through this time."

29 - HELP ME

Hunter jerked awake, reaching for the ringing phone. A call in the middle of the night was never a good thing. In the dark, caller ID was useless. "Hello?" she managed, struggling to sit up and turn on the light.

"Mom, help me." Logan's voice, filled with terror, chilled.

"What's going on?" Hunter forced calm into her question.

"I hurt so bad."

"Where?" Hunter now on her feet, started for the bedroom door. The cord on the phone stopped her mid-stride.

"My stomach." Logan's fear radiated through the dark like a black light to illuminate Hunter's own stark terror.

"Sophia? Call for Sophia. I'm hanging up. I'm coming." Hunter paused before hanging up. "Logan, I want to hear you call for Sophia."

"There's so much blood.' Logan's hysterical cries galvanized Hunter to change tactics.

"I'm hanging up. I'm calling Sophia. I'll be there as fast as I can."

Her daughter's sobs intensified.

"Logan, listen sweetheart. I'm hanging up and calling you from my cell phone. I can talk to you while I drive over, okay?" She imagined Logan nodding, prayed that was the right image and disconnected.

Grabbing her cell phone, she made a quick stop in the bathroom while flinging on a pair of pants and top. Shoving her feet in a pair of sandals, she grabbed her purse and flew down the stairs.

She called Sophia and let the phone ring and ring. No answer. She called Grant who answered on the second ring.

"I don't know what's going on. I'm on my way over there because Logan is hysterical. She says she's in pain and there's blood. I can't reach Sophia."

"I'll call Sophia and meet you there," Grant stated and hung up.

In the car, she turned the engine on, backed around and then called Logan's phone. Panic churned and vomit rose in her throat. *Answer, answer, answer* she pleaded as she sped through the night.

Hanging up when no one answered and it didn't go to voice mail, she startled when her phone instantly rang.

"Sophia's with her," Grant said. "Where are you?"

"I'm about five minutes away. What's going on?"

"Sophia isn't sure. She's called Doc S and Gabby. Both are on their way. Logan refuses to have 911 called."

"She doesn't have the right to refuse," Hunter started.

"She does have the right, Hunt," Grant said. "She has the legal right to refuse. I'm banking on her changing her mind when you show up."

"I hope and pray you're right." Hunter sent prayer upon prayer to The Goddess. "Please be with her. Please help her. Please, please, please."

She noticed silence from the phone and knew Grant had hung up and was on his way. *Just a little bit further.*

Sophia's house was easy to find in the middle of the night. Lights blazed from every window. Before Hunter reached the front door, Gabby arrived.

Together they entered bedlam. Sophia's usual calm demeanor was frazzled. While she had Logan on the couch, hips and feet in the air, the trail of blood from the hall to the couch was heart-stopping.

Grant came in the door behind them. The scene before him ashened his face. "Good God," he muttered.

"I've put a baggie of ice on her abdomen like Doc S said but it doesn't seem to be helping." Sophia's hands shook as she repositioned it.

"Mom?" Logan called. "Mom help me. I don't want to die. I'm sorry I was bad. Please Mom, don't let me die."

Phone out, Hunter dialed 911 but before she finished the call, Doc S came in.

"Let's see what's going on here." Doc moved quickly to Logan's side. "I'm not going to ask you to leave, but I do want you to move away from the foot of the couch. Perhaps over by the doors to the back?"

"Mom?" Logan's panicky voice called to her. "Mom, don't leave me."

A quick nod from Doc S and Hunter moved so she could lean over the back of the couch, hold Logan's hand, smooth the hair from her sweating face. "I'm right here, sweetheart. I'm not going to leave you. Doc is here and will help you too. Sophia and Gabby and your dad are all here."

"I'm not alone." Logan's gaze locked with Hunter's.

"No you are not alone. What's the rest of it?"

"I am loved by many," Logan whispered. A moan escaped as her knees drew up towards her abdomen. "It hurts so bad," she whimpered.

"I'm right here. Your dad's here. Gabby and Sophia are here. What's more important, Doc is here."

Doc's fingers covered Logan's pulse, her eyes watched Logan's breathing. "Tell me what happened."

"I woke up and felt bad cramps," Logan started. "I got up to get some aspirin from the bathroom and that's when I saw all the blood. Am I going to bleed to death?" Logan choked the question, new tears coursed from the corners of her eyes into her now matted hair.

"No, you're not going to bleed to death," Doc stated. "How long ago was that?"

"I called Mom when I was in the bathroom with the light on and saw how much blood there was. And the pain was so much worse."

Logan's grip on Hunter's hand crushed as another wave of cramps claimed her.

"She called me about thirty minutes or so ago," Hunter offered.

Grant had his phone out. "You called me thirty-seven minutes ago. I called Sophia thirty-five minutes ago. Does that help?"

"Thank you." Doc S turned towards Grant. "All information helps." She turned back to Logan. "Piecing things together it has been less than an hour since you woke in pain and realized you were bleeding. The pain is like cramps but worse than you've ever had. You are still bleeding, still having severe cramps. Without further examination, I suspect you're having a miscarriage."

Doc waited a moment, let her news sink in, locked eyes with Logan before continuing. "I want you to go to the Emergency Department and get checked out. If I'm right, it's important your body is able to slough off all the lining of your uterus.

"Your choice right now is only whether your mom finishes dialing 911 and you go by ambulance or whether you go by car." Doc S kept her gaze on Logan until, after another wave of pain ebbed, she nodded.

"Which is it?"

"All the blood?"

"If you want to go by car," Hunter interjected. "That's what we'll do. We can put plastic and towels down on the seat. It isn't that big a deal."

"Can you and Dad and Gabby and—," she took another deep breath when a cramp seized her.

"We can all come but not in the same car." Hunter glanced at the others and saw heads nod.

"I'll meet you there," Doc S said. "I've privileges at University Hospital so if you go there, I'll be able to see you."

"That's the plan then. Do you have plastic?" Grant asked Sophia who was already moving to the garage.

"Out here," Sophia said, continuing on.

"I'll get a blanket," Gabby said. "Much better than a few towels."

"Get two of them so she can have one under her hips," Doc S said.

As preparations to transport Logan in a car were made, she alerted University Hospital they were coming. "They are expecting you," she announced before she left.

It took almost ten minutes to get everything set. The decision was to use Hunter's car since Grant's was a rental. He would drive so Hunter could hold Logan's hand. Gabby and Sophia would follow in Gabby's car.

Grant carried Logan out and with Hunter at the other side, managed to set her on the backseat. A few minutes more to buckle her in while keeping her sideways and her hips elevated.

Hunter worried about Logan's safety if they were in an accident but said nothing when she caught a glimpse of Grant's grim face in the dim light of a street lamp.

Holding Logan's hand, Hunter kept up a running commentary of where they were. At the corner of Sophia's street, Gabby had flicked her lights and pulled around Grant. Sophia motioned them to follow which was quick thinking on their part because that meant she could concentrate on Logan and not have to give Grant directions.

When they pulled into the Emergency Department parking area, Doc S was waiting with an orderly. Logan was efficiently loaded onto a gurney and with Hunter still holding her hand, rushed into the hospital.

During the quick exchange, Doc S pointed to a space where Grant could park the car and told him how to get inside.

Funny how in a crisis bits and pieces of non-related images come floating through. Hunter was grateful the women in her morning session had suggested she cancel her classes for the week. She was grateful Logan was at Sophia's and had someone with her. She was thankful Gabby was able to come. But most of all she was blessed that Grant was in their lives.

Less than a month had passed since she turned and saw the ghost of her past.

Less than a month had passed since the darkness of her past was exposed to the light.

Less than a month had passed since her and Logan's lives were turned upside down.

Knowing The Circle was there and would support her and love Logan no matter what happened was a gift beyond measure.

"Mom?" Logan's sleepy voice interrupted her musing.

"I'm here." She leaned over and placed a soft kiss on Logan's forehead.

"Is Dad still here?"

Hunter felt his strength before his hand rested on her shoulder. "I'm still here." His voice had a husky note and she heard a slight quaver in the last word.

Doc had explained that Logan was miscarrying and the doctors wanted to keep her overnight for observation, to check and make sure her body had completed the job. They'd given Logan something that made her a little drowsy, dulled the pain enough her body no longer jerked into a jackknife position.

"Why did this happening?" Hunter asked Doc S the question on everyone's mind.

"We never know exactly, especially this early." Doc looked around, her gaze momentarily resting on each of them. "If you are wondering if she'll have problems getting pregnant and carrying a child to term, I doubt it. Sometimes our bodies know or maybe our guardian angels know or maybe, if you believe like Gabby does, the Goddess knows this is not the time. Some people believe a child chooses his or her parents. If that is what you believe, then you can say the child changed his or her mind.

"Do not think," she cautioned "this means it is over. Logan is a sensitive and thoughtful young woman. I've no doubt she'll have very mixed feelings about this event in her life. This is not the end of it."

Grant stood beside her, his arm around her shoulders. Gabby and Sophia had been on her other side. The terror she'd felt when Logan called now gone. The pain she'd felt when Doc had announced the test results showing Logan to be pregnant also gone.

What took their place was a bone deep numbness. The thought crossed her mind that if Logan's pregnancy had gone to term, she'd be a grandmother and Grant a grandfather. It was painful to acknowledge he'd have been a good father and he'd have been a good grandfather. A spike of guilt stabbed through her. She had kept Grant from Logan and she had prayed for a miscarriage. *Does it ever matter if our intentions are good?* She battled the 'if only' and 'what if' thoughts, beating them into submission for now.

The ED doctor agreed with Doc S's diagnosis. Logan was prepped and wheeled off to surgery where they checked to make sure her uterus was clean.

When Logan was back in her room, Hunter and Grant curled up in chairs. Their arms through the railings, they held their daughter's hands. Even though Hunter hated hospitals, nothing could drag her away from Logan's side.

Soon after, Sophia and Gabby left. Gabby was taking Sophia home and, Hunter knew, helping Sophia clean everything up. It had been a hellish night for them also.

As dawn peeked through the curtained window, she glanced across the bed at Grant. His weary smile and thumbs up eased her worries.

Logan stirred and her eyes fluttered open. "Am I going to be okay?"

"You are going to be more than okay," Grant answered.

Hunter stood and stretched before leaning down and kissing Logan's cheek. "Your body will heal first. In time all of you will be healed and you'll see life as good."

Logan smiled at her mom and held her dad's hand. "I am loved by many but especially I'm loved by you," she looked at Hunter, "and you," she said looking at Grant.

A wave of quiet overlay the exhaustion. The light of love was stronger than anything else. Logan was loved by many as was she. Was Grant? Hunter lifted her face until her eyes met his. *No, I don't think he is or ever was loved by many. Maybe that is a gift he'll receive while he's here.*

A nurse bustled in, pulling the curtain for privacy, ordering them out while she checked Logan's vital signs.

In the hall, they stretched and paced until they could return to the room. Shortly afterward the doctor made rounds. She checked the chart, asked some questions, visually checked for bleeding, clots and the like. "Want to go home?" she asked Logan.

"Can I?" Logan asked eagerly trying to sit up.

"You can. I'll write the orders. Read them carefully even though the nurse will go over them with you. You need to take it easy for a couple of days. You've had some excessive bleeding. Not enough to require a transfusion but enough that your body needs a few days to regroup."

And that was it.

Two hours later, the three of them left the hospital.

"Where to?" Grant asked Logan's reflection in the rearview mirror.

"Home," Logan said. "I want to go home." Her voice was firm but when Hunter turned to her, she saw doubt on her face.

"If you mean back home above the studio, I'd like nothing better." She reached back and patted Logan's knee.

"Are you sure?" Logan asked.

"I've never been surer of anything." Hunter knew Sophia was home and figured she'd have Grant stay with Logan and she'd go over to pick up whatever was needed. At that moment all she could think of was the school work.

"I think I'm doing pretty good learning my way around, but I could use some help getting back to your part of town," Grant said to no one in particular.

Hunter checked where they were but before she could respond, Logan directed him into the right lane to turn onto the freeway ramp and reminded him of their exit.

Grant and Logan joked back and forth as he deftly moved the car through traffic. He pulled in behind the studio. Hunter got out, turned off the alarm and unlocked the door as Grant helped Logan out of the back seat.

They were home.

The sound of those three words was music. She wanted to dance a jig or at least twirl a few times. Instead she held the door open and waited until Grant and Logan passed through. Closing the door behind them, she locked it and followed them upstairs.

Logan didn't want to be in her room and opted for the couch. Grant offered to make a grocery store run when Logan asked for apricot juice and peach yoghurt.

"This is what's available right now." Hunter listed what was on hand. "I'll go to the store in a bit when I go over to Sophia's to pick up your school books and anything else there you want here."

"As if I want my school books." Logan joked. She sobered and added, "Will you be angry with me if I'm not ready to go back to school yet?"

"No," Hunter replied. "However, I vote to postpone serious conversations until later today or even tomorrow. It's been a long night and I think we all could use some rest.

Her phone rang. She listened, nodded before saying, "That sounds good." Hanging up she said, "That was Sophia. She still has the dinner from last night including the decadent chocolate cake. We're invited to come over.

"Is that okay with you?" she asked Logan.

Logan pleated the blanket across her legs. "I made such a mess," Her cheeks pinked with embarrassment.

"My guess is there isn't a sign of it. If I know Gabby and Sophia, the floors were mopped and a couple of loads of laundry done before going to bed."

"Do you really think—?"

"I know you are loved by many, including Sophia and Gabby," Hunter interrupted. "You know Sophia would not have called and invited us to dinner if she was upset or mad or angry or any of the things you are worried about.

"And this solves the issue of getting your car, Logan's things, etc. We can make a store run now and rest up before heading over there. Soph mentioned an early dinner and suggested we eat at five."

Hunter waited for nods of agreement or understanding before heading to the kitchen. A pad of paper and pen in hand she wrote: peach yoghurt, apricot juice. "What else do we need at the store?"

The combination of Logan's familiar voice along with Grant's soothed and the list was quickly made. "I'm just going to go get this now," she said reaching for her purse.

"Let me do this." Grant took the list from her hand. "I'd like to stop by the motel and take a shower. I also need to check emails and all. I'll stop and get groceries on my way back if you both can wait an hour or so for these things," he added and waved the list.

And so it was almost like being a family. She snuggled on the couch with Logan, grateful for this time with her little girl. *My not so little girl.* She tightened her hold a fraction. Logan relaxed against her, her head resting on Hunter's shoulder. Tilting her head, she placed a soft kiss on Logan's temple. "I love you," she whispered relishing the closeness, rejoicing that her daughter was home. *Home for now. There isn't that much time before she's off to college.* Hunter staved off the idea of Logan across the country attending Smith College. Knowing Grant would be close enough to see her often did not soothe but it didn't rankle as it once would have. *We've come a long way. So much more to sort out, to work out but maybe with time... .*

30 - BECOMING A DAD

*B*ooting up his computer, Grant checked his emails. The president of the firm had forwarded a couple of messages from important clients and added his own dire warnings about the drop in billable hours, meager (if any) bonus checks unless Grant returned immediately. His assistant had sent one from her home computer urging him to return post haste; things at work were not going well for him.

It was useless to try and explain to anyone in the firm or his family why he was in Fremont, Oregon instead of home doing what he was supposed to be doing, what was expected of a Parker IV. Three emails from his mother expressed her disapproval and upset that he wasn't there for this or that social event. One terse email from his father: "To: Grant Hayward Parker IV From: Grant Hayward Parker III Re: Family Obligations. The message? "Remember who you are!"

Of course he remembered who he was and what was expected of him by both his family and the firm. He'd been here in Fremont for four weeks. It had been an intense and tragic time and he couldn't remember feeling more angry or helpless in his entire life. But he also couldn't remember feeling more accepted for who he was underneath the Parker name. How freeing.

He hadn't shaved or even thought about it until he got back to his room and took a shower. Looking at the scruffy face in the mirror, he'd actually laughed and almost didn't shave, almost decided to grow a beard. Why did he shave? Habit. Also if he grew a beard he wanted it to be because *he* wanted to grow one and not in some sort of delayed adolescent rebellion.

Taking some time, he outlined a response to his assistant, the firm's president, his mother and father. Six drafts later, he called it quits. *Need to sort things out better before I send anything back.*

At the grocery store, he found everything on Hunter's list. Out of habit he added a couple of bottles of wine before remembering Hunter didn't drink it. Putting them back on the shelf, he looked in the candy aisle for chocolate—no Godiva or hand-dipped Belgian chocolates. He settled for a local dairy's ice cream. The Burgundy Cherry flavor added to the basket, he paid for the food and headed back to the studio.

At the top of the stairs, Logan's crying and Hunter's soothing voice stopped him in his tracks. Not sure what to do next, he paused. Before he sorted things out, Hunter appeared, took the sack of groceries from him and started back into the living area.

She gave him a helpless look and shrugged—as if he was supposed to be able to interpret that.

"Hey, Logan, what's going on?" He thought that a fairly neutral question.

"I can't stay," Logan sobbed, her words a bit muffled because her forehead rested on her knees.

"Tell me about it." Grant perched on the arm at the end of the couch.

"I'm not her anymore," Logan choked out.

She looked up, a picture of misery with a tear-stained face, runny nose, blotchy skin, disheveled hair and wrinkled top.

"Help me understand what 'I'm not her anymore' means." Grant leaned forward a bit as if being closer would help him figure out what was happening.

Logan shook her head and sobbed.

Hunter said, "The best I can figure it out, her room belongs to who she once was and is not her room anymore."

"Is your mom right?" Grant asked.

Logan raised her head. "I know it sounds stupid."

"I don't think it sounds stupid. I think it sounds like a problem that easily can be solved." His chest swelled with a pride he'd never felt at the look of hope on Logan's face.

"We'll just change the room around and then it will be your room, okay?"

"What do you mean?" Logan asked, the tears abating, curiosity blooming.

"Pictures, posters can come down now. I can move furniture around in a new arrangement. And, if you want, we can get new bedding and curtains so it's a whole new look. If you want, we can get paint and change the color."

It was hard to stop talking, to stay seated and wait for her to say something but he did. He kept his gaze on his daughter, making sure he blinked so he didn't appear to be staring.

Logan looked over his right shoulder and it was obvious she was checking with her mom. When she looked back at him, she smiled. "What will you do with everything?"

"That depends," Grant said. "There may be a few things you do want to keep, some things you may want packed up and stored in case you want them at another time in your life. Of course there will be those items you want gone. Those items can be tossed or donated. Your choice."

It struck him then that he had no idea what Logan's favorite color was, if she liked more modern or traditional styles. There was so much to know about the young woman sitting at the other end of the couch.

"My favorite color is green. I like green and white together with maybe a pop of blue. Curves—if there is a pattern it must have curves."

Logan turned to Hunter, "Mom, can we cleanse my altar enough or do you think I should create a new one?"

"We can cleanse everything either by smudging it, washing it in salt water, or you can drum or ring bells to move energy."

Grant stood and started down the hall. "I'm going out to get boxes and green. When I return, I'll bring things out of the room and you can decide if you want to do the smudge and stuff, pack it, or if you want me to take it away."

He stopped in front of Logan's room and poked his head inside. "I think this is doable within a couple of hours. Worst thing Logan is you'll sleep on the couch because it isn't quite finished"

A spring in his step, a tuneless whistle on his lips, Grant headed down the stairs. Once in the car, he glanced in the rear view mirror as he started to back out. The face looking back at him had a silly grin on it. "I think I'm getting the hang of this fa—dad-thing."

THE SHOPPING TRIP took longer than he thought because he had a bad case of decidiphobia when it came to picking the bedding: too many color and pattern choices for a new-to-the-position dad. A sales clerk helped but in the end he asked a couple of teenage girls in the adjacent aisle what they thought.

And that's what he bought—two sets of bedding just in case the pale green with dark green accents was wrong. The other set was a dark green bottom sheet with a printed top sheet in varied greens with a dark blue vine or something along with bright red and pink flowers. When he'd seen it, it reminded him of Logan. He added six pillows of varying shapes, sizes and colors, a navy rug and a hummingbird shaped desk lamp.

It took two trips to get everything upstairs. That prideful grin was back as Logan eagerly opened every sack and declared the contents perfect. Hunter suggested she pick one set of bedding and two pillows. Logan looked over at him, he looked at Hunter who rolled her eyes and turned away.

Logan beamed.

All he managed before they left for Sophia's was to get the pictures and posters off the walls. Left to do was moving the items off her desk and nightstand into the living area.

"Let's see how everyone is feeling after dinner," Hunter said when Logan pleaded for him to come back and finish up tonight.

Without any directions, he drove directly to Sophia's. No wrong turns, no debates at a street corner which way to turn. A bit surprised at how at home he felt in this new place, he was pleased Hunter did not seem watchful, waiting for him to make a mistake. When he glanced in her direction, she was either talking to Logan in the back-seat or she smiled at him.

Over dinner, he reminded himself he would have to return to Providence and that trip would be sooner rather than later. The thought did pop into his mind that maybe he didn't have to return, maybe he could remain here, spend time with his daughter, see what developed between Hunter and him. *Wishful thinking.* Even though he stuffed the fantasy of living in Fremont in the back of his mind, he saw more clearly why he never married, what kept him from committing to anyone else.

One of his strengths as an attorney was his skill as an observer. He'd been doing a lot of that. Each of the men he'd met was deeply in love and fully committed to his wife. Yes, there were things they'd like to be different.

But they each respected their wife, respected her spiritual path, respected her independence and need to be her own person, respected her relationships within their women's circle. The fantasy of creating a family with Hunter and Logan reappeared.

Would it be worth it? Would it be worth it to learn about and respect Hunter's spiritual path, to respect and support her independence and her relationships within The Circle?

If I had the unconditional love they have, it would be. His chest tightened and his throat closed. He cleared his throat and took a deep breath. *Have I ever been unconditionally loved?* An image of himself as a young man laughing, running along the shore, racing in and out of the ebbing and flowing water, a young girl with braided chestnut hair bleached in places by the summer sun, keeping pace. *Perhaps, perhaps I have.*

Sophia's Garden
Sunday
May 01, 2005

ichael and Elizabeth's plans to join them in Fremont for Beltane had changed at the last minute. Her doctor said travel by air at this stage of her pregnancy was not advised. E's feet were swelling and it was important she spend several hours each day with them elevated above her heart—impossible on transatlantic and transcontinental flights.

Because of the Kentucky Derby in six days, Michael was in the States. He had three entries all together. His friend, Paddy was here with one horse. Their plan was for Paddy to remain in the States for the duration of the Triple Crown races. Once Michael saw his horses settled for the second leg, he'd turn things over to Paddy and return to Ireland. Racing was not more important than the birth of their first child.

Once again, the men and children were present. Jackson's Italian architect friend, Giovanni Migliori was in town. Not a stranger to their ceremonies, he settled in with the men and children.

A sadness rested on Hunter's heart. It was bittersweet to see Madison Michelle and to think of Elizabeth and Michael's impending parenthood. Logan's spontaneous miscarriage was a blessing and yet —and yet.

Last night when they'd had dinner with Sophia, Logan had been quiet and subdued. Surreptitiously she'd inspected the floors for blood. Hunter had been right and all had been scrubbed clean. Sophia had even put clean sheets on the bed and with Logan's belongings packed and waiting for them, it was almost as if her daughter had never been there.

Not yet ready to sleep in her old room, Logan stayed on the couch another night. Grant had helped carry things in but had said his good nights soon after. With Logan dozing, Hunter had slipped into bed. Even though exhausted, sleep had not come easily.

Every decision has an element of risk and pain. While she'd still do what she did, remembering the many struggles, the many sleepless nights, doubts assailed. *Did I really do the right thing all those years ago? Should—.*

"Can I help?" Gabby slipped her arm around Hunter's waist.

"Do I look that grim?" Hunter did a swift self-check and knew she not only looked grim but tearful.

"Pretty much." Gabby pulled her closer in a side hug. "Always remember whatever happens you're not alone."

Hunter's laugh was harsh. The others turned her way. "We say that to everyone."

"Because it's the truth. No one in The Circle has faced adversity alone. That will not change with you."

Drawing her attention back to the circle, her feet at shoulder width she raised her arms to the sky.

"May the Goddess in all her wisdom guide us through this time of plenty," Hunter said. *Where did that come from?* She shook her head, quelled the urge to speak again because Ashley's soft southern drawl sounded.

"May the Goddess continue to bless us with an abundance of love and gratitude."

"May we find comfort in the changing of the seasons," Sophia said.

The friend she's been helping must not be doing well. Hunter's thoughts drifted and she missed Diana's prayer.

She centered her attention back to The Circle in time to hear Lily say, "May this time of growth and renewal, of life and love bring us our heart's desire."

"May we know with a certainty that whatever comes our way, we will never have to face it alone," Gabby said ending this part of their Ceremony.

They dropped their arms and moved to a space beyond the living circle. Once settled on the ground, the talking stone in the center, they shared what they were grateful for and what they wanted to manifest during the next turn of the wheel.

"When we celebrate Beltane, I'm reminded of new beginnings, new starts, new growth. Soph's garden is budding and blooming. I need a mini-vacation to rejuvenate," Gabby started. "Work has been hectic and I'd love a whole week to myself. A friend of mine has a cabin and that's where I'd go. No phone, no television. There is running water and electricity because of a pump on the well and a generator. And with the propane stove to cook on, it isn't too rough. I don't think I can do this anytime soon, but I'd be ever so grateful if I can get away before Summer Solstice."

"I'm reminded at this time of the year how very blessed I am. Charlie is so close I can drive down to Eugene and have lunch with him. He and Jackson have created a loving relationship. While he still talks to his dad, I think he really values Jackson's advice. Eleanor is back east with her daughters. Jackson and I do enjoy having the house to ourselves but I miss her." Lily's gaze dropped to the stone, a soft blush on her cheeks.

"I've got my surgery scheduled for the Monday after school is out," Ashley said. "Y'all have been so important in my life. I can't imagine Daniel and me figuring things out without you. My kids?" She smiled and tapped her knee, "need to remind myself that they're 'our kids' these days. Y'all can see and hear how happy they are, even Anthony has times when the joy just flows. I'm enjoying each moment of every day of my new life."

"Matthew and I are now celebrating seconds." Diana picked up the stone. "Last year was his first Beltane. This is the second May we've lived together. I'm staying focused on the positive times we shared a year ago because as you all know, some of it was horrific. Between now and Solstice? Fremont Community College has renewed my contract. I'd been worried they might not because I didn't want to teach this summer. Worried about that for nothing! Something to work on—worrying about things that have yet to and might never happen."

"The friend I've been helping the past couple of years is not doing so well. I see him and know how blessed I am to be able to breathe, breathe deep, breathe often—take air deep into my body and exhale. I've become quite fond of him," Sophia said tears welling. "Between now and Solstice, I will make sure I see him more often, send him notes, make sure he has healthy food to eat. He still smokes, even with the diagnosis of end stage emphysema, and refuses to consider changing that. But, at heart he's a good man and I want his passing to be as peaceful as possible."

"Between now and Solstice, my prayer is that my path becomes clearer. When Grant informed me I have resources and unless I want to work, I don't have to, I decided to reduced my class load and teach only on Monday, Wednesday and Friday. I know I can't sit still but do I want to teach six days a week? Do I want to teach morning, afternoon and evening classes?

"My life right now seems to have so many possibilities it feels confusing and chaotic and overwhelming at times. My priority remains to support Logan as she finishes high school and makes decisions on her future. I know my role as her mom is changing. I pray I will handle these changes with grace."

Hunter placed the stone back in the center. Diana's clear voice started a song. "Beauty is …". They stood, and still singing strolled back to the house.

Before they reached the patio, Ashley's Rose charged out,

dancing among them, adding her voice to the song. Hunter looked up, saw Logan with Grant beside her, his hand on her shoulder. They watched her as she separated from the others and approached them.

"How often do you do this?" Grant asked. "What if it'd been raining? Do you always do that," he gestured towards the yard, "on the Sabats?"

Hunter smiled. Grant had obviously been doing some research or listening closely to use the word "Sabats". "We meet every couple of weeks in addition to the Sabats. If it'd been raining, we'd have either stayed out for the prayers around the living altar and come under the patio covering for the rest or just stayed inside."

"In Oregon, Dad," Logan added, "rain can be such a light mist you hardly even notice it or it can be so hard you'd be soaked in less than a minute."

"Do I need to get an umbrella?" Grant asked.

Logan and Hunter laughed. "Oh Dad, an umbrella tells everyone you're a newbie. Real Oregonians don't use umbrellas—well, not very often. I don't remember using my umbrella—well, I did use it when I was all dressed up for the Winter Recital. Wearing a hooded jacket just wouldn't have worked."

"No umbrella then." Grant, his arm still around Logan, reached out with his other to Hunter. "I think we men have done a fantastic job on the food." He dropped his arms to his side before gesturing them through the door. "Shall we?"

Hunter watched Grant's reaction as a spirit plate was created, prayers of thanks were said, and Rose took the plate outside. He didn't seem to bat an eye or raise a censorious much less questioning brow.

The day wound down. Everyone drifted off. Tomorrow was a school day so Ashley, Daniel and the kids were the first to leave. An early morning meeting at work had Gabby leaving with them. Fussy baby had Diana and Matthew whisking away with M2. Lily, Jackson and Giovanni stayed longer. Jackson, Grant and Giovanni were deep in conversation. She, Lily and Sophia decided to have another cup of tea.

Inviting Logan to join them, Hunter was glad when her daughter curled up in a chair, a mug of tea and a couple of cookies in hand.

Hunter noticed Giovanni had watched Gabriella but didn't engage in his usual banter. *I wonder what's going on there?*

"Soph? If you're going to do some baking tonight, I can help," Logan said.

"You've already been a big help, my dear," Sophia said. "My freezer is full, so no baking tonight."

They left when Lily, Jackson and Giovanni did. Midway down the driveway, Logan turned back and hugged Sophia. Hunter watched her daughter say something, kiss Sophia's cheek, watched as Sophia hugged Logan long and hard.

Grant's arm rested on her shoulder. "You're staring."

"I'm trying not to be jealous." Hunter slapped her hand over her mouth. "I-I-I—."

"Glad I'm not the only one with those feelings." He turned her towards him. "Look me in the eyes." He tipped her chin up with the tip of his finger. "What color are they?"

"Blue-grey or maybe grey-blue, why?"

"Thought they might be tinged with green if they weren't a bright luminescent green. Glad to know they haven't changed and I don't have to wear dark glasses all the time."

Hunter laughed. "If the color changes, I'll let you know."

Grant dropped them off, waited until they were inside and the door locked. She'd agreed to flash the light so he'd know all was okay. Upstairs she hugged Logan and watched her settled in on the couch. While Grant had purchased bedding, there still needed to be some cleaning out and rearranging before Logan was comfortable in her old room.

Before sliding between the sheets, Hunter stood in front of her altar. The array of stones and figurines comforted. Arms bent at the elbows, palms facing the sky, she closed her eyes. "Thank you Goddess and God for being with me these past weeks, for staying with me even when I wasn't paying attention. Thank you for taking care of Logan, for being with her when she was lost and showing her the way home. Thank you for bringing Grant into our lives."

Before getting into bed, Hunter checked on Logan one more time. Tiptoeing across to the couch, she bent and placed a soft kiss on Logan's cheek as she slept. "I love you," Hunter whispered.

Settling down in her own bed, Hunter faced thoughts that had surged through her mind the last couple of days. Something had changed between Grant and her. Something she didn't want to examine much less explore. Something she couldn't ignore.

Grant made the call to Ms. Lawford, the attorney Matthew and Daniel recommended as 'the' person to talk to about custody. He'd made it clear he didn't want custody but he did want to be known legally as Logan's father. The Oregon Revised Statutes were clear about the procedure but he decided to err on the side of caution. Talking to an attorney and confirming what the process was made sense, especially when Matthew, Daniel and even Jackson described her as *the only* attorney they'd talk to about something this important.

Ms. Lawford was a direct, no nonsense person whose demeanor softened slightly when he mentioned he'd been referred by Daniel O'Donnell and Matthew Houston. Now he sat in an almost shabby anteroom waiting. There was a handwritten sign up saying to have a seat, she'd be back shortly. He'd already been waiting fifteen minutes because he'd arrived early.

The door opened and a middle-aged woman with a briefcase in one hand marched in. "Mr. Parker." She continued across to the door to her office. Unlocking it, Ms. Lawford waved him to follow her in.

Organized chaos greeted him as he stepped into her office. As he passed through the doorway he noted it was a reinforced frame and a metal door with a deadlock as well as a lock on the knob. He was sure there was a security system somewhere because she'd waved the hand with the key as she came in the outer office door. *Interesting.*

"How can I help you?" Ms. Lawford inquired putting her briefcase down beside her desk, gesturing him to a seating area by the windows.

"I'd like to check out the process in Oregon for being recognized as the legal father of a minor child. Actually she'll have turned eighteen by the end of the month."

"I understand you are an attorney," Ms. Lawford countered.

"I'm a corporate attorney licensed to practice in several states along the Atlantic seaboard but I'm not licensed to practice in Oregon."

"Considering it?" Ms. Lawford asked. "Coffee? Water?"

"Considering what?" Grant replied. "No, thank you, I'm fine."

"Considering opening a practice in Oregon?" Ms. Lawford fixed a cup of coffee and sat opposite Grant who'd chosen a chair instead of the couch.

"Why the interest?" Grant asked, deciding this interview was drifting into an interrogation.

"If Mr. O'Donnell, Mr. Houston and Mr. Montgomery referred you, you must be asking about Logan Compton because Hunter is the only woman in the circle who has a child who fits 'still a minor but will turn eighteen by the end of the month'." She smiled and sat back waiting for his response.

Grant recognized a superior strategist when he met one and Ms. Lawford was that: smart, observant and disarming. He couldn't imagine one of the men calling and giving her a heads up. He hadn't mentioned any names other than that the referral had come from them. This meant she had more than a passing acquaintance with the other women.

"They told me you are the best." Grant leaned back against the chair's cushions, crossed his feet at the ankles. His steady gaze didn't waver as he looked for reactions to his statement.

When she laughed, he was surprised. "I will tell you a secret," she announced leaning towards him in a conspiratorial manner. "Those seven are the female version of the three musketeers—all for one and one for all."

It was his turn to laugh, or at least chuckle. "Even someone less observant than either you or I could see that. If it isn't too much trouble, I'll take that offer of water."

Ms. Lawford stood and marched to the small refrigerator near her desk. *Hunter glides. Ms. Lawford marches. I'll have to pay attention to how Logan moves. A dad would know that.*

"Have I passed scrutiny or are there other hurdles for me to jump?" he asked after taking a swallow and recapping the bottle.

Eyes lit with humor, Ms. Lawford laughed. "You passed when I made the appointment with you. If you think any one of those men would have referred you to me if you hadn't been thoroughly vetted, you are mistaken."

"Perhaps they find me lacking and referred me to you to warn me off or discourage me or—," he waved his hand in the air, "whatever else you could think of to do."

"Not a chance. They are protective of their wives and children but that net of protection includes all the women and children and, I would guess, now includes you. I'm not sure why but I dare say I'm correct.

"Now, I'm assuming you want your name on the birth certificate?"

"I'm willing to adopt her if necessary but it looks like there is a process for being recognized as the legal as well as the biological father without going through a home study and the adoption process."

"Correct. A notarized statement from Hunter acknowledging you as the father as well as your notarized statement claiming to be the father is enough. If you want it more official, you can ask for a short hearing before a judge or in most cases, whichever judge is handling domestic court issues on the day your paperwork is filed will just sign the order."

"It seems like it should be more complicated." Grant looked past Ms. Lawford to the diplomas on the wall behind her desk. The urge to rub the ache in his chest was strong but he was not going to let her know how he felt. The question he'd asked himself about being unconditionally loved popped unbidden. *Could Logan love him unconditionally? What would it be like to follow a dream?*

"If you want it to be more complicated, I'm sure I can come up with something to satisfy you." Ms. Lawford grinned. "Usually people want things simplified."

"I'll talk to Hunter and Logan. If they are agreeable, will you draw up the statements for us all to sign?" Grant's gaze rested on Ms. Lawford as she took a moment to consider.

"You could do that yourself," she remarked.

"Maybe, but I think it better for us as a family to have the legal aspects of things handled by someone else." He smiled his most charming smile. "You've come highly recommended."

Ms. Lawford laughed. "I'd be delighted to draw up the papers and even file them for you if you want. And if the three of you decide you want a short hearing in front of a judge, I can arrange that also."

"Thank you." Grant stood. "We'll see what Hunter and Logan want in terms of the hearing. I'll let you know when I've talked to them and we're ready to move forward."

"And do consider setting up a practice in Fremont. We can always use a good lawyer." Ms. Lawford accompanied him to the door.

"My practice in Rhode Island is pressure-filled. And even though this is counted as a vacation, I'm still connected to the firm through emails and phone calls. I'm not sure if I moved to Fremont, I'd practice law. If I did move here, I'd want something different, less intense." Grant faced Ms. Lawford and extended his hand. "I appreciate your time and expertise in this matter. We'll add your fee for today onto the rest of the billing?"

"Initial consultation is free," Ms. Lawford said.

"This was more than a consultation. You gave me answers and a direction on what I asked about. Even more you asked me questions I will take the time to think about and answer."

"I can add thirty minutes to my billing, if that is what you'd prefer." Ms. Lawford shook Grant's hand. "And I'll repeat myself, we can always use a good lawyer in Fremont."

∼

GRANT CALLED AHEAD and checked with Hunter about getting takeout for dinner. She said she had food and it wasn't necessary. He agreed and repeated it was something he'd like to do. The third time they went on this communication merry-go-round she said she and Logan loved Mexican and gave him the name of their favorite take-out place.

In hindsight he could see the fallacy of his thinking, the error in his approach. He'd vacillated between asking Hunter first and getting her agreement and then together they could ask Logan versus he'd approach them both at the same time.

In the end, he decided to talk to Hunter alone and that delayed things for two days because he left before Logan went to bed and he'd been unable to catch her alone for any length of time. Their quarters above the studio were sufficient for the two of them but sound carried so the one time he found Hunter alone in the studio, he hesitated to say much. She was drumming and dancing and he'd knew that was the main way she managed stress and worked out problems.

Talking to her on the phone Friday morning, he asked if he could schedule a time for them to talk. Of course she wanted to know why and his statement that it wasn't something he wanted to talk about over the phone didn't go over well.

Logan had a follow-up appointment with Doc S that evening. Hunter arranged for Gabby to be there also and if everything was going well, she'd take Logan out for an ice cream treat.

Thankful that Doc S gave them a thumbs up when she came out and Logan had a smile on her face, Plan A was in place. Logan and Gabby left for ice cream. They were getting a quart of vanilla and one of peach. Hunter had bananas and chocolate sauce and maybe some caramel—they'd bring the ice cream home and fix sundaes.

The drive back to Hunter and Logan's place was quiet and a bit strained. Not at all an auspicious beginning but he was optimistic. Logan wanted a dad and he wanted to be it. Hunter had been accepting and this past week she'd stepped aside and let him handle things like changing Logan's room around so she was comfortable

188

back home. That was a good sign he thought pulling into the parking spot.

Upstairs he checked his watch and paced while Hunter listened to three messages on her answering machine, made notes, got the chocolate sauce out to warm, looked for caramel sauce. *Is she avoiding me? One way to find out.*

Grant stepped in front of her as she crossed the small kitchen and rested his hands on her shoulders. "Please, come sit with me for a few minutes." His voice calm, he looked her in the eyes. "I'm not going to bite and I don't think what I want to talk about will be upsetting."

Hunter pivoted and with her long legs crossed to the couch in mere moments. He followed, deciding to sit next to her.

"I made an appointment to see Ms. Lawford earlier this week," he began. The look of panic on Hunter's face was his first indication all was not going as he'd hoped it would.

She was on her feet, pacing, hands waving in the air although no words were said.

"I wanted to see what the procedure was for me to be recognized as Logan's legal father. Nothing more than that, I promise," he said debating whether to stand or remain seated.

Hunter whirled, stared daggers at him, hands fisted on her hips, "And why would I agree to that?" she hurled the words at his head.

"Because you love your daughter and you know she's always wanted a father," he said only then realizing they were not alone.

"I don't want a father," Logan shouted. "I never wanted a father."

Gabby stood between Logan and the hall. "Put the ice cream in the freezer first and then we can talk," she said in a calm voice. "We've interrupted your parents so after the ice cream is put away, we need to find out if they need more time by themselves to talk."

Logan stalked to the freezer and shoved the quarts inside. She stalked to where Grant sat, "You do not bully my mom! I don't want a father. Fathers are—." Her face crumpled and tears flowed. "Father's don't care about you. They don't try to find you."

Grant stood. He reached out towards Logan and then pulled his hands back. His chest tightened, his throat closed and moisture gathered in his eyes. *How did I screw this up so badly?*

"I didn't mean to create problems," he began, his voice a bit shaky from the tightness in his chest. "I guess I want to be a part of your lives more than you want me."

He turned away, reached for the jacket he'd tossed on the back of the chair when he came in. "I'll go now. You have my phone number. If you want or need something, just let me know." He stumbled ever so slightly, reached out to steady himself and found Gabby's hand in his.

He glanced her way not trusting the moisture in his eyes to not turn into tears. The movement was minimal but he was certain she shook her head.

"Listen up," Gabby said. "You," she pulled on Grant's arm, "sit back down."

"You," she pointed at Logan, "sit here in this chair."

"You here," she directed Hunter to another chair. In this configuration, they were situated at the points of a triangle.

"Here's the deal. I've heard Logan talk about wanting a dad for years. So," she said looking at Logan. "What's going on here?"

"I don't want a father," Logan insisted.

"What's the difference between a father and a dad?" Gabby asked.

"I've changed my mind," Logan said. "I think Rose has it right and what I want is a papa."

"What's the difference between a father, a dad, and a papa?" Grant's brows scrunched together, his head tilted to the side looking from Hunter to Logan to Gabby.

"Logan, this is a good question. What's your answer?" Gabby asked.

"I don't have one." Logan began to cry.

"What's the point of this—? Hunter gestured to the scenario. "It's only upsetting Logan."

"And why is that?" Gabby's hand rested on Hunter's shoulder. "Why is Logan so upset about having a real dad or father in her life? I think that's a very good question.

"Logan," Gabby said in a quiet firm tone. "Where are you right now? Going forward? What is the message your body is giving you right now? Is it true?"

Logan looked up at Gabby. "I don't know where I am right now because I'm scared."

"Scared about what?" Hunter asked leaning forward.

"Scared I'm wrong. Scared you'll be mad at me if I say 'yes'. Scared he won't stay, that he'll leave and never come back."

"Hunt?" Gabby prodded.

"If you really want Grant's name on your birth certificate, I can deal with that. I'm not sure I can handle you changing your name or leaving me to live with him," Hunter said in a shaky voice watching Logan as she talked.

"Grant?" Gabby asked looking in his direction.

"I'm new to this father or dad or papa stuff and I'm botching it bad. Being a part of all this," he gestured around the room, "is more complicated than I ever realized.

"I don't know how to show you you won't be wrong wanting me in your life because I do have to return to work at some point. That point is sooner rather than later. I wanted an official place in your lives before I have to leave." His gaze traveled between Logan and Hunter. "I have parents and siblings but I don't have a family."

At Logan's questioning gaze, he added, "Your mom was right to leave. If I'd known about you I would have tried to find you, tried to convince your mom we should marry. As it was, she thought I was involved with someone and she left to protect you. If we'd talked, we'd have married and remained in Rhode Island. I don't know that we'd still be married. I don't know that we'd even still love each other. What I do know is you would not be the fantastic young woman you are if your mom had stayed."

Tears trickled down Hunter's cheeks. She cleared her throat, opened her mouth to speak but no words emerged.

"Mom? Are you okay?" Logan's anxious voice asked.

Hunter nodded, her gaze locked with Grant's as she stood. In some ways it was like a choreographed scene, she stood and he did also. She took a step forward as did he.

Her arms slid around his neck, her head nestled against his shoulder, his shirt dampened from her tears. He held her as if she were transparent porcelain and would break if he pulled her close. "Thank you," she whispered in a voice thick with tears. "Thank you for understanding."

Gabby nudged Logan and pointed towards Grant and Hunter. She nodded when Logan looked a question at her.

Grant looked over Hunter's head at Logan and held out a hand in welcome even while believing she'd refuse.

Logan stood and took the two steps to stand next to him. He wrapped his arm around her. It wasn't instantaneous but she did relax, rest her head on his chest and in time put one arm around his waist, the other around Hunter's.

Gabby gave him a finger wave and turned to leave.

"Don't go," he heard himself say. Two words and the spell broke. Hunter sniffed and wiped her face with the back of her hand. She stepped away and grabbed tissue, handing some to Logan.

Logan backed away and sat down on the couch. He took a chance and sat next to her, not crowding her but definitely there.

"Where are we?" he asked. "I need some help to navigate this situation."

"If Logan agrees, her birth certificate will be changed and your name added," Hunter said. "Logan?"

"Do you promise not to go away and never come back?" Logan speared him with a look so reminiscent of her mom his breath caught in his chest and words refused to form. A nod, a deep breath, a solemn vow. "I will do all in my power to be the best—," he paused not sure what to call himself. "What do you expect of a dad or a papa?"

"I want my dad to listen to me. To try and understand me. I want my dad to be a talking dad not a yelling one. I want him to be kind and not hit mom or me or, really, anyone. I want him to want to be around me, to do things with me and to be part of my family when that's okay with mom.

"He needs to know mom is first in my life because she's always been there for me. I want my dad to come to the important events in my life although crossing the stage at high school graduation won't be on the list. I want my dad to be my cheerleader, someone who'll encourage me to do my best and move forward in my life.

"There's probably more but that's all I can think of right now." Logan finished but her gaze remained on Grant.

"All I can promise is to do my best. I won't knowingly hurt you or your mom. When I return to Rhode Island, we'll have a time when we talk on the phone and we can always do email. I can't promise right now when I'll be back but I will come back because I want to be your cheerleader, I want to attend all the important events in your life and I want to be a part of your family as much as you and your mom will let me." He eased his grip on Logan's hand, blinked to quiet the plea he sent to Hunter with his eyes.

"All anyone can do is their best." Hunter moved to sit on Logan's other side. "When do you think you'll have to leave?"

"Sometime next week. I hope at the end of it but there are problems at the firm. My assistant was just fired and they've appointed another woman to take her place. It's punishment because I left and didn't return when they wanted me to," he said in answer to the question on Hunter's face.

"My parents are threatening to hire a private detective. Again, I've not come home when ordered. My father—," he grimaced and turned to Logan, "I'm glad I'm going to be a dad and not a father," he said giving her a side-hug. "Well suffice it to say he is not happy with me at all."

"If you need to leave earlier—." Logan twisted her hands as panic flared. "I don't want you to get into trouble." Her high-pitched voice wobbled on the last word.

"A dad keeps his promises." He took Logan's closest hand in his. "And this dad said he'd help you study for those mid-term tests." He looked over Logan's head, met Hunter's searching gaze. "It's nothing new, Logan. They're just trying to reel me in because I've stepped outside the expectations for a partner in the law firm and a Parker the Fourth."

Tears welled in Hunter's eyes and she reached behind Logan and patted his shoulder. "I see things haven't really changed," she said in a quiet stricken voice.

"Not really," Grant replied. "It's just easier to deal with, to see the manipulation when you're older." He stood without releasing Logan's hand. "I do have some work to finish up and send off tonight," Grant said. "I'll be back tomorrow and we'll hit the books."

"Come first thing and I'll make breakfast," Hunter said.

"Something more than yoghurt and granola?" Grant teased.

"Mom makes an awesome omelet." Logan covered a yawn with her hand.

"Yes, she does," Gabby testified.

"Okay." Hunter stood and stretched, a smile graced her face and she twirled in place. "Omelets for breakfast. Omelets stuffed with what?"

"I'll pick up shrimp," Gabby said. "A shrimp omelet with Swiss cheese would be fantastic."

"I'll stop by the bakery," Grant offered, "and get some croissants or —, I'm sure I can figure it out." He turned and gave Logan a hug. "Get some sleep. Your brain will need it."

She laughed and hugged him back.

"Thank you," he said against Hunter's hair as he pulled her into a hug. The spicy scent she wore reminded him of making love under the hot summer sun. He stepped back, his hands sliding down her arms to hold her hands for a moment. He turned to leave. "See you all in the morning."

"I'll walk out with you." Gabby picked up her purse and followed him down the hall.

Outside, Gabby stopped and put her hand on his arm. "I'm glad you're here and in both of their lives. Logan especially needs you but in her own independent way, Hunt does also. Do not," she emphasized these words by shaking her finger at him, "do not disappoint them."

She turned away, a wave over her shoulder along with the words "See you in the morning."

Grant waited while Gabby unlocked and got into her car. Once her engine was running, he got into his. This time next week he'd be either back east or about to leave.

At the motel, a sense of resoluteness infused him. He sat at the computer, checked emails and responded to those that needed his input.

He emailed his assistant, Karen, at her home email address asking her to consider herself on a paid semi-vacation. There were some tasks he wanted her to do for him.

First task? Buy a digital camera and head out to his place at the shore for the day. Why? He wanted pictures from the dock out front and from the back deck. He wanted pictures taken throughout the day, pictures to capture the sunrise and sunset, pictures to capture the light beating down on the water at noon and slanting across the horizon just before sunset.

Second task? Email the shots to him.

Third task? Download the pictures to a CD and send that to him using one of the overnight services.

Fourth task? Take a week off because she'd be very busy when he got back.

His postscript? He'd ask his housekeeper, Mrs. Ripley, to unlock the place so Karen and her husband could spend the day there.

After clicking 'send', Grant went over some paperwork. Lounged on the bed, his laptop propped against his knees he methodically dealt with the business at hand.

Sleep was elusive.

Hunter would recognize the pictures he wanted made into art work for Logan's bedroom wall. Why was he was willing to risk a negative reaction to her seeing them? Because in those few minutes when he held her in his arms the sense of family and belonging and home stole his breath away. *If this is what being a real part of a family is all about—.*

He didn't remember falling asleep but the buzz on his alarm told him it was seven. A crick in his neck and bent glasses were signs he'd fallen asleep while working. *I've got enough to get by if I lived a more modest lifestyle—I've got commitments and obligations to deal with before I go down that path.*

A hot shower, a quick call to Mrs. Ripley and he was out the door.

Stopping at the bakery, the smells of baking bread, cinnamon and other spices reminded him of Hunter. He bought an almond-paste-stuffed pastry ring and a loaf of peasant bread. It would make excellent toast the sales clerk said.

As he pulled into his parking place, he grinned. *My parking place.* Grabbing the bakery sacks and his laptop from the car, his steps were light as he unlocked the door and started up the stairs.

"I'm here," he called out.

"Dad's here." Logan's footsteps pattered down the hall towards him.

Grant's steps faltered when her smiling face appeared at the top of the stairs. His chest constricting wasn't new but the feelings of a profound happiness were. He continued up the stairs, exchanging quips with his daughter. *My daughter.* He found himself just saying the words internally from time to time. At the top of the stairs, Logan gave him a hug and then tugged him along the hall.

"Mom'll start the omelets once she's out of the shower," she chatted.

He hung out at the table where he could see into the kitchen area after depositing his contributions on the counter. A ringing of the bell and he jogged down the hall and down the stairs to the door. Gabby was there with shrimp. Behind her was Sophia.

"I know you stopped at the bakery, but believe me, as good as that might be, Soph's pecan sticky buns are better," Gabby said.

His mouth watered at the thought of soft, yeasty, pecan and cinnamon with a bit of caramel rolls. "I'll put my pastry in the freezer," he said and started back up the stairs.

As the only man sitting around the table, it wasn't as uncomfortable as he thought it might be. He was included in the conversations, asked his opinion, listened to, drawn into a discussion. *This is what*

Logan is talking about. Being included. In my family? In Hunter's family? Never. And this informality would never be accepted.

Breakfast finished and dishes cleared Hunter and Gabby left Sophia behind. They were going down and calling students. While she was clear she wasn't teaching a full schedule in the future, it was important to her to finish what she started with this group of students. Starting now, Hunter figured she'd be able to have her spring recital in late June instead of mid-May.

Logan got out her books, Sophia looked over the paper she'd written while Grant quizzed her for the government and economics mid-terms she'd take shortly. Before Sophia proctored the test, they mapped out her study schedule through the next week.

"Dad has to go back to Rhode Island next weekend," Logan informed Sophia.

"You can practice your speech final and your oral report on your senior project with any of us. I think your dad helps you the most with government, economics and math," Sophia suggested.

"I've been working on my part of the senior project and I'll have it ready for you to take to the others by Monday. I'll be ready to do my oral report then also," Logan shared.

Standing, she rounded the table and gave Sophia a long hug. "Thank you so much for talking to my teachers and helping me with-with-with everything."

"Your dad helped too. Remember he was on the conference call with your teachers and me last week. Because you'd done so much on your own with your dad's help to catch up, they were impressed and more willing to work with you." Sophia reached up and patted Logan's shoulder. "I appreciate the thank you and especially the hug. Can't get too many of them these days." She laughed. "If I didn't know you better, I'd say you were procrastinating."

Logan returned to her seat. The morning passed. Veggie sandwiches on the peasant bread he'd brought were their lunch. He wandered down to see what Hunter was up to when Logan and Sophia started the mid-terms.

Gabby had left after lunch to catch up on errands.

He found Hunter in the studio, drawing out a routine on a white board—or that's what he thought she was doing with the squiggle marks and arrows.

"I'm going for a walk," he announced.

She waved a green marker in his direction.

Outside he started down the block, crossing at the light in the direction of the running path. He wasn't dressed to run other than he had tennis shoes on. Not real running shoes but they'd work if he decided he wanted to increase his pace.

So this is what being a dad could be like. He stopped at the playground on the right just before the path began. Kids on swings their moms and dads pushed, a toddler, held safe by a dad, on a teeter-totter, mom on the far end pushing down and letting it up. Sadness welled as the thought surfaced that he not only never had these experiences, he never would.

The sadness faded with the realization that he'd never have had these experiences with Logan to begin with. There would have been a nanny to take her to the park or perhaps Hunter could have managed to get away once a week or so. He'd be a father not a dad. He'd be working, at meetings or maybe as with his own father, spending time with a mistress.

I think being a dad in the here and now will be better.

Grant pulled out his cell phone and dialed Ms. Lawford's number. The message he left: "Go ahead with the paperwork. Seeing the judge by the end of the day next Friday is imperative because I have to go back to Rhode Island next weekend. Let me know if there's anything I can do to expedite things."

When he hung up, the readout on the phone said he had plenty of time for a leisurely jog around the park. He stuffed the phone in his pants pocket and started off.

33 - HE'S GONE

Sunday
May 15, 2005

*H*unter, her arm around Logan's shoulder, watched Grant disappear down the concourse. It was ten on Sunday night and Grant was taking the red-eye to LaGuardia. From there he'd take the commuter train to Providence and a taxi home. If all went well, he'd be in the office before nine. He'd delayed his return as long as he could. Wrapping his arms around both of them, lingering before heading through security showed her how hard it was for him to leave.

Her lips still tingled from his parting kiss. Not even close to a peck on the cheek. The full impact of the kiss, his scent, the feel of his arms and chest pressing into her—it was the last thing he'd done.

That kiss.

Striding away.

Never looking back.

"I think Dad will miss us." Logan shifted closer, her head on Hunter's shoulder.

"I'm sure he already misses you." Hunter hugged her daughter.

"No, Mom, he'll miss you too." Logan pulled away, linked her arm in Hunter's and started walking away. "Come on, Mom. He isn't coming back."

Hunter heard the catch in Logan's voice. "He will be back. He won't be able to stay away from you," she assured her daughter. "I've seen how he looks at you, how important you are to him."

Logan stopped in mid-stride pulling Hunter to a halt. "Mom, he looks at you—I can tell when he sees you as you are now and I can tell when he sees you in his memories."

Hunter pulled Logan close. "Perhaps we can agree that he'll miss us both?"

Logan nodded.

Swinging away, she grabbed her mom's hand. "If I wasn't almost eighteen, I'd race you to the car," she said and grinned.

"Glad I'm not almost eighteen, because not only will I race you to the car, I'll beat you." Hunter loped off.

"No fair," Logan called out, easily catching up.

Matching steps they jogged through the airport and to the parking garage.

"Guess it's a tie," Hunter said spotting the car.

"Not even." Logan sprinted the rest of the way, a gleeful laugh trailing behind.

Hunter slowed, thankful the old Logan had showed herself. From time to time she appeared. Not daily, much less multiple times a day, and not for very long but it gladdened her heart that she came at all.

"Want to drive home?" she asked her daughter when she reached the car.

"Yes!" Logan fist pumped the air, rounded the trunk and hugged Hunter close. "Thanks Mom."

SOPHIA AND GABRIELLA were waiting for them when they pulled into their parking spot. Hunter wasn't really surprised to see them.

However, what did have her eyebrows flying up and her eyes widening was they both toted packages.

"What about work tomorrow," Hunter said turning off the alarm and unlocking the door. She stood to the side so everyone could precede her.

"We won't be long," Sophia said.

"Keeping a promise," Gabby added.

Upstairs, coats divested, tea kettle on to boil and a plate of Sophia's peanut butter cookies at hand, they settled around the table.

"Open it and all your questions will be answered," Sophia said, handing a smaller package to Hunter.

"I don't understand." Hunter held the six by eight box turning it this way and that.

"Mom, just open it," Logan encouraged. "I'll do it if you don't want to," she said reaching for it.

"No you don't." Hunter held her arm out to the side. "I'm perfectly capable of opening it on my own."

The plain brown paper easily pulled away, the plain white box gave no clues. Lifting the top off the box, revealed a photo album.

Hunter took it out and opened the cover. The first picture was of the paternity papers. The second and third pages showed each of them signing the papers before a notary.

Over the next ten pages were photographs of them with Ms. Lawford, in front of Judge Peterson, in a group hug, posing for the camera big smiles on their faces.

The next picture was of Grant and Logan at this very table. Logan bent over a book and Grant's posture and gesture showed he was explaining something. Another picture was of her and Logan in the kitchen. One more was of the three of them off for a run.

When she turned to the next page, it was blank as were the rest of the pages.

"Mom, this fell out." Logan handed her a piece of paper.

The words blurred. Hunter waved it back at Logan. "What does it say?"

"Many more pages to fill as a family," Logan choked out. "I guess he really will be back." She took the tissue Sophia offered, wiped her face and blew her nose.

The shrill of the tea kettle signaled a welcomed break.

"How?" Hunter asked after fixing her cup and returning to the table. "How did he do this?"

"Grant asked us to take pictures with our phones at the signing. And, he also asked me," Sophia said, "to take pictures of him with Logan."

"Soph and I decided to add a few more than he asked for because it seemed he wanted to capture his time here."

"And the note?" Hunter asked.

"We gave him the album yesterday to check out. He gave it back and we wrapped it up. He asked us to give it to you after he left—well, that album and this." Gabby gestured to the larger package. "This one is specifically for Logan."

Logan jumped up and tore the paper off the two foot by three foot box. Tugging the top up, she gasped. "This is so beautiful." Her mouth formed an 'o' and her eyes widened. "Look." She pulled the framed picture out and set it on the chair she just vacated. "Here's another one," she exclaimed. After putting it in front of the first picture, she got the last one out.

"It's called a triptych," Sophia said, rising and rounding the table. "They go like this." She held the two pictures already on the chair up and stood next to Logan who held the third one.

"Gabby, why don't you hold the picture Logan has so she can see the scene?" Sophia suggested.

Logan handed the picture to Gabby and moved to stand on the opposite side. "Wow, that's so beautiful." Logan leaned across the table, her gaze shifted from one picture to the other and back. She stepped back a few steps to see the panoramic scene.

"Mom, come see what Dad gave me for my room." Logan held her hand out.

Hunter gripped the table top as she rose. She'd seen enough of the first picture to know the scene. Somehow Grant had photographs taken of the view from his deck. It was a house they'd often fantasized living in as they jogged down the beach. The light on the water shimmered in the noonday sun. Sensations of dashing into the cool water, of lying on the hot sand, of ardent kisses and flaring passions assaulted her body. She staggered.

"Just sat too long," she said regaining her physical balance if not her emotional equilibrium.

"That's the view from the deck at your dad's place at the shore." A stab of awareness at how easy it was to speak the east coast word—east coast people go to the shore; on the west coast they go to the beach or maybe the coast.

"Really?" Logan asked. "That's really what he sees?"

"Really." Hunter slipped an arm around Logan's shoulders. "Now when you wake up in the morning you can see the same view your dad does when he's there."

"He doesn't live there all the time?" Logan's head tilted to the side, her brows scrunched as she scrutinized the scene more closely.

"No, he has a place in the city near his work and this place at the shore. Then his family has a summer place in Maine and a winter place in Florida." Hunter listened to her voice, listened for jealousy, listened for negativity. What she heard was a neutral, factual recitation of the Parker family properties.

"Here," Gabby said. "Let's hang them in your room. Soph and I have work tomorrow and this is at least a two person job."

Logan chattered as she and Gabby took the pictures to her room. Moments later Logan dashed out and rummaged through a kitchen drawer. "Found one," she called back to Gabby, heading back to her room with a hammer.

Sophia rested her hand on Hunter's shoulder. "More tea? I think what we have is now cold."

"I'm good for now, but help yourself," Hunter said. "I'll just take care of these." When she picked up the large box, a smaller package fell out. *More pictures.* "Logan, your dad put an envelope of photographs in the box. Mind if I look at them first?" she called out over the rapping of the hammer.

"Go ahead," Logan replied. The next words were indistinct.

"She talking to Gabby," Sophia said patting the chair next to her.

Hands trembling, Hunter opened the envelope. Memories flooded of times past and her vision blurred. The sun rising off the front dock greeted her. The view memorialized from dawn to dusk. This house sat at the end of a spit of land. Sunrise over the water from the dock; sunset over the water from the lawn.

"Come see, Mom, Sophia, come see," Logan called out, her eagerness apparent.

Sophia linked arms. "You are doing so well," she said to Hunter as they crossed to the hall and to Logan's room.

"Look Mom," Logan said pulling her to the center of her room. "I get to see them every morning when I get up and at night when I go to bed. Aren't they great?"

Hunter internally steeled herself to face her past. And there it was, right in front of her. Bright with the sun sparkling on the waves, a fishing boat in the distance. Together they made up a panoramic view and it was spectacular.

"Have you really really been there?" Logan asked without looking at her.

"I have." Hunter said. "A very long time ago."

"Do you ever want to go back?" Logan asked still gazing at the pictures.

"It's one of those times and places we can never return to." Her strength faltered and tears threatened. Sophia squeezed her hand.

"Tomorrow is a work day and I'll be over after school to pick up your senior project. I'll check and see when you need to call in and give your oral report to your teacher so pay attention to the phone," Sophia said to Logan before turning and giving Hunter a long hug.

"Your dad left you these." Hunter managed to say as she put the envelope on Logan's dresser. "I'll see you two out," she said to Sophia and Gabby and left the bedroom.

Long hugs and call if you need to talk and I'll check on you tomorrow at the bottom of the stairs left Hunter drained. She wandered along the hall to her studio, her finger tips tracing a path down the wall. Inside she picked up her drum and began a slow, steady beat.

In time to the beat she circled the room in what she called the 'shuffle step': a step she'd adapted from one she'd seen used by Native American dancers at a PowWow. The next loop around the room was different: three steps and a pirouette. Alternating, she rounded the room over and over and over until her arms were weak from holding and beating the drum and her legs showed signs of fatigue.

Upstairs she peeked in on Logan who was asleep, the sheets and blankets from Grant tucked under her chin. The urge to step inside just enough to look at the triptych was strong.

She turned away.

Grant was gone and yet he wasn't. At some point during all that had been going on, he'd called. His message was simple. "I already miss you. I'll be back."

A note next to the phone from Logan. "Dad called me. He misses us and hopes I can come and visit."

Bile rose in her throat. Hunter dashed to the bathroom, lost the little in her stomach.

In her nightmares she lost Logan to the life she'd fled.

In her nightmares she was faced with the choice to join her or lose her forever.

In her nightmares, Grant's arm was around Logan's shoulders and she was nowhere to be seen.

Grant expected he looked about how he felt—drug through the knothole backwards. He'd dozed on the plane and on the train but the chauffer had to wake him when he reached his downtown condo. After a quick shower and shave, he stood before his bedroom's full length mirror adjusting his tie.

Once on the plane he'd opened the package Gabby had given him after he'd swore on all that was holy he wouldn't until he got home. Inside was a duplicate of the photo album he'd put together for Hunter and Logan. This one had only two blank pages and didn't start with a photo of the paternity papers.

The neat print under the first page said Logan was seven years old. She was in a soccer uniform, a ball tucked under one arm, a bright smile on her face. In the next two pictures, she was flanked by two boys. *Diana and Lily's sons.* He squinted and held the album at an angle to better see Logan walking across a stage. The notation beneath: Eighth Grade Promotion. A note from Sophia explained that these were copies of pictures she and Gabby had from over the years that they wanted to share with him.

Where was it now? Tucked into a shoe box under a stack of like shoe boxes in his closet. Why? *I don't want to share them.*

Until now he'd just accepted he didn't really have any privacy. He employed the same cleaning service his parents used and he knew the woman who weekly cleaned his place reported anything unusual to his mother.

His six weeks in Fremont were the first time he'd ever felt free of family expectations, that he had a private life. But as he strode out to the waiting car, he wondered if that had been a myth.

"Good morning," he said as he walked right past his new assistant and on into his office.

"I've organized," she started as she followed behind him.

Grant cut her off. "I'll let you know if I need you."

"I can get—."

"I believe I said I'll call you if I need you." He stared her down.

"Of course, Four," she said, using his office nickname.

"Mr. Parker will do." Grant walked back to the door and stood to the side until she left. Then he firmly shut the door behind her.

At his desk, he perused the neatly stacked files. He turned his calendar back to the day he'd left. One by one he turned the pages seeing indelible images of his time in Fremont, of Logan and Hunter on each page. He missed them with an intensity that hurt.

Too early to call. Hunter may be up but Logan would still be asleep.

His thoughts were interrupted by a sharp rap on the door immediately followed by its opening. Herb, the firm's president, stood in the entrance. Behind him was the assistant, hand-picked he knew by the man in front of him.

"Welcome back." Herb's face was wreathed in a jovial smile. "We expect you to have lunch with us today so we can bring you up to date on things. We've got the prospect of landing a couple of new clients, right up your alley.

"I'm sure Cathy misunderstood your instructions, Four. You'll need some help catching up."

"Actually Herb, the misunderstanding is that she is my assistant. I've had Karen as an assistant for over five years. She's kept track of things for me while I've been on vacation. Other than what's happened between last Friday and this morning, I am up-to-date on things."

Herb frowned. "Your old assistant was fired. She was a distraction, creating problems."

"Really? And what distraction and problems would that have been?" Grant asked keeping his face neutral but aware of the pounding pulse in his temple.

"No need to go into that, Four. Cathy is experienced and able to provide you with *everything* you need."

Grant thought Herb winked. Hoped he was wrong. Knew he wasn't.

"I've already got everything I need," he said. "My job description authorizes me to hire and fire assistants and secretaries. You may have fired her, but I've hired her back. Either she returns to this office, or I'll just work with her at a remote location.

"It's amazing what people can do these days. If you have a computer, you can work from home. It's something I've been considering trying out myself." Grant remained standing, his gaze locked with Herb. He resisted the urge to bounce up and down on his toes, to do something to release the fuming fury that was building. *I can't believe this type of interaction didn't used to bother me.*

"I'll expect you at The Fontaine at eleven-forty-five," Herb said, the 'or else' implied. He spun on his heel and stalked out.

"Are you sure you won't need me for anything?" Cathy asked, emphasizing the last two syllables.

"Positive," Grant said. "You may want to check in with human resources to see if there is another opening, or perhaps talk to Herb about one."

Cathy, a pouty look on her face, turned and left her hips swinging in silent invitation. When the door closed, Grant ran his finger between the starched cloth and his neck and pulled. *One battle down, how many more to go?*

Grant picked up his cell phone and dialed Karen. "I'll be sending you some paperwork later. Tomorrow we'll draw up a contract and set out the terms of our working agreement."

He listened, nodded and then said "If you want to draw up a draft, I've no problem with that. Let's plan on breakfast at The Deli."

Over the next two hours, both his mother and father called inviting him for dinner. "A welcome home gathering with family," his mother had said.

Eleven-twenty sharp he closed the file he'd been working on, went into the attached bathroom and washed up. His hair was a bit shaggy having missed two of his usual bi-weekly trims. The bright smile he'd seen the past couple of weeks when he shaved, the whistle on his lips, the sense of happiness, of freedom were gone. *How did I do this without complaint for so many years?*

Eleven-forty-five sharp he walked into The Fontaine. Of course he was the first one. He was tempted to walk out, leave a message with the maître d that he had pressing business, keep on going out to his place at the shore. He could be there in an hour. While the thought intrigued, the reality was he would barely get there before needing to return because of dinner tonight with his parents.

When the clock struck twelve, he rose and started towards the door. Of course just as he left the restaurant, Herb and the other partners arrived. It was as if they'd waited in the shadows until he got up to leave.

"Sorry about that, Four," Herb said. "Important call came in at the last minute."

"Not a problem." Grant stood to the side and brought up the rear as the others followed Herb into the restaurant.

The 'bring him up to date' and 'possible clients for him' never did get discussed. They did talk about billable hours and if things didn't improve bonus checks that para-legals and secretaries counted on would be skimpy or nonexistent. No talk about their own checks being short.

How did I just go along with this? It was May, bonus checks didn't get determined and paid out until November or maybe the first week in December. It would appear this lunch and the talk of financial doom and gloom was for his benefit, was to let him know he'd been found lacking. Especially when they went around the table and each person reported what their billable hours were for the month of April.

"Actually I had forty billable hours in April and considering I was on vacation, I'm good with that," he said when his turn came.

"And what do you think your hours will be this month?" Herb asked, skewering him with a calculating look.

"Higher than that." Grant schooled his face in a neutral mien and kept his tone mild.

The maître d approached the table. "A call for Mr. Parker," he said looking at Grant.

"Thank you," Grant said and stood. "I'll take it outside."

"The young lady said no matter what you were doing to interrupt," the maître d said. "I hope—. "

"You did as you were asked," Grant said reaching the phone on the stand next to the maître d's desk. "Parker here."

"Karen here. Did I time this call correctly?"

"Perfect. I'll take care of it," he said a bit loudly for the maître d's benefit. Hanging up the phone, Grant handed the man a hefty tip, thanked him again for calling him to the phone and walked out.

DINNER WAS MORE of the same. His mother had invited Debbie and Sunny, her handpicked candidates for Mrs. Parker IV. He wasn't surprised and not even upset. He was polite, distant, endured the glares from his mother when he avoided spending any time with either woman.

Debbie had been a friend of Hunter's in high school. She'd married and divorced twice, had four children, and he'd guess liposuction if not cosmetic surgery. It was impossible not to compare Hunter to the two women.

Looking at Debbie, he saw what his life with Hunter would have been. Their marriage would not have been happy and by this time they'd most likely divorced. Debbie's eyes, especially after two before-dinner cocktails, several glasses of wine during the meal and at least two after-dinner drinks, mirrored desperation. About thirty-six with four children and two divorces under her belt, her prospects were not good. Most of the men his age were already married or looking at the twenty-something's in their social circle.

Perhaps because they had been a couple, Sunny was not subtle. Whenever she could, she touched, stroked and he figured if given the chance, she would grope.

His mother was blatant in her attempts to match-make when she informed both women he'd be delighted to escort them home.

Used to Mrs. Parker III's machinations, he'd suspected something along those lines when he walked in the door and saw it was not 'just family'.

He sent the women home in his town car. To say his mother was not pleased was an understatement of epic proportions.

His father, Three or Mr. Parker III invited him into his study. The hypocrisy of his father grilling him on the bimbo he'd obviously taken up with rankled. Grant either ignored the question or refused to answer. There was no way he was going to mention Hunter or Logan to either of his parents.

Finally the evening was over. He let himself into his condo, grateful it was empty, grateful he had no relationship to break off. He was also grateful that while it was midnight in Providence, it was nine in Fremont.

He changed into the most disreputable pair of sweats he owned, poured himself a Drambuie on the rocks and settled down in front of the gas fireplace. Thankful he had both Logan and Hunter on speed dial; he keyed in Logan's number and sipped his drink.

She answered on the second ring, "Dad," her excitement streaked across the miles. "I love everything," she chatted on. "Mom said the pictures are the view from your place at the beach—I mean the shore." She laughed. "Mom said you say 'shore' back there not beach. Is she right?"

Grant rested his head on the back of the chair as weariness claimed him. He just wanted to hear their voices. For right now, that was enough.

He managed short answers, realized right away that Logan didn't need more than that from him tonight.

"Grant?" Hunter came on the line.

"Yeah," he said.

"Have you been drinking?"

"I had two glasses of wine with dinner and am currently three sips into a Drambuie on the rocks. So the short answer is 'yes' the longer answer is 'I'm not drunk.'"

"It's midnight there. Are you okay? I thought you'd have crashed by now," Hunter's questions and comments soothed. No inquisition, just concern.

"I'm about ready to go under," Grant said, his eyes closed. "Just wanted to check in and see how you were doing."

"Logan is thrilled with the pictures. And I'm grateful for the album. It hadn't occurred to me to record the occasion but I'm glad it occurred to you."

He felt connected to Hunter across the miles even in the silence that followed. He was fading fast. What registered was she was glad. He wasn't as sure what she was glad about.

"Grant," Hunter said. "Grant?"

"I'm still here. Got to go before I fall asleep on you. Give Logan a hug from me, okay?"

"I will do that. Take care of yourself. Get some sleep."

"Good night," he said and hung up. Tomorrow was another day, a day that promised to be even more challenging. He expected his mother to show up with another single woman in tow. He expected his father to make some pointed remark about his responsibilities to the Parker name. He expected Herb to be circling.

In his dreams he was looking out the window in Ms. Lawford's office, a file of some sort on the desk in front of him. A framed picture of Hunter and Logan in the upper right corner and next to that, another of he and Hunter, waves tickling their feet.

By lunchtime, Grant was ready to turn in his resignation. Herb had been waiting for him when he got to the office at seven. A bit worse for wear with six hours sleep on top of the previous night spent flying across country, he gritted his teeth, refused on principle the coffee Cathy brought in and listened to Herb drone on. Lights were flashing on his office phone, his cell was vibrating and his head was pounding.

"Herb, I can see calls on hold." Grant gestured to the phone on his desk. "We can finish this discussion later."

"Cathy," Herb barked, "Take care of those calls."

"Cathy," Grant said, "Do not touch that phone." He stared at the woman caught in the power struggle. When she turned to look at him, he said to Herb. "Cathy is not and will not be my assistant. I'm sure she's very good at what she does but I do not want to train someone new to my way of doing things.

"Either we set a time to finish what you have to say or we can agree that you've said all you need." Grant stood and gestured towards the door. "I have work to do and an appointment I'm late for."

Closing the door behind him, he texted Karen he was on his way; checked the phone lines that were blinking, noting no one was on any of the six lines. The dream from last night was vivid in his mind's eye as he strode out the door.

"If Logan comes east to school, I want to be here for her. If not? Then leaving the firm is looking better and better every day," he muttered as he started towards The Deli ten blocks away.

Karen was waiting, a worried look on her face. Grant waved her first question away. "Let's order first."

Their order taken, he handed Karen a single sheet of paper. "I made a couple of changes to the draft you sent me." He nodded towards the document now in her hand.

Rhode Island was small, the legal community smaller. He imagined the discord in his office caused by his refusal to work with another assistant was general knowledge and would be seen in a less than professional light. *How to approach that?*

Karen saved him the trouble. "My husband is concerned about this arrangement." She set the contract down on the table and leaned forward. "He wants me to find another position. I told him I owed you at least this meeting."

The waitress arrived with their food so he had a few minutes to consider what to say while he added a dollop of catsup to his hash browns.

"I thought of the complications these changes could bring," he started. "As you can see, I've indicated all work will be done electronically or by courier. We will have to meet, but we can easily do that in a public place."

"Client confidentiality?" Karen asked.

"Can be handled by giving each client a number. If we are discussing the research needed for number eight no one else will know who that is." He took a bite of omelet mentally comparing this one to Hunter's. It failed.

Grant paused in mid-bite, put his fork down and elbows on the table, templed his fingers. "I did hear you say your husband is concerned." He sighed and leaned back in his chair, rubbed his temples with his fingers. "I won't disagree with your husband about looking for another position. I'll write a recommendation for you today. While I hope you won't use it, I totally understand why you would."

"Thank you. I won't leave you in the lurch. I know a couple of paralegals who would do a good job for you. And," Karen smiled, "I know you well enough to suggest someone who won't need a lot of training. You do have your quirks."

"Like doing my own research?"

"That would be one of them. You ferret out the cases and then ask me to read and make annotations." She chuckled and took a bite of her scrambled eggs. "You do know you've changed in some ways— subtle changes but noticeable."

"I'd like to hear your observations." Grant smiled and added, "I think." He took a swallow of coffee and sat forward so Karen didn't have to speak too loud.

"You used to be comfortable—physically that is. Now you are almost squirming as if you want to take your tie off. You used to be more formal, business-like and it isn't that you've really changed but you have. I can't really tell you what's different, only that something is. You've always been professional and I don't see that as different—," she stared right at him as she finished, "whatever you did, whatever happened while you were gone was good for you. I think the real Grant Haywood Parker the Fourth is peeking through."

One of the things he valued about Karen was her keen observation, her skilled assessments and her direct language. He would miss her.

"The more I think about it, the more I know you need to find another position. It occurs to me that things at the office will get worse rather than better and I don't want you caught up in the gossip and the drama.

"What do you think about asking Martha to be my assistant?"

"She's a legal secretary not a paralegal."

"But I love to do research, remember?"

Grant relaxed when Karen grinned. "She'd sure keep you in line."

"Too true." He put his hand out, "You can give the contract back. I'll send you a letter stating that while you've provided exemplary service, my needs have changed. I'll include a severance package and a letter of recommendation.

"Now to deal with Herb and hire Martha."

"What's Herb doing to you? He thinks highly of you."

"Not since I didn't return on the next plane when he told me to. Not since I refused to accept Cathy as my new assistant."

"Cathy?" Karen laughed. "Martha will suit you much better. I could say more but I won't. Just go with Martha and you'll be just fine."

"Martha lives on the block behind me. If she has questions about accepting, tell her to come talk to me." Karen handed the contract back to Grant.

They finished their breakfast, had another cup of coffee before leaving. Karen insisted on paying for her own breakfast. Grant took note of the amount and planned to add it to her severance package.

On the sidewalk, he wished her well and they shook hands. Walking back to the office he told himself change was good. Karen's words about the effect of his time in Fremont rang true. He had changed. He was less inclined to just play along, to engage in the gamesmanship needed to navigate the professional shoals.

Grant stopped by Martha's desk, two floors down from his own, on his way to his office. The firm kept three legal secretaries on staff to do miscellaneous work, back up secretaries assigned to specific attorneys and to fill in when someone was sick or on vacation.

"I'm looking for someone to keep me organized, remind me of appointments and type briefs," Grant said, looking directly at the older woman.

"Research?" Martha asked.

"I like doing my own so unless there is an inordinate amount of it, I'll do it. And," he continued when her mouth opened and she appeared to be raising an objection, "if there is more than I can do, I'll borrow a paralegal or hire someone part time."

"Word is you aren't staying around," Martha said.

"Word isn't always correct," Grant responded. "And should word ever be correct you'll be one of the first to know." He started towards the elevators, turned around and took the few steps back to Martha's desk. "Karen said to stop by if you have questions," he said leaning down and speaking in a voice pitched low so only Martha could hear. Straightening, he started back to the elevator. "Let me know if that figure is okay. I really want you to work for me so your salary is negotiable."

"You'll have my answer in the morning," Martha said. "I'll either be at the desk outside your office or I'll be here."

"Perfect." Grant continued on his way.

Although confident Herb would hear the news before he got off the elevator, Grant still stopped by Herb's office to tell him in person. Of course he had to wait—thirty minutes—but he had expected some form of punishment.

Herb was not pleased but Grant insisted he only needed the services of a legal secretary and Cathy's talents would be wasted if she were assigned to him.

Yes, it was unusual for an attorney of his stature and experience to do his own research but he loved doing it and he needed to add something he enjoyed to his job.

Herb capitulated, patted him on the back like a benevolent father and assured him that being back at work would help him get back in the routine of things.

Grant knew 'the routine of things' meant to do what he used to do and stop being an independent pain in the butt.

Two messages from his mother waited for him. He called her back, told him he was way behind at work and needed to work long hours the rest of the week. "I'll come for dinner on Sunday, mother. Before that just won't work out."

"What's wrong?"

"Nothing. I'm behind at work. I'll see you Sunday."

She'd hung up after a lengthy pause. He left the office at six, picked up Chinese take-out on the way to his condo. He was in bed and asleep by nine.

Martha was at the desk outside his office when he arrived at eight. She'd already checked messages, appointments and had a list of tasks waiting on his desk.

He grinned. "You're perfect. Just what I need."

Martha had been at the firm longer than he had, knew the politics, what was needed and what was expected. She was priceless.

The morning passed quickly. He had the maintenance staff come in and rearrange his office. A work table was added under the windows. The large couch removed in favor of two more chairs so he had flexible comfortable seating for four.

Martha checked out volumes from the firm's law library for him. By the end of the day, they decided her hours would change from eight to five to nine to six. He'd stop any research by four so she'd have two hours to type up his notes for him and return any volumes to the library.

He left for home that night with a spring in his step even though he'd worked a twelve hour day.

At nine he called Logan and left a message. He tried Hunter's number. Disappointed when he couldn't reach either of them, he started to fix a drink intending to spend the next couple of hours with a scotch on the rocks, watching something on television.

What did I do in the evenings when I wasn't with Logan and Hunter? Work. He booted up his laptop and sent emails to his daughter. Three short ones.

"How are you?"

"Miss you."

"Give me a call. You have my number. Don't forget the time difference but if you want to talk, you can call anytime."

He poured the drink down the drain, rinsed out the glass and left it on the drain board. Tomorrow the cleaning service comes. That thought galvanized him to double check where he'd stashed his photo album. Deciding it might still be discovered because his mother was really upset, he stuck it in his briefcase. With Martha guarding his office, it was safe there.

In vivid dreams, he, Hunter and Logan ran down a sandy beach, waves crashing on high cliffs in front of them. They were definitely in Oregon.

He woke wondering if it was possible to convince Hunter to move back to Rhode Island. *Not a prayer.* But maybe a visit? *Need to check on what the Knight-Compton family is doing these days.*

By the end of the week, with his routine established something was definitely wrong. He missed his daily runs with his daughter or Hunter or both. He missed coaching Logan with her studies. The two nights he'd talked to her on the phone weren't enough. It might help if he had her picture on his desk or the mantle in his condo or even his beach place but he wasn't ready to deal with the firestorm that would bring.

GRANT LEARNED that Hunter's mother had had a stroke while he was in Fremont. The scuttlebutt was she'd recovered but it wasn't certain if she'd ever be fully functional again. He debated on letting Hunter know and decided against it. What could she do? Without Hunter's permission, he'd never let her mother know he'd found her daughter much less anything about Logan.

The idea that Hunter would give him permission to tell her mother anything was ludicrous. *I'll check things out first. When I really know what's going on, I'll know better whether to tell Hunter anything.*

ixed feelings: elation and jealousy warred. Hunter was on an emotional rollercoaster and at this moment was in a deep pit of jealousy. After another restless night, she checked emails, drank a couple cups of tea and checked voice mail messages. With the morning now half over, with no improvement in mood, she left their quarters.

Worried if she didn't get back in control, she'd act on the turmoil Hunter raced down to her studio. One step inside the door and she moved, began the most physical routine she knew. Leaps, spins, intricate footwork with her arms stretched high over her head carried her down the long room and back up to her starting point. Over and over and over and over—sweat dripped, muscles burned and still Hunter exerted herself in an effort to block the fear.

Exhausted, she slowed the pace, lowered her arms and began a long cool down process. It wasn't so much the fear of *what if.* It was much more the fear of *when.*

When would Logan ask to go see Grant in Rhode Island?
When would he offer to take her to tour Smith College?
When would she be left alone?
When would she lose her daughter?

After the 'when' came the 'what'.

What would she say when Logan and Grant asked?

What would she do if asked to come too?

What would she do when she was alone?

What would that mean?

At thirty-six she'd never truly lived alone because she counted the months of her pregnancy as living with Logan.

Somehow in her mind, it made a difference if Logan was away at college even at Smith. Why? Because if she went to Smith, Grant would only be a few hours away. It made a difference because she wouldn't be close enough to spend a weekend with her or even take her out to dinner during finals week.

Petty, I'm being petty. I've had her for eighteen years and I'm upset that Grant will be able to see her more frequently over the next four years? I'm disappointed in myself.

But it was more than that.

What if she decided to stay in the area?

What if she found the love of her life, married and remained there?

What if I—.

Stop, stop, stop! You are driving yourself crazy with these thoughts.

The cool down process complete, she leaned against the barre. *What can I do now? I can release the 'what if' thoughts. I can remind myself I am not alone.*

"Mom?" Logan stood in the doorway. "Are you okay?" She hurried to Hunter who was pushing away from the wooden rail.

"I'm fine," Hunter said, thankful she'd caught her breath and could speak. "I just needed to move, to do something and thought I see if I remembered an old routine."

"And did you? Remember?" Logan asked standing beside Hunter.

"I did." Hunter gestured to the wall of mirrors. "Just look at you. So grown up."

"I remember when you first brought me here. I had to stand on tip-toe to reach this." Logan rested her hand on the barre, lifted a leg and bent her head to her knee.

Hunter's laugh was a bit shaky at the memory of those early years of Logan eagerly following her around and mimicking everything she did. "Those were special times."

Logan, both feet now on the floor, gave Hunter a hug. "They were the best of times."

"You're showing off," Hunter said. "A Tale of Two Cities" opening lines are classic."

"But true. Fremont is only one city but the best of times and the worst of times in my life have been here." Logan hugged her mom again. "I'm so sorry I ran away, if…," her voice trailed off.

Hunter waited a heartbeat before filling the silence. "You do know you're using a word that isn't helpful. We all have "if's" and regrets. Dwelling on them doesn't help us move forward with our lives or make good plans for our future."

"I know. It's just that sometimes it seems like I'm in the middle of "if" before I realize it."

"And to get back on track?" Hunter asked, her arm around Logan's shoulder.

"Sometimes I can just tell myself to stop thinking like that but other times it's harder. You come down here and drum or dance or both."

"Sometimes I go for a run." Hunter leaned over and kissed Logan's temple.

"Sometimes you call and talk to someone. I don't have anyone to talk to," Logan said.

"Yes you do. You have Gabby, Doc S, Sophia or anyone else in The Circle and you have Grant and you have me." Hunter noticed Logan's frown. "What about your friends? Miranda and Melissa?"

"I just can't talk to, talk about, I just can't!" Logan bent at the waist, holding herself.

"Then you don't have to talk to them about what happened." Hunter rested her hand on Logan's back. "I do know that Miranda's dad drinks and has hit her mom and even hit her. Do you know how she was able to talk to you and Melissa about what happens in her family?"

"We saw her bruises and kept asking her about them." Logan

straightened. "My bruises are here." She placed one hand over her abdomen. "And here." She placed her other hand over her heart.

Hunter wrapped her arm around Logan's shoulder and gave her a side-hug. "You are a wise young woman. You do what your heart and body tell you to do. I will support you regardless of your choice as will your dad, as will The Circle." She leaned over and kissed her daughter's temple and steered them towards the door. "We can talk as we go upstairs," she said keeping close contact with Logan. "And I need a shower after that workout."

Logan relaxing against her, Hunter saw as a signal to change the subject. "Want to see if Gabby can come over? If the two of you need some alone time, I can come back down here and work on the details for the Spring Recital."

"Take your shower, Mom. Maybe we can go out to eat? That Italian restaurant Dad took us to sounds good to me."

Thankful the stairs were wide enough for them to walk up side-by-side, Hunter swallowed down the fear. "Italian does sound good. Their tiramisu was really good."

"Not as good as Giovanni's," Logan offered in a normal almost upbeat tone.

"No, not as good as his," Hunter agreed. "But since we don't have his tiramisu as an option, I'm up for Italian."

She heard the phone ring while she was in the shower. A light knock on the door while she dried off.

"Mom? That was Lily. She said Jackson is making enough spaghetti for two armies and begged us to come over," Logan giggled. "She always exaggerates."

Hunter ran a comb through her damp hair after pulling on a pair of tan slacks and print top. Socks and tennis shoes finished her outfit. A glance in the mirror and she decided to finger fluff her hair to give it some volume.

"Can we, Mom?" Logan asked as soon as she opened the bathroom door. "Can we go to Lily and Jackson's? I bet Jackson has his home-made ice cream and toppings for dessert."

The eagerness on Logan's face, in her voice, in her posture gladdened Hunter's heart. "Of course we can." She pulled Logan into a long hug. "I think spending time with Lily and Jackson is an excellent idea. And," she stepped back, "if Jackson is fixing spaghetti for two armies, I'm sure Lily has called everyone else. We haven't all gotten together since Beltane."

AFTER DINNER AND BEFORE DESSERT, they had an informal circle. As the men were cleaning up the kitchen, the women were in a semi-circle in front of the fireplace. Logan and Rose as well as Madison Michelle were next to or on the laps of their mothers.

With Logan there Hunter did not talk about her fears or jealous feelings. Sophia, who was on her right side, slid an arm around her waist as Logan, who was on her left side, animatedly talked about her earlier conversation with Grant.

"He's really, really proud of me," Logan said recounting Grant's reaction to her news that she'd passed all her courses and would get her diploma.

"He's going to send me something for my birthday and graduation." Logan did a little bounce in her seat. "I know I'm saying the obvious, but I'm really really excited." She turned to Hunter, "Do you think it's a car?" she asked, eyes shining with excitement, her voice a squeal of delight.

Sophia patted Hunter's back. The light touch distracted her for the half-second needed to think before speaking. "I've no idea what your dad is getting you," she said in a measured tone. "However, I'm sure whatever it is, you'll be thrilled with it. I think he hinted around about a new pair of running shoes." Hunter grinned. "Maybe the second part is a new pair of running shorts that are color coordinated with the shoes."

"M-o-o-o-m," Logan drew the word out as only a teenager could do. "You are so-o-o not funny."

"If I may," Sophia said, waiting for Logan's nod before continuing. "Your excitement, your anticipation of what is coming is delightful to see and part of the gift from your dad."

"He just laughed when I tried to trick him into giving me a hint," Logan said, a mock pout pursing her lips.

At that pronouncement, Hunter did laugh. Laughed with tears in her eyes. Laughed and cried at the same time. Memories crowded one another.

"Mom?" Logan's happiness evaporated in an instant with Hunter's tears.

"I'm okay," Hunter said in a shaky voice. "Grant is a master at keeping a secret." *And so am I.* She leaned over and kissed Logan's cheek. "I'm okay. Just remembering something from the past is all."

"About Dad?"

Hunter nodded, not trusting her voice.

After they shared where they were in their lives at that time, they went around the circle one more time with each woman talking directly to Logan.

"It's been amazing to watch you grow and change and become a talented young woman," Lily said.

"Seeing your connection to the Goddess and God strengthen, I know your roots are deep and will keep you anchored as you go forward with your life," Diana added.

"Always remember you are loved by many, for that certain knowledge will sustain you through the dark times that come in everyone's life," Gabby said, leaning forward, her gaze riveted on Logan's.

"Your gifts are many," Ashley said, an arm around Rose. "You can reach others when no one else can and draw them back to the light. Always know how grateful I am for that."

"And I'm really proud of you, Logan," Rose said. "I love you lots." Rose slipped away from her mom, came around to Logan and launched herself into Logan's arms. A smacking kiss on the cheek was followed by "I really really love you."

She jumped off Logan's lap and continued around until she once again sat next to her mom. "We should have a sleepover. We haven't done that in forever."

Logan squirmed in her seat, struggled to maintain eye contact with each woman who spoke to her. Her whispered 'thank you' barely heard even by Hunter who sat next to her. There was something about Rose's exuberance that helped her accept the love being offered. "We'll figure something out over dessert, okay?" Logan finally said to Rose.

When Rose happily nodded, Sophia said, "Your commitment to finishing your group projects early enough so the others were not inconvenienced, your commitment to graduating, the time and energy, the dedicated hours you spent catching up and showing your teachers you deserved to have that diploma were inspiring. I know you didn't do all that in a vacuum, I know you had support and encouragement at all times, but still—there are other people young and old who, even with support and encouragement, do not have the perseverance to stay the course.

"While we all know while you were gone there were dark times, it isn't important for any of us to know the details. What is important is for you to remember that if you can move far enough beyond whatever happened to you to accomplish all you have, there is nothing you can't do if you decide to do it."

Hunter put her arm around Logan and gave her a side-hug. "Always remember I love you." She looked over at Lily and smiled. "Wherever you are, when you look into the night sky, always know I see the same Grandmother moon, the same stars and I'm sending my love to you wherever you may be."

Logan turned and wrapped her arms around her mom. With her head on Hunter's shoulder, she looked around at the other women. "I am so very blessed to have each of you in my life. Knowing I am loved by many has made a real difference. When I go to bed, I fall asleep with your names drifting through my mind "I am loved by many" is how I start and then I whisper your names."

Hunter patted Sophia's knee. "I don't know where we'd be if you hadn't sent that flyer out all those years ago. Each of you has been and is a blessing in our lives."

"Blessed Be," Lily said. The sacred words were murmured by

everyone except for Rose. "Blessed Be," she said loudly a beaming smile on her face.

A MESSAGE from Grant was on her voicemail. Looking at the clock and factoring in the time difference, she decided to call him the next day. The next morning she saw he'd left another message on the office answering machine. Figuring he'd be sleeping in or out for a run, she waited until evening his time to call.

He answered on the second ring. "Can't talk, will call you later." The silence reinforced the fact he'd hung up. *What's going on?* She'd heard other voices in the background. *A party?* No music or at least she didn't think there was music. *Of course, some social event. Weekends were full of back-to-back social events.*

She noticed her cell phone needed charging. Plugging it in to the charger in the living room, she busied herself with housekeeping. While Logan vacuumed and dusted, she wiped down the kitchen and bathroom and together they did the laundry. One of the things she'd like to do was add a laundry area upstairs. As it was they used the washer and dryer connected to the studio.

Tired both emotionally and physically, once the last load of laundry was folded and put away, she dropped into bed and was asleep before she pulled the covers up.

WHY DOESN'T SHE ANSWER? Grant checked the time, did the easy math. "I should have left the table and talked to her when she called," he muttered. Of course he knew why he hadn't done that. He wasn't prepared for the inquisition that would follow. Even saying it was work related would only have reduced the questions from three dozen to one.

Grant ran a hand through his rumpled hair, wished for a glass of scotch but reminded himself he hadn't needed a drink while in Fremont. Here he had the habit of ending the day with a drink in his hand. Right now heading out to the shore, taking a run along the sand, clearing his head seemed the best way to deal with the restlessness.

His mother's words as she'd pecked him on the cheek when he left still irritated. "Your mood needs improvement. If you were going home to a wife I'm sure it would," she'd said.

The implication that sex would make it all better soured the already difficult evening. His mother had not invited several single women, no, she'd hit him with a sledge hammer by inviting three couples (constraint on her side). He'd dated them all. One he'd lived with for three years. The other two he'd had flings with. The less than subtle message was 'see what you're missing?'. He also knew the husbands. Knew they knew of his previous involvement with their wives. They were a bit cool towards him, often touched their wives, the clear message 'hands off.'

As if. I've never been involved with a married woman. His mother's plan had more than backfired, it had exploded. More than ever he was determined to never marry anyone she picked out.

Turning away from the window, he strode to the bedroom he used as a home office and unlocked his briefcase. The photo album was buried beneath three files he'd brought home. Grant took it back to the living room, turned on the gas fireplace and slouched in the leather chair semi-facing the flames.

At this point he didn't even have to open it to see the pictures he'd leafed through and stared at so many times. He loved looking at Logan. He picked up his cell phone and tapped in the code before clicking through and listening to voice mails.

Grant held the phone to his ear as he opened the cover and turned the pages. He had changed their order. Logan's pictures were first. Hunter's were in a second section and the few of the three of them in the very back. He listened to Logan's messages. He'd heard them so many times he knew them by heart. Listening to her voice, seeing her pictures was a painful exercise and yet he did it several times each day.

Pitiful. He was pitiful. He was pitiful and miserable. He couldn't even say he was loved by many. "I am loved by my daughter." He turned to the picture of her in her running outfit, hair in disarray, a brilliant smile on her face. Hands on her hips, she'd turned back when she'd beat him. Her exuberance magnificent. He missed her fiercely.

What are you going to do about it? His short list was send her a ticket to come see him. Until he had some time to show her around, that wasn't wise. What would she do each day while he was at the office for ten to twelve hours? He certainly didn't want to leave her to his mother. His other option was to fly out to Fremont. He could do that for a long weekend.

Next weekend was Memorial Day Weekend and with Logan's birthday on May 31, the urge to spend the time there surged. His mother had a house party planned at their place at the shore and expected, actually she'd demanded, he be in attendance. *And are you looking forward to attending?* No, he wasn't.

It should be a no brainer to head out for the long weekend and celebrate my daughter's birthday. But it wasn't that easy. Between the relentless pressure at the firm and from his parents to conform, to pop back into the mold, to become his old self, sleep was elusive as was his appetite. If he took off there would be even more pressure, more of his parents' interference.

Maybe if Logan came out? *I could ask Karen to show her around when I was working.*

Grant looked at the phone, willing it to ring. It didn't. Frustration tightened his muscles and he got up from the chair. The condo had an indoor pool and workout room. He changed into a pair of dark blue trunks, pulled on a matching set of sweats and tennis shoes. In the elevator he punched the button for the amenities floor.

He caught sight of himself in the full length mirror just inside the locker room. An image of him in well-used sweats he'd picked up at a thrift shop in Fremont juxtaposed with the image in the mirror. *Damn I look good.* He forced a toothy smile. It faded. *Damn I feel like crap.* He looked at the well-dressed, successful and to some, handsome man in the mirror. Truth was he was miserable. Caught between the routine of habit and years of just doing what was expected, Grant looked at the blue-grey eyes of the man in the mirror and saw loneliness and misery.

Ninety minutes later, he didn't even look because he hadn't changed. He'd worn himself out with swimming laps and racing five miles on the treadmill.

His mind worried the possibilities. In the end, he determined that until Logan made and acted on a decision, he'd stay put. The last thing he needed was to be in Oregon with his daughter in Massachusetts.

Back in his condo, he didn't pick up the album. Once in bed, his mind opened the cover. He went all the way through this time, falling asleep with the picture on the last page—the three of them. He was in the middle, Logan and Hunter on each side, his arms around their shoulders, wide grins on their faces they posed as a stranger took the shot. The backdrop Multnomah Falls. The roar of the water crashing into the pool lulled him to sleep.

37 - MEMORIAL DAY WEEKEND

*H*unter tried calling Grant the next day. The message he'd left last night while she and Logan were over at Sophia's baking cinnamon rolls was terse. "Sorry I couldn't talk. Call me." A second message an hour later "Sorry I missed you again. I'll try tomorrow."

Taking the initiative didn't help. Grant didn't pick up when she called him. He did call Monday night but she had a second class for her students because the Spring Recital was fast approaching and everyone needed a little more time. Upstairs after class she checked her phone. He'd left two messages. The second saying he wouldn't be available after midnight his time—it was five after nine when she heard that message. He'd sounded tired, exhausted, stressed, worn out or worn down—she moved the charger next to her bed and plugged her phone in.

Tuesday she was in the shower when he called the first time. She was in the bathroom when he called the second time. Both messages ended with, "It's crazy around here. I'll try later."

Grant had sent emails to Logan during this time but they arrived in the wee hours of the morning Fremont time.

"Dad's having a hard time," Logan commented Tuesday night as they fixed a salad for dinner.

"He does seem to be very busy," she'd replied.

"I miss him," Logan said. "I wish he were here."

Hunter missed him too. It had been easier with him around because he engaged Logan, did things with her so she wasn't left alone. Now that she'd completed all of her assignments, she didn't have a study routine. Charlie, Lily's son, was coming home for Memorial Day Weekend. Hunter hoped when Logan saw Charlie, he could pull her out of her shell, help her ease back into her old life. She still had not reengaged with any of her high school friends.

On a few of their runs on the path around the park, they'd seen a few of Logan's friends in the distance. A wave was all she'd managed.

An intense restlessness consumed the remainder of Hunter's day and long into the night.

While she wanted Logan to reclaim her old life, she was realistic enough to know it might not happen in Fremont. If she did go to Smith College, Diana's son Bill was a student at Boston College so she'd know someone in the area. Grant was a couple of hours away and Eleanor had mentioned Jackson's sisters and their families would welcome Logan into their homes, especially on weekends.

Hunter pasted a smile on her face, fought the jealousy, argued with the fear her daughter would no longer want her or be close to her. *I need to talk to Lily and Diana. They've great relationships with their sons now.* "And," she reminded herself, "you have a great relationship with your daughter. Stop creating trouble."

Wednesday she waved at her last student and locked the door. Turning off the lights in the front office and in the studio on her way to the back stairs, her phone rang.

She sat on the bottom steps and answered.

"Made it," Grant said, his exhaustion weighting his words.

"I just said goodbye to my last student. You sound beat."

"Where are you?" Grant asked.

"Sitting on the third step from the bottom in back, where are you?"

"Sitting on a bench a block away from my place."

"It's ten o'clock there."

"Yep, I mean yes, it is."

"Grant, are you okay?" Hunter hunched over the phone, pressing it closer to her ear as if in that position she was closer to him

"Just tired," he said in a bone-weary voice.

"I'm flattered you've made so many efforts to reach me and sorry our schedules are so disparate but shouldn't you be in bed?" She stood and paced down the hall to the front door and back.

"When we've talked, I'll do that. I'm sure you'll think I'm paranoid but I don't feel like I can call and talk to you in my condo much less the office."

Hunter stopped. "Do you think someone planted one of those listening devices?"

"My parents are acting very strange. Something's up but I don't know what."

"So you're sitting on a bench in the city park a few blocks from your place so you can talk to me without being overheard. Did I get that right?"

"Yeah, I mean, yes."

"Grant, stop correcting yourself." Hunter continued to pace, one hand holding the phone to her ear, the other wrapped tightly across her waist.

"Habit," he said.

"One you can break any time."

"Hello, officer," Grant said in the distance.

Hunter could tell he no longer held the phone up because many of the words were indistinct.

"What are you doing this weekend?" he asked now back with her.

"Charlie's coming home. He's Lily's son. I know he and Logan will be hanging out. I'm figuring I'll be spending some time over there also, why?"

"May I come see you?"

Hunter heard the words and also the anguish underneath. "You are welcome here in Fremont whenever you want to come. I know there is room at Lily's and Diana's."

"Don't want to put anyone out. I can get a motel again."

"Grant, let us know your flight and we'll pick you up. Do not make a reservation anywhere. We'll work it all out when you get here."

"Are you sure you don't have plans?"

"I'm sure I don't have any plans that can't easily include you," Hunter said. "And remember, you are missed by many."

"I'll try to remember that. And thank you. I'm just incredibly tired right now."

"Come as early as you can and stay as long as you can—Logan misses you."

"And you?"

He spoke in such a soft voice she could have pretended she didn't hear him but she'd told him the truth. He was missed by many and she was one of them.

"I am one of the many who miss you." Her voice soft, she added, "See you very soon."

Hunter paced up and down the hall, considered going into her studio and drumming, movement was what she needed. Movement would quell this restlessness. Jogging up the stairs she saw Logan hanging back.

"I didn't mean to eavesdrop." She looked guilty. "You were talking to Dad?"

"I was. He's coming for a visit over Memorial Day Weekend. If he comes in earlier on Friday, you'll have to pick him up while I'm teaching. Will that be okay with you?"

"You'll let me drive by myself?"

"You do have your license." Hunter draped an arm around Logan's shoulders. "You have a license, you know where the airport is, you know what your dad looks like—I think you are the perfect one to pick him up if I'm unable to."

"I think Dad would be happier staying with Lily and Jackson. Madison Michelle still wakes up in the middle of the night crying."

"They'll have Charlie home," Hunter said.

"But the downstairs has two bedrooms and an office and the upstairs has the bedroom at the top of the stairs. Charlie stays in the downstairs bedroom next to the doors out to the lower deck. Dad can stay upstairs, you know in the room Lily was in after her accident."

"We'll check with them and see if that works out." Hunter patted Logan's back. "If we need to, you and I can double up and your dad can have your room."

"Really?! Really, Mom? You'd let Dad stay here?" Logan bounced with excitement. "That would be awesome."

"It will be a challenge with three of us and one bathroom." Hunter smiled. "We may have to put a timer in there for you."

"I'd be really quick if Dad was here," Logan started, before she caught the twinkle in her mom's eyes. She turned and hugged Hunter tight. "I love you so much, Mom." She stepped back, rested her hands on Hunter's shoulders. "Even when you tease me like that I still love you." She leaned in and kissed Hunter's cheek. Moving on into the kitchen she called out, "I'm making grilled tuna sandwiches for dinner, okay?"

"Sounds perfect."

GRANT REFUSED to look at his reflection as he strode through the airport in the early hours of Saturday morning. He'd taken the last plane out of New York Friday night, literally running to catch it before boarding closed. No first class seat, he was scrunched in the middle of a five seat row. Of course every seat was filled, he had no leg room, he couldn't even stretch. It was the longest flight of his entire life.

He said he'd call when the plane landed and meet them on the arriving flights level.

"Dad, Dad, Dad," he'd heard someone calling as he strode past security and on into the terminal.

"Grant?"

That stopped him in his tracks. He turned just in time to brace himself for Logan's launch. She wrapped her arms around him and hugged him so tight it hurt to breathe. Over her head he saw Hunter, a worried look in her eyes.

"You look dead on your feet." She took Logan's arm. "Let's get your dad out of here."

Logan stepped back and looked at Grant. "You look awful. Are you sick?"

"A little sleep, a hot shower and shave and I'll be good as new." The truth of those words evoked little energy. He'd made it to Fremont, to his family and that was enough. Logan's constant chatter as they made their way out of the airport distracted him from his exhaustion. No need to stop by baggage claim, he hadn't brought much, his laptop, a couple changes of clothes—all in his carryon.

He'd worn his tennis shoes, been seen in public in a pair of jeans albeit his good ones, a chambray shirt, again newish, no tie, in need of a shave because he was in a hurry and didn't take the time to do that before he rushed to the train station and on into New York.

The world still turned.

Martha would be there Tuesday morning as usual. His calendar showed no client appointments until one. If he flew out Tuesday on the first plane, he could make it to his condo, change and be on time for the meeting.

He'd put a new out-going message on his voice mail saying he was unavailable until Wednesday. An email to his parents said he wasn't feeling well and was turning his cell phone off until Tuesday. Trotter, the doorman's instructions? "Mr. Parker is not to be disturbed under any circumstances." He could only hope the ruse worked.

A feeling of dread underlay all his cloak and dagger thinking. Here in Fremont he hoped to have the space and freedom to sort it out.

At the car, a simple request. "Let me sit in back. I know you live close but I need a short nap so I can complete sentences."

Logan drove. He remained conscious enough to compliment her on her driving before his head nodded and he slept.

When he woke, the smell of coffee tantalized. "Where? What?"

"We're almost to the Montgomery House." Hunter handed a cup of coffee back to him.

"Is this the real thing or decaf?"

"The real thing with a double shot of espresso," Logan said.

He reached for the cup making sure he had a firm grasp before nodding to Hunter. "You may want to hold off and not drink that if you want to sleep a bit more. We can heat it up later in the microwave."

"I'll be okay," he said.

"You look worse than I've ever seen you. What's going on?"

She looked at him with such compassion. *She would understand.* "Promise to wake me at noon?"

"Promise." She reached back for the coffee. "A wise decision."

Jackson met them at the door, pointed to the stairs and followed him up. The door to the room at the top of the stairs was open. He turned to thank him and realized he didn't have his laptop or carry-on.

"Here you go, Dad," Logan said, following Jackson in and carrying his luggage. "You get some sleep. We'll wake you at noon. That's a promise." She put his laptop on a small table next to the door and his carry-on at the foot of the bed.

"Bathroom's through there." Jackson pointed him, literally turned him so the door to the bathroom was in front of him. "Fresh towels, razor, whatever. If you don't find it ask, I'm sure we have it.

"We'll check on you at noon but don't count on a huge effort to wake you. You look like hell." Jackson clapped him on the back. "We'll try to send you back looking human."

Grant used the bathroom, washed his face and hands, stripped down and because he figured Logan would come in and check on him, pulled on a pair of sweat pants.

At some point he heard voices, maybe heard his name? Paralyzed by the drug of deep sleep, he didn't respond.

It was three o'clock when he did open his eyes. He'd missed three more hours with his daughter, with Hunter. Opening his eyes, she was there.

"Coffee?" Hunter held a steaming cup of coffee but did not hand it to him.

He struggled to untangle himself from the sheets and realized they weren't wrapped around him as they had been every night at the condo. Maybe he wasn't refreshed but he was better. Just seeing her—.

Which meant she was seeing him. He needed a shower, a shave, clean clothes—the list sped through his mind in a flash.

"You do need clothes and you could comb your hair. Otherwise, you're fine."

How did she know? But of course she did. It was why he had come. He needed someone who understood.

Hunter handed him the coffee, he sipped the steaming liquid. "I burned my lips. Kiss them and make them better?"

She laughed, a genuine light laugh. "Put some chap stick on them and they'll be just fine." She backed away, laughter dancing in her eyes. She twirled once before she reached the door. "Most everyone is here. Some are downstairs, all the way down, watching movies. The rest of us are hanging out on the deck off the dining room trying to decide what to do for dinner. Jackson is considering grilling hamburgers. What do you think?"

What did he do when there was a group of friends around? He fixed drinks, circulated, chatted. What would he do here?

"Stop thinking, Grant. Do you want hamburgers or steak?"

"What's easiest? I don't want anyone to go to more trouble."

"With Charlie, Sophia, Diana and Matthew and the baby, Ashley, Daniel, Rose, Anthony and James, Gabriella, Logan and me here, adding a hamburger or steak for you isn't going to create a problem." She'd ticked the names off on her fingers.

Framed in the doorway, she paused, her gaze locked with his. "It's just a decision about steak or hamburger. What else is worrying you?"

"I'm just uncomfortable. I show up and everything is out of—,"

A soft smile of understanding curved her lips. "Worried the numbers are off here?"

Grant shrugged.

"We don't care if there are the same number of men and women at the table or they are alternated in the seating. Here, the only expectation of you is that you state your preference, whatever that is. So, the question remains—hamburger or steak?"

"Is it really that simple? All the time is it really that simple?"

"Pretty much. If there is an expectation, you know in advance as in "everybody bring something we're having a potluck" but that isn't what's happening today."

Grant watched Hunter and listened carefully to the words for any underlying message. He didn't hear any.

"It may surprise you with our past and all, but I think everyone genuinely likes you. I've never seen Jackson, Daniel or Matthew welcome someone they didn't like. I've seen them polite but you know that is very different than welcoming."

Grant nodded in agreement. "I'm taking a quick shower and shaving because I'll feel cleaner if I do. Should be there in twenty."

"I'll time you." Hunter started out of the room. "Nope, I'll tell Logan to time you." Her laughter floated through the air as she closed the door.

Showered, shaved, clean clothes on, he was still tired but the utter exhaustion was gone. A squeak when he opened the door. Logan stood on the other side, hand raised to knock.

"You're late," she announced.

"You're early," he replied.

"Am not," she said and danced away.

"Are too," he said and grabbed for her.

She turned and scampered down the stairs calling out as she went. "Dad's up. Charlie, come meet my dad."

Halfway down the stairs, he looked over the railing. Logan had a young man by the hand, dragging him along—Charlie. He could see bits and pieces of Lily in him. *Can people see bits and pieces of me in Logan?*

At the bottom of the stairs, Logan stood to one side, "Dad, this is my friend, Charlie Hughes. Charlie, this is my dad, Grant." She looked up at him. "Should I use your whole name? I know I'm supposed to introduce the older person to the younger one."

"Grant is fine." He held his hand out and shook Charlie's hand. "So you're home for the weekend? How far away is your school?"

And that was that. As he walked towards the group on the deck he reviewed his impressions of Charlie, especially his impressions of Charlie and his daughter. *They're just friends.* He accepted a beer from Matthew. *But Hunter and I started off like that—just friends.*

Logan and Charlie darted off when the next movie was slated to start.

"Who all is down there?" he asked Hunter, a ridge of tension shifting down his spine.

"What do you mean?" she asked the clarifying question before answering.

They were standing next to each other on the upper deck looking out at the view.

"Downstairs? Is there an adult down there?"

Hunter gave him a strange look. "Grant, Charlie and Logan are down there with James, Anthony and Rose. Nothing is going to happen. And, Daniel pops down every so often to see if they 'need' anything." She quirked her fingers around the one word.

She leaned into him, rested her shoulder against his. "Relax, Dad. Logan is fine. She hasn't had a panic attack when with any of us for over a week. She feels safe with everyone who is here. And just so you know, as an added precaution they are only watching PG movies."

He hung out with Jackson and studiously watched as the charcoal was laid just so and the fire built until the coals were raked out to cover the bottom of the grill. There was wine and beer, soft drinks, iced tea, tonics of various flavors. It was 'help yourself' although he did notice whoever was making a kitchen run announced that and offered to bring things back.

Jackson took orders and cooked hamburgers to the individual's preference. Grant liked his medium rare and so did Jackson. Theirs were cooked last. Potato, pasta and tossed green salads were on the breakfast bar along with pickles, olives, slices of tomato, onion, avocado. If someone wanted cheese, Jackson added it just before the meat came off the grill so it was melted just a bit.

Grant had Jackson add a slice of horseradish cheddar to his burger. By the time he'd added the extras, he knew he couldn't take a bite without making a mess.

"Just squish it together and take a bite. Make sure you have several paper napkins. Don't worry, Grant," Hunter said coming to stand beside him. "Look at Matthew." She nodded towards Diana's husband who was just sinking his teeth into a towering hamburger.

He chewed and swallowed. "Best burger ever, Jackson," Matthew said before taking another bite.

Grant looked around him. No one was using a knife and fork. No one was taking a dainty bite. No one was worried about a drip of sauce on their hand much less their plate.

"Like this?" Grant pressed the top bun down on the rest of the ingredients, picked it up, chose a spot and bit down. His eyes closed in bliss as the flavors of meat and grease and horseradish, onions, pickles, lettuce tomato—well, everything he'd added melded in his mouth.

Who knew eating a homemade hamburger could be so decadent? So freeing? Even life changing?

Monday morning Grant woke to Logan's voice calling him from the other side of the bedroom door. He'd initially thought he'd stay at the Montgomery's Saturday night because he was so tired. Sunday had been a relaxed day of hanging out with the men while the women had one of their circle meetings. He still didn't understand exactly what they did.

The men were at Daniels and the women at Sophia's. The Men included James, Anthony and Charlie. The Women included Rose, Logan and Madison Michelle. A couple hours passed and they loaded into two cars—he joined Daniel, Matthew and Jackson in Daniel's extended cab truck. Charlie drove Jackson's black Jaguar with James and Anthony. Where? To Sophia's where a potluck was in progress. Tables and chairs set on Sophia's patio provided a relaxed place to capture a beautiful day.

Plates full, the other men paired up by sitting next to or near their wives. He decided to "go with it" and settled between Logan and Hunter.

He carefully listened as they discussed Summer Solstice and everyone going to Ireland. He remembered one of the women, Elizabeth, lived there with her husband, Michael. That was also Lily and

Jackson's wedding anniversary—their third. The energy flowing between them clearly said "you are the one."

Each of the men seemed to have a particularly close and intense connection with their wives. So connected the men seemed to know when something was needed.

Matthew picked Madison Michelle up and went inside. Diana had not said a word or even leaned towards him or handed him the baby. *Had she even started to get up herself?* Daniel stepped away and checked on the children. *Maybe they have a secret code and Ashley tapped his foot under the table?*

Would he ever be that tuned in to another person much less a woman? *I am.*

Hunter leaned close. "What's so funny?"

"Not funny," he responded in a quiet voice. "I just realized something about myself that I like."

Hunter leaned away her brows scrunched as she perused his face. "Whatever it is, it looks good on you."

He relaxed back in his chair, cognizant he did have that connection with Logan and Hunter. Perhaps not as deep as the other men, but he did know when they were happy, worried, upset. Of course he always knew when his parents were upset and angry. What was different was he knew when the people around him right now were happy, content, pleased.

People he knew back home said or acted as if they were happy, content, pleased. He'd come to distrust that those were real feelings. Here on Sophia's patio, surrounded by people who in many ways were strangers, he trusted the faces they showed him.

Sunday night, back at the Montgomery's, he stood out on the deck, Hunter by his side. Logan was downstairs watching movies with Charlie. He no longer worried his daughter was in danger. They were friends and right now, nothing more than that. A memory from long ago of being friends with the woman beside him warmed. He stepped closer and put his arm around Hunter's shoulder.

"I was just remembering when we were friends."

"Those were special days." Hunter leaned against him. "I remember those times and rebelled against them coming to an end."

"Was I part of your rebellion?" Grant breathed in her spicy scent, relished the weight of her against his side.

"No." Hunter shifted and lifted her face so she could see his. "No, you were not part of my rebellion."

Time to be honest. "When I left to go back to school, I got sucked back into the insanity. I believe you saw me with some other woman but I have no memory of it. I should have searched for you but it was easier to believe the story you'd decided to finish your schooling in Europe. I know I failed you, failed us." Grant held her close.

"Just before I left for Rhode Island I was out on a run at the park close to your place. I saw a mother pushing her child on a swing. That simple act reminded me of all I've missed in Logan's life." He felt her stiffen. "Please listen." He waited until she relaxed.

"Go on."

"Think Hunter. Think about what our life would have been back then. What would the chances have been for either of us to take our daughter to the park on a sunny afternoon to play on the swing? It occurred to me you might have accomplished that from time to time, maybe even once a week. But where would I have been?

"Where I have been. At the office. Working sixty hour weeks. And time off? I've never had a true vacation until I came here to Fremont."

Hunter frowned. "What do you mean?"

"My vacations were always connected to business. The skiing trips to Gstaad were scheduled so I could cozy up to prospective clients; weekends at the shore spent entertaining current clients. Work always in the back of my mind if not the forefront—until I came here."

"What's happening back home now?" Hunter asked. Her stomach was queasy and her eyes watery because she knew he spoke the truth. She would have been on several committees, doing charity work, courting the wives of potential clients, etc. She'd watched her mother and even Grant's mother live those lives.

"Mother throws every single woman of a marriageable age in my direction. Most recently she had a dinner and invited women I used to date along with their husbands just to show me what I'm missing. Father thinks I need a mistress."

"And you? What do you think you need?"

He wanted to say 'you' or 'you and Logan' but it was more than that. "I need breathing room. I need time to just be myself and do what I want. I need time to jog along the shore and watch the sunrise or the sunset. Does that sound crazy?"

"No. The crazy part is you thinking that could happen there. Neither your parents nor the firm will accept that you should have, much less deserve, a life of your own making. It just isn't the way things are done. At least not how I remember it."

"I know I want you and Logan in my life. Exactly how that will happen, I'm not sure. Logan still wants to go to Smith and if she does, I want to be close to her."

"And, I'd feel better if you were closer if Logan does go to Smith. She would be delighted to have a dad come see her on campus and do dad things with her." Hunter said the words without a shaky voice, without tears, without a queasy stomach. She settled back against his side.

They were both startled at the sound of the doorbell ringing. Grant glanced at his watch. It was nine.

Dread snaked through his bowels as the voice at the door registered. *How the hell?!?*

Hunter turned, a shocked looked on her face. "What have you done?" She cried out, pulled away and darted down the steps to the deck below.

Pounding on the lower door, her urgent voice called out to open the door.

Her voice dimmed.

Grant knew her mind was racing with ways to hide Logan.

Jackson's voice. "You've got company."

"I heard." Grant took a step towards the door. He paused next to Jackson. "I've no idea how they found out whatever they think they've found out."

In the dining room, Grant saw his parents propping suitcases along the wall and taking coats off. "I'll get them out of here," he muttered to Jackson who'd followed him into the house.

"Mother, Father, don't bother taking your things off." Grant strode across the room. He ignored his mother's offered cheek and his father's outstretched hand. "Did you rent a car?" He didn't even wait to see their answer. His phone out, he dialed the cab company and ordered a taxi. Lily, who was closest, gave him the house number. Did he see sympathy in her eyes? Jackson's were bright with fury.

"We'll wait outside." Grant grabbed his mother's suitcase and opened the front door. He stood to the side, an expectant look on his face.

"I will not be treated this way," she said in her most formidable tone. "Especially not by you." She spat the last word. "My son the lying hypocrite."

"Outside Mother," he ordered. "We will finish this discussion in private."

The room was quiet as a graveyard. His lungs failed to fully expand, his heart beat slowed, he was dying inside.

Glaring at his parents, Grant stood ramrod straight by the door and waited. Neither his mother nor his father moved.

"Who is she?" His father hurled the words into the silence.

"Out now!" Grant stabbed at the doorway. "I will not discuss anything with either of you here."

"It's all right, Grant," Hunter said, appearing from the downstairs, her hand on his arm. She turned to his parents, "Mrs. Parker, Mr. Parker."

His mother scowled. "Honey? Honey Knight Compton? You are a disgrace to your family's name. Why your poor mother—."

"Mother, listen to me and listen well. If you ever want me to set foot in your house again, you will cease speaking, pick up your purse and leave."

"Your mother is very ill. She may not live much longer," his mother said while she picked up her purse, took a step towards the door and waited.

"Thank you for sharing that," Hunter said in a lofty formal tone. "I do appreciate your having coming all this way to inform me."

"The taxi is here," Grant announced as a pair of headlights swung into the driveway.

He looked up to make sure his father was coming and saw Logan peeking around the corner, tears streaming down her face. Discombobulated by the sight, he glanced at Hunter who'd also seen their daughter.

"Get them out of here," she muttered in an aside to him.

He was a dead man.

"Again, thank you for bringing the news of my mother to me in person," Hunter said ushering both Mr. and Mrs. Parker out the door.

HUNTER SHUT the door behind Grant, careful not to slam it. Tears streamed down her cheeks. *How could he?* was mixed with *Did he know?* was mixed with *He didn't know.* She was angry and confused and hurt and—beneath it all the sense of betrayal.

"Mom, were those people my grandparents?" Logan stood, hands fisted on her hips, chin jutted in anger, her eyes shone with pain.

"Let's see if we can move away from the door and, perhaps, even sit down," Lily coached, nudging Hunter towards the living room couch.

"Come on, Logan," Charlie said. "We'll see what's going on together."

A sullen Logan marched to a chair across from the couch where her mom now sat. She plopped down, arms folded a mutinous look on her face.

Lily rubbed a soothing circle on Hunter's back, accepted a mug of tea from Jackson and set it within easy reach on the coffee table. Jackson handed Logan and Charlie glasses with juice diluted with seltzer water, a favorite of theirs. He returned with a mug of tea for Lily and his own glass of water. He sat halfway between the four, sipped his drink and waited.

The silence was uncomfortable. Hunter knew if she didn't speak, Lily would—eventually. But what to say? The betrayal in Logan's posture, in her eyes cut her to her core. *How could he!? How could he do this to me? How could he betray me? How could he abandon me?*

"I don't even know where to begin." Bile in Hunter's stomach threatened to make a hurling appearance. Sitting rigidly straight, hands locked so tightly together her knuckles were white, so tightly together she couldn't reach for her cup of tea. If she let go, even an inch, she'd unravel.

"Who were those people?" Logan enunciated each word.

"They are Mr. and Mrs. Grant Hayward Parker the Third. He goes by "Three" and she goes by "Mrs. Three"."

"So they are my grandparents." Logan sagged back against the pillowed chair, the anger leeching out.

"Yes," Hunter said, watching the anger leave.

"So Dad is ashamed of me," Logan said, despair filling in the cracks where anger had been.

"No!" Hunter leapt up, crossed and kneeled before Logan. "No, that is not it at all." She reached and held Logan's hand even when she tried to pull away. "Your dad is not ashamed of you. He's very, very proud of you."

Logan jerked away, the despair gone, confused anger paramount. "Then why didn't he want them to meet me? Why did he take them away?"

Charlie put his arm around Logan. "I think I know the answer to that." He looked at Hunter who nodded.

"You see, when I wanted to go live with my dad in Ohio, it about tore my mom apart. She and Dad didn't get along and she worried about me. Really, really worried," he emphasized.

"We were already doing things with The Circle and you know how careful we are about whom we share some of that stuff with." He waited. Gave Logan's shoulder a little jiggle. When she nodded, he continued.

"I saw your dad Saturday when he first got here. He was a mess. You were worried about him, right?"

Logan nodded.

"So, think about it, Logan. Where had he been? Who had he been with? What had happened to tear him up like that? My guess is he was with his family and whatever happened there is why he was in such bad shape.

"When I was first in Ohio with my dad, it was like walking on—not egg shells because the egg is already broken—but raw eggs hoping nothing broke. Of course they did. No matter how good I tried to be, I wasn't good enough. Dad would get mad, he'd yell and say mean things about Mom and how she didn't raise me right and if I didn't do as they did I'd end up a loser and wasn't it a good thing I'd come there so they could whip me into shape."

Hunter had moved back to the couch when she realized Charlie had more to say than a sentence or two. She grabbed Lily's hand knowing this was the first time she'd heard this truth.

"I know there were times Mom felt I'd betrayed her because in some ways I had. Maybe not at the core but that first year, I never stood up to my dad and told him not to talk about my mom that way. I never did that until I saw Bill take his dad on.

"And, I still pick my battles with my dad. He will never change his mind about Mom because he thinks she lied to him and tricked him into marrying her—well, that's a story for another day or maybe one that never needs telling." Charlie glanced over at his mom.

"What I want to say is, your mom loves you and always has. And I'd bet your dad loves you too. I don't know why they want to protect you or even what they want to protect you from, but my guess is that's what's going on.

"What parents don't always get is that sometimes we have to experience something on our own, get bumps and bruises, get knocked down so we can learn to get back up. Sometimes protecting us isn't the best thing to do. Sometimes like when we're learning to walk or ride a bike, they need to let us try and be there to catch us when we fall."

Charlie stopped talking but remained next to Logan, his arm around her.

"You are very wise, Charlie," Hunter said, still gripping Lily's hand. "Do you know how hard it is to push the bike and then take your hands off, see your child wobble and even fall? To kiss the scrapes and bruises and stand by when they want to try again?"

Charlie shook his head. "I'm guessing at some point in my life I will."

"It's one of the hardest things I think a parent does. But it's also a necessary part of being a parent." Hunter took a shaky breath, her gaze moved from Charlie to Logan.

"I will do my best to explain what my fears are if you spend time with either Grant's parents or mine," she said.

Jackson rose. "Someone's here." He crossed to the door and opened it. Grant stood alone on the other side.

"May I come in?"

Jackson stepped aside.

Striding across to the chair where Logan sat, he squatted in front of her. "I'm so very sorry. I never meant to hurt you. My parents are not always very nice people and I just didn't want you to have to deal with that."

"I can handle it, Dad." Logan raised her head and looked over at Hunter. "I'm eighteen and it should be my choice whether I meet and get to know my grandparents or not—." She stopped, looked back at Grant, "Do you think they really want to meet me?"

The urge to look over at Hunter was strong but he held his daughter's gaze. "We'll find out tomorrow. The only way I could break away from them and not have them follow me back here was to arrange to have breakfast with them at the hotel. A public place will help keep them at least polite if not welcoming."

"They don't want me?" Logan said, her voice trembling.

"Right now they don't know about you," Grant said. "I just wanted to protect you from the nastiness that comes with being around them."

Hunter sat on the arm of the chair next to Logan. "So, tomorrow will be like riding that bike with your dad and me there in case you fall. We'll catch you and dust you off. Be prepared for us to discourage you from getting back on."

At Grant's quizzical look she added, "Charlie had a story he told about parents trying to protect their kids but that sometimes it's important for them to learn how to deal with the scrapes and bruises of a fall."

"I get it." Grant stood, held out his hand and shook Charlie's. "Well done."

The somber mood mellowed. Jackson had come to Lily's side and was whispering in her ear. She nodded, slipped an arm around his waist and laid her head on his shoulder.

Hunter and Grant were flanking Logan who was hugging Charlie. When Logan stepped back, Charlie gave her a thumbs up and stepped to his mom's side.

"I'd like to see you home," Grant said. "Actually I just want more time with you both before breakfast."

"We'll be fine, Grant," Hunter said, "Get some sleep. We'll pick you up at eight so we can easily talk before meeting your parents at the hotel at nine."

Logan approached and gave him a hard hug. "I can handle it Dad. Don't worry about me."

"I missed a lot of years of worry so that means I have to worry more and harder and longer than your mom to catch up," Grant said hugging her back.

"You're so funny, Dad." Logan laughed. At the door, instead of going outside with her mom, she turned back. Taking Grant's hands in hers, she leaned close and said "I'm moving forward with my life. They won't stop me from doing that. The worst that can happen is they won't like me. If that happens, I'll still have you and Mom, so I'll be okay." She squeezed his hands and stepped back. "You're doing a great job as a dad."

Breathing just got difficult, virtually impossible. Moisture welled in his eyes. Frozen feet stuck to the floor. Grant watched his daughter and her mother leave arm in arm. Hunter had the drive home to talk to Logan. He'd be ready with what he had to say come morning.

A hand clapped him on the shoulder. "What about a nightcap?" Jackson said.

Lily and Charlie were on the couch, engaged in an earnest discussion. "They've things to work out right now," Jackson said. "We can go up to my office. Comfortable chairs and a bottle of excellent cognac."

"And are you able to fill me in on what I missed?"

"Not a problem." Jackson gestured towards the stairs. He detoured a few steps, leaned over the back of the couch, gave Lily a kiss and patted Charlie's shoulder.

Hunter was right. There was a difference between being polite and being accepted. He'd had his doubts but no more—here he was accepted. The feelings of betrayal no longer ruled. He had a place to be himself. If nothing else came out of his search for and finding Hunter and Logan, he had that now and it was a gift to treasure, a gift worth more than money or status.

39 - BREAKFAST

The hotel door automatically opened when Grant, Hunter and Logan approached. Not really the jaws of death—much too dramatic an analogy. It was obvious Logan wanted to make a good impression and it was obvious Hunter had talked to her. His daughter was scrubbed clean, a minimum of make-up, her hair straightened with a plain headband holding it away from her face. She wore her best dress, stockings and sandals.

Her mother, on the other hand, wore a free flowing print skirt with a color-coordinated top, long earrings, mascara and lipstick. On her bare feet a pair of sparkly sandals caught the eye as she walked.

He wore what he had: a pair of jeans, a shirt with no tie and his tennis shoes. The hotel was one of the best in town but did not require a tie for their breakfast buffet.

Mr. and Mrs. Parker III were waiting in the lobby for them. They stood when his party came in the door but did not approach. *The better to scrutinize and find fault.*

"Mother, Father, I'd like to introduce you to my daughter, Logan." Grant laid a protective hand on her shoulder. "Logan, Mr. and Mrs. Parker the Third."

"I'm pleased to meet you," Logan said holding out her hand.

"You look just like your mother when she was your age," Grant's mother said. His father stood silent. Neither took Logan's hand.

"You remember my mom?" Logan gestured to her mother.

"Of course I remember, Honey," his mother said, a sniff in her tone.

Introductions complete, he linked his arm through Hunter's and held Logan's hand as they proceeded to the restaurant. Conversation was stilted until, in answer to his mother's question about her future, Logan mentioned considering Smith College.

Not that his mother accepted her newest granddaughter, but she was impressed. Not everyone got into Smith. It was excruciating to watch Logan attempt to meet his parents' unspoken judgement. Of course the 'niceties' were second nature having been drilled into him since childhood. He was secretly pleased when Hunter reached in front of him for the salt instead of asking to have it passed.

His mother's eyebrows arched so high they almost disappeared into her hair line.

"We're a bit more informal here in the west," Hunter said in response to the unspoken criticism.

"Manners, good manners are always in vogue," his mother replied.

"Are you leaving this afternoon?" Grant interjected, looking at his parents.

"We'll go back when you do. We brought the jet," his father replied, a smile playing around his mouth. "Heard you came out coach."

"You heard correctly. Going back the same way," Grant said, earning a direct look of disapproval from Three.

"We'll expect you for dinner then," his mother said.

"I've got plans. I'm not sure when I'll have the time to see you. Work, you know. Shoulder to the grindstone and all."

A sharp jab in his side caught his attention. He glanced over at Hunter. She was not pleased with him. A slight nod in her direction to let her know he'd got the message.

"I may be able to stop by next Sunday." Both of his parents nodded their approval. "However, there is to be no discussion about my daughter or Hunter unless I bring it up."

His mother's mouth opened to object. He didn't give her any time. "If you can't agree, I won't come. If I'm there and you bring them up, I'll leave. No reminders, no second chances. I'll get up, even in the middle of dinner, even in front of your friends and walk out."

"Don't you think that rather harsh?" Three said. "After all we're curious to who this young lady is," he nodded towards Logan, "and what happened to Honey, here."

"If Hunter wants you to know anything about her, she's perfectly capable of telling you. If it's that important to you, ask her yourself.

"As for my daughter, she's off limits to your prying. You may not inquire about her mother through her. And, you may not quiz her about her upbringing or in any way criticize anything about her."

"Dad," Logan said, her hand resting on his arm. "I know you're trying to protect me but I'm okay with them talking to me about stuff. I have a cell phone and they can call me. They can email me, if they do that kind of thing."

Her earnestness lowered his guard.

"Do you really think I want to harm this child?" his mother spoke now. "Really Grant. Have I ever done anything that wasn't for your own good?"

He and Hunter had talked briefly last night and had agreed to pick their battles. She nudged his thigh with hers. This wasn't one of them she messaged.

Three's appetite was not dampened by the undercurrents swirling around the table. His mother picked at her food which was normal. Hunter, who had taken small helpings from the buffet, made a good effort leaving less than a fourth of the meal on her plate. Logan pushed food around and he wasn't sure she'd taken more than a couple of bites. His plate? His plate was untouched. As much as he hated to see the food go to waste, he couldn't eat a bite.

An hour in, Hunter excused herself. His mother popped up. "You can show me where the facilities are." She gestured to Hunter to go first.

He almost went after them but stifled the urge to leap up because that would leave Logan alone to deal with his father's inquisition.

"Where did your name come from? I know your mother's parents but have never heard it before," Three asked Logan.

"You'll have to ask my mother," Logan said. She glanced up at Grant. He smiled back.

"Why do they call you 'Three'?" she asked his father. "That seems strange to go by a number."

"Your father is known as 'Four'," his father said. "We tend to be long-lived so after there were three Grant's in the family, we decided to use the numbers. I'm Grant Hayward Parker the Third. Your father is Grant Hayward Parker the Fourth. When he has a son, he'll be Grant Hayward Parker the Fifth."

"So you'd call him Five?" Logan asked.

His father grinned. "That's the plan. Of course your father has been derelict in his duty to the family. Now that the secret is out and we know about you, he can marry and have that son."

Grant was eternally grateful in that moment he had not eaten anything because he almost lost the water and coffee he'd had when his stomach clenched.

"Here comes Mom," Logan said leaning towards him.

Following his mother, who had a very pleased look on her face was Hunter who did not share the same look.

In fact, Hunter did not sit down when his mother did. "It's been delightful seeing you again after all these years," she said in an icy, formal tone. "Logan, we need to go now. Grant?"

Her toe didn't tap but the coiled energy bubbling inside her was about to explode. He stood, took Hunter's elbow in his hand and rested the other on Logan's shoulder.

"I'm sure you both have a lot to think and talk about on your return trip." He dropped his hand from Logan's shoulder, pulled out his wallet and dropped three twenties on the table. "This should cover our share of the meal."

His hand back on Logan's shoulder, he half-turned away before saying in a lethally quiet voice, "Do talk things over, do think things through. I'm serious about what I said about discussing my private life or the private life of Hunter or Logan. If you want to see me, let me know. Do not," he speared his mother with a look, "Do not expect me to attend any social events until further notice. I will stop by next Sunday for an hour or so if you can refrain from discussing these topics."

"Grant," his mother said, "Don't you think you are being a bit too, oh, I don't know, overbearing? Until I hear Honey and Logan tell me I'm not to speak about them—," she paused a triumphant look on her face.

"If you can speak about them out of the context of my private life, so be it. If they want to talk to you, they can call or email you. My boundary is I will not discuss either of them with you, period."

"Logan," his mother said. "I know Four, I mean Grant, believes he is doing what is best for you. Your grandfather and I would love to have you come and visit, get to know us on your own without his prejudice interfering. Please consider this an open invitation. We'll always have room in our house and in our hearts for you." While speaking, she'd stood and moved behind her husband to stand in front of Logan and press something into her hand.

"We will see you next Sunday, Grant. It was a pleasure seeing you again, Honey. Please think about my offer."

Hunter pushed past him, blocking Logan from his parents as she took her hand and towed her behind, striding towards the door.

Grant didn't look back as he lengthened his stride. He caught up with them in the lobby. Furious tears lit Hunter's eyes. "Where's Logan?"

"She said she had to use the restroom, couldn't wait until we got home." Her toes beat a rapid tattoo on the marble floor.

"What else? What happened when you and my mother were gone?"

"Do you know your mother has a cell phone?" she said through clenched teeth.

He nodded.

"Would it surprise you to know she didn't have to use the restroom? That she used that as a ruse to be alone with me?"

He shook his head and waited.

"She called my mother," Hunter seethed. "Called her and told her she was with me and then shoved the phone at me. I could hear my mother saying something. I put it down on the counter and started to walk out. Your mother said "your mother is dying, won't you talk to her and make amends with her?

"Did you know that?" Hunter spoke in a low furious tone, tears streaming down her cheeks. "Did you?"

"I'd heard she'd a stroke but that is all. She was home so it was hard to find anything out without it looking suspicious. It isn't like I've seen either of your parents other than at large social events in over a decade. Why would I be calling on her?" Grant explained.

"You could have told me." She took the handkerchief he offered. "I was shocked. And then I did pick the phone up. She sounded so weak and then she cried and asked me to come home. Who knows what the truth is anymore."

Grant put an arm around her shoulders and held her close to his side. *Where is Logan?* Not that he expected her to do anything, he just wanted her here so he could take them away. Jackson had told him to bring them back if he thought that a good idea. Right now he was grateful for the suggestion.

Logan came walking across the lobby, her eyes as big as saucers. "Do you know what grandmother gave me?"

He shook his head. Hunter wiped her eyes and blew her nose. "What?"

"She gave me a check for ten thousand dollars so I can come see her any time I want."

What do you say to something like that? He had no experiences to draw from. Hunter's silence signaled she was stunned.

"Jackson, Lily and Charlie are waiting for us," Grant said grabbing the lifeline of that invitation. "Lots to share." His hand on Hunter's elbow, he slung his arm around Logan's shoulders and started out.

They'd used valet parking so when the attendant came with the car, he took the keys, rounded the car to the driver's seat while the valet parking staff made sure Hunter and Logan were seated.

"I think I need to go home," Hunter said.

"We're going to Lily and Jackson's first," Grant responded. "We can talk about what to do next once we're there."

It took a few wrong turns and a few corrections via Logan before he got on the right street up the hillside to the Montgomerys' house. Parking the car in the driveway, he turned off the engine. Hunter still looked in shock, Logan was still ogling the check.

He tooted the horn a couple of times. The front door opened and Lily and Jackson came out on the steps. He motioned to them. Jackson turned back but Lily came forward. She opened Hunter's door, picked up her purse and said, "Let's go in. I think this is a brandy tea day."

Grant made it out, opened the door for Logan who still looked at the check. He gently pried it from her hands, "Let's go inside." He helped her out of the car, something that felt strange.

"Can Grandmother really afford to give me that much money?" she asked in an awestruck voice.

"Yes, she can. So can I and so can your mom if you need it." He wanted to say his mother was just trying to buy her but Charlie came out and took Logan's hand. "You've got lots to tell me, I can tell," he said and led her into the house.

Stuffing the check in his pocket as he approached the door, Grant paused to hear what Jackson had to say. "Don't know what happened but Hunter is almost as bad as she was when Logan took off."

"Where are they?"

"Out on the deck."

There was a view through the house, out the back windows to the distant mountains. Silhouetted against their snow-capped peaks were Hunter and Lily, backs to the house they looked east. While he was watching, Lily patted Hunter's back. Hunter nodded. *Whatever that exchange means.*

"It may be better if I let them sort it out," Grant said stepping into the house.

"Hungry?" Jackson asked.

"What do you have?"

He settled at the kitchen island where he could see Hunter and

Lily in his peripheral vision as Jackson started with the day's menu. In the end, he waited until everyone else was ready to eat.

Jackson puttered around the kitchen making ice cream after learning Grant's favorite flavor was peppermint. "I've got all the fixings. You'll need a dish before you leave."

40 - PLANS AND PREPARATIONS

While Lily and Hunter talked on the deck and Charlie and Logan talked downstairs, Jackson and Grant talked in the kitchen. The easy camaraderie and conversations he and Jackson shared as the ice cream mixer droned on and on communicated to Grant he was not judged for what happened last night and this morning. At one point, Ms. Lawford's words pop up into his mind, words that left him with a question. Did he still want to be an attorney? And if he wasn't an attorney what would he do?

With his investments, savings, equity in his condo and house at the shore, he didn't have to work, especially if he lived a more modest lifestyle. But what would he do with his day? Going for a daily run would not fill his time. If Hunter agreed, he could manage her investments, keep her books, things she had to do but didn't enjoy.

Grant delayed his return to Providence until Tuesday afternoon. The few extra hours gave him time to celebrate Logan's birthday on her birthday. What does one do for an eighteen-year-old young lady? He could ask Hunter for ideas but he didn't. He wanted this, her first birthday gift from him, to really be from him.

After agonizing over what was right, what was appropriate, what would suit, he gave her a bouquet of eighteen roses of various colors and a gift certificate for a day at a spa—hair, facial, pedicure, manicure and massage. A gift certificate for two in a card, tucked into the bouquet delivered to her door by an upscale florist.

Why two? Because while Logan was now able to handle some things fairly well, being alone without panic attacks wasn't one of them. This way, she and her mom could have a spa-pampered day.

As he boarded the plane for Rhode Island, he still seriously questioned going to see his parents on Sunday and whether he could be civil to his mother.

The way she'd blindsided Hunter and bribed Logan was typical. *I'm not surprised, just pissed.*

BECAUSE HE HAD PROMISED HUNTER, he did drop by his parents' place the following Sunday. He'd called and reminded his mother of the agreement—no questions about Hunter, Logan, his time in Fremont and no one else present. There were three cars parked to the side in front of the garage when he pulled into the circular drive.

After debating whether to go in or just drive away, Grant decided to go in to confirm his suspicions and if they were correct, to clearly communicate with his parents he was serious about the boundary he'd set.

One sharp rap on the door and Grant walked in. Voices came from the back of the house. He continued on, determined to show his mother he would not be coerced into whatever scheme she had cooked up.

Through the screen doors, he saw his parents and another couple out on the patio. He stepped out.

"Grant, you remember the Knight-Comptons," his mother called out to him.

"Of course I do," Grant said striding across the space. "I heard you had a stroke," he said, extending his hand to Hunter's mother. Shaking her hand, he was surprised at how strong her grip was. "It's good to see you out and about."

He turned and offered his hand to Mr. Knight-Compton. The older man stood, shook his hand and said, "It seems we have things to discuss."

"Actually," Grant replied. "I won't be staying." He nodded to his father who had also stood, ignored his mother. "I'll see myself out."

"Grant, Grant," his mother called after him. He heard her footsteps on the tile as he lengthened his stride in an effort to escape before she caught up to him. *Why?* The question halted his progress a few feet from the front door.

"Grant, really! You are being unreasonable and rude," his mother charged.

"I told you I would not stay if anyone else was here." His tone matter-of-fact, his gaze fierce. "I also told you that if you could not keep that agreement, respect my wishes, I'd leave."

"But they are Honey's parents. They are eager to know more about her. To meet their granddaughter."

"Then that is something they need to figure out how to do on their own." Grant continued on to his car thankful his mother didn't follow. He was fairly sure she'd give Hunter's parents if she hadn't already done so, all the information she had about Hunter.

He pulled over to the side of the road. *I need to let Hunter know what's going on so she isn't blindsided again.*

IN THE BACKGROUND a cell phone rang, the distinct tone reminded Hunter she hadn't turned hers off. Refocusing on Sophia's living room and their Ceremony, she stared at varying hues of citrine in the center of their altar. The multi-colored fluorite being used as their talking stone warmed in her hands.

"I don't know if Grant can or even would take time off to go with us to Ireland for Summer Solstice. I'll check that out with him." The sound of her exhale filled the silence.

"I've taken a big step and contacted a couple of dancers I know in LA to see if they are interested in relocating to Fremont and teaching.

I really want to take most of the summer off to spend time with Logan before she goes to college. Once she does that, my time with her will be even more limited."

Hunter gripped the fluorite, her knuckles white. "Sunday Grant's parents showed up at Lily and Jackson's. Grant's mother blurted out my mother was very ill before he got them out of there. He told them we'd have breakfast together the next morning. I don't know why I was blindsided by what happened next but I was.

"Grant's mother came with me to the restroom and called my mother while I was in the stall. When I came out, she shoved the phone at me, told me my mother was dying and I needed to talk to her to make amends. Remember, I've had no contact with my parents for eighteen years but I still recognized my mother's voice as I put the phone down. It sounded as if she was crying so I picked it back up. She was very teary, very—not like herself at all and she begged me to come home. I can't do that—at least not yet. I haven't forgotten much less forgiven what happened all those years ago.

"Logan, on the other hand, does want to meet her and spend time with Grant's mother." She rubbed her forehead with the stone and fought back tears. "I-I-It's my worst nightmare come true," she choked out. "Grant's mother gave her a check for ten thousand dollars. Logan was and is awed by that amount. She did let Grant take it with him because he promised to open an investment account and match it.

"What if after all this time, I lose her to them?" She looked at each woman for an answer she wasn't sure even existed.

Ashley leaned towards her, "First you will grieve but then you will look around you. At least that's what I'm doing since Anthony wants to go live with Art. And after—," she stopped and took a deep breath. "What's important is that both Lily and Diana had times when their boys looked like they were turning away. I know those were hard times for each of them." She handed the stone to Lily, who sat closest to her. "How did y'all manage that?"

Lily took the stone, looked over at Diana who nodded. "We kept our hands and hearts open to them. We reached out even when we heard nothing back. We looked for little things to keep us connected to our boys."

"Those little things," Diana added, "were simple. We remembered the good times. We kept and reread the notes or emails we did get. We kept their pictures on the mantle, next to our computers, in our wallets. And we always sent them our love and prayers filled with wishes that their highest good was being served."

"And," Lily added, "when we did have contact, even to this day, we do not discuss their fathers. If they want to talk about an old memory, we would, but nothing about what's happening today. I know Charlie has talked a couple of times to Daniel or Matthew because he knows I won't discuss whatever the problem is and he doesn't want to put Jackson in a difficult spot."

"Bill has talked to Giovanni because I won't talk to him about Dennis either. If they are having problems, they have to figure them out on their own. I'm just grateful both our boys have men in their lives they are comfortable talking with."

"But Logan?"

"Logan has people, Hunter. She has all of us and while I can see that in some cases she wouldn't talk to any of us, she has talked to Gabby and Sophia about some things. She also has that doctor she can call. She's an intelligent and resourceful young woman. If she needs to talk to someone, she'll figure it out," Lily reminded her.

Hunter put her hand out and retrieved the stone from Lily. "My Spring Recital is June 18th and I hope everyone can come." She added, swiping away the last of her tears. "Back to what we were discussing—our plans for Solstice. Logan and I will be there. I'll extend the invitation to Grant and let everyone know whether or not he can come. She rubbed the fluorite on her forehead again, fidgeted as she handed the stone to Gabby.

"I have confidence that Logan will see through any attempts to buy her off. Maybe not at first, but she will see it before too much time passes. She loves you and loves the life she's lived in Fremont. I don't see her easily leaving all that behind which would be a not so subtle requirement for her to be accepted by her grandparents." Gabby rested her hand on Hunter's knee. "Trust all is as it should be.

"I will also be in Ireland. I've told Jordan, the team leader, that I'll be gone for two weeks starting June twentieth. Elizabeth is due any time and I am looking forward to getting to know our newest niece."

Updates completed, Solstice plans finalized, they stood. Hands at shoulder height, palms facing up they closed the circle with prayer.

"Guardian Spirits, ancestors, Goddess and God, thank you for your presence here with us today. We feel your energy and know you support our highest good as we move forward with our lives," Sophia said.

"We ask that you watch over us until we meet again," Hunter added. She listened for the next voice but heard none. It wasn't common but it did happen that few words were said when they closed a circle.

"If there are other words to be spoken at this time, we are listening," Gabby said.

The quiet continued a moment longer.

"Blessed Be." They chorused.

They claimed their contributions to the altar and Sophia cleared the space by picking up and folding the variegated yellow and orange tie-dyed cloth that served as the foundation.

In the family room, food was laid out on the counter, a spirit plate created and taken into the garden as an offering of gratitude for the abundance before them.

Hunter wavered for a minute and then decided to check her phone. Seeing Grant's number she debated but in the end listened to his voice mail message.

As she was hanging up, her phone rang again. She recognized the Rhode Island area code and consciously decided not to answer.

There must have been a look on her face or something that alerted the others because Gabby was on one side and Ashley on the other. When it rang again, Lily took the phone from her hand and turned it off.

"There, now you won't even have to hear it ring. You can listen to any messages when you are up to it," Lily said handing the phone back. "And if I overstepped, let me know and I'll turn it back on."

Hunter took the phone and put it back in her purse. "That was either Grant's mother or my own. I've no idea what to even say."

"Maybe there isn't anything for you to say. Maybe your job at this time is to listen," Sophia said.

Gabby's phone rang. She stepped out on the patio to answer it. "What's up?"

"Mom isn't answering her phone?" Logan said. "My Grandmother Compton is crying because she can't talk to her. I told her I'd tell Mom to talk to her."

"Logan, your mom will talk to people when she's ready. Your job is to tell them she isn't available, period. No explanations, no excuses, no apologies."

"But, she's crying really hard," Logan said, her voice quivering.

"Then don't answer unless you can say only that your mom isn't available to talk right now. If you think I'm off base, ask your dad. He'll know better than anyone what to say."

"Got to go, Gabby." Logan's voice wavered but she continued on. "The kids want me to help them with a project to surprise Ashley when she gets home. Do you know when that'll be?"

"Maybe in an hour or so," Gabby replied. "I can call you when she leaves if that will help."

"No, if we have an hour, we'll be good," Logan said. "And, Gabby? Thanks. It's just really difficult when she's crying so hard I can hardly understand her."

"My best advice is to talk to your dad about all this," Gabby repeated.

Monday
June 20, 2005

G rant exited the plane at Limerick, Ireland's Shannon International airport. Waiting for him? Hunter and Logan. Surrounded with hugs and kisses, at least from his daughter, Grant's mood lifted. He'd made the right decision when he informed the firm he'd be gone for the next ten days.

What about clients? What about emergencies? What about—? He answered them all with "Do what you'd do if I was run over by a truck." *Freedom. I'm addicted to the freedom of being myself.*

At baggage claim, he grabbed his suitcase and followed Hunter and Logan out to the curb. Lily, Jackson, Ashley, Daniel and their kids, Gabriella, Sophia, Diana, Matthew and the baby were all there.

"We're ready to go." Jackson took the lead. "We decided to hire transportation to Kinslow. Mick offered to send Seamus, but this will work just as well."

Jackson gestured and two vans pulled forward. The drivers helped load luggage into the back of each vehicle. Ashley, Daniel and the three kids climbed in with Hunter, Grant and Logan. The other van held Lily, Jackson, Sophia and Gabby along with Diana, Matthew and Madison Michelle.

Grant struggled to stay awake. The drive was soothing even with the excited voices of the younger children. He dozed and startled awake more than once as brilliant images flashed through his dream-state.

Last week Hunter talked to him on the phone bringing him up-to-date, reminding him that Eleanor was already in Ireland, making sure he understood he could participate in their Solstice Ceremony or not. Whatever his decision, it would be okay.

When the van turned and passed columns topped with horses, Grant knew they'd arrived. Not only had the entrance to the stud farm been described, but the delighted cries of "We're here!" echoing from Rose verified it.

A dark haired man and a woman who held a newborn baby were in the drive as the vans rolled to a stop. Grant hung back deciding to help unload the luggage while greetings, hugs, handshakes and the inevitable cooing over the baby ensued.

"Grant." Hearing his name, Grant turned from helping with the bags. Jackson motioned him forward.

Making sure the piece he'd been handling was upright; he nodded to the driver and took the few steps to where Jackson stood.

"Grant, this is our host Michael Murphy, also known as 'Mick'. And, in case you haven't figured it out, the new mother beaming in delight, is Mrs. Murphy or Elizabeth or E."

"Thank you for allowing me to be here, Mrs. Murphy," Grant said. *Another baby brought into a world of love.*

"Call me Elizabeth or E." Elizabeth beamed and shifted the baby to her shoulder.

"Michael, this is Grant Parker, Logan's Dad," Jackson continued the introduction. "Not sure what all Hunter and Logan told him about what's happening here but I assured him we'd answer any questions as best we could."

Michael Murphy's handshake was firm, his mouth curved in a smile of welcome, his blue eyes lit with humor. "And its welcome you are," he said, his Irish brogue distinct. "I've got a map of the place for you inside. Since E's been holding gatherings, I've added the out buildings to the map of the house."

"That's a great idea. Grant will easily be able to get around." Jackson turned back to the pile of luggage, slung a backpack over one shoulder and picked up the handles to two suitcases. "Need some help getting this all inside," he said looking pointedly at James and Anthony. "You boys are big enough to help take luggage upstairs." He waited until each boy had their own backpack and suitcase. "You can come back for more after you deposit that in your room," he reminded them.

Grant took the map Michael handed him as he entered the main foyer. The central table had a crystal bowl in the center and four horses in some pattern. He stopped for a moment and studied the design.

"The horses are in the four directions," Elizabeth said stopping beside him. "Once you are settled, if you are interested, I'll tell you the story of how this all came to be. For now you look about ready to drop so Maeve and I will lead you to your room, won't we sweet," she said kissing the baby's head.

Grateful he didn't have to make heads or tails out of the map, he followed Elizabeth up the main staircase and down the hall to the left. As he passed a room where he could see Diana, Matthew and Madison Michelle with Matthew holding the baby while Diana unpack, he stumbled. Not from tiredness although that was a factor.

Across the hall was a room with Ashley and Daniel. Next to them, James and Anthony. Logan and Rose shared the room next to Diana and her family.

His mind raced to figure out what was so different about being here. He'd been to any number of 'house parties'. *But staff showed me to my room, carried my bag.*

Next to the girls? Sophia and across the hall from her, Gabriella. Lily and Jackson were next with Hunter's room across the hall from them. His room was located next to the Montgomerys and diagonally across the hall from Hunter.

Chattering, calling out, checking in—the noise of friends coming together and he was included. *Included without strings.*

Elizabeth was talking to him. "We use the room across from you for gathering but if that bothers you at all, let us know. We can easily find another place to meet."

"There she is," Eleanor Montgomery said as she drew near. "Now E, you need to rest a bit. I know you'll want to be up and about later." Eleanor whisked Maeve away.

"You think if you take her I'll follow?" Elizabeth said a mock frown on her face. "Dinner's at six and the dining room is clearly marked on the map." She turned away and trailed behind Eleanor.

Hunter stepped out of her room and crossed the hall. "We'll make sure he finds his way, E." She glided across his room and looked out the window. "Your view is of the front gardens and some of the paddocks."

Grant joined her and leaned against the casement.

Hunter reached out and rested her hand on his arm as she continued to look at the view "Remember you may hear a humming and see a shimmering light. It's hard to explain The Lady, the energy here. If you have questions, you only have to ask. Any one of us will do our best to answer."

Catching his gaze in his reflection, she added. "I'm very glad you're here and I hope you can stay for the full ten days."

"That's the plan. I can't explain it but I do need to be here for some inexplicable reason." He placed a hand over Hunter's. "I will do my best not to jump to conclusions, judge, or hare off without talking to you first."

"That's good to know." She smiled up at him. "I am grateful we have this time here with Logan to see what happens when we're not caught up in our daily lives. That is one of the main blessings of this place—we can connect with that part of us that knows we are spiritual beings living a human existence."

Grant left it at that. He didn't know that he believed everything the women talked about but he did know it brought them comfort. Without her drumming, her prayers and The Circle, he wasn't sure

Hunter would have survived the time Logan was missing. *If these ideas and practices bring Hunter peace and joy and seem to be helping my daughter heal, can they really be bad?*

A minute or so later, she'd left to check on Logan. He pulled the curtains shut after opening the window and breathing in the fresh clean air. In the darkened room, he took off his shoes and stretched out. It was a bit chilly so he pulled up the quilt from the end of the bed and curled on his side. Hearing a quiet hum in the air, he drifted off to sleep.

UNEASE, dis-ease whatever it was, Grant decided he needed to talk to someone if he was going to keep anything resembling an open mind to what was happening around him. His nap had been full of lucid dreams of a woman in flowing blue robes, a crescent tattoo on her forehead, arms out stretched.

"Welcome," she'd said. "You belong here as do the others." Even upon waking the clarity of the vision and the voice stayed with him.

Who to talk to eluded him. He'd instantly quashed the idea of talking to Hunter or Logan. One of the other women? "I've a few questions but don't say anything to Hunter or Logan." While those words were what popped into his mind, they definitely would create problems.

Why didn't he just talk to Hunter? *Because I don't know what the consequences will be if I'm too skeptical. What if I say or do something that destroys the fragile connection we've created.*

Following the map back to the main stairs, he encountered Jackson lounging in a chair at the top of the steps. Problem solved or so he hoped.

"Feeling better?" Jackson asked, rising.

"I think I can stay awake through dinner," Grant replied.

"Good to know." Jackson started down the stairs. "You can put the map away for now. Thought you might want to join us in Michael's study for a taste of Irish whiskey."

"Thanks for the invitation. By the way, who constitutes "us"?"

"Us men. We thought you might," Jackson paused, looked over his shoulder and gave Grant his full attention. "We thought you might have some questions about what happens here," he said with a vague wave of his hand.

Jackson had reached the black and white marble floor before Grant gathered himself enough to start down. Joining Jackson, Grant followed his lead down a wide corridor.

One knock and Jackson opened the door and stepped in. They were the last to arrive. Michael, Matthew and Daniel lounged on various chairs and couches around the room, glasses in hand.

"Welcome," Daniel said.

"Glasses and decanter are on the sideboard," Michael said. "Help yourselves."

"Just so you know," Matthew added. "Dinner is at six. The women want a couple of hours after dinner to gather and set things up for tomorrow."

"Do you know what the general plan is for tomorrow?" Grant asked, pouring three fingers of excellent Irish whiskey in a Waterford crystal glass.

Jackson, who had already poured his drink, turned to the others. "Mick, he's only been to Beltane and in comparison to ceremony here—."

Michael pointed to a vacant chair. Jackson was already settling on the empty end of the couch—Daniel slouched on the other.

"Ye may have met The Lady, long blue gown, blue crescent tattooed on her forehead," Michael started. "She's an old spirit, the energy of the sacred feminine who has inhabited these lands since the beginning of time.

"I can see by the look on your face she's come to you, made you welcome."

Grant nodded and took a sip of his drink. *What the hell?*

"This land has been in my family for generations. I met Elizabeth because she'd had visions of The Lady calling her to come to Ireland. Our road was more than a bit rocky, but we overcame the obstacles and are now blessed to have wee Maeve. Elizabeth insisted she be named after my gran," he ended his face beaming with pride.

"Don't think I knew that was your grandmother's name, Mick," Jackson said. "But I'm not surprised that E would insist." He turned to Grant and added, "The women knew each other long before any of us came into the picture." Jackson gestured widely to include the other men. "I had serious problems accepting Lily's gift or perhaps it's more her view of the world. However, it isn't as important that I believe everything as it is that I love her unconditionally."

"Elizabeth also has a gift and I fought accepting it and in the process almost lost her." Michael sipped from his glass. "I think each of us came to a point where we had to suck it up, admit we loved the hardheaded women and figure a way to have them in our lives. I thank The Lady and God every day Elizabeth and I were able to find our way."

"Just think of their core belief that everything, including us, is part of the sacred," Matthew added. "That's what helped me stay with Diana, that and a few other things. It would have been easy to turn away or at least distance myself because she freaked me out more than once. I'm glad I hung in there—well, for the most part. I've a woman I love and who loves me unconditionally. I've a baby daughter. Life is good."

"I know that having the time to get to know and understand what The Circle was about before Ash's cancer returned helped me be there for her. It also gave me a footing for being Rose's papa because she is certainly her mother's daughter." Daniel laughed. "I can't imagine my house or my life without them. No patter of little feet in my place."

"No, it's like a thundering herd when they tromp down the stairs all at the same time. And, Rose?" Matthew said.

"Just wait until Madison Michelle is charging through life," Daniel replied.

Grant looked at the faces of the other men and saw they were teasing each other. The old hurt of not having these stories to tell about Logan burned in his chest. He took a healthy swallow of his drink, noted that it was almost gone, considered getting more but decided against that. A buzz was already zinging through his sleep-deprived brain.

"So, if I want to be a part of Hunter's life, I—what? What do I need to do?" Grant leaned forward in his chair like an athlete at the starting line of the biggest race of his life.

"At the very least, you need to stay out of it," Daniel started.

"You need to accept whatever it is as important to her," Matthew added.

"Be able to see how it all supports her, brings joy to her life in the good times and provides an anchor in the bad," Jackson said.

"In the end, understand these beliefs and practices are integral to who she is. Your rejection of them will be seen as a rejection of her," Michael finished.

"That isn't to say you have to adopt any of it as your own." Daniel stood, wandered to the bank of windows that looked out over the back patio. "But be open to it. I've found joining Ashley in creating a spirit plate or saying prayers for health or someone else's well-being has only strengthened our relationship."

"Research has shown that focused prayer, which they see as energy, does have an effect," Jackson commented. "Lily stays up on those things because of her business."

"Your advice then is to keep an open mind and not dismiss whatever happens out-of-hand?"

"Pretty much," Matthew said. The other men nodded.

Grant was quiet as he absorbed what was shared with him. *If I want whatever Hunter and I've created so far to have a chance to grow—I do want that but—.*

"Got it," he said. "So is the hum a part of all this?" Grant made a broad swipe with the hand that held his empty glass.

"'Tis indeed," Michael said. "And the fact that you've seen The Lady and hear the hum is a good sign. She accepts you. If you need help in knowing what to say to Hunter, The Lady may give you the words—if you are open to hearing them."

A bell rang in the distance. "Dinner." Michael stood. "I know Seamus would appreciate our delivering our glasses to the dining room if not the kitchen. He's taken it upon himself to dote upon the wee one and that takes up a lot of his time and energy," Michael said and chuckled.

Grant caught up with Jackson halfway down the hall. "Thanks for waiting for me."

"Least I could do. Passing it forward."

"Who helped you understand it all?" Grant asked.

"Lily and my mother. Thankfully I was intelligent enough to figure out that to win her I had to win over the others. You've made good inroads there because of your acceptance of Logan and your ability to move forward with Hunt."

"I realized fairly early that if we'd married back then, Hunter wouldn't be who she is today. I'm not even sure we'd be married. And, those things I think I've missed? I still would have missed them. No time to play in the park, go for a run, or even have dinner with your children in that world.

"For all the trauma and challenges I created by the way I introduced myself into her life, I have a better relationship with Logan than I ever had with my own parents. Because Hunter raised her far away from that life, she's turned out to be a fantastic young lady.

"In my world, neither my friends nor I had dinner with our parents. I had a nanny when I was really young. By school age, she was gone and I either ate by myself or—let's just say I had more dinners with our cook than anyone else until I came home from college."

"Not even when you were in high school?" Jackson asked.

"In high school, I was invited to sit with the adults on special occasions and was scrutinized for social manners from the time I walked into a room until I left. The next day, my mother would sit me down and critique my performance, correcting what I did wrong, for example picking up the wrong fork or not speaking evenly to the women on either side of me. I may have learned excellent manners, but the meals at your place, when you grilled hamburgers or made spaghetti—I have fond memories of."

"When you're next in Fremont, we'll do it again," Jackson offered.

"I'd like that," Grant managed before Jackson stepped away and embraced his wife. Grant stepped to the side and observed the couples form. *These men truly do love their women.* He winced. *Not sure that's an acceptable way of describing their relationships.*

Dinner was delicious, conversation lively and his energy level was sapped as the evening went on. After a decadent dessert of fresh peach cobbler with ice cream and a peach brandy sauce drizzled over the top, the women trooped off to the front parlor. Logan and Rose were invited which meant the men were left to their own devices.

Grant helped clear the table.

"Exhausted?" Matthew asked as they headed back towards Michael's study.

"Pretty much," Grant replied.

"Call it a night," Matthew advised. "We'll find out what's going on tomorrow at breakfast."

Grant veered off and started up the stairs. "Thanks."

"Remember, we've all been where you are. Ask and we'll answer. Or—go ahead and ask Hunter or Logan."

AFTER A RESTFUL NIGHT of deep sleep and comforting dreams, Grant was standing at the window when he heard the knock. "Come in," he invited.

"You're up." Hunter stood in the doorway.

Grant turned from the window. She was dressed in her running outfit. "I was considering getting the map and going for a run before breakfast. Looks like you have the same idea."

"You'll have Logan and me so no need for the map."

The three of them headed out through the kitchen, confirming breakfast was a buffet and everything would be available by eight. A few stretches to warm up and off they went at a leisurely pace.

"About today," Hunter said as they loped along the drive. "We'll be going to The Sacred Grove around three this afternoon. We're hoping you'll be willing to remain with the younger children."

"She means James, Anthony, Rose and the two babies," Logan said.

"I'm not very experienced with babies."

"That's okay, Dad. Eleanor will be here. She and Rose will take care of the babies, but James and Anthony will need watching."

"Watching? What does that entail?" Grant asked as the fleeting sense of relief at having no responsibility for babies fled.

"There's a lot of things they can get into." Logan loped beside him. "The best thing is to take them to the stables. They love the horses and Dickens and the other grooms are really good about setting limits. You'll be their most favorite person in the whole world if you'd go riding with them. Maybe ask Seamus to fix some sandwiches? Of course one of the grooms would go along so you didn't get lost." Logan grinned. "You can do it, Dad. I've confidence in you." She laughed and sprinted ahead.

"It isn't nice to throw your dad's words back at him," Grant called out after her, deciding to keep pace with Hunter.

"Are you disappointed you won't be down in The Sacred Grove today?" Hunter asked.

"Disappointed and relieved," Grant said, deciding on honesty.

Hunter laughed. "The decision last night was to let you get used to things instead of throwing you in the deep end."

"Thank you, I think." Grant smiled at the analogy Hunter used. *The same one I did.*

"What will you be doing and how long will you be gone?" Grant asked.

"We each will prepare in our own way, meet up about three and then proceed down the path to The Sacred Grove. We do prayers of gratitude for The Light. We'll sing songs. Because of the babies, we won't be there until it's totally dark. But time has a way of warping when we're with The Lady. It always seems as though we just got there when it's time to leave. When we return, hours and hours have passed."

"You say prayers and sing songs for hours and hours?" Grant said, perplexed that those two activities would take so long.

"We also share where we are in our lives, what we want to manifest between now and the Winter Solstice. Last year we celebrated Winter Solstice in Fremont because Diana was too far along in her pregnancy, Ashley was too weak from fighting the cancer and I was too tightly booked. It's looking like this year we'll celebrate it here.

"Just so you know, Summer Solstice is Lily and Jackson's anniversary and Winter Solstice is Elizabeth and Michael's. The next anniversary coming up is Diana and Matthew's on Lammas, that's the first of August," Hunter informed him.

Logan came into view, loping towards them. "Slug-a-bugs," she challenged as she trotted by.

"Excuse me," he said to Hunter. "I've got a daughter to beat. It isn't nice to challenge your old dad," Grant said as he sprinted by Logan.

"We'll see who makes it back to the kitchen entrance first," Logan called speeding by him.

Grant lengthened his stride, caught up to Logan and matched her pace.

"Waiting to sprint at the end," she taunted. "I've got a pretty good one myself and my legs are younger."

"Mine are longer," Grant challenged and edged ahead.

THE LADY GREETED them as they entered The Sacred Grove. Forming a semi-circle around the fire, the women raised their arms skyward, palms out and prayed.

"We are the light,

"We are the source,

"Through us love flows throughout the world"

Three times three the prayer was repeated as was their practice.

Here, the restlessness that often consumed Hunter lessened until it was gone. The urge to get up and move was softer and when she did rise, her feet moved over the grassy circle leaving no footprints behind. Bending low, reaching high, swirling and twirling she danced to the music swelling inside her. When the music faded, she slowed and stopped.

The Lady appeared before her. "You are a blessing to us all. Never forget your gifts, the gift of grace, the gift of the beauty of movement, the gift of seeing past the superficial to what lies below."

As The Lady faded, Diana began singing. The song of the goddess waiting to be recognized, to be remembered was one of Hunter's favorites. "Perhaps," she mused, "it's because of the dancers. Or maybe because it is the one we were singing when Logan returned to us from the streets."

Michael, Jackson, Matthew and Daniel had remained off to the side but now joined the circle around the spring.

Sitting next to Elizabeth, Michael rested one hand on her back, "I want to manifest between now and the dark solstice, more of what I have. My life is full of love. Love of my Elizabeth and of my wee one, Maeve. Having you all here to celebrate this longest of days, is a great gift to us," he smiled, his brogue thickening, "to all three of us."

"It feels so right to have everyone here, to welcome Logan into the arms of The Lady, to see how each of the younger ones have grown and changed. At this time last year I was distraught and for a time lost my faith. Because of all of you," Elizabeth gestured around the circle, "I wasn't in the darkness for long. I still mourn that little life but I do know if I'd carried that wee one, our Maeve would not be here. It is impossible not to be grateful to have her with us."

"Celebrating our anniversary with all of you is the right thing for Lily and me to do. Why? Because without you, I'm not sure we'd even have one." Jackson leaned over and kissed Lily's cheek. "That would be a real loss because this woman is the best thing that ever happened to me"

"I love you, too." Lily shifted to lean against Jackson's arm. "Between now and Winter Solstice, I plan on creating more time with the man I love. It won't happen right away, but as soon as Ashley can help out, I'm backing off a bit. I'm talking to another guardian, because Ash isn't sure she wants to take on that level of responsibility. But I'm open to other options. I don't mind being the guardian and having a back-up named in the paperwork so if I'm spending time with Jackson, the other person can make the decisions."

"As soon as we return to Fremont, I'm having the surgery so it will most likely be September when school starts before I can really help Lily out," Ashley said. "My life is full of love and that's why I know I will manifest good health in the future. And, I know whatever comes my way I'll not have to handle it by myself." She reached out and took Daniel's hand in hers.

"What I want to manifest," Daniel said, pressing a kiss to the back of Ashley's hand, "isn't anything I have control over. I want a healthy, cancer-free wife who has regained her health and vitality. What I can manifest is a way to show her every day she is loved. I also want to be okay with Anthony's decision to move to Alabama to live with his dad. And, if that comes to pass, to make sure James and Rose—well, that all of us will be okay with that decision and will welcome him back if he changes his mind and returns to us."

"I can't imagine a better life," Matthew said, his arm around Diana's shoulders. "I'm good if we can maintain this bubble."

Diana laughed. "I can imagine a better life. While I have no actual control over it, if Madison Michelle sleeps the night through sooner rather than later, my life will be better. However, I know, even when somewhat sleep deprived, that time will pass, she will sleep through the night and all will be well. I want to manifest continued joy and happiness with my husband, son and daughter. I want to manifest teaching classes three nights a week and one Saturday a month. My plate will be as full as I want it to be with that."

Seeing her circle sisters and their husbands, hearing the declarations of love and commitment was difficult for Hunter. Last night she'd asked that Grant be excluded saying he had no real experience and inviting him into ceremony in the sacred grove was too much. Logan had countered saying Grant could handle it, but in the end, Hunter's wishes prevailed. Now she wondered if she'd made the right decision.

"I want to manifest more time with my dad," Logan was saying. "I want to get to know my grandparents, aunts, uncles and cousins. When we meet at Winter Solstice, I want to stand up and recite my connections to ancestors many generations back."

Hunter quelled the urge to dash ice water on Logan's words. The idea of recounting her ancestors and including her mother? A shimmering light surrounded her; calm infiltrated the nausea connected to that idea. "All will be well. You trust, you believe and all will be well." The message from The Lady was clear. *If* "No, not if. You decide to and you will."

"I still want to manifest some time at a special place outside of Fremont. My commitments didn't allow me to take the time before Solstice as I'd first planned. A week should be enough. It's the perfect place for me to deal with some personal issues I want to work on," Gabriella said. "There is something sacred about that space as there is here."

Sophia looked at Hunter, an eyebrow raised in question. Hunter smiled and waved her hand in a motion for Sophia to speak.

"I have watched my friend's disease progress over the last several years. Even though it's difficult to see his decline, I do believe death is a natural part of The Wheel of Life. I see this cycle each year in my garden.

"I'm talking to him about what he wants in the end. Where does he want to be? Who does he want with him? Completing his Advanced Directives. Before I left, he did seem to be listening to what I said. At times it's as if he thinks he'll die the day after he makes these decisions.

"One of the most difficult things for me to accept, even though I know it's true, is that I cannot make him do anything. He continues to smoke and he only follows the doctor's orders when he wants to. The only thing I do have control over is being his friend. To me that means telling him the truth as I see it in a kind and supportive way. Finding my way to that being enough has not been easy for me."

Hunter was now the center of attention as all heads turned towards her. What did she want to manifest?

"I want to manifest someone to take over Twinkle Toes for the summer so I have extra time to spend with Logan." She smiled at Elizabeth and Diana. "It wasn't very long ago she was a baby, so tiny, so delicate. I was so scared to be her mom. The best advice I was ever given was to relax and love her. I may not have got the 'relax' part down very well, but I've loved her from the moment I found out about her."

The music of the bubbling spring, the sound of the wind through the trees, Hunter drifted in the light of the filtered sun. The shimmering radiance of The Lady enveloped them all. "It is time to go. You are needed elsewhere."

Their prayer was said times three before they filed out, down the path leading to the south entrance from whence they came.

Usually we come in one gate and leave by another, Hunter observed as she passed out of the tree-lined path. They circled the grove, west, north, east and around to the south again before following Elizabeth and Michael up the path to the patio above.

Hunter didn't hurry, Logan was within sight. She didn't have a baby to feed or younger children to check on much less an older mother or mother-in-law. Reaching the back entrance to The Manor, she was surprised to hear Eleanor calling her name, a sense of urgency in the tone.

Hurrying forward, she found Eleanor, worry creasing her forehead. "Grant has fallen." Eleanor looped her arm through Hunter's. "We've put a call in for the doctor. It seems he has a concussion. He doesn't make a lot of sense right now."

They were ascending the stairs now, a worried Logan had rushed ahead.

"So the doctor hasn't checked him out yet."

"He is on his way but won't be here for a bit longer," Eleanor said. "We've got an ice pack on the swelling and a bandage on the cut. Grant will be fine but he is not happy about staying down and quiet."

"No, he wouldn't be," Hunter said. "Logan and I can handle things from here," she added now outside Grant's bedroom door. She took a deep breath, huffed it out and opened the door.

Grant was not in bed but sitting in a chair. No ice pack on anything but she did see the bandage on his cheek. Logan was pacing, arms waving, her worried words easily reached the doorway. "Dad, you have to."

Hunter stepped into the room. "Actually, Logan, if your dad wants to be a stubborn jackass about this, that's what he'll do. If he doesn't care his choice worries you as well as me and is *against* the doctor's orders, he'll continue to do what he wants."

Grant glared at her. "I fell off a horse. It isn't as if—."

She raised her hand to interrupt. "You have a concussion. Why would you put yourself at risk? Why would you worry the people who love and care about you?

"At least until the doctor comes and confirms what is obvious, consider doing what was advised." Hunter stood next to the bed, fluffed the pillows and stood back.

"I'll help you up, Dad," Logan offered taking his arm.

"Don't," Grant snapped.

"Your dad isn't a very nice person when he's in pain," Hunter said. "Reminds me of the time he dove in the ocean and hit his head on a submerged log. Lucky he wasn't alone," she said sweetly.

Grant winced as he stood, shuffled across the floor and reluctantly climbed on the bed. "Do not put covers over me," he ordered.

"I wouldn't think of doing that without you asking me to," Hunter replied.

"Dad?" Logan hovered nearby.

"Your dad is just fine." Hunter's tone was all business. "If anything, he's bored. Perhaps you can find something to read to him while we wait for the doctor? And ask Seamus about something to drink— maybe a glass of iced tea?"

Logan hurried out.

Hunter considered shutting the door but decided against it so she had the element of surprise. The lambast she planned on would never have been delivered in their families with a door open.

"Don't you ever worry your daughter like that again." Hunter rounded to the foot of the bed to better see him. "And don't look away. You scared her and then you acted like a jerk. Look at me," she ordered. "Even from here I can see your pupils are uneven. That's a sure sign of a concussion and you are smart enough to know they can be dangerous. Why would you ever risk brain damage or even death! What is wrong with you?"

Hunter turned away as tears streamed down her cheeks. "I thought you wanted a daughter. I thought you wanted to be a dad." She turned back. "If this is your idea of how to accomplish that, you are wrong."

Grant's mouth opened. "Don't," Hunter said. "Do not say anything to me. Save it for the person you've hurt the most."

Arms folded across her chest, she stood at the window, looked out at the view, wishing she saw the doctor's car coming down the drive.

Hunter wished she had a mirror or could see Grant's face reflected in the window. Was his mouth agape because she'd rounded on him speaking frankly and with the door open? Was his mouth pursed to keep an angry retort from spilling out? Was he looking thoughtful, considering her words? Of course she could turn around and look but—.

Logan dashed in followed by Seamus with a tray with three glasses of iced tea and a plate of scones. "This'll do until dinner." He put the tray down on top of the dresser.

Logan placed the pile of books at the foot of the bed before scooting a chair from the sitting area closer. One-by-one she picked up the books reading the titles to Grant before setting them in a row.

"Which one, Dad?" Logan asked.

"You can pick." Grant reached over and laid his hand on Logan's. "Sorry I was so curmudgeonly."

"It's all right, Dad, you've had a lot to get used to here." Logan picked up a book and opened it.

Hunter watched Grant relax against the pillows as Logan began to read about Ireland. She remained across the room, keeping an eye out for the doctor. From time to time, Logan stopped and asked her dad a question. He frowned and succinctly answered the first couple of times but said nothing more. When she saw his lips quirk in a little smile at the third question, she relaxed. *We've weathered this one. But even though he's figured out why Logan is quizzing him, this is far from over.*

"Mom, you know Dad really shouldn't be left to figure things out on his own. He still gets a little fuzzy-brained. I can help him. He needs me, Mom."

As much as she wanted to rail against Logan's plea, Hunter knew there was some truth in it. "We can call his parents and they'll come meet him at the airport."

"Mom, we really don't need to bother them with all that. I can make sure Dad gets to his place and that Grandmother and Grandfather know he's home," Logan argued.

"We can certainly change our flight from New York to Fremont so that we can make sure your dad gets home safely," Hunter countered.

"Mom, you're not listening. I want to stay with Dad. I want to make sure he's okay. I don't want to just drop him off and leave. You can't stay. You've got Alyssa coming to check out the studio in two days. That's barely enough time for you to get home as it is. You can always come later, that is if you want to. I can wait to tour Smith College until you come," Logan offered.

They were at the Shannon airport when this was brought up. Logan didn't want her luggage checked through to Fremont. Hunter wasn't even sure Grant knew of his daughter's plan so that was a place to start.

"Let's see what your dad has to say," Hunter said, swiveling around and marching to where Grant sat, Jackson and Matthew on either side. *This doesn't look good if those two are with him.* Jackson looked up as she approached but it was Matthew who stood. As he passed by her, he paused and said, "Problem with thinking right now."

Hunter took Matthew's seat, placed her hand on Grant's arm. "Ready for twenty questions?" she joked.

"No, my head is pounding and—," he stopped and looked at her, his eyes blank.

"Maybe you need to change your ticket and stay here until you're better?" Hunter said. "Logan can stay with you and when you are in better shape, the two of you can fly back together."

"Excellent idea," Jackson said already starting to stand. "I'll check it out with Michael but I already know the answer is 'yes'."

Jackson crossed to where Michael and Elizabeth were saying their goodbyes to the others. Hunter watched him, saw Michael and Elizabeth look over and both heads nod.

"I'll pull their luggage out of the pile," Jackson said as he approached.

"Logan can help," Hunter offered staying next to Grant. She leaned her shoulder against his, "Logan is really a very good little nurse. She'll hover but remember that is her way of showing you she loves you. I admit I have problems with hovering but remembering it's a sign of love is the best way I've found to not become a snappish curmudgeon."

Logan and Jackson were soon back, tugging suitcases behind. Standing to the side, Jackson's arm was slung around Logan's shoulder, his head tilted down towards her. She looked up at him and nodded every few words. *I wonder what that's about.*

Grant stirred. "I must have dozed or something," he said. "Is it time to go through security?"

Hunter's heart ached hearing those words. "Change in plans." She tucked her arm through his and rested her head on his shoulder. "You and Logan are staying here a bit longer."

"Why?" he asked, clearly confused.

"Because," Hunter took a deep breath, reminding herself that the truth, when said with compassion was always best. "Because your brain needs a little more R&R time before you fly off and get back to work. We all thought you'd recovered more than you really have because just this trip from The Manor to here and your brain is struggling.

"Logan is going to stay with you. The doctor is going to come back and check you. In a couple of weeks when you really are better—." Hunter cleared her throat and swiped away the tears dampening her cheeks. "She wants to go home with you," she said on a shaky breath. Her stomach churned. There was so much more she wanted to say especially comments like "I'm not sure that's a good idea" but she swallowed each and every one of them. Along with everything else, her worry and fear dumped on him was the last thing he needed.

Hunter turned to wave when she'd passed through security. Logan stood next to her dad, a protective arm around his waist.

"We're going to rearrange our seating assignments," Gabby said, matching Hunter's pace down the concourse.

Hunter nodded. All those words tumbling around in her mind and she couldn't sort them out well enough to speak. *At least for the next couple of weeks I know she's safe.* That became her mantra as she waited for boarding, got to her seat, and settled in for the long trans-Atlantic trip.

Either Gabby or Sophia sat with her. The three of them changed seats every now and then, pacing up and down the aisle, doing deep knee bends and standing on their tiptoes. Screaming her frustration wouldn't help and there was no way for her to move her body enough to rid it of this toxic energy. Hunter tried going inward and dancing different routines in her mind—the ones requiring the most endurance—at best it took the edge off.

At LaGuardia she eschewed the tram and jogged from one gate to the other. Grateful for a shorter flight and the knowledge she'd be in her own space in a few hours, Hunter plopped into her seat, snapped the belt on and pulled out the safety card. Checking where the exits were, she exchanged it for the magazine in the seat pocket.

The sounds of a fussy baby in front of her broke into her thoughts. Madison Michelle was held in the air by her dad, Hunter waved and the baby smiled.

"You're hired," Diana said through the crack between the seats.

"Feel free to hand her back to me any time." Hunter walked her fingers along the top of the seat. "The distraction will do me good."

Taking turns entertaining M2 did help pass the time. She carried the baby up and down the aisle a few times, played peek-a-boo and in general enjoyed the feeling of success when Madison Michelle chortled at her antics.

Finally they landed in Fremont, disembarked the plane, got their luggage and headed out to long-term parking and their vehicles.

"It feels so good to be moving!" Hunter exclaimed. She stopped and twirled before grabbing the handle of her suitcase and starting off again.

"Why don't we stop at the deli and get sandwiches?" Gabby asked. "I don't have anything fresh to eat and really don't feel like cooking."

"I like that idea," Hunter said. "I can put off going to the grocery store until later. The deli has small cartons of milk and I've got cereal at home so breakfast is taken care of."

"Or you can both come over in the morning and I'll fix waffles and thaw a few pecan sticky buns," Sophia offered. "I do think the deli idea tonight is a good one. Gives me time to get home, put things away and make that grocery list."

"Looks like we have a plan," Gabby said, hefting her bags into the trunk.

HUNTER STOOD in the middle of the living room, after leaving her suitcase by her bedroom door. *It doesn't feel right without Logan here. Keep moving.*

Unpacked, a grocery list made for tomorrow, Hunter put her deli sandwich in the refrigerator for later and headed downstairs. In the studio, she cranked up the music. Swaying to the beat, she picked up her drum and started to move. Free style dancing fit her mood. Swirling, twirling, leaping interspersed with intricate steps, she circled the floor over and over. Sweat dripped from her chin, her shirt clung to her damp body, her muscles burned and still she danced and beat on her drum.

The flashing lights in the studio pulled her out of the zone.

Sophia and Gabby stood by the switch.

Hunter stalked over to the sound system and turned it off.

"Have you eaten your sandwich yet?" Sophia asked into the silence.

Hunter shook her head.

"Good," Gabby said. "We've brought ours along. Seems Soph and I've gotten used to eating with other people around."

"Time for you to take a shower if you want," Sophia said. "That'll give the brownies a bit more time to thaw." She held up a foil covered plate.

"Are you hovering?" Hunter gasped out the question.

"Of course we are. It's your turn," Gabby said in a sweet voice. "But hovering has its rewards. More of Sophia's treats, a few more updates from Elizabeth and extra calls and time with me. Oh, and invitations to dinner from Diana and Lily."

"I'm sure I'll look back on all this and be grateful. I'm just not there yet." Hunter glided across the studio floor to the door. "I will take a quick shower. Make yourselves at home," she called out over her shoulder as she strode down the hall.

LOCKING the door and turning the alarm on, Hunter leaned back against the door. Sophia and Gabby had stayed a couple of hours, doing their best to engage her. If she wanted to talk, they would have listened but her worries and fears were too scary to put into words. And at this moment, Logan and Grant were safe at The Manor.

Emails from Logan and Elizabeth as well as one from Eleanor assured her the doctor had been by and seen to Grant. Their reports included the doctor's recommendation that Grant not travel for at least two more weeks. Of course he hadn't wanted to comply. He had duties and responsibilities in Rhode Island.

Elizabeth's added postscript said Michael had written an email to Grant's law firm, implying he was considering using them for his state-side business. It went out from his email address but had Grant's name on it. And yes, Grant had read it over and typed his name at the bottom. Why?

Hunter smiled as she read the longer email noting E was answering questions she knew Hunter would be asking. Why? Because Grant was saying he was fine and had to get back to the office. Even the doctor telling him he shouldn't travel at this time wasn't helping. It was only when Michael talked to him about becoming a client, Grant settled down.

That made sense to her. Grant was driven. *But he has changed. He's set boundaries with his parents. He didn't even take his laptop to Ireland and he never checked in with the office—Don't drive yourself crazy over this. Unless you choose to fly back to Ireland, you need to let this go for now.*

Alyssa would be here tomorrow afternoon. While doubts popped up, in the end she wanted the flexibility to spend more time with Logan before she went off to college. With Alyssa coming on board, she could offer classes Monday through Saturday both during the day and in the evenings.

Freedom and flexibility. If Logan did go to Smith, with Alyssa here she'd be able to fly back to spend a weekend with her. If she chose a college closer to home, she'd also be able to flex her time to better fit when Logan had time off.

Grant would recover and Logan would return with him to Rhode Island. It was inevitable she'd meet her maternal grandmother. *My mother.* The cracking sobbing voice of her mother when she'd had the phone shoved at her echoed in her head. *I can't forgive them for what they did.*

Grant's words came unbidden. "The reality is, if we'd married, I still would have missed Logan's childhood. I wouldn't have been at the park pushing her in the swing. I wouldn't have changed a diaper. I'm not even sure I would have ever held her."

If he can forgive me, can I ever forgive?

July 12, 2005
LaGuardia Airport, New York

*G*rant linked his arm with Logan's as they headed to baggage claim. His vision blurred from the pounding pain in his head. Three weeks from the fall off the horse and while he still had moments when his brain seemed to slow, the worst of it was the raging pain in his head.

Debilitating.

And at times like this in a busy, noisy environment, it affected his vision and gait.

Maybe he wasn't as ready to deal with work and family as he'd thought? Maybe he should have spent more time in Ireland? Maybe he should have gone with Elizabeth and Logan to the Sacred Grove? Maybe—? Doubts assailed and doubled his discomfort.

A shimmer of soft light flickered at the corner of his vision. The Lady's soft voice quieted the painful roar. *All will be well. Trust.* His vision cleared, his gait steadied.

Grant looked for the Parker Party signage as they passed by security. He'd hired a service to take them to Providence and his condo. It was the only plan Michael agreed to. Grant knew it was the more prudent choice but—. If he didn't hurt so bad, he'd smile at the thought of Michael badgering him these past three weeks to sit, rest, relax and enjoy the time with his daughter.

There were the times when she withdrew, curled into herself and he was grateful Elizabeth and Eleanor were there. He knew the nights she had trouble sleeping because she had a haunted look about her. Sometimes she and Elizabeth went to The Grove. Even if she didn't say anything, he knew because for the rest of the day, she had a calm, peacefulness about her.

There were also the times when she was so like her mother at that age, once he even called her "honey."

She'd startled.

Did that creep call her that? He didn't ask.

He did invite her to sit with him in the gazebo. With glasses of Seamus's lemonade to sip and the pitcher nearby, he talked about her mother, who Honey Knight Compton was in a different place at a different time. When he said she reminded him of her mother at this age, his daughter beamed.

Inwardly Grant winced at what his and Hunter's mothers would do when Logan was in their direct orbit. *Crush as much of her spirit as they can.* For a brief moment while sitting in the gazebo he reconsidered his decision to stay out of it, let her find out for herself why her mom had left.

"Dad, there's someone with a sign." Logan's voice pulled him out of his thoughts. She tugged his arm and pointed to a uniformed woman holding a sign in the air.

"That's us." Grant veered towards the driver. "Give her a wave so she knows we're her fare."

Logan waved, energetically, and Grant caught the reprimand "Young ladies do not…" before it spilled out. He'd heard it enough times directed at his two older sisters. The words "young ladies" or "young men" or worse "gentlemen" meant a lecture on etiquette, deportment or expectations of a Parker were forthcoming.

The driver took over, leading them to baggage claim, taking their tickets and grabbing their luggage. Pushing the cart out to the curb, she hailed a town car. The trunk opened and she began stowing their gear while another driver appeared and opened the door to the back seat.

"Thank you for using Lincoln Car Services," the first driver said, sliding into the passenger seat.

As the car pulled out into traffic, Grant rested his head on the back of the seat and closed his eyes. The throbbing pulsated through his entire body.

Through the pain, he half-listened as Logan struck up a conversation with the drivers, asking them about the sights along the way. After a few stiff and formal exchanges, they relaxed and pointed out landmarks, sharing a bit of history with her. Through squinted eyes, he saw Logan's look of wonder as she saw sights she'd only read about or seen in a movie or on television.

At some point, he must have dozed.

"Dad, we're here," Logan said, excitement bouncing in her words. "Oh look, I think that's Grandmother."

Grant's stomach clenched at the announcement.

The door opened. Logan clamored out. The contents of his stomach almost hurled. She hadn't slid to the edge of the seat, swung her legs around and stood with grace and elegance.

"My dear, just look at you," his mother was saying. "In your excitement to be here you must have forgotten the proper way to exit a car. No worries. Next time I'm sure you'll remember."

Head splitting, stomach churning, Grant forced himself forward before his mother said more. Logan's worried look and stiff posture when he reached her side added another level of pain to his pounding head. "Thank you for meeting us," he managed, taking Logan's arm. "It was a long trip and we need to rest. Perhaps this weekend?"

He gave Logan the keys to the condo, gestured her forward before saying to the doorman, "Trotter, please make sure my daughter and our things get upstairs. Just have them put everything in the living room."

Logan, keys in hand, kissed her grandmother's cheek and was first through the entrance into the building. Trotter nodded his way before following the now loaded luggage cart being pushed by one of the drivers inside.

Grant relaxed knowing Logan would be upstairs in his home when he got there. Trotter would make sure of it.

However, before he could join her, he had his mother to deal with. She was eyeing him in an almost concerned way which helped him know in advance what her tactic would be.

"No, Mother, Logan and I are not coming to stay at your place, either in town or at the shore. We have plans for the next few days. Again, if you'd like us to come out to the shore on the weekend, we can certainly spend a day with you. I'm sure you understand that I want to show her my place also."

"You look like hell," his mother said her tone sharp and commanding.

"Thank you for sharing your opinion. I'm actually travel weary and would like to spend some time with my daughter without the drone of the plane engines, the coughing of other passengers and crying babies. So again, please note your options are our coming by your shore place either Saturday or Sunday. We will not be spending the night but we will spend the day.

"You do know how to reach me. I'll confirm the date and time when you decide." Grant stepped around his mother and started into the building as the driver exited.

More grateful than usual the elevator required a code, Grant punched in the numbers and stepped in when the doors opened. Trotter, who was back at his post, would lose his job if he gave the code to Mrs. Three. At least for now, he and Logan were safe from her machinations.

The door to his condo was open, Logan standing in the entrance looking for him. She smiled and stood to the side as he walked in.

"I figured out which was your room because I snooped," she said. "The one with all your shaving stuff in the bathroom—at least I hope that's true. I put your suitcases in there and my things in the other bedroom.

"I love your views. This is a great place. And Trotter seems to be the best ever. What is his title? I said 'Mr. Trotter' and he said just 'Trotter'. He told me all I had to do was ask and he'd make sure I got whatever I needed. That's what concierges do but he said he was the doorman."

In his own place, his daughter safe from her grandparents, he slouched in his favorite high backed chair. Logan puttered around. He heard kitchen cupboards opening, water running but was in too much pain to open his eyes.

"Not much in the way of food. We'll get take-out tonight and get groceries tomorrow. There's a pad and pencil on the counter—start a list, okay?"

"I will after you take this," Logan said.

He startled a bit thinking she was in the kitchen instead of right beside him. Opening his eyes, he saw she held a glass of water in one hand and pills in the other. The pain pills would put him out and even though he knew that would be for the best, he shook his head.

"Food first. The drawer next to the refrigerator has a stack of take-out menus. What sounds good to you? A deli sandwich, Chinese, Thai, Indian, Italian?"

He closed his eyes again when Logan turned away. The drawer opened and closed. The thick carpet stilled the sound of her footsteps. The air shifted. He peeked when he heard the papers riffle. She was perched on the footstool next to his chair.

"What's your favorite?"

"Pizza from Luigi's. They deliver so we don't even need to go get it."

"They've got a lot of choices," Logan said.

"What do you like the best? And, the deli on the corner has great corned beef and cabbage as well as Reuben sandwiches so we can do pizza another time."

"But do they deliver?"

"They'll bring it to the door of the building because it's only a few steps away. Trotter will call up and let us know it's here and we go down and get it from him."

"What about paying for it?"

"I give Trotter some money at the beginning of the month to take care of these things for me. He'll just pay them out of that and keep the receipt. If I'm getting low, he'll let me know and if I've a balance, he lets me know that too."

"Do you pay him?"

"I do. And, he gets a tip from me each time I order this way."

"Let's do the deli sandwich. My mouth watered when you mentioned the Reuben."

Grant led her through the process of ordering, had her call down to Trotter to let him know food was coming and she'd be down to pick it up. He observed her concentrating, making sure she did it 'right'. Where was the light-hearted young girl he'd seen glimpses of when they ordered a sandwich from the deli in Fremont?

"It's just a sandwich," he'd said at one point.

"I know but I've never done this before," she said a note of exasperation in her tone.

"Of course you've ordered sandwiches. You ordered several when I was with you."

"That was different," she said. "I want to get this right. I've so much to learn."

The unspoken words *if I'm going to fit in; if I'm going to be accepted.*

Grant's head throbbed but he stayed with his decision. He'd limit contact and be supportive but not interfere. *She needs to know what her mother endured for the first eighteen years and what I've endured for close to forty.*

A WEEK HAD PASSED, his head still pounded if he did much of anything. He'd checked with his own physician who said this was normal for as severe a concussion as he'd obviously had. Recommendation? Take it easy. Don't overdo. Cut back at work.

Martha had caught several mistakes he'd made at work. Simple mistakes that showed he still had problems thinking. When she approached him on the second day he was in the office for the third time, Grant asked to meet with the other partners. He asked Martha to inform them of the mistakes she'd caught. He reminded them of the concussion and presented the letter his doctor had written. The consensus was if he needed more time off, he should take it.

"I know if I work from home, I'll be able to concentrate. Also," he'd added. "Martha will review my work, check my voice mails and bring important calls to my attention. I see this operating much like we did when I was in Fremont." Grant stood, ushered Martha out the door, not waiting for discussion. He left a new outgoing message on his phone telling callers to leave a message or to contact Martha. That done, he gathered his laptop and left.

Because his vision was still affected from the pounding in his head, he'd stopped driving. Martha had ordered a taxi and it was waiting at the curb.

Directing it to his mother's house, he took another pain pill. Taking the edge off the pounding in his skull was important if he was to deal with his mother.

Logan was spending time today with his mother and he was fairly certain Hunter's mother was in attendance also. It was almost lunch and he expected that scene to be excruciating as the two women corrected Logan's lack of knowing which of the four forks to use when.

He knocked on the front door, opened it and as he entered, called out. "I'm here."

The door to his father's study was closed which meant he was ensconced inside.

Grant strode down the hall to the back patio where his mother liked to have lunch on warm days. He'd been right. Mrs. Knight-Compton was seated to one side of Logan. She was leaning towards his daughter, pointing and talking. Logan was sitting stiffly no part of her body touching the chair back.

"Grant, we're surprised to see you this early. Your father—,"

"Is in his study. I'm sure doing something important. I don't want to disturb him. And, I'm hungry so I think I'll join you ladies." He continued to the table.

"Good afternoon, Mrs. Knight-Compton." Grant nodded towards Hunter's mother. "I see you've met my daughter."

A maid came forward and set another place at the table. He actually had a whole side to himself because both of Logan's grandmothers sat closer to her than normal. *The better to provide instruction.*

A cart with platters of fish and bowls of salad and vegetables was rolled to his side. He helped himself to the shrimp and added two spoonfuls of pasta salad to his plate. A sourdough roll and a pat of butter completed his meal. "I'll have an iced tea," he said to the maid who had placed a glass of ice water within his reach when she'd laid out his place setting.

Logan sat across the table from him, rigid, a mix of fear and determination on her face and in her eyes.

"Mrs. Knight-Compton, you look well." He picked up his knife, cut a small piece from the pat of butter and after pulling a matching piece from the roll, buttered it. Setting the knife down on the bread plate, he placed the bite of roll next to his shrimp.

He chatted with the two women while keeping an eye on Logan. His ability to engage them, after all they wouldn't want to appear rude, kept the focus away from her. However, she did not eat one bite. She did sip her water, placing the glass exactly back on the spot it had come from.

Grateful he hadn't taken more food given how hungry he really was, he cleaned his plate, wiped his mouth and placed his napkin over his now empty plate.

"It's been delightful spending time with you," he said to Hunter's mother as he rose.

"An excellent meal as always." He tilted his head in his mother's direction.

"It's time for us to go, Logan." Grant rounded the table and pulled back her chair. "Say your goodbyes to your grandmothers." He reached out and took her elbow in his hand, nudging her up.

"Thank you, Grandmother Parker," she said. She stiffened. "I mean," she turned towards Hunter's mother, "It was nice meeting you, Grandmother Compton." She shifted to face his mother. "Thank you for a lovely lunch, Grandmother Parker."

"Much better," his mother said, "Don't you agree," she added addressing Mrs. Knight-Compton.

"I do indeed," Hunter's mother replied. "She is coming along nicely."

"Now Grant, you and Logan must come to dinner—," his mother started.

"We'll see you again at the shore next Sunday. Perhaps Logan and I'll invite you and father to a brunch. I'll have to check with staff and see what we can do," Grant interrupted.

"You do mean to include the Knight-Comptons," his mother said her arched brow and glare sending a clear message.

"Of course, I just assumed that any invitation to you and Father to spend time with Logan and me would include the Knight-Comptons," he said smoothly.

Grant knew by the purse of her lips and the continued glare, he'd irritated his mother. Clearly she'd wanted to train Logan so she could claim the accomplishment. *You should have seen the poor child before I stepped in. She didn't know one fork from the next.*

He did stop at the study door, knocked and waited until his father called out.

"We're leaving now," he told Three from the doorway. "Expect an invitation to our place on the shore this weekend. We've informed mother but wanted to let you know as well. And, the Knight-Comptons will also join us." His father did not look happy but before he said anything Grant added, "Shall I close the door or leave it open?"

"Closed, please."

Grant did so, took Logan's hand and went out the door. They walked a couple of blocks and then sat on a stone wall while he called a taxi.

She'd been silent since saying goodbye to his father. He slung his arm around her shoulder. "Don't worry."

"Won't the girls at Smith know all about the forks and everything?" She chewed her bottom lip.

"Some will."

"I'll be laughed at."

"Not necessarily."

"I'll embarrass the family." She looked down at her feet.

"I'm family and you won't embarrass me. Your mom is family and you won't embarrass her," Grant said.

"But Grandmother Parker and Grandmother Compton said it's my duty to show society what a real lady is like."

Grant noticed Logan still sat ramrod straight. "Just relax," he said and rubbed her back.

"If I don't sit this way all the time, I'll forget when it matters and slump or slouch."

"Logan, you are not going to slump or slouch anywhere it matters. I slouch in my chair at home."

"But you've had years of practice. You can afford to slouch from time to time. I can't. What if I forget and do something awful?"

The taxi pulled to the curb. Grant held out his hand inviting Logan to accept it by wiggling his fingers. The pain and panic in her voice twisted his gut. The urge to interfere more than he had just done strangled his voice. Holding her hand, he helped her into the taxi, got in after her and gave the driver the address to the condo.

"Here's the deal," he said as the taxi drove off. "You and I are going out to the shore for the rest of the week. If we feel like it, we'll drive up and take a tour of Smith College. If we don't, we won't."

"What about work?"

"I'll still do some work but it'll be like I did when I was in Fremont. Checking in with Martha on how things are in the morning and then again in the afternoon. She'll call me if there is something that can't wait."

"Is it because of me? Did I do something wrong?" Logan asked but looked out the taxi's window.

Grant saw tears clinging to the corners of her eyes, heard the quaver in her voice, the pain of humiliation and doubt.

"No. The doctor in Ireland and my own doctor here have said I need to take more time off. And, Martha caught a couple of errors I made this past week. Everyone agreed it would be better if I worked from home."

"Are you sure I—,"

He interrupted her. "I do not want to hear you belittle yourself. You are my daughter. I'm just getting to know you. I see you as perfect just the way you are. And, if I decided I wanted to take the summer off and just hang out with you, there is nothing wrong with that."

The idea of taking the summer off and just spending it with Logan spontaneously spouted from his mouth and the words as they replayed in his mind soothed. *I wonder if—*

∿

"THIS IS REALLY where you and Mom sat around a bonfire?" Logan asked again, looking in wonder at the circle of stones, burnt wood inside.

"This is where we spent many an evening roasting marshmallows, building s'mores—," *and making love.* Thankful he stopped at s'mores, Grant let the memories come, sharing the appropriate ones with his daughter. They strolled along the beach. He still not up to jogging or running because, even though his headaches were improved they were still constant.

Logan ran ahead and back, her face shining with wonder, picking up pieces of driftwood, ocean smoothed glass. "You look just like your mom did back then," he'd said once when she'd come back a piece of blue glass in hand.

"I'm emailing her every night and letting her know what we're doing. Would it be okay if I asked her to come visit?"

"Of course it is. I think that would be a great idea." He wrapped an arm around Logan's shoulders and she matched her stride to his and slipped her arm around his waist as they turned back to the house.

"I love it here at the shore," Logan said.

"It's a magical place." Grant thought of the magic he and Hunter created that summer—and part of that magic was at his side.

"Grandmother Parker and Grandmother Compton have said they'll come early so they can help me get ready for the luncheon tomorrow."

"I have no idea why. Food for six is being catered in. House is clean."

"I think it's to remind me about etiquette rules and make sure my makeup is done right." Logan pulled away from his side.

"We're at the shore. You don't have to wear makeup. A pair of shorts and top is fine. Comb your hair, maybe pull it back into a ponytail is all you have to do. This isn't a debutante ball."

"What about shoes? Do I have to wear stockings and heels?"

The mothers would probably wear stockings and heels along with creased pants and matching tops and jackets. Their hair would be styled and they would be wearing makeup. He rethought his earlier commitment to himself to stay out of it.

"I've told you what I think is appropriate and if you decide to go with what I've said, I'll say something to them if they start in. But it's up to you."

Grant stayed out on the deck when Logan went inside. He put aside the idea to call Hunter. Alyssa had decided to stay and was even now moving up to Fremont. *We'll see how things go this weekend.*

44 - A MOTHER KNOWS

Something was wrong. Hunter knew with a certainty something was wrong with her daughter. What was wrong was another matter. She'd asked Lily, Diana and Sophia to lunch at her place—just in case—. Just in case what? Tears or the compelling need to scream or jump up or… . These women were her friends, her soul sisters, they'd understand.

With Alyssa now teaching, she left the front door unlocked.

"We're here." Sophia's voice sounded at the bottom of the steps.

Hunter met them at the top, hugging each one in turn.

"This is a feast." Lily eyed the counter filled with sandwiches, salads and beverages.

"Help yourselves." Hunter stood aside until each woman filled her plate and sat at the table. "I really appreciate your coming," she said, her back to them. "I didn't think I could talk about this in a restaurant." She put the sandwich back, leaving a spoonful of each salad on her plate. After pouring a glass of iced water, she joined them.

"So what's going on?" Diana asked.

"That's part of the problem. I just have this feeling that something is wrong with Logan but I can't tell you what it is. I thought because you two," she gestured to Lily and Diana, "had times when your sons were across the country you could help me figure it out. And, Soph, you know Logan and teens so I hoped you could also shed some light on what might be happening."

"Bring us up-to-date." Sophia took a bite of her sandwich.

"She's spending time most days with her grandmothers. Grant is working from his house at the shore and Logan is living with him there. But his parents and mine also have houses nearby—an easy walk. From what I can glean in limited conversations with her, Logan spends the time Grant is working with one or both of her grandmothers."

"Limited conversations? Logan?" Sophia commented. "She's more on the loquacious side from my perspective."

Both Lily and Diana nodded their heads.

"I remember when Charlie went to live with his father, he became quiet and closed off. It was a loyalty issue for him." Lily reached over and patted Hunter's hand.

"Bill became so distant. I thought I'd lost him. It wasn't as much of a loyalty issue as he just didn't know how to deal with the toxicity of his parent's marriage," Diana said.

"Both Charlie and Bill worked it out so they could have the strong relationship with you that they have now," Sophia said. "I think something else is going on with Logan because you," she nodded to Hunter, "have certainly given her permission to create a relationship with Grant and to attend college across the country. What else do you think could be going on?"

"I'm not sure. She no longer volunteers much of anything, not even about something she and Grant do and never says anything about her time with her grandmothers." Hunter's stomach lurched. Putting her fork down, she folded her napkin and stood.

"When she was first there, she seemed so excited about meeting family and seeing another part of the country," Diana said, looking up at Hunter. "I could ask Bill to call her. Maybe she'd talk to him."

"I know Charlie would call her also," Lily added. "Do you think that might help? Someone more neutral to talk to if there is something going on?"

"Have you talked to Grant about your concerns?" Sophia asked.

"Not specifically. I've asked him about his concussion and how things are going in general. I don't want to appear nosy. It's their time to work their relationship out so I've tried to keep my part of the conversation on the light side."

"Are you comfortable asking if he knows why Logan isn't talking very much to you?" Sophia asked.

Hunter shook her head. "I did comment that Logan seemed a bit distant when I talked to her. His answer was vague, something about she has a lot going on, what with meeting her aunts and cousins and getting to know her grandparents." Hunter's gaze swept around the table. "He alluded to her working on issues from when she ran away."

"That makes sense. When you think about it, it hasn't been that long—four months is all," Sophia said.

"I think there's more to it," Lily said.

Diana nodded. "It feels more like it is connected to being there in Rhode Island, or maybe being at the beach, I mean shore."

"There've been no real problems with communication when the three of you were here in Fremont or even in Ireland. And, correct me if I'm wrong, but when they first got to Providence, she was open and shared her excitement at seeing that city, Grant's condo, going out to the shore. So when did things change?"

"When they more-or-less moved to the shore," Hunter said. "I think within a week of them staying out there full time, I noticed the difference." She'd moved to the calendar on the wall and was looking back at the July dates.

"She seems not just distant but almost stilted as if she is thinking about every word before she says it out loud." Hunter turned from the calendar, her focus far away as if she could see all the way from Oregon to Rhode Island.

"Has Logan talked any more about going to Smith College?" Sophia asked. "There might be a hint of what's happening if you talked to her about that."

Hunter returned to her chair. Her head tilted, she dredged up that conversation from her memory. "The last time I mentioned it, she was hesitant and I just—well, I spoke into the silence and told her it was okay with me if she decided to attend another school. She still had time to make up her mind—not a lot of time but a few weeks at least."

"What happened then?" Lily asked.

"She said 'thanks Mom' and that she had to go, her Grandmother Parker was due and she still had to fix her hair and do her makeup." Hunter gasped and grabbed Lily and Diana's hands, her gaze bore into Sophia's steadiness. "That's it!"

Hunter surged to her feet dragging Lily and Diana up with her. "That's it. That's what's wrong!"

"Fixing her hair and putting on make-up?" Sophia asked now standing, her forehead furrowed in confusion.

"Think, Soph," Diana said. "She's at the beach, hanging out with her dad, taking runs, maybe swimming in the surf from what Grant and Hunter have said. And now she has to fix her hair and do her makeup?"

"If her Grandmother Parker is taking her to lunch or shopping?" Sophia's quizzical look communicated she had no idea what Hunter and Diana were talking about.

"It's about pleasing someone else because you want them to like you and you're afraid they won't if you are yourself," Lily stated. "Of all of us, you have been the truest to who you really are. Each of us," Lily gestured to Hunter and Diana, "have become chameleons to be accepted, to be loved. Logan has never had that experience. She's been unconditionally loved by many in her life and she knows that."

"But Grant?" Sophia asked still puzzled.

"Grant was raised this way, with these expectations. He's never had the freedom to do as he pleased and still know he'd be loved and accepted," Diana said.

"Except when he was here," Lily shared. "He made a comment to Jackson that he'd never experienced the same level of freedom that he did here. He didn't phrase it like that. He used the word "expectations". I remember, he told Jackson when we were grilling on the back deck he couldn't remember a social event where he wasn't expected to do anything except enjoy himself."

"That's sad," Sophia said.

"But true," Hunter responded. "Being Grant Haywood Parker the Fourth, he would be expected to, at the very least, schmooze with other guests to enhance the family name or cultivate relationships for the law firm. He would be expected to always circulate, always ask women to dance, refill the men's drinks, etc."

"Daunting for someone like Logan," Diana said. She put her arm around Hunter, "Does this help?"

"Yes," Hunter replied.

"What are you going to do now?" Diana asked.

Bile rose in Hunter's throat, speech impossible. She took a sip of her water hoping she didn't choke on it. The fear that clawed in her bowels, the bile in her throat stark reminders of her past; a past she'd worked so hard to escape.

A memory of Logan trying so hard to please Grant's mother when they were at breakfast, flashed. *Times how many put downs?* There really was only one answer.

Could she?

Could she do it?

Could she do it alone?

Would she be alone or would Grant stand by her? She'd not fought for that to happen eighteen years ago. Would she fight for that to happen now?

Would Logan's desire for an extended family trump everything so she'd stay regardless of the price she was paying? Would she lose her daughter to the life she'd fled?

Hunter paced to and fro as questions raged through her mind. At one point she stopped and did ten deep knee bends to clear the oppressive energy from her body. There really was only one answer.

"I have to go to Rhode Island." Hunter stopped in mid-track and looked at the others, saw nods of agreement, soft smiles on their faces.

Lily was the first to speak. "You know you will be in our prayers while you are gone."

"And only a phone call away," Diana added.

"Perhaps now is the time to finish what you were too young to do that long ago summer. Perhaps now is the time to speak your truth to your parents so if Logan decides to stay and go to school at Smith you will be comfortable spending time with her." Sophia stood in front of Hunter, placed her hands on her shoulders, looked her in the eyes and said, "You do know you are strong enough to deal with whatever comes your way."

Hunter wrapped her arms around Sophia, who shifted and enveloped her in a hug. "I do know I am loved by many and am supported by everyone in The Circle. I can only hope I am strong enough to face my past."

"Your love for Logan and Grant's love for you will see you through," Lily said.

Hunter stepped away from Sophia and turned towards Lily, an incredulous look on her face. "You are hallucinating."

"I don't think so," Diana added.

Hunter looked at Sophia who nodded in agreement.

"I'm not saying he even realizes it," Lily said, "but the way he looks at you?"

"He feels guilty," Hunter began.

"It didn't look like guilt by the time he left in May," Diana said. "He does have a certain look on his face when he looks at you and another one when he is watching you and Logan together. Even Matthew commented on it."

"Jackson said Grant wants to be a good dad to Logan and sees you as a good mom so he watches you for clues to help him out," Lily said.

"Do you want some time to think things over on your own or do you want one, two or all three of us to stay?" Sophia asked.

"I am a strong and independent woman who is fiercely protective of her daughter." Hunter's voice rang with conviction. Her straight spine and raised chin emphasized her determination. "I must be prepared that nothing I do will persuade Logan she does not have to turn herself into someone else, that if her grandparents don't like who she is, that is their loss."

"And you will be in our prayers and we'll be only a phone call away," Diana said.

Hunter walked them out to the sidewalk. Back inside she stopped, wrote a note to Alyssa to come upstairs when classes were over. Restless, she glanced at the clock and saw she could get a thirty minute run in before Alyssa would be available.

Changing into shorts, t-shirt and running shoes, Hunter headed out. Feet pounding on the lake path, she found the zone and ran and ran. Along the far side of the lake, she slowed so that when she reached the end and was back on the pavement, her pace was once again that of a jogger.

Alyssa was waiting for her when she came in the front door. She waved to Alyssa to follow as she continued down the hall, getting her speaking voice back.

In the living room, she turned and looked at Alyssa. At thirty, Alyssa looked twenty. Her honey-colored blond hair was pulled into a high pony-tail. She was wearing a Twinkle Toes shirt, tights, and dancer's shoes. A questioning look on her face, she crossed to the table and sat.

"Anything wrong?" Alyssa asked.

Hunter noticed an edge to her voice and quickly responded. "Not with you.

"Here's the deal. I need to go to Rhode Island and check on some things. I could be gone a couple of days or a couple of weeks. Are you okay with covering everything for that long?" Hunter asked in a forthright manner.

"You'd trust me to run everything for a couple of weeks?" Alyssa asked her eyes wide.

"Of course I'd trust you. But this is more than you signed on for so—,"

"Will you be back before the summer recital?"

"Yes. Everything is really up in the air right now. If I can, I'll be back sooner. At the least I'll be here for the Recital."

"I can do it. I promise I can handle this for you." Alyssa stood and stepped forward, taking Hunter's hands in hers.

"For us," Hunter said. "Remember the deal we made. I want to cut back my teaching time so I have more flexibility. Since we can offer more classes, there is profit sharing in this for you.

"I know I've been distracted and haven't talked to you much. I'm sorry if you've felt unsure of your status," Hunter added. "You are amazing. As amazing as I thought you'd be. Am I right, do you want to stay and work with me?"

Alyssa dropped Hunter's hands and twirled in place. "Yes, yes, yes."

Hunter laughed and hugged her friend. "Good. Let's celebrate!"

"I found a great Italian restaurant a few blocks away," Alyssa said, a bright smile on her face.

"Let me shower, change and make a couple of phone calls. How about," Hunter glanced at the clock on the wall, "we meet out front in an hour. Will that work for you?"

"See you then," Alyssa said over her shoulder as she headed towards the stairs. "My treat!" she laughed.

"Dutch!" Hunter shouted after her.

The sound of Alyssa's laughter as she headed down the hall echoed upstairs.

A shower did not ease the feeling that something was wrong with Logan. Hunter looked in the mirror as she patted on moisturizer. *I'm going to Rhode Island.* Finished she returned to her room and the altar on her dresser. Arms raised in prayer. *Goddess and God be with me on this journey. Help me fix whatever is wrong.*

45 - CONFRONTATION

Things do change in eighteen years: new paint, new buildings, new roads everywhere. The hired town car sped along roads once familiar but now less so. Lost in memories Hunter was oblivious when the town car pulled up to the house on the shore. The driver opened her door and handed her out, unloaded her luggage from the trunk and set it by the front door.

Ringing the bell, she added three loud raps. Tilting her head, Hunter listened for footsteps. Silence.

By this time it did occur to her that her plan to surprise Grant and Logan with her arrival might have a flaw. She hadn't taken into account no one would be home. Leaving her suitcase by the door, Hunter wandered along the wraparound deck.

Overlaying every bush, rock and view was a memory of that magical summer. She'd prepared herself for the memories but the reality was more, much more. Her progress slowed as the wonder of their love infused her every pore. Dramatic? Yes, it was dramatic and perhaps even romantic.

As she neared the back corner of the deck, voices reminded her of where she was and why she was here. Hunter grabbed the railing to steady herself as the sound of her mother's voice echoed down the years.

"Do remember to sit up straight. You never know who might walk by and see you. You don't want them to think badly of you."

But not that summer. Or not all summer. Grant and I escaped.

Hunter halted, not wanting her presence detected. Even without seeing anyone, she knew the critical words said in a critical tone were directed at Logan. Hunter strained to hear her daughter's response.

"I'm sorry, Grandmother Compton. I will do better."

Was she hanging her head, defeated?

Was she looking up, defiance flashing in her eyes?

Was she leaning forward, eager to please?

A soft footstep behind her warned her she was not alone. The scent of sea air and heat told her who had joined her. "Come with me," Grant said in a low tone near her ear.

His hand on her elbow, Hunter turned and allowed him to guide her back along the decking and through a door into a room that obviously was his office.

"I'm glad you're here." Grant stepped closer, his arm sliding from her elbow to around her waist. "Very glad."

"You could have told me what was going on. I'd have been on the next plane if you'd told me what was going on." Hunter pulled away and turned to face him.

"Would you? Would you have hopped on the next plane or even one in a few days and flown out here?" Grant challenged back. "You would rather not be here right now."

"But I am here right now and I will stay here until I know what's wrong with my daughter." She saw him flinch but was not about to sooth his feelings. "What is going on?" Hunter asked but immediately held up her hand, "No, let me guess. Your mother and my mother are "helping", she finger quoted the word, "our daughter learn the rules of society."

He nodded.

"And you are witnessing their incessant criticism and doing nothing."

"That is not true," Grant said before Hunter could take another breath. "I talk to her after her time with them, ask her if she wants me to put a stop to their badgering. She has continually begged me not to interfere."

"I don't believe that," Hunter started.

"She says she wants to know these things, they'll make her a better person, help her fit in at Smith or other places in the world," Grant rushed on.

Hunter paused. She knew what happened to Logan when she was on the streets tore a gaping hole in her daughter's self-esteem. *But how does sitting with at least two inches of space between your spine and the back of the chair make you a better person, help you fit in?* She turned away, a soft sigh escaped. *Just because I don't like what he's saying doesn't make it a lie.*

"It's difficult to watch. But if you say something she'll jump to their defense," Grant added.

Hunter whipped around. "You've got to be kidding?"

"Wish I was."

Hunter plopped down on the closest chair. "I couldn't stay away."

"I'm glad you came," Grant repeated crouching in front of her and taking her hands. "Very glad."

He stood. "Let's get your things and settle you into one of the guest rooms."

GRANT LEANED against the doorframe as Hunter unpacked her suitcase, putting some items in the dresser and hanging the others in the closet. "Want to change before we go out back?"

She stopped, checked her face, hair and clothes and shook her head. He smiled. She wasn't giving an inch.

"Let's go," he said offering her his arm.

She sailed past him but waited at the archway for him to catch up. "This way?" she asked nodding to the left with her head.

"Yes. Shall we go out the door together? Do you want me to go first? Or do you want to go first or alone?"

Hunter tilted her head, a considering look on her face. "I think I'd like to go out together." She held out her hand, and gripped his when he reached her side.

"Ready?" Grant stopped a few feet from the French doors out to the back deck.

Hunter lifted her chin, inhaled and exhaled through her mouth and nodded.

He opened the door and stepped out. She matched him stride for stride as they continued to the lower deck where Logan and her Grandmothers sat.

"I've a surprise for you," he said as they started down the four steps from one level to the other.

"Mom?" Logan screeched. She was half-way to her feet when she stopped, sat down and after looking at her grandmothers said, "Mother, it is good to see you."

His mother's triumphant smile was matched by Mrs. Knight Compton. Hunter didn't miss a step or stumble. She approached the older women, giving each an air kiss and a "so good to see you again" fake greeting.

Her hand tightened and he knew she struggled with how to greet their daughter.

"Come and give your mom a hug," Grant said, reaching out to Logan. "She's traveled a long way to surprise you."

Logan stood, smoothed her sundress and sedately walked to where they stood a few feet away. He pulled her close and whispered, "It's allowed to show surprise and excitement."

Logan nodded. She wrapped her arms around Hunter and held on tight. "I'm really okay, Mom," she said in a soft voice in Hunter's ear. "Honest I am."

"Good. That means you and I can go running and dance on the sand and swim in the surf and make bonfires on the beach with your dad," Hunter said.

Keeping an arm around Logan's waist, Hunter looked over at her mother. "I'm sure you and Mrs. Three have things to take care of at home."

She turned, her gaze locked with Grant. "Do you mind inviting your parents and mine for dinner tomorrow night?"

"Excellent idea." He moved to Logan's other side, his arm around her shoulder completing the family tableau.

He expected an argument about being asked to leave, but after a quick glance between the grandmothers, they gathered their purses, said their good-byes, air kissed all around and left. "I'll walk you out." Grant escorted each woman up the few steps and towards the house.

When he returned five minutes later, Hunter and Logan were walking along the beach, shoes in hand. Hunter saw him and waved to him to join them. He shook his head and started to turn when he heard Logan call out "Dad?"

Jogging down the final steps and onto the sand, his heart raced with elation. As he neared he saw the laughter in Hunter's eyes and the wariness in Logan's.

"Last one to the log," Hunter challenged, pointing down the beach at least one hundred yards, "has to either buy or fix dinner."

He listened to Hunter's laughter as she shot off down the sand.

"Mom," Logan called out. "You've got to wait. You can't just call out a challenge and take off."

"Oh but she can." Grant drew a line on the sand with his toes. "So it's between us. One of us will be last. Will it be me or you?"

He jogged off, realized Logan was not with him. Stopping, he turned back. She was standing at the line, tears in her eyes. "What's going on?" Grant asked coming up to her, putting an arm around her.

"What will people think if they see us acting like heathens?" Logan wiped her eyes with the back of her hand.

"They'll think we're having fun," Grant said simply. "And, before you tell me something else one of your grandmothers told you, remember our first days here?"

Logan nodded.

Hunter came up to them, bent and put her hands on her thighs. "What happened to the two of you?"

"Our daughter was concerned about what people would think if they saw us acting like heathens." Grant leaned towards Logan, "Your mom and I were some of the best heathens or hooligans this beach ever saw."

Hunter laughed. "We were at that."

"And, while your mom may not meet with everyone's approval here, she meets with mine as do you and that's what matters."

"Grandmother Compton said Mother left because she didn't want to shame the family, because she wasn't accepted in society. She said if I did well and was accepted—,"

"That is hogwash, crap, crazy—." Grant's raised voiced interrupted. He blew out a harsh breath and made a concerted effort not to shout. "Your mom was accepted. She was liked. People loved being around her. Why? Because she was brave. Brave enough to stay true to herself, to her dreams and talents. Brave enough to take off and have you and raise you to be the awesome young lady you are.

"Now you and I lost the race so we've got to do dinner," he said changing the subject. Slinging his arm around Logan he pulled her close. Opening his other arm, he invited Hunter in.

He couldn't imagine Hunter moving here, even if they lived in this house full time. But he could imagine him living in Fremont. The catch was still—where would Logan be? If she did go to Smith, he'd stay put for another four years.

DINNER OVER, they were sitting on the dock off the front of the property watching the sunset when she heard the car doors slam shut. Hunter glanced over at Grant who'd already stood and looked ready to do battle.

She smiled in his direction and started back to the house motioning to him to stay behind with Logan, who had also stood. Seeing Grant's hand out to stop Logan helped Hunter move forward.

"Mother, Father, I'm surprised to see you since the invitation was for tomorrow night," Hunter said in her more formal tone.

"Don't you speak to me like that," her father started.

"And I'd appreciate your having a civil tone when you speak to me also," Hunter countered.

"I am your father and I'll speak to you as I please," he sputtered.

Hunter continued to the house, stopping on the top step. Turning back she said, "Come in, please. I'm sure you have a great deal to say and we wouldn't want just anyone to hear it."

She led them to the left, into the formal living room, turned on lights and waited until her mother sat on the couch. Hunter chose a chair across from her mother.

Her father paced and shouted, railed and ranted and even cursed a time or two. What was she thinking when she took off? What was she thinking coming back? Of course he didn't care to hear what her answers were.

Hunter had prepared as best she knew how. She dredged up every defense she'd ever erected in her childhood but they failed her.

She used to be able to sit erect, listen well enough so that when her father did expect an answer she could give one. Tonight even listening was beyond her. So when her father stopped and looked expectantly at her, she looked back.

"Well?" he said.

"Well what?" she responded.

"Don't be insolent with me. What do you have to say for yourself?"

Hunter stood and faced him. "If I thought either of you truly wanted to hear an answer to that question, I'd say something. However, I'm sure neither of you do. If you have more to say, Father, more hateful critical words to hurl my way, get it over with because this is your one chance.

"If you cannot keep a civil tongue, speak in a respectful manner to me, then the invitation to dinner for tomorrow night is rescinded."

She resumed her seat, relaxing back against the cushions. "Do go on." She motioned to her father to continue.

"Your posture, Honey," her mother interjected.

"Is not your concern," Hunter replied. "And, I no longer answer to

'Honey'. I go by the name 'Hunter' and if that isn't okay with you I really don't care."

"Your legal name is," her father started.

Hunter stared at him and said, "My legal name is Hunter Knight Compton. Honey Knight Compton died eighteen years ago when her parents forced her to choose between keeping up appearances and having a child."

"It wasn't like that," her mother started.

"Really?" Hunter's laugh was scornful.

"No, we just wanted what was best for you," her mother continued.

"Best for the image of the Knight Comptons. Not what was best for me."

"What was best for the Knight Comptons was best for you," her father stated looming over her. "What would you have if not for your ties to this family?"

"What I do have, which is a successful business, a daughter who is wonderful just as she is, a group of friends who stand by me unconditionally, is in no way connected to this family," Hunter countered. "For your information, on the west coast the name Compton or even Knight Compton doesn't garner any special attention."

"You didn't put that together on your own," her father said rocking back on his heels, a menacing smile on his face.

"Tell me more?" Hunter met his stare.

"Your grandmother set up a trust."

"Yes, she did and until this past month, I've never touched a penny. I've supported Logan and myself from the work I did. At times I waitressed, worked in a child care center and danced."

"Until I thought I might need money for Logan's college education, I had no direct contact with the people who oversee the trust. In May, Grant helped me learn about the trust. That's when I learned the trust owned the building." She laughed. "I've been paying myself rent for years. The first money I've spent from the trust was to purchase my ticket here.

"All these years I've supported Logan and myself. We've had lean times. I've gone to bed hungry to make sure she never did. I know because I've done it that it is possible to create a good life, to live according to your own strengths and beliefs, to grow into the person you can become instead of turning into someone's expectation of who you should be. Logan and I are proof of that."

She stood before her father. "Do you have more to say or not?"

"I'll—"

"No, you won't. You will not speak to me whenever and however you choose. You will only speak to me with respect and if you cannot promise that, then you need to leave and not come back tomorrow or ever."

"Compton," her mother said, standing next to her father, her hand on his arm. "Leave it. We've been without our daughter in our lives for too long."

"I will not have her," he stabbed his finger at Hunter, "talk to me that way."

"You've made your point," her mother said. "I think we need to leave now."

"I'll leave when I damn well please," her father shouted shoving her mother's hand off his arm.

"That's enough!" Hunter strode to her mother's side. "You may not treat anyone like that in this house. Leave now!"

"I'll leave when I damn well please," her father said again, arms folded across his chest.

"Fine, stay in this room for as long as you want," Hunter took her mother's elbow.

Her mother must be in shock. That would explain why her mother did not resist as Hunter towed her from the room. "This way." She nudged her mother out to the back deck. They stopped at the upper railing.

"Your father does love you," her mother said.

"I was told by one of my friends that there is a difference between the feelings of love and the actions of love. Whether he has feelings of love for me or not, he does not treat me with love."

"It's his—"

"Don't Mother. Don't make up excuses for him." Hunter breathed in the salty air, letting it out on a sigh. "If we are ever to repair the damage of the past, we have to find a new direction. I'll never measure up to your standards because they aren't mine and don't and won't serve me. I'm asking you to consider loving me and loving Logan for who we are, not who you think you can change us into.

"And if you are talking to Mrs. Three, please pass that along. I don't know whether Logan will go to Smith or return to Oregon or go somewhere else but whatever her decision is, I hope you can find a way to love and support her for the wonderful young woman she is.

"The world will not come to an end if she picks up the wrong fork or shows excitement or anticipation for a special event or person. You may be surprised at how much beauty is in the world and how much joy and laughter you can experience if you let yourself."

Hunter saw Grant and Logan coming from the beach and moved around her mother to stand on the top step. She welcomed his arms around her, supporting her.

"I love you Mom," Logan said giving Hunter a hug.

"I'll let you know if your father and I will be joining you for dinner," her mother said, her formal tone tinged with ice.

"I'll walk you out," Logan said following her grandmother into the house.

"You were magnificent," Grant said against her hair.

"So you heard everything?"

"Pretty much."

Hunter leaned into Grant, let him bear her weight, relished his hand stroking her back. *I wonder what he'd do if I tipped my head back and kissed him.*

Grant, Logan and Hunter loped down the beach on a morning run before breakfast. Mrs. Ripley was fixing omelets and would come back to put together the evening meal. Within an hour of the Comptons leaving last night, the phone had rung. His mother stated they would also be coming for dinner.

Instead of reminding his mother they weren't invited, he'd made the decision to include them. He appreciated Hunter wishing she'd been consulted but the reality was it was time to deal with all of them.

Logan had been silent last night, heading to bed as soon as she'd come back in from seeing her grandparents to their car. The greeting she'd bestowed on her parents this morning was formal. "Mother" "Father" no 'Mom and Dad'.

Grant didn't seem bothered by it but Hunter was. The closeness she'd always had with her daughter was absent and she missed her even though she was only a few feet away.

Efforts to engage Logan in conversation failed, rebuffed by short answers to open-ended questions and a quick 'yes' or 'no' to closed-ended ones. What had happened to the light-hearted, spirited young woman who was her daughter? Part of her light was dimmed by her time on the streets but she was regaining that. This dimming was more insidious to Hunter's mind because Logan was dimming her own light.

Grant had a business meeting in town, Logan was ensconced in her room, which left Hunter to her own devices. She checked emails and answered the ones from The Circle with a short answer: "Some is worse and some is better. More tomorrow."

What did she mean by that?

The better was with Grant. The comfort of his arms, the accolades he rained upon her for how she stood up to her parents.

The worst? Logan. It never occurred to her Logan would so totally shut her out. That first spark of joy Logan showed upon her arrival was gone. *Will it ever come back?*

Grant wasn't due back until two; Logan was still hanging out in her room, a "do not disturb" sign on her door. Hunter was at loose ends so she wandered into the kitchen to get a glass of iced tea. Mrs. Ripley was chopping ingredients for a soup.

"I'd love to help." Hunter eyed the stalks of celery and onions on the chopping block.

"You can do the celery or onion," she said. "You know which knife is best for chopping?"

Hunter laughed. "I've been cooking for Logan and myself since she was born. I may not be the best cook, but I do know my way around a kitchen." Hunter picked a knife out of the rack and started on the onion. "What are you fixing? I've no idea what Grant's favorites are or if Logan now has something she adores she's only had here."

"Mr. Grant likes his seafood: shrimp, lobster, crab, salmon, scampi —so I have some casserole recipes and I fix them in ramekins and freeze them. That way he can easily heat them up. He also likes my red sauce. I make it from scratch. He can cook pasta." Mrs. Ripley laughed. "He loves freshly grated cheese too."

"In Fremont he helped fix dinner and made a pretty good tossed green salad," Hunter offered. "But I didn't know he could cook pasta."

"It must be fresh. That way he only has to boil the water and it cooks in a few minutes."

"He raved about your macaroni and cheese," Hunter said.

"Of course, his two favorite things—pasta and cheese. I cooked for him when he was a boy and I remember how much he liked it. It was our secret. Not for his parents. They'd have been horrified to see him eat something so plain."

"Homemade macaroni and cheese is not plain. It is rich and creamy and Logan and I add bits and pieces of other things to it."

"What do you add?"

"Leftover bacon chopped up fine, peas, left over chopped up chunks of chicken are our favorite extras. The bacon and the peas add a bit of color the chunks of chicken a different texture."

Who would have thought chopping vegetables, stirring a roux, kneading bread and chatting with Mrs. Ripley would be so relaxing? But it wasn't the activity. It was the sharing. Mrs. Ripley had story upon story about Grant's childhood and his current lifestyle to tell and Hunter was an avid listener. She didn't just listen, she also shared what she and Logan were doing at similar times.

The aroma of freshly baked bread permeated the house, the soup was simmering on the stove, a shrimp and pasta salad was in the refrigerator along with a pitcher of sangria. Cookies hot from the oven cooled on a rack. Hunter and Mrs. Ripley were sitting at the kitchen island, sipping iced tea when she heard Grant call out.

"We're in the kitchen," she said, her voice raised so he could hear her.

"Ahh, the place smells fantastic," Grant said coming into the kitchen. He grabbed a plate from the cupboard and approached the cookies, loading his plate with half a dozen, he eyed the bread.

"Bread is for dinner." Mrs. Ripley stood and took her glass to the sink, rinsed it and put it in the dishwasher. "You know what to do?" she asked Hunter. Seeing her nod, Mrs. Ripley turned to Grant. "Ms. Hunter has been a good helper today. She'll make sure everything goes smoothly." She patted his arm. "I'm going home now."

Grant took her place on the stool next to Hunter. "What have you been doing with yourself?"

"Answered emails and helped out in the kitchen."

"You didn't have to do that."

"I know but I needed to keep busy and it is soothing to do something repetitive like chopping vegetables and talking."

"Did she tell you stories about me?"

Hunter laughed. "What do you think?"

Grant's scowl lacked ferocity, "I could fire her."

"And lose your mac and cheese source? I seriously doubt it." Hunter stood. "Are you through for the day?"

"I am."

"Want to go for a walk on the sand?"

"Sure. By the way, where's Logan?" He said eating the last of his cookies.

"She went to her room when you left and hasn't come out. She has a 'do not disturb' sign on her door and I'm honoring it."

"I'll go talk to her," Grant said and started towards that wing of the house.

"Grant? Just do what you'd normally do if I wasn't here. Don't ask her why she's stayed in her room or about me, please."

He nodded. "I'm going to change into something more appropriate for a walk on the sand," Grant said, loosening his tie and starting off.

He may not be a quick change artist but Hunter noted he was trotting down the steps towards her in short order. He approached, slung his arm over her shoulder and started towards the point. She matched his stride, comfortable in their silence.

"I hollered at her closed door that I was home and going for a walk. Invited her to join us," Grant said as they continued along the water line. "Give her time."

"How much?"

"Don't know. She's become very protective of her grandmothers, thinks their instruction will benefit her, believes being accepted into society is a good thing and will make life easier for her."

Hunter stumbled. Grant's hold tightened. She steadied herself. "So her overhearing me set boundaries with my parents was not necessarily a good thing."

"No, at least not right now."

"Have I lost her?" Hunter's voice broke. "After all I've done to provide her with a place to grow and be who she is, have I lost her to them?"

The restlessness she'd curtailed while working in the kitchen hit like a lightning storm, sending bolts of energy through her. Pulling away from the haven of Grant's arm, she charged down the beach. At the point she kept going until the dock blocked her path.

"This way," Grant called out.

Hunter followed him up some steps carved into the bank, across the drive and around the side yard. He veered to the right and took another narrow path that led back to the beach. Back on the sand, he slowed.

"Want to do that again or," he nodded to the left, "head that way or stop?"

"Not stop, you choose."

Grant loped back towards the point, Hunter matched his stride. At the tip a line of rocks divided the narrow spit of land. They wound their way through them again but stopped on the other side. Hunter slowed and turned towards the last of the rocks. It was low tide so the water did not pound against the rocks sending spray in all directions. But it did lap at this last one.

"I loved this place. That last summer was magical." Hunter balanced on the next to last rock to keep her shoes dry. "Do you ever wonder why our parents let us have that time?"

She turned to Grant, taking his hand to step down to the sand. "Before then the noose was tight. From what I see now, the noose tightened around you again. Why?"

"Why did they reel me in?"

"No, why did they let us run free that summer?"

"I've never thought of that." Grant linked arms with her.

"Until I came back, I hadn't either. But it's odd."

"An anomaly because they'd never done so before and have never done so since. I've fought for any freedom I have."

"Do you have freedom? True freedom to be yourself?"

"I have time out." Seeing her quizzical look, he went on. "I have times and places when I'm alone where I allow myself to relax and put the responsibilities and expectations aside. But when I'm around people, whether at work or at a social gathering, I'm always aware of what is expected of me."

"And you live up to those expectations."

"Yes."

They walked along, passed by the house and continued along the water's edge.

"Are you disappointed in me?" Grant asked.

"No, I see you as knowing who you are underneath the mask."

"If you'd stayed—,"

"If I'd stayed, if we'd married, I'd have lost myself and I don't know that you would have kept hold of who you are. We'd have been sucked into the whirlpool of expectations and into the darkness. We'd have lost the ability to see the world from other perspectives."

The sand ran for miles along this stretch of the shoreline. Houses they knew from that long ago summer passed by, the house of Grant's parents came into view. Time to turn back.

"Want to race?" Grant asked.

"Not really but I'd like a bit faster pace back. I've a shower to take, a dinner to check on. I do remember how to set a table for a more formal occasion. Or at least I think I do."

"I'll double check it if you want me to—or not. It's up to you because it doesn't matter to me if everything is lined up just so."

Hunter's pace was a slow trot. "Good to know." Shoulder to shoulder, in tandem they moved down the beach comfortable in the motion and the silence.

SHOWERED and dressed for a casual evening, Hunter turned and checked her image out in the mirror. Her hair was pulled back in a chignon, her multi-colored print tunic over black tights, was set off by bright pink flip-flops. No stockings, no heels, no nail polish, no make-up—*a compromise of sorts.*

Hearing Logan and Grant's voices but too far away to make out the words, she slowed her pace. At the entrance to the back patio, she stopped in her tracks as her breath whooshed out in an exhale that left her reeling. Logan was moving from one place setting to the other, moving silverware, glasses, napkins—standing back, head tilted as she studied the layout before stepping back and making another slight change.

"You don't understand, Father," Logan said in the most formal and tight tone Hunter had ever heard. "Grandmother Compton and Grandmother Parker will notice if it isn't just right. I don't want to disappoint them. They've worked so hard to teach me the right way to do things."

Grant had looked in her direction, shaking his head, signaling her to stay back or stay out of it. Her stomach rebelled. She turned and dashed, barely making it back to her bathroom before everything she'd eaten, everything still in her stomach erupted. Weak, she sagged against the toilet, reached for a towel to wipe her face.

A soft knock on the door frame.

Hunter looked up to see Grant, a concerned look puckering the space between his brows. "It'll be okay," he said, reaching down to help her up.

Tears welled and she shook her head. "I've lost her."

She hung on to the vanity, ran water and rinsed her mouth, used some mouthwash to get rid of the foul taste and washed her face and hands. "Please help me," she said motioning into the bedroom.

Grant supported her to the chair she indicated, handed her the cell phone on her dresser as she asked. "I'll be okay but I don't think I can eat anything. Please make my excuses."

"Hunter, don't give up." Grant knelt beside the chair and took her hands in his. "Don't give up. She'll understand in time."

"I don't think I'm strong enough. If I'm going to be there for her when she finally understands," she swiped at the freely flowing tears, "I can't stay."

"We'll talk after everyone is gone." Grant rose. "Don't worry, Hunt. I'll watch out for her and do my best to protect her from the worst of it."

"I know you will and I thank you for it." Hunter stood, wrapped her arms around him and kissed his cheek. "I'm so glad I came. The memories of our summer are precious and give me much pleasure."

Grant pulled her close, wiped the dampness from her cheeks with his thumb. Tilting her head, his lips found hers with a scorching kiss that heated her lips. "I've wanted to do that since I first saw you in Fremont."

"When you were yelling at me?" Hunter said and smiled.

"Before that. When I saw you dancing, I wanted you with a passion that matched if not exceeded the best of our time together that summer."

She kissed him, her tongue sliding along his lips. He opened and she darted in. His groan and tightening grip sent flurries of excitement tracing down her spine. *If only...*

The doorbell rang. He pulled away. "Later," he said his voice gruff.

She smiled and said nothing.

When the door closed, she sank into the chair, tears running down her face. She picked up the phone and made a call. If she stood next to the window opposite from where she sat, she could hear the voices of the Parkers and Comptons along with Logan and Grant. A few minutes later the phone rang.

"Yes, thank you. I owe you."

To reach the closet, she did need to pass by the window. Her mother's voice, "Much better, Logan. Don't you think so?"

"Much better," Grant's mother said.

She continued to the closet, pulled her suitcase out and began to pack. With her luggage in hand, Hunter eased through the house and down the front steps. Continuing down the drive, she waited at its entrance. A taxi appeared, she waved it down.

Looking back was more than she could manage so she kept facing forward. When the cab turned onto the main highway, she closed her eyes and let the tears fall.

The drive was over two hours and her tears were spent before they arrived at the airport. Hunter got out at the first stop. Towing her suitcase with the smaller carryon perched on top, she made her way to the line at the ticket counter.

Her cell phone rang as she waited. A glance showed her it was Grant. Unable to face him, she tucked it back in her purse.

Lily had done as she'd requested and a first class ticket for the next flight to Fremont was waiting. With her ticket in hand, she strode to the gate. She was on the red-eye to Fremont and would be there before morning after a long layover in Chicago.

At least I'll be home tomorrow. At least I've got Twinkle Toes. But most of all, I've got The Circle. She braced one hand on the back of a seat at the gate and did ten deep knee bends, then ten twists and ten side bends. Her phone rang twice. She didn't stop.

When she was ready to board, she checked the phone. All the calls were from Grant. She turned the phone off, stuck it in the bottom of her purse and marched down the gangway.

Chicago. I'll listen to his messages in Chicago. Maybe even text him. Tears welled but she turned her face to look out the window, not wanting anyone to see them.

Maybe not in Chicago. Maybe I'll listen to them when I get home. Maybe ....

Grateful. Grateful. Grateful. Hunter's lungs filled with gratitude as she came through security and saw Lily and Sophia waiting for her.

"Gabriella and Ashley are at your place fixing breakfast. Diana will be along as soon as M2 has eaten." Lily wrapped Hunter in a long hug.

"Me next," Sophia said, stepping up when Lily moved to the side.

"How was the flight?" Lily asked as they started towards baggage claim.

"Smooth, uneventful, long," Hunter replied.

"We tried to call and leave a message but you had your phone off, even while in Chicago," Sophia mentioned.

"Oh." Hunter reached in the bottom of her purse and dragged her phone out. Turning it on she said, "I didn't want to talk to anyone back there so I turned it off and forgot to turn it back on."

"So Logan didn't know you were leaving?" Lily asked once they were walking to the parking garage.

"I'm sure she's relieved I've left," Hunter said in a shaky voice willing the tears back.

Conversation was superficial—travel stories and weather updates.

The aroma of breakfast greeted her when she came through the back door. Alyssa stuck her head out of the studio and Hunter waved.

"Come on up after class and have some breakfast," Sophia invited.

Alyssa smiled and waved, ducking back inside.

Upstairs Hunter was greeted with hugs, divested of her suitcase and carryon and settled at the table.

Her cell phone rang. "It's Grant," Lily said. "I can answer it if you want me to."

"I can't talk to him yet," Hunter managed.

"Not a problem," Lily said and walked towards the bathroom. "Hi Grant." The rest was lost when the door shut.

"So, how's your appetite?" Ashley asked. "We've the makings for omelets or we can do something simpler like scrambled eggs with various omelet fillings added. Also on the menu we have decadent pecan sticky buns courtesy of Ms. Bakery herself, Sophia Denton."

"Tea, mimosas and orange juice are the beverages," Gabriella said squeezing another orange into juice.

Home, surrounded by people who loved and accepted her just as she was—travel weary, rumpled, probably a stain somewhere. It didn't matter to any of them. *How could Logan give this up?*

"You will be okay." Ashley gave her a side-hug. "We're here and we won't leave until we're kicked out."

Sophia handed her a tissue. "Talk when you want or don't. We're here for you however you need us."

Words she needed and wanted to hear. Words that said she did know her place in The Circle. Words that comforted because they said she was not alone.

Lily came out of the bathroom, set the cell phone on the table. Her bright blue eyes held fire. "It would be helpful to know your view of all of this," she said to Hunter. "I'm not saying you need to talk now or to all of us or anything like that but Grant is furious, to say the least."

"Furious because I left?"

"Furious because you gave up and left him alone to deal with all the whatever it is that's going on there," Lily replied.

"I did leave him to deal with it on his own but I didn't give up.

Well, maybe I did," Hunter amended, trying to see the situation from Grant's perspective.

"Let's eat first and then I'll catch everyone up on what happened," Hunter said. "Besides, Diana will be coming and that way I'll only have to talk about it once."

~

A BABY-PUKED-UPON Diana arrived apologizing for not having showered. She stepped into the bathroom and changed into a clean top.

She looked at Hunter. "Do you mind if I have a minute to catch up to myself. I really want to be present for you."

Champagne was opened, mimosas made, juice poured and tea steeped. Hunter decided to splurge and fixed a mimosa. The blend of fresh squeezed orange juice and the effervescence of the champagne was a special treat.

"You know I thought something was wrong because Logan really wouldn't talk to me and neither did Grant—or at least he wasn't answering my questions. So I went back to see how things were for myself.

"Logan really wants to please her grandmothers to the point she is tying herself into knots over it. She almost ran to greet me when I showed up but stopped, sat back down, schooled her features and formally said, "Mother, it is good to see you." My Logan called me 'Mother' then walked sedately to where I stood."

Hunter's voice shook as she went on to explain how difficult it was to hear her mother and Grant's mother correct Logan in the same tones she had heard all her growing up years. "It tore my heart to see Logan try so hard. Not knowing or not believing there will always be something to correct.

"They want her perfect and she thinks if she can learn what they want, she'll fit in. She'll be accepted for those accomplishments. It's as if she no longer sees that being accepted for who she is is more important than being accepted for what she does, who she knows, how much money is in her bank account.

"I set clear and firm boundaries with my parents and she was upset because I would not or could not understand that what they were doing was for my own good.

"It may seem like a little thing. I'd set the table for dinner because Grant's parents and mine were invited. All the right number of forks, spoons, glasses, etc. were on the table, a low display of flowers in the center. I'd showered and changed and was coming back out when I saw Logan hovering around the table making minute changes here and there in an effort to make sure everything was just perfect."

Hunter reached for two forks, set them side by side and shifted one a fraction of an inch apart. She tilted her head and moved it back, almost to where it had been. Then frowned and lined them up again. "It's like that. Broke my heart to see her so fretful over getting the place setting so precise. I barely made it to the bathroom before I lost everything in my stomach.

"The grandparents came and I overheard the grandmothers criticizing her. Oh, they said she is making progress. Offered her hope that one day she'd succeed enough so they'd praise her.

"I called Lily, packed and left. I told Grant I couldn't watch her try to please them but not that I was leaving," she said when she saw Lily's brow raise. "I told him it broke my heart to see her try so hard because I'd tried for seventeen years to get it right and always failed." She inhaled a shaky breath. "He said she'd come to understand they will never be satisfied."

"So you left," Sophia said. "No note?"

Hunter shook her head.

Diana reached over and took Hunter's hand. "If you've never lived with constant censure, it's hard to understand how it destroys your sense of self."

"Hearing my daughter criticized, images of too many times when I was the recipient of the unrelenting disapproval and denigration overwhelmed. I was seventeen again. I had to leave."

"Didn't you mention that you talked to your father also?" Sophia said.

"I did. He started in about how ungrateful I was. How I couldn't make it without the Compton name, etc. and I told him to stop. He demanded I talk to him with respect and I said the same thing—he needed to talk to me with respect and if he couldn't manage that then I didn't want to see him again. During this exchange, my mother reprimanded me about my posture."

"Your posture?" Ashley looked incredulous. "You have great posture, Hunt."

"This posture." Hunter sat rigidly straight with two inches of space between her back and the chair.

"Now what?" Sophia asked.

"I don't know that Logan will ever come home to Fremont but I do know if she does, I want to be at my best for her. If I'd stayed, well, I was already struggling with anger, fear, loss, memories and the sense I was failing my daughter because I hadn't stayed and raised her back there."

"So you've returned, will work at Twinkle Toes, and just pick up where you left off?" Gabby asked.

"No, Alyssa is here and she's doing a fantastic job. I have some freedom and flexibility. I thought I'd see if I can support some of you for the time being. I can help out with Madison Michelle so you and Matthew can have a date night. I can do the same for you," she said to Ashley.

"I thought I might be able to put together a couple of simple gentle exercises for some of your clients, Lily. Ones they can do to their favorite music. I want to be of use. I can weed for Sophia and I want to talk to you," she looked at Gabby, "to see who I need to talk to at the Youth Shelter. I can volunteer an evening or maybe even offer a drop in weekend dance class.

"One of the benefits of now understanding and accessing the trust my grandmother left me is I don't have to work so hard at Twinkle Toes. So, think it over and let me know what you'd like me to do."

"Am I interrupting," Alyssa called out from the bottom of the stairs.

"Not at all, we're just getting ready to have breakfast," Hunter replied.

Lily lingered after breakfast and everyone had left. "Do you remember when I first came home after the accident?"

Hunter nodded. "I ask because you may remember that Eleanor and Jackson left me several messages on my cell phone. My advice to you is that sooner rather than later you listen to Grant's messages and give him a call."

"I will tomorrow. I promise. I just need a few hours to unpack and settle back in, catch up with Alyssa, go for a run and get a good night's sleep." She walked Lily to the back door where Sophia waited. "You said he was furious. I really don't understand why. I can understand upset but furious?"

"He loves you and you've abandoned him," Sophia said.

"He didn't say that!" Hunter's eyes flew open in shock, her exclamation rang in the hallway.

"No, not in words. He wants to be a good dad to Logan and is insecure, isn't sure he's doing a good job. He thought the two of you would handle things together. He kept saying "and after"—then he'd catch himself and stop but a few sentences later he'd say the same thing. Does that make sense to you?"

Hunter nodded. *After that kiss. How could I have left after that kiss?*

48 - HEALING AND ICE CREAM

August 08, 2005
The Shore House, Rhode Isand

Crouching in the shrubbery beneath Logan's open window, Grant heard muffled sobs. Her grandmothers had taken her shopping, to lunch and then brought her home. They'd come inside and had her set the table for a formal dinner and create a menu for a society luncheon. Obviously she hadn't met their standards. Obviously she hadn't figured out she never would. Obviously it was time for him to do something.

He crept out onto the lawn, stood and stretched. The sand beckoned but he didn't have on his running shoes. *To hell with it. I have to do something or I'll—.* Another bolt of understanding slammed into his gut. He scrubbed his face with his hands, turned back to the house and jogged inside.

At Logan's door he called out, "Going for a run. Come with me." He purposefully didn't end with a question in his tone hoping in her current state she'd splash some water on her face and come. *And why does she need to splash water on her face?*

He knocked. "Hey Logan."

Grant waited and hearing nothing, he knocked again. "I know you're in there. Please answer." Checking his watch, he waited. A minute is a very long time.

"I'm worried. I'm coming in," he announced as he knocked a third time and opened the door.

Logan was curled around a pillow in a chair. Frantically she tried to dry her tear stained face with her hands, straighten her skirt and stand.

Grant crossed the room in giant strides. He kneeled before her and pulled her into his arms. "Hey, sweetheart," he said "tell me what's so awful you won't go for a run with your dad."

"I-I-I-can't," she stammered fresh tears soaking his shirt.

"Then let me tell you what's wrong, okay?"

He waited until he felt her nod against his shoulder.

"You've tried so very hard to learn what your grandmothers say are important things for a young lady to know."

"But I've failed," Logan sobbed. "I'm-I'm-I'm an embarrassment."

"Actually, the truth is you aren't an embarrassment. It's impossible to meet their standards because they change them on you. Today the knife is supposed to be a certain distance from the plate, the spoon, etc. Tomorrow the distance is slightly different, so when you meet today's standard tomorrow, it will be wrong. The catch is, they'll never tell you. They'll only correct you.

"Imagine living with these shifting standards for seventeen years, never measuring up."

"Like Mother?" Logan lifted her head to watch his face when he answered.

"Exactly." Grant kissed the top of her head. "I understand more every day what your mother did to try to save you from a life of failing to measure up to shifting standards."

"She's never called me since she left," Logan said as new tears fell.

"Think about what was happening when she did leave," Grant said. "And while you're thinking back to that time, change into shorts and we'll go for a walk."

"I need to—,"

"Do nothing more than change into shorts. Stay barefooted if you want. We'll stay between here and the point if that's more comfortable for you," he offered, seeing the anxious fretting consume her.

"I'm getting mac and cheese from the freezer. It's like medicine and makes everything better." He walked to the door. "I'll wait. If it's that important for you to shower, put on makeup, etc. just for me, I'll wait. Understand though that I love you just as you are. I love you with no make-up, tears in your eyes and snot running from your nose."

"Ddaadd!" Logan drew the word out, every syllable infused with horror. She charged to her bathroom. "Oh Goddess, I'm a mess."

"But you are my mess and I love you even when you are or maybe even more so when you are a mess," Grant said and closed the door. He waited for feelings of doubt and insufficiency to pop up but none did. *I'm glad I paid attention when The Circle talked about how important it is to tell someone you love them especially when they're struggling.*

GRANT HEARD A CAR DOOR SHUT. His and Hunter's mother's voices were easily heard as they went up the front steps to the house. He and Logan had walked to the point and raced back. They'd had mac and cheese and were sitting on the dock, waiting for the sunset. Waiting to make ice cream sundaes and eat them by the fire pit off the back deck.

"You stay right here," he said as he stood. "I will send them on their way. You've spent enough time with them today."

"I—,"

"Will stay here," he repeated a bit more firmly. He saw her begin to muster up an argument. "Do me a favor and check in with your body and see how you feel. When I heard their voices, I saw you tense. Check that out while I'm gone. If you didn't tense up and you did remain relaxed and at ease, you can go in and call them."

The grandmothers were coming back out the front door onto the porch as he went up the steps.

"My goodness, Grant, where do you have her?" his mother asked.

"Yes, we really must talk to her tonight. The debutante ball is in two weeks and she needs more practice," Hunter's mother added.

"Here is how things will be from now on," Grant said escorting each woman back down the steps and to the car. He opened the passenger door and ushered in Mrs. Compton. Holding on to his mother's elbow he rounded the car, opened the driver's door and remained blocking her from passing by him until she subsided and got in.

He leaned down until he was eye-level. "Neither of you will say anything to Logan unless it is a compliment. One word of correction or criticism and you will not see her for forty-eight hours. If, after that time out, you continue to correct and criticize her, the time out will be increased to one week."

"Now Grant, you know we are only trying to help her be successful when she enters society," his mother started. "She has made such progress. I know it has been difficult but if she'd had any—."

"I will only repeat myself one more time. Listen carefully. If you offer one word of correction or criticism you will not see her for forty-eight hours. And, if I didn't make it clear before, you can no longer see her alone. I will be with her and I will be watching. If you call her on the phone, I'll listen in. One word of correction or criticism and you will not see her for forty-eight hours.

"This is not negotiable. There is no bargaining. This is an edict." He straightened and stepped back.

"You are not thinking as a father should," his mother said.

"No I'm not," Grant agreed. "I'm thinking like a Dad. Good night, ladies. Pleases do think carefully about what I said because I will enforce it."

He stood in the drive until his mother drove away before turning and heading back to the dock.

"I listened," Logan said.

"Of course you did," Grant said. "And I hope you heard and saw how I set boundaries with them." He leaned towards her, "And remember, that's pretty much how your mom did it with her father when she was here."

"That's how you've made it?" Logan asked. "You seem to not be affected by any of it at all."

"I used to be. Growing up I had it drummed into me what my responsibilities were as Grant Haywood Parker the Fourth. And until I spent that time in Fremont with you and your mom and the others, I followed along as I was meant to do. Other than a few occasions when I retreated to this house, I attended every social event I was expected to. I worked enormous hours as I was expected to. The only thing I didn't do was marry as I was expected to."

"Why?" Logan asked, taking his hand as they walked to the house.

"Because I never met anyone I wanted to spend my life with."

"But you had girlfriends. Grandmother Parker was talking about a Deidra, who was going to be moving back to Providence after her divorce and she hoped you'd marry her."

Grant laughed. "I will remain single the rest of my life before I marry her or anyone else my mother picks out for me.

"Ready for that ice cream sundae?" he asked. "I know it pales in comparison to what Jackson makes from scratch but it's the best store bought brand I know."

"We could make our own," Logan offered.

"Good idea. Tomorrow we'll go shopping for an ice cream maker and tomorrow night we'll have our own for dessert."

"We can make homemade sauces too. Jackson makes all kinds but most of us love his chocolate sauce on his peppermint ice cream. Maybe we can email him and see if he'll share the recipe." Logan's smile of anticipation grinned at him as she danced backward into the house.

"I think we should call him because that way we can plead and maybe he'll pity us and share." Grant bent his head, a hang-dog look on his face, a whine beginning in his voice.

"You are so funny, Dad," Logan said and giggled. "But you are so right. Jackson won't be able to say no if we plead."

They did call Jackson who took his time before agreeing to send them the recipe for the chocolate sauce. "The ice cream is a secret recipe. You'll have to develop your own."

Grant had taken the phone when Logan scampered off to turn on the computer. "Thanks," he'd said to Jackson. "You don't know how important having a recipe for chocolate sauce is right now."

"Ice cream sundaes smooth out almost every problem," Jackson had replied. "Be sure and bring your recipes for peppermint and vanilla ice cream out with you. We'll have a competition."

"Blind taste test?" Grant asked a teasing tone in his voice.

"It's the only kind I agree to because I know my ice cream is superior and I'll win," Jackson said and laughed.

"You're on. Logan and I will perfect our recipe and then come and challenge you."

"Good to know we'll see you again."

"Thanks again," Grant said and ended the call.

"Really, really Dad, we'll take on Jackson?" Logan stood in the doorway, her eyes wide with excitement.

"Not only will we take on Jackson, we'll win." He crossed the room and gave her a high-five.

The next night as they sat eating their homemade sundae, they discussed what needed improvement.

"I think a bit more vanilla. Sophia said you need vanilla to bring out the other flavors." Logan's eyes closed as she took another mouthful.

"Okay, but not too much more. I can barely taste the peppermint."

"Maybe add more peppermint and a little more vanilla?"

"I think we need to consult with Mrs. Ripley," Grant conceded.

"Or maybe call and ask Mom. When we make it at home, it tastes pretty good."

"Pretty good won't beat Jackson," Grant said.

And so it went all week long. Either or both of the grandmothers stopped by every day, using various strategies to draw him away so they could talk to Logan in private. He knew them too well. As they became more exasperated, he was more relaxed. Logan was always more formal around them but she wasn't as tense and there were no further tears—or none that he knew of.

They'd missed Hunter's birthday. Although they'd called and sent flowers, they weren't there.

"You know your mom missed seeing you on her birthday." Grant started the conversation off with the obvious.

Logan nodded. "But we sent flowers and called."

"What about surprising her?"

"With what?"

"I was thinking of asking her to meet us in Boston so she can see Smith College. We've done the tour but she hasn't. We could take her out to dinner at a great restaurant and maybe go dancing. You and I've been practicing and I bet she'd be surprised if we danced. We'll get rooms at the Parker Hotel so after the tour we can change before we go out. What do you think?"

"Do you think I'm ready?" Logan asked, anxiety twisting her mouth.

"You are perfectly ready" Grant reached over and ruffled her hair.

"Daad," Logan exclaimed. "You—," she looked over at him and laughed. "You are the best dad ever. I think it's a great plan but I don't think Mom will go for it."

"Leave that to me, okay?"

Logan nodded. "Ready to try tonight's peppermint ice cream?" she asked heading into the kitchen.

"Maybe we should go for a run first," Grant called out after her, patting his belly.

49 - BOSTON

After their run and ice cream, Logan had headed for bed. Grant headed to his office and the phone. With the Summer Recital on the twentieth and something called the Fourteenth Moon Ceremony over Labor Day weekend, the timing was tight.

First he called and talked to Jackson and Lily. Next he called Hunter and proposed the Boston trip suggesting maybe Jackson, Lily and Charlie would like to come.

When he hinted Logan had a surprise for her, Hunter's hesitation evaporated. Plans set, reservations made, he enjoyed the next four days making sure his work at the office was completed by noon. With Martha working for him, it was easy.

Grateful he'd made it clear he was taking on no new clients; Grant also carefully shifted the clients with the heaviest workloads to younger more eager associates. He remained available to them for consultation but these young lawyers were diligent and professional and he doubted he'd get many calls. Not only did this change offer them the opportunity for more experience but also more billable hours.

The partners were upset with him but that only fit into his longer term goal. Within the four or so hours he daily allocated to the firm, he easily completed what needed his personal attention.

Another one of his goals was to educate Logan on money management which in his world was known as investments. His mother had gifted her with ten thousand as had he. Not to be outdone, his father had matched it as had both the Knight Comptons. Her account sat at a little over fifty thousand dollars including interest.

Grant soon learned Logan had an aptitude for investments but needed a calculator to do the math. Interesting she understood the strategy even though her math skills were weak. He'd upgraded her phone to one that did more than make and receive calls. He smiled looking at the oblong mini-computer in his hand. *That's what phones are becoming, mini-computers.*

❧

Saturday
August 13, 2005

LOGAN DROVE THEM TO BOSTON. It was a different experience to be in the passenger seat and Grant enjoyed the scenery. She pulled over when they reached the city and asked him to drive the rest of the way. They checked into the Parker Hotel and then drove to Logan International Airport.

"How does it feel to have one of the busiest airports in the country named after you?" Grant asked as they drove past the sign welcoming them to the airport.

Her lighthearted giggle gladdened his heart.

They parked in the parking structure and were waiting outside security when Hunter, Lily, Jackson and Charlie came through. The look of pure joy on Logan's face tightened his chest as she dashed forward and hugged her mom, then keeping one arm around Hunter, hugged Lily, Jackson and Charlie.

Logan stayed close to Hunter, held Charlie's hand, and was so close to skipping or twirling right there in the airport, emotion clogged his throat and words were hard to speak.

Hunter had looked over at him with wonder and gratitude shining in her eyes. He'd smiled back, gave her a thumbs up and turned to Jackson and Lily.

The late afternoon was spent on the Smith College campus where the tour guide showed them the dorms, various buildings where classes were held and talked about the enlightened education women received at the school.

One thing Grant was grateful the grandmothers had done was take Logan shopping. When she showed him her new clothes, there was an ankle-length navy blue gown that looked fantastic on her. Matching sandals had medium height heels. She also had sparkly clips for her hair that matched the dress. The outfit was perfect for an evening of dining and dancing at an exclusive restaurant.

He and Charlie shared a room, Logan and Hunter next to theirs and Lily and Jackson across the hall.

Grant rocked back on his heels as the elevator door opened and Logan and Hunter walked out. Charlie's indrawn breath of appreciation matched his own. Grant approached the women who were the focal point of his life.

"Absolutely stunning!" He kissed Logan's cheek. "What do you think of our daughter?" he asked Hunter.

"She's amazing."

"As is her mother." Grant reached for Hunter's hand and as he held it, brushed his lips across her knuckles. An inward smile warmed his heart when he heard her sharp intake of breath.

Lily and Jackson arrived and the six of them went out to a waiting limousine.

They arrived exactly on time to the upscale restaurant, were ushered to their table and waited upon with just the right amount of attention. The food was excellent. Grant had the pasta seafood medley. Logan had laughed when he ordered but then ordered the same thing. Jackson had steak and lobster, Lily had the Atlantic salmon and Hunter had scampi and wild rice. Charlie followed Jackson's lead.

As dinner progressed, conversation easily flowed around the table. Logan and Charlie were included, listened to and encouraged to speak. At ten-thirty plates were being cleared away. Grant stood and rounded the table to where Logan was sitting.

"Will you do me the honor of this dance," he asked.

She beamed up at him and nodded. Rising she said, "I'd love to." As they crossed to the dance floor she asked, "Is this Mom's surprise?"

"Part of it." It was a surreal moment, holding his daughter in his arms, leading her out to dance. *I have a first that her mother could never have had.*

The music came to an end. Placing her hand on his arm, Grant led her back to their table. "Thank you for the dance," he said bowing before her.

"Thank you." Logan's eyes shone with unshed tears.

"Happy?" he asked making sure he wasn't misreading something.

"If we weren't here, I would hug you," Logan said.

He slipped his arms around her and pulled her close. "Never let being in public keep you from hugging your dad, your mom or someday your husband and kids."

Logan held him tight. "Thank you," she said lifting her head so she spoke closer to his ear because the music had started again.

When he stepped back, Charlie was next to Logan.

"May I?" he asked.

"I'd love to," Logan said.

Lily and Jackson were also making their way to the dance floor.

"Our turn." Grant held his hand out to Hunter.

"I am beyond words to tell you what I felt seeing you and our daughter dance," Hunter said. "She's, she's—."

"Yes, she is," Grant replied, holding her a fraction of an inch closer. "Now I'm going to ask you a question and I don't want you to yell at me."

Hunter looked at him, her turquoise green eyes squinting before she nodded.

"Just how close is our daughter with Charlie?"

"Jealous? Worried?"

"Uncertain if I should be worried," Grant replied, his cheek resting against her temple.

Hunter leaned back. "I told you before they are friends. That hasn't changed. She, Bill and Charlie have always been friends but I think she and Charlie are a bit closer. Are they close enough that she's talked to him about what happened? I don't think so. Are they close as in forming a romantic attachment? I don't think that either—he is a wonderful young man and although I wouldn't discourage that happening I wouldn't encourage it either."

They danced until one, made their way out to the limousine and back to the hotel.

"Sleep in, everyone," Grant said as they ambled down the hall to their rooms.

"No plans for tomorrow?" Hunter asked.

"Not plans but options"

Hunter's eyebrows rose when she saw his conspiratorial wink at Logan.

"Let's plan on meeting around eleven in the lobby. We can decide what we want to do for breakfast then."

"Eleven? What about ten?" Logan asked.

"Perfect," Lily said.

"Do I get any hints about the options?" Charlie asked as they entered their room.

"None," Grant said. "You need to be surprised along with everyone else."

"Logan won't be surprised," Charlie said. "I saw you wink at her."

"That doesn't mean there isn't a surprise for her too," Grant said.

Grant and Charlie met up with Logan, Hunter, Lily and Jackson in the lobby. They decided to walk to a nearby deli for breakfast. At noon, the van Grant had ordered pulled up to the hotel. The tour guide presented their options. Since this was a private tour, they could see what they wanted. The Old North Church, Faneuil Hall, Concord and Lexington along with a stroll along the waterfront, Beacon Hill and Boston Commons all made the list.

Dinner that evening was at a local tavern noted for sandwiches and local craft beers, in distinct contrast to the elegant restaurant where they'd dined last night. An outside seating area was open to the general public which meant minors could sit there. The humidity was bearable so they straddled the benches and sat at a long wooden table that easily held the six of them.

Back at the hotel, Grant informed everyone that tomorrow's surprise meant they would check out of the hotel.

"We'll meet in the lobby at seven and stop for breakfast at eight." He saw Hunter say something to Logan who shook her head. Smiling he went on to his room, leaving the others to wonder what tomorrow would bring. When Charlie came in, he was in bed and dozing.

As they were packing in the morning, Grant asked Charlie about driving in Boston. "If you mean will the crazy drivers bother me, not really," the young man replied.

Meeting up with everyone in the lobby, he relished the look of anticipation and adventure on everyone's face. Even Hunter was caught up in "what's next?"

He hailed the Bell Captain and gave him the ticket for his car. Ushering everyone outside, he saw the second car he'd rented for the occasion. When his car arrived, he directed that Logan and Charlie's luggage be put in his trunk, the remaining pieces in the second car.

"Surprise for the day is a road trip." Grant tossed his keys to Charlie. "Those two are taking my car and following us. We'll regroup at breakfast."

"Are you sure?" Hunter nodded towards Charlie and Logan who had already gotten in his car.

"I am. Logan drove all the way up here until we hit city traffic. Charlie is comfortable driving in city traffic so they'll be just fine." He escorted Hunter to the car they were using.

"Men in front and women in back or are we dividing up?" he asked Lily, Jackson and Hunter.

"We are not doing men in front and women in back," Hunter said huffily. "If you want to divide things that way, the women will be in front and the men in back."

"Let's do it this way." Grant gestured to Hunter to sit in the passenger seat. "We can change things around at breakfast."

Before Grant got into the driver's seat, he checked on Charlie and Logan. "If we get separated, call me," he said reminding them again of the road out of town and the name of the restaurant.

BREAKFAST at a little place in Plymouth was an event. The food delicious and the guessing about the rest of the day's activities kept the conversation lively.

Grant almost told everyone the plan but decided to keep things a secret for the time being. He knew Hunter would know where they were going within a few hours as would Logan.

Late in the afternoon they approached Providence. He took an exit and headed towards the shore. Hunter had become stonily quiet as they crossed into Rhode Island. Lily had never been to the east coast so it was all new to her. Jackson had been raised out here, spent summers at the shore, had sisters' who still lived in Massachusetts. One of the reasons the Montgomerys had come on this trip was to spend a few days visiting Jackson's sisters and their families.

He pulled into the circular drive in front of his house. Lights were on just as he'd asked. He expected food would be ready also. He, for one, was starving.

Charlie and Logan pulled in behind, got out of the car and stretched.

"Grab your bags. Logan, you and your mom are sharing your room. Show Lily and Jackson the second master and Charlie the guest room, okay?" He waited, saw her nod before he retrieved the luggage from the trunk and headed inside, bags in hand.

Mrs. Ripley was waiting, a pitcher of iced tea on a tray on the kitchen island, his favorite pasta and seafood salad, her pasta and red sauce with meatballs on a platter next to it. The aroma of freshly baked bread filled the room. Two loaves, still warm from the oven, were wrapped in towels in bread baskets.

Candles on the back deck, a fire going in the fire pit, a bar set up in case Jackson or Lily or even Hunter wanted something stronger than iced tea.

Grant washed at the sink, took the towel Mrs. Ripley handed him and greeted everyone when they, following their noses and Logan, found the kitchen. He introduced Mrs. Ripley and invited everyone to dish up, gestured to the back deck and stepped back.

"I suppose you have homemade ice cream for dessert," Jackson commented as he helped himself to the spaghetti and red sauce, meatballs and seafood pasta salad.

"Contest does not begin until Logan and I are in Fremont. I

wouldn't ask your wife to vote against you." Grant's stern facial expression was at odds with the laughter in his eyes.

"What's this all about?" Hunter asked.

"Dad and I've been experimenting with homemade ice cream and we think our recipe for peppermint ice cream and maybe even our vanilla is as good," Logan paused, pressed a hand to her mouth to stifle the giggles, "as good as Jackson's. Dad and Jackson have a bet—well, sort of a bet."

"You?" Hunter looked askance. "You cooking in the kitchen? I didn't know you knew how to do anything except heat something up in the microwave."

"Too true, you don't know what a culinary genius I've become." Grant winked at Logan. "Why Logan and I have been cooking up all sorts of things."

Charlie and Logan took their plates and sat near the fire pit. The adults took over the table on the upper level.

"You made this seafood salad?" Lily asked. "I love it."

"Wish I could claim credit. Mrs. Ripley put all this together. I can cook pasta and I can cook seafood so it is a dish I've learned to fix. Bread, red sauce and meatballs? Not even. I can do a tossed green salad. I've perfected my chopping and dicing skills this past month."

"We're going for a walk," Logan called out as she and Charlie left the fire pit and walked out towards the water.

"This is a magical place," Lily said. "I can see why Logan has wanted to stay for the summer. And this is where you grew up?" she asked Hunter.

"My family has a place up the shore. Grant's parents' place is a few doors closer. It can be a magical place," Hunter allowed. "I'll clear the table," she said and stood.

"If we take things inside, Mrs. Ripley will clean up the kitchen." Grant picked up his own plate and silverware and headed inside.

That done they walked down to the fire pit, stood around it and watched the flames.

"Grant, Grant," Charlie called.

Grant sprinted off the lower deck and down the sand. "Coming!"

He saw Logan standing stiff, surrounded by his mother and Hunter's. He charged up to them

"That's it. Logan, you go back to the house. Now," he said, pointing behind him. He turned, saw Hunter and said, "Take her back to the house. She will not see either of these harridans for the rest of the summer."

"You can't—," his mother started.

"Keep you from your granddaughter?" he finished. "Watch me."

"But Grant," Mrs. Compton whined. "She's—,"

"She's perfect just the way she is and since you can't see that and can't appreciate that and since you *were warned* that's it. You are banned from my property. If I need to I will have a restraining order filed against you, leak it to the press so everyone knows how vile you both are."

"I don't think they're vile." Hunter stood beside him and tucked her arm in his. "They are misguided. However, I totally support the idea of a restraining order."

"Do I get any say in this?" Logan asked.

"Of course you do." Hunter turned and reached out to include her daughter.

Charlie by her side, Logan stepped next to her dad. "I know you are only thinking of what's best for me. You want me to fit in and not be an embarrassment to your families. I know all that but I also know I am who I am. I have faults. I'll never be perfect in your eyes. But," she leaned into Grant. "I am perfect in my dad's eyes and in my mom's eyes and in the eyes of my friends. I'm perfect because they look at me with eyes of love and that blurs some of my faults.

"Maybe when I'm older, I'll be able to set the boundaries my mom and dad have set but I don't seem able to do that yet. And that tells me I can't spend time with either of you." Logan turned around and walked back towards Grant's shore house.

"Logan," the grandmothers' chorused. "My dear, don't—."

"She's made her decision, Mother, Mrs. Compton." He slipped Hunter's arm through his. "Do you have anything else you want to say?"

"Not really. Well, there is one thing. It may be hard for you or Father to understand why being a Knight Compton isn't as important to me as it has always been to you; why being accepted as part of society was never my goal; why living the life you chose for me was what I rebelled against. It was never my goal to hurt you or shame you. My goal was always to choose my own path. A deep sadness lodges here," Hunter rubbed her heart, "when I think about all we've lost because you didn't understand."

"And are you happy? Are you glad you struggled, scrimped, saved?" her mother asked in an imperious tone.

"Since the tradeoff was choosing my own path, yes, I am happy for every minute of my life." Hunter's voice rang with her clarity.

"But Logan didn't have fashionable clothing, didn't know all the rules of etiquette until we stepped in," Mrs. Parker said, her criticism dripping from each word.

"Not as you see them, that's true. And, if you will recall, Mother, my choices were an abortion or adoption," Hunter replied.

"You could have married Grant," her mother shot back. "If you had said who the father was, you could have been married. Logan would have had two parents and lacked for nothing."

She glanced up at Grant and saw the same thought cross his face that had just dawned on her. *They wanted us to have that time together.*

Looking back at her mother, she said, "Logan lacked for nothing as it is. She's had love and acceptance from me and others. Now she has even more because she has that from her dad. Because she is loved and accepted unconditionally, she's always had more than the trappings of society could ever provide.

"We have guests and we are being rude by staying here instead of tending to them. I'm sure you understand why we are returning to them now." Hunter turned away and started back down the beach, Grant by her side.

"You remember asking me why our parents had left us alone that summer?"

"I do," Grant replied. "And now I think it was on purpose; a plot to merge the Parker and Knight Compton families."

"I don't think we would have made it. We would have lost—I know that if we'd married and things had gone bad my memories of our summer would have been tainted. As it is, I look around here and the memories come. They are bittersweet. They have pain laced within them. But there is also joy."

"By the way, you were magnificent." Grant leaned towards her.

"And so were you," Hunter said. "You really were in her corner."

"Who did you talk to when you had doubts about what you were doing?" Grant asked matching her stride.

"I didn't always have someone to talk to. But I always went back to "love". Was my decision based on my love for her? Were my words said from a loving space? And what did it matter if someone thought I was wrong? Who were they? Were they someone I needed to pay attention to?"

"So if someone in the grocery store frowned?"

"I ignored it but if her teacher made a suggestion, I listened. And then I watched other mom's interact with their kids. If I caught myself thinking 'I wish my mother had done that' I paid attention."

The house was in sight, four silhouettes backlit by the fire pit waited at the bottom of the steps.

"Mom, I don't belong here," Logan said as Hunter approached the steps.

Grant stumbled, caught himself with Jackson's hand on his arm before he fell.

"What about Smith College?" Hunter asked.

"I was also accepted at the University of Oregon and Fremont State, I do have options."

"And your dad?" Hunter added, looking his way.

Grant remained a couple of steps back hoping his face was not illuminated by the fire light. The bleakness that crawled through his gut iced him from the inside out.

"Dad can visit. Maybe we can find a place, somewhere in between, to meet until I can handle the grandmothers." Logan looked miserable but determined.

"Of course your dad can visit any time he can get away."

Grant waited to hear Hunter say something to him about moving to Fremont. Waited for Logan to come and hug him, ask him when he could visit. Waited for an invitation that, as the moments ticked by, wasn't going to come. He'd burst into their lives without an invitation once before, he'd learned his lesson and wasn't going to do that again.

"Need a drink?" Jackson's soft voice came from behind his left shoulder.

"Drink for sure but need to move first—and stop me after two." Grant started walking towards the point. "I don't want to get drunk and miss whatever time I have left with her."

Jackson fell in beside him, his quiet presence helped.

The tide was in. Grant stood just outside the water line. A buoy sounded in the night. Lights along the horizon showed ships out at sea. Painful questions circled: the kind that have no answer but are still asked.

Where did I go wrong? Should I have stepped in between Logan and the mothers earlier? Should I have talked to Hunter about the idea of moving to Fremont? Should I have tried to stop Logan from leaving? How will I manage without my daughter here? How can I go back to what my life used to be?

Each question created a sharp numbing pain. Tears threatened but a Parker doesn't cry. His knees shook but a Parker doesn't fall to his knees in a lump of weakness. A Parker doesn't... .

The deep mournful sound of the buoy echoed in every cell in his body. The water rushed, nibbling just beyond his toes and then slipped away. He'd gotten close. He'd rushed out to Fremont, nibbled around the toes of fatherhood and now watched it ebb away.

JACKSON STAYED with him when they returned to the house and his office. Two scotch on the rocks and they stopped. No real conversation; there weren't any words to fill the gaping hole now left in his life.

The next morning, Grant sucked it up, put his game face on and played the perfect host. The iron bar held his head on his neck, the 'T' keeping his shoulders back. The cold mass in his gut rejected anything but water. He waved Hunter, Logan and Charlie off on their run down the beach.

For a moment he worried that the grandmothers would attack again but a glance at his watch told him it was too early for them to be put together enough to be out in public. There was a positive side to the "image is everything" view of the world.

Mrs. Ripley appeared and made omelets, French toast from the bread she'd baked yesterday and set up a bowl of fresh fruit and a pitcher of fresh squeezed orange juice. He picked up his glass of water and went out on the dock.

Logan had packed her Fremont clothes last night. The clothes and mementoes she'd acquired while in Ireland and here with him would be shipped. Her excited chatter about Twinkle Toes and returning to Fremont drifted across the deck as they ate Mrs. Ripley's breakfast.

Pleading work and needing to get caught up, Grant ordered a town car to take Charlie, Logan and Hunter into New York to LaGuardia.

Lily and Jackson were driving the rental car back to Boston where they planned to spend the rest of the week with Jackson's sisters. Eleanor was flying in to Boston from Ireland late in the week. The Montgomery family reunion was planned for the weekend of the twentieth.

Standing at the railing, looking out to the horizon, even the fresh sea air did nothing for his pounding head. If only, if only, if only but neither Logan nor Hunter asked about him moving to Fremont. In fact this morning they didn't ask him about anything, even visits.

His original plan had been to become a part of his daughter's life. He'd succeeded at that. It was his fantasy to move to Fremont and create a family with Hunter and Logan, not theirs.

The image of the chaos he'd created when he first barged into their lives quelled any urge to share that fantasy with them, to tell them he wanted to move to Fremont, would willingly give up this life to be with them.

The risk of losing what he had was too great.

Grant stood in the driveway, waving as the vehicles drove away. He wandered through the side yard and down to the sand. Kicking his shoes and pulling his socks off, he tossed them up on the steps. Off he ran, as if the demons from hell were after him. Even his common sense told him he was overdoing it but he didn't care. If he just reached the zone, the pain would be gone. He'd have that time of euphoria. But no matter how far or how fast he ran, he never found the zone.

51 - 14TH MOON

Fourteenth Moon Ceremony
Labor Day Weekend
September, 2005

There was something peaceful and serene about setting up tents up in the shade created by a circle of tall fir trees, footsteps softened by an inches-deep covering of needles, the whisper of wind through the overhead branches. Hunter shared one of the tents with Gabriella, Sophia and Lily. Diana, Elizabeth and Ashley were in the next tent. Logan camped, as was the tradition, with the other maidens, all young women who'd had their first menses.

A path through the trees led to another circle within a grove of aspen. A fire pit to one side would be lit and cared for throughout ceremony. On the opposite side of the fir grove a food tent was set up. Tables and chairs scattered in the general area gave the women a chance to socialize during meals or other times when they weren't in the sacred circle.

Hunter volunteered to drum as the women entered the circle; to tend the fire; to help with the food—anything to keep involved, to keep busy, to keep unwanted thoughts at bay.

In the early afternoon, she waved the cleansing smudge around her before entering the circle for the Matron Ceremony. The other matrons, all women who had had children and still had their monthly flow, settled on the yellow sheets and blankets covering the ground.

Sitting cross-legged, Hunter relaxed and imagined a place where she was safe.

Safe and comfortable.

Safe and free.

Safe and loved.

Unbidden the curve in the bank along the Rhode Island shore came to her. The vision wasn't from the past because she'd paid attention to that spot when she was on the beach and knew the land had eroded over the years so the shape was different than it had been all those years ago.

It was the epitome of the place where she was safe, was loved, was free and it wasn't empty.

The hunched figure now in that space was the reason she'd felt safe, free and loved. Then the figure rose and walked away leaving that sacred space of love, safety and acceptance empty.

Hunter heard a moan. Arms surround her. She sagged against Lily, took tissues from Sophia and after wiping her eyes tried for a smile. Failing that, she buried her head in arms that now encircled her knees. "I'm okay," she whispered taking deep calming breathes in through her nose and exhaling through her mouth.

In ceremony it was always an option to share or not. Hunter chose not to. One of the blessings about sacred women's circles was the honoring of such decisions. As she left the circle, she was not mobbed with questions about what happened, although a concerned Logan did come and walk with her to her tent.

"I can bring you dinner if you want to rest," Logan offered.

"Not sure I can eat anything right now," she replied.

"I'll check back with you before they put the food away just in case," Logan said. A long hug and a soft "I love you, Mom" and Logan was gone. She was alone.

Lily returned to the tent, a plate of fruit, cheese and a few rice crackers—"just in case." When Sophia wandered over, she pulled a bottle of seltzer water from a pocket. Gabriella appeared with a mug of hot tea. That she accepted and sipped. Chamomile.

Still in a place of distant visions and memories, she sat through the Crone Ceremony. What one of the wise women said seemed to register, to resonate.

"Wisdom is knowing what of your past you can mend, can reclaim and what of your past to let go."

The curve in the bank was part of her past, part of her past with Grant. Was she to reclaim it or let it go?

Sleep eluded her. Wrapped in a blanket, she sat outside the tent, watching the night sky, listening to night sounds: the hoots from owls, the scuffle of small animals in the undergrowth, the howl of a coyote. Sitting in the quiet, in the stillness, she let the thoughts and images appear and fade. The urge to dance or drum, to move, to do something absent, she waited for a feeling of unease to claim her. It never did.

Hunter still sat outside when the sun came up. A golden red globe inching its way across the blue sky, its face fractured with the shadowed outline of mountains and trees.

It was an interesting space to be in—there but not there. The curve in the bank in her inner vision, she packed, helped take the tent down and clean up the grounds. Logan offered to drive home. She accepted.

NEITHER UPSET NOR surprised when she heard Lily and Diana's voices, she managed to stand up by the time they reached the top of the stairs.

"You know you don't have to talk," Diana started. "Lily and I met up outside without even talking to each other."

"Brought you a container of Sophia's peanut butter cookies and another one with her pecan sticky buns. She had her sick friend to help but asked me to bring these to you." Lily placed two plastic containers on the kitchen counter. "Mind if I fix a pot of tea?" she asked Hunter.

"No, go ahead." Hunter curled up in the chair she'd inhabited before their arrival. Chilled even on a warm late summer day, she pulled a throw around her shoulders.

"I know it was only a few days, but tell us how Madison Michelle is doing?" Lily asked Diana.

"M2 is with Matthew. They're out checking work sites." She laughed and pulled out a picture of the baby in a front facing carrier, a mini hard hat on her head. Matthew was pointing at something and M2 appeared to be looking in that direction.

"At eight months, her receptive language is miles ahead of her expressive skills. I'm not sure that means she understands construction terms," Lily said and laughed. "More like mama, dada, bottle, bear or whatever her favorite toys are."

"It's a wonderful and strange gift to have this little girl in my life." Diana smiled and put the picture back in her wallet. "I was unsure of what it would be like at my age to have an infant who will be a toddler before I know it. When I look back on life with Bill at this stage it was almost like being a single parent. Matthew changes diapers, gets up with her at night, feeds her, plays with her. I'm so grateful I reached out for him.

"You do know," she said looking at Hunter, "that I almost didn't. I sat in front of his place for some time and almost talked myself into driving off. Whatever gave me the strength to go to him and tell him I loved him—." She laughed "Did you know I asked him to marry me?

"Now why did I say all that?" Diana sat back, a curious look on her face. "I came to keep you company, not regale you with stories about my almost not-marriage."

Lily invited Hunter to join her on a trip to the Monterrey Bay area.

"Thanks for the invitation but that is your time with Jackson. And Logan has some things to do to get ready for college. She couldn't get into the dorm because she registered so late. Friday we're going apartment hunting in Eugene." She sighed. "If we can't find something close to campus, I may have to get her a car."

"Charlie is also checking with his friends to see if anyone needs another roommate," Lily reminded her. "What if I check my schedule and move things around so you and I can both go down there with the kids?" Lily suggested.

"Just what they want," Diana said and laughed.

September 05, 2005
Rhode Island

"And just why are you here?" Martha interrogated Grant Tuesday morning when she came in with his mail. "You look like hell. And, I'm working harder because you are not paying attention to what you are doing," she lectured.

Grant knew he looked like he hadn't slept because he hadn't. He knew he was making mistakes because he was. He knew—. "Leave it." He scrubbed his face with his hands. "Just leave it, Martha."

"No, I'm not going to leave it." She marched back to the door, shutting and locking it. Turning towards him she fixed him with a piercing stare. "You are going to listen to me."

She crossed to his desk, pulled up a chair and leaned her forearms on the top.

"I've known you since you came to work here. You've done everything expected of you and more. Rising through the ranks to partner in short time. You are admired and emulated by some of the younger attorneys. Every support staff wants to work for you because you are fair and professional.

"In all that time, I've never seen you happy and seldom seen you content. Even when you had some woman in your life, you were never as happy as you've been this summer. Think about it and ask yourself why would you try to stuff yourself back into a mold that never really fit you when you could reclaim that happiness."

Grant paced the office. "Happy? You think I was happy trying to figure out how to parent an eighteen year old I barely knew?"

"I saw you happy and I saw you parenting your daughter who adores you," Martha countered.

"She starts college later this month. She's moving forward with her life and doesn't really have time for me."

"Pity party, pity party," Martha said in a singsong tone. "Really, I thought you could do better than that. Answer this then: What keeps you from moving closer to her, being able to spend Dad's Weekend with her? Make a date and take her out for lunch during finals?"

"I've not been invited for anything more than a visit. What's more, when I just showed up the first time I made a royal mess of everything." Grant rubbed the back of his neck with one hand the other fisted on his hip. "And I've a house, condo, job, obligations, connections," he continued, ticking them off on one hand.

"You can sell the house, the condo, quit, get rid of your obligations. Those connections that mean something to you, keep them. You already have connections in Fremont to build upon. Maybe another job is waiting for you?"

Grant frowned noting Martha had ignored the first part. "And what will you do if I leave?"

"I'm your secretary, not your obligation. I'll be just fine." She caught his gaze and held it. "I'll be just fine if you leave. Will you be just fine if you stay?"

Martha rose, put the chair back in its place, strode to the door, unlocked it and walked out.

Would he be okay if he stayed?

No, no I won't be okay if I stay.

whirlwind of activity consumed the rest of Grant's day. He put his condo on the market, called a contractor he'd worked with before to meet him at the shore house that evening. A call to Ms. Lawford had a positive outcome. With his background in financial investments, trusts, etc., she was sure they could work something out. That night he wrote out his letter of resignation giving the firm four weeks notice that he was leaving.

The next morning, he called Martha in to his office. "I've an answer to your question. If I stay I will be miserable. I've turned in my resignation, given them a four week notice. And, I've other news.

"I'm having caretaker quarters added onto the shore house. The person who lives there will also need to be able to take care of business dealings I still have in the area. I'm offering that position to you. A generous salary and benefits come with the deal. This weekend, come out and see the place. The new quarters will be ready before Halloween but if you accept, you can move in sooner and use one of the bedrooms until it's done."

"What's this?" Herb charged through the door waving a piece of paper. "You're giving us notice?"

"That's what it says. And, I'm trying to tempt Martha to leave with me." The last vestiges of the cold lodged deep in his gut seeped away to be filled, not by emptiness, but by the warmth of hope.

"Four, what the hell is going on here," Herb shouted. "You can't just leave."

Grant looked at the man who at one time had been his mentor and for a brief moment wondered what happened. His soft yet firm voice reflected the calm infiltrating every cell. "I only have a few clients now. I'm not interested in building more billable hours. If you want to discuss setting up a west coast office in Fremont, I may consider it but right now, I'm not even sure I want to be an attorney."

News of his resignation spread like a fire storm through the three floors in the office building the firm occupied. Ten minutes from when Herb charged out of his office, his father called demanding an explanation. Considering his father didn't even work for the firm, Grant was surprised.

"Let's have lunch," Grant said. "I'll tell you more. Invite mother and I'll tell you both."

His father ordered him to come to the house for dinner. Grant declined, offering to pay for their dinner at a restaurant in town.

Before the end of the day, both of his parents had made several calls but he'd held firm. They refused to meet with him in a public place and he refused to meet with them in private. When he checked in with Trotter later in the day, he learned his parents were lying in wait for him. "Call me when they leave," he requested.

Grant spent the evening in a quiet little restaurant and bar a mile away. When he got the 'all clear', it was eleven.

Of course the next morning they were waiting for him when he left for work. He stood on the sidewalk, refusing their offer of a ride to the office. He once again invited them to lunch or dinner at a restaurant of their choice. At one point his father's face was a reddish purple and Grant wondered if Three would have a stroke right there on the sidewalk.

By the weekend, thankfully his parents were exhausted. In his entire life he'd never defied them to this extent. While he'd set boundaries with Logan, this was different. His father had stayed out of that. In his entire life, Three had never gone toe-to-toe with Four and lost.

To put them out of their misery and to give himself a break, on Sunday he wrote them a short email. Points made were:

1. I want to live my own life without the obligations of being Grant Haywood Parker IV of Rhode Island.

2. I want to find out if I can create a good life for myself based on who I am as a person and not on my name.

3. I want an on-going close relationship with my daughter.

4. I'm selling the condo, creating a caretaker suite at the shore house and moving to Fremont.

INSTEAD OF TRAVELING to Eugene to apartment hunt for Logan with Lily, Hunter was on the plane.

Destination: Rhode Island.

Purpose: To reclaim, if possible, her relationship with Grant.

No surprise visit this time, she'd called ahead and asked him to meet her at the shore house saying she wanted to talk to him with no one else around.

The town car circled the drive, stopping in front of the steps. The driver helped her out, deposited her suitcase next to her and drove off.

For the first time since she made the decision, made the call, doubts assaulted and she questioned her impulsive plan. She replayed the phone call with Grant in her mind. Had he been reluctant, pleased, neutral when she'd asked to meet him here? *He didn't sound excited...*

What was she thinking coming all the way out here? Was it possible to reclaim that long ago summer? Was it wise to even try? Her stomach lurched at the thought he'd coolly listen to what she had to say and then send her away. *He either will or he won't. Standing here—.*

At the bottom of the stairs, she took a deep breath. Shoulders back and chin up, she marched up onto the porch.

She didn't even have to knock.

He was waiting for her.

Hunter wanted to launch herself into his arms. Feel the sense of safety and homecoming she'd imagined but Grant's arms were not out-stretched.

Instead, he stepped to the side and gestured her into the house. Hunter left her suitcase in the entryway and walked on through to the back deck. Leaning on the rail, she breathed in the salt air.

Moments later Grant was at her side, his back to the ocean, his elbows resting on the top board.

"What's going on?" he asked not looking at her.

"I need to talk to you."

"So you said."

Hunter remembered the words of the Crone at the 14th Moon. "Wisdom is knowing what of your past to reclaim and what to let go." She'd known when she heard those words that what they'd shared that summer was worth at least the effort. *Which is why I'm here.*

"Will you walk with me?" Hunter turned to Grant and held out her hand.

He didn't take it, didn't touch her in any way but he did follow her down to the sand.

One of those times to trust. Rather like the 14th Moon when my dancing and drumming wouldn't have helped me sort things through. I needed to be still and quiet.

She started along the sand, her hands tucked into her pants pockets, comforted that he matched his stride to hers.

They walked in silence.

"Let's sit here," Hunter said as they approached the curve in the bank.

"Time to talk?" he asked.

"Time to be. Time to just be together." *The words will come when the time is right.*

The space was small enough their shoulders and arms touched. The space filled with his scent, with his heat. Uncertainty leached from her body and she relaxed against him.

Grant's sigh was more a whoosh of breath than a soft exhale.

"I've missed you." Hunter tipped her head back the better to see his profile. "I'm here because of something one of the Crone's, an elder woman of the 14th Moon circle, said. She talked about wisdom being our knowing what of the past to let go and what to at least try to reclaim.

"We're not the same people we were back then but what we had was so—." She sighed and started again. "I don't have words adequate to express what our summer together meant to me. The sense of freedom, of safety, of knowing I was loved unconditionally was a gift that I treasure to this day.

"I want to at least try to reclaim a part of that summer with you. I don't have any expectations really other than we'll spend time together and see what happens."

"What do you mean? See what happens?" Grant shifted to see her.

"That's the beauty of it. No expectations."

"You'll move here?"

"If that's what is needed to see if we can reclaim what we had, yes I will." Hunter stood. Reaching back, she took his hand and holding it firmly, said "Need some help?"

Grant bounced up, wrapped his arms around her and kissed her, a deep heated kiss. Her toes curled into the sand, her arms slipped up around his neck and she kissed him back. The magic of being in his arms again swirled around her.

Drawing back to catch their breaths, Hunter looked into his blue grey eyes and saw the promise of a future together.

"Do you know why I've never married?" Grant's gaze locked with her turquoise-green one.

She shook her head.

"Because every time I thought about the future, of waking up with someone for the rest of my life—the only face I ever saw was yours."

"Do you know why I've never married?" Hunter's gaze locked with his blue-grey one.

He shook his head.

"Because no matter how hard I tried, I could never erase the feel of your arms around me, your lips on mine, your body pressed against mine, your voice whispering in my ear."

Grant rested his forehead against hers. "Does it seem strange to you that after all that has happened, I still love you? That I want to spend the rest of my life with you?"

"No," Hunter whispered. "No," she said more forcefully. "It doesn't seem strange to me at all because I came back here to see if I could reclaim what we had, to see if the magic was still there between us."

"And is it?"

Hunter tipped her head and kissed his jaw, nibbled at the stubble of his beard, sucked his earlobe. "I think it is."

"Just the physical attraction?"

"Just?" Hunter stepped back. She laughed and shook her head. "No, not 'just' the physical attraction. There is so much more."

Grant sank to one knee and held her hand to his heart. "Hunter, will you do me the distinct honor of becoming my wife?"

Hunter joined him in the sand. "I will become your wife if you will become my husband."

He laughed "No man and wife for you?"

She wrapped her arms around his neck, kissed him fully before she replied. "Equal terms, a partnership."

"I can do that," he said. "You may have to remind me if you see me slipping into old patterns. I want this future with you and Logan enough to make the changes."

Fall Equinox
September 21, 2005

They'd come full circle. Holding hands during the flight home to Fremont, Hunter gazed at the jade cabochon encircled by tiny pearls on her ring finger. Her right hand stroked the matching pearl and jade pendant dangling from a simple strand of pearls around her neck. Grant's ring finger sported a simple gold band. Inside, hidden from view, was an etching of what looked like a wave but was really a curve in a sand bank.

Once in Fremont, they still had to face everyone who would be understandably upset they'd missed the wedding. In the end it was an easy decision to get married on this day. The fall equinox, when the days and nights shared equal space, was a metaphor for their new life together.

Sharing equally the joys of being Logan's parents.

Sharing equally the challenges of creating a new life together.

Sharing the freedom of loving someone and knowing you were loved in return.

Grant, who technically had two weeks remaining of his four week

notice, left Martha in charge of the caretaker renovation. He'd transferred every client file and assured everyone he would still be available on a consulting basis.

Logan was starting college next Monday. Being there was a first he
refused to miss. His old obligations, whether to the firm or his family,
were definitely on a backburner if they weren't already boiled dry and
tossed out.

"I love you," he whispered in Hunter's ear. He noticed the shiver,
the slight blush in her cheeks. "Do you know what I want to do right
now?" He let the breath from his voice caress her neck.

Hunter knew he was enjoying the tease and when they landed and
were home, he'd follow through. "I do know what you want to do," she
said in a breathless response. "And this is what I want to do." Her low
sultry tone stroked his ear as her fingers stroked his palm. "Well,
maybe not just to your hand."

"Truce," Grant choked out.

Hunter laughed. "Truce." She snuggled next to him.

It was dark when they arrived in Fremont. No one met them
because no one knew they were flying in tonight.

Logan was in Eugene moving her things into an apartment she and
Charlie were sharing with two of Charlie's friends. Lily and Jackson
had met them and vouched for them. Hunter trusted the Montgomery's decision about the young people. Grant was looking
forward to his role as a dad in this first in Logan's life. Meeting the
roommates and checking them out for himself would happen before
the weekend.

They took a cab to the studio. Hunter unlocked the door and
turned off the alarm while Grant paid the driver and got their bags.
Martha would send more of his things once he decided what he
needed.

On the beach, Hunter had said she'd move to Rhode Island to
recapture what they'd had. She'd been willing to move to be with him.
Knowing her relationship with her parents and siblings was still fractured and might never be whole, her commitment to "them" meant
a lot.

Long into the night they'd talked. He shared his idea of moving to Fremont and working with Ms. Lawford. Her tears that she and Logan had never even guessed that was an option were kissed away.

Logan was their north star.

Grant had joked about getting a unit in the same apartment complex; Hunter was sure there was a thread of seriousness to the statement. Being in Fremont was close enough, he finally allowed.

Settled on the couch in the upstairs living quarters, Grant scrolled through his digital camera for the pictures of their wedding. He'd paid the couple waiting behind them to take them. Paid them enough to pay for their honeymoon and then some he thought, remembering the stunned expressions on their faces as he gave them four hundred dollars to take a few pictures of the ceremony.

He called Hunter to join him and breathed deeply of her cinnamon scent. She snuggled next to him as he scrolled picture by picture.

He was talking to a judge he knew in this one.

Hunter and he holding hands.

The judge holding the marriage ceremony binder.

The next four they were saying their vows.

"I now pronounce you husband and wife," Grant said as he checked out the next picture. "I'm sure this is where the judge said that." He kissed her temple. "Let's see what comes next"

"Let me guess." Hunter tipped her head so she looked in his eyes. She curled her hand around his neck, pulled him closer and kissed him. "I think this was next."

Grant laughed, "You are close but not quite there." He put the camera aside and pulled her onto his lap. "If my memory serves it was more like this." His lips met hers, his tongue foraged and his hands feasted on her lithe body.

Nineteen years after their summer of loving, their summer of freedom, they were back in each other's arms.

Hunter had flown to Rhode Island to see if the past could be recaptured. Grant had shown her the present could be better than the past. She wasn't naïve anymore and she didn't expect their road to always be a smooth one. After all they'd lived most of their adult lives answering only to themselves.

What had convinced her to take a chance, to leap into the air not knowing if her partner would or could catch her was the certain knowledge that if she didn't take the leap, she'd never know.

As Grant's questing hands and skillful mouth roamed, her heart soared. He was well-worth the taking the leap.

LEARN MORE ABOUT THESE BOOKS

Get the Latest News about New Releases, Special Events, Special pricing/sales

You have just finished reading *Hunter: The Drum and The Dancer* the fifth book in the Sacred Women's Circle series.

Be the first to learn about future releases, any pre-release pricing or sales and special events by signing up for my mailing list here. I do not spam and you are free to unsubscribe at any time.

For More Information on The Sacred Women's Circle series check out:

My website: www.JudithAshleyRomance.com
My blog: www.JudithAshley.blogspot.com

Lily: The Dragon and the Great Horned Owl
Elizabeth: The Lady and the Sacred Grove
Diana: The Queen of Swords and the Knight of Pentacles
Ashley: Dragonflies and Dreams
Hunter: The Drum and The Dance
Gabriella: Chaos to Symmetry
Sophia: Every Ending Is A Beginning

A REQUEST

If you enjoyed reading about *Hunter*, I'd be grateful if you would spread the word by telling friends and family, posting on social media and writing a review. Any and all of the above will be greatly appreciated and are a perfect way to support me..

ABOUT JUDITH

What do you do if you see visions and hear voices? If you're Judith Ashley, you write these stories down.

It helped that her visions and the voices were of seven women creating a sacred women's circle, a haven from whence they deal with the issues and struggles many of us face in everyday life.

It also helped that Judith experiences firsthand the healing power of supportive relationships and spiritual practices.

Judith's Prayer for you: *May your dreams manifest in "right time" and may you know the peace of unconditional acceptance, support and unconditional love.*

http://www.judithashleyromance.com/

.

facebook.com/JudithAshley.Romance

twitter.com/JudithAshley19

bookbub.com/authors/judith-ashley

WINDTREE PRESS

For more books from the heart in fiction and non-fiction please visit
Windtree Press

http://windtreepress.com